P R I D E

WILLIAM WHARTON

"Mr. Wharton has a special gift for portraying filial relationships, and his portrait of Dickie and his father . . . possesses a sweetness and felt emotion that leaves a warm, pleasant afterglow in our minds."
—Michiko Kakutani, *The New York Times*

"*Pride* works its magic by allowing the darkest and most threatening forces to invade a luminous and enchanted landscape. William Wharton knows precisely how to cast such spells—and his magic words are extracted directly from the American grain."
—*Sun-Times* (Chicago)

"William Wharton is better than a good storyteller. His descriptions of processes and things . . . are often intensely real, wonderfully effective. . . . *Pride* could be filmed in sepia."
—*The New York Times Book Review*

"Superbly plotted . . . a truly memorable novel."
—*The Pittsburgh Press*

QUANTITY SALES

Most Dell Books are available at special quantity discounts when purchased in bulk by corporations, organizations, and special-interest groups. Custom imprinting or excerpting can also be done to fit special needs. For details write: Dell Publishing Co., Inc., 1 Dag Hammarskjold Plaza, New York, NY 10017, Attn.: Special Sales Dept., or phone: (212) 605-3319.

INDIVIDUAL SALES

Are there any Dell Books you want but cannot find in your local stores? If so, you can order them directly from us. You can get any Dell book in print. Simply include the book's title, author, and ISBN number, if you have it, along with a check or money order (no cash can be accepted) for the full retail price plus 75¢ per copy to cover shipping and handling. Mail to: Dell Readers Service, Dept. FM, 6 Regent Street, Livingston, N.J. 07039.

P R I D E

WILLIAM WHARTON

Published by
Dell Publishing Co., Inc.
1 Dag Hammarskjold Plaza
New York, New York 10017

Laurel ® TM 674623, Dell Publishing Co., Inc.

ISBN: 0-440-37118-X

Printed in the United States of America

October 1987

10 9 8 7 6 5 4 3 2 1

PROLOGUE

ON October 6, 1938, in Wildwood, New Jersey, a lion, part of a "Wall of Death" motorcycle act, escaped from his cage on the boardwalk and killed a man.

On that day, Neville Chamberlain was negotiating with Adolf Hitler, giving him a large part of Czechoslovakia called the Sudetenland. It was Yom Kippur, the Day of Atonement. Jews throughout the world prayed, fasted, repented, atoned. They had little idea how, during the next seven horrible years, there would be much for all to atone.

Ann Sheridan sued for divorce and Martha Raye prepared to marry David Rose.

* * *

There was much labor unrest. The Great Depression was slowly lifting, and working men, though glad to be working again, were asking for a fairer share in profit and a promise of more job security. The A.F. of L. was preparing to shut down auto plants. The C.I.O. in Johnstown, Pennsylvania, was battling company police at the steel mills. There was a garbage and trash collectors' strike in Philadelphia, involving police intervention, violence, and labor retaliation.

The day that lion escaped, I was one month short of my twelfth birthday. The previous summer I'd seen the "Wall of Death" motorcycle act. It was the summer, also, when I first experienced a sexual as compared to a religious ejaculation.

There are some events that mark watersheds or cusps in life. The escape of that lion was one for me. It became a subconscious symbol, a foreboding, of all the violence and violation possible in life.

I began having a recurring nightmare. It haunted me for more than six years and lasted until W.W. II, when I went off and gathered material for worse nightmares.

In my "lion nightmare" I'm living on a street much like the one described by Dickie in this book. I stand behind the front door to our house and look out through the glass panes, across our porch, down our front steps. Lions are strolling, stalking the streets, the lawns; they lurk silently between porches.

My mother and father, my sister, my grandparents, aunts, uncles, cousins, friends, and neighbors are walking around. They pay no attention to the lions.

With great trepidation, I dash out to warn them of the danger, their peril. But they ignore me, laugh, insist the lions are only friendly kittens.

In despair, I scamper back behind the security of my

impervious front door. I watch as those I love are mauled, killed, destroyed by these marauding beasts.

Invariably, I woke from this dream sobbing uncontrollably, swallowed in a deep sense of loss.

This novel, despite the factual reality of the original tragedy, is a work of fiction. The characters, situations, sequences, and events are products of my imagination. Any relationship to real events is purely coincidental.

Perhaps, in writing this, I am trying at last to exorcise *my* lions in the night, my personal succubi, or perhaps I'm still helplessly attempting to warn people of hidden dangers from behind my seemingly secure front door. I don't know; it doesn't matter.

But let us now begin, as Dickie Kettleson tells us about *his* pride, *his* territory.

WILLIAM WHARTON

PART 1

WHERE I live, in Stonehurst Hills, there are rows of houses with alleys between them. These aren't the same kind of alleys they have down in Philadelphia at my grandfather's house. Those rows down there are older, were built before so many people had automobiles.

The rows we live in here, in Stonehurst, were built *after* the world war, when people started needing garages because they had cars.

At my grandfather's, the alleys are only narrow walkways, wide as an ordinary sidewalk, with metal fences along the edges. There are gardens outside the back of each house, little tiny lawns, with flowers in the summer, lots of sunflowers and hollyhocks.

Also, at my grandfather's house, you open two slanted cellar doors in the back garden and go down steps into the cellar, because those houses are built on flat streets, not hills.

Our alleys here were mostly built so cars could get into the garages. These garages are built under each of the houses. The alleys are wider, but, even so, it's hard for two cars to pass in our alley, especially where there are still old-style porches with steps sticking out.

In our alley, the pavement's cracked up so there's nothing but pebbles and broken chunks of pavement. Also, everybody puts trashcans, ashcans, or garbage cans back there and the street cleaner never comes down the alley so it's all dirty and smelly.

The kitchens in our rows open onto the back porches. These porches are at least ten feet up in the air. If it weren't for them, you could walk out the kitchen door, step off a brick cliff, and kill yourself.

Whenever we'd knock down one of those old-style porches, my Dad'd always nail a few boards across the kitchen door, temporarily, so somebody wouldn't forget and wind up smashed dead.

Our side of the alley is higher than the other because these rows are built along the side of a small hill. I guess that's why they call this part where we live Stonehurst Hills. It's a nice-sounding name for just rows of houses.

Our back porches are built out into the alleys and aren't much. Each house in our row is sort of a reversed twin of the one next door. The old-style back porches were built so there was only one set of steps going up to each pair of houses. I don't exactly know why they built those steps anyway; it's easier, and makes more sense, to go through the kitchen, down the cellar stairs and out through the cellar door; that's what everybody does.

The back porches are mostly used only to walk out on and hang clothes. Each house has a pulley clothesline going across the alley to the back of a house on the next street.

Our pulley has a line across to the McClosky place on Greenwood Avenue. *They* have one coming across to our place. All down the alley there are these pulleys with clotheslines.

The McCloskys are probably the only people we even know over on Greenwood Avenue. Nobody knows anybody on another row. In fact, I'm afraid to *walk* along Greenwood Avenue; there are some mean, tough kids living there, especially down near the end on the other side of the areaway. Practically none of them go to St. Cyril's where I go; mostly they go to Stonehurst, that's the public school.

I don't know when everybody agreed to put up those pulleys but it gives each house a chance to hang out clothes. In winter, or when it rains, we hang clothes in the cellar. On Mondays, in good weather, when most of the women in our neighborhood do the wash, you can hardly see down our alley for the wet clothes hanging out. Walking down that alley, coming home from school on Monday for lunch, there are so many clothes dripping it's like walking through a rainstorm. And, on any day, there are almost enough clothes so you feel as if you're walking under a tent.

There are fifty houses in our row, on our side of the street, the seventy hundred block of Clover Lane. There's just that narrow areaway going through the alleys halfway down. The areaway is between 7048 and 7046. Our house is 7066.

The houses across the street, in front, uphill from us, have the odd numbers. There aren't any numbers on houses in back alleys, the way there are on front. I know the McCloskys' house must be 7067 Greenwood though I've never checked. It has to be.

As I said, we live on a hill. You wouldn't know it,

walking along any of the streets like Clover Lane or
Radbourne Road or Greenwood Avenue because they're
all straight around the side of the hill. But going the *other*
way, it *is* a hill. Radbourne Road is higher than Clover
Lane and even the other side of Clover Lane is higher
than our side. Our front lawn is flat but the lawns on the
other side of the street are hills. It's nicer having a flat
front lawn for a garden but the hills are good for playing
King of the Hill or digging tunnels.

One time I went into the front bedroom of Jimmy
Malony's house across the street on the hill side. I looked
out his window there and could see all the way down the
hill, all the way to Baltimore Pike almost. It was something I hadn't expected. Jimmy'd taken me up to his parents' room to show me some of his mother's underwear
but the view out that window interested me more.

We can't see over top of the houses on Greenwood
Avenue from *our* back bedrooms. Those houses are a little bit lower than our houses, so we drive *up* a small hill
to get into our garage and they go *down a* little one to get
into theirs. Still, we aren't high enough so we can see over
the houses on the other side of our alley. We just look
smack into their windows surrounded by brick wall.

There are twelve steps up to the front porches of
houses on the high side of Clover Lane. When you're on
the front porch of Jimmy Malony's house you look right
across into the bedroom windows of our side, but the
street with the lawns and everything make it a long way
across, so they probably can't see anything, even with a
spyglass.

It's down in the alley where the iceman comes. He carries
ice up the porch stairs if there are steps left: I mean if
Dad and I haven't built the new kind of porches without
steps. If we *have,* the iceman comes through the cellar
and up the cellar steps.

Most everybody has a yellow card in the kitchen window if they want ice; sometimes it's in the cellar window. It has 25, 50, 75, and 100 printed in the corners. You turn it up to how many pounds of ice you want. If you don't want any, you turn it backward. A few people are starting to have refrigerators now and don't have cards in the windows.

If you're in the alley when the ice truck comes, the iceman will always chip off a piece of ice for you, or sometimes there are pieces of ice splintered off from where he's split a chunk of ice before. The floor part of the ice truck is wooden, soaked wet all the time and with shining silver metal tracks to make the ice slide easier. The iceman can cut off perfect cubes of ice or larger pieces just using his icepick. Sometimes it only takes one or two swings and he gets it cut through. He has a pair of big ice tongs and uses them to pick up the ice and throw it over his back onto a wet burlap sack. Our iceman is short, but he's really strong. I don't know where he lives and he doesn't speak much American.

Also, the man who sells fruits and vegetables comes through our alley. His truck is old and painted dark green. He stops the truck and yells, "Fresh fruits, fresh vegetables," but if you didn't know, you wouldn't know what he's saying: he runs it all together and practically sings. He's Italian and is hard to understand.

When Mom sends me down to buy something from him, she always tells me to watch the scale and check the change because he'll cheat me. But, so far as I can see, he cheats himself more than anybody. He always throws one more of anything onto the scale after he weighs it and charges for only the two pounds or whatever it is you've bought. Also, he usually gives me some fruit to eat, for free. He does this for everybody, not just me.

Down our alley also comes the man who sharpens knives and scissors and the man who scrapes horseradish from big horseradish roots. He mixes it in jars while you stand there; you have to bring your own jar. My dad loves horseradish. It makes me cry. I think it'd even make a horse cry. The ashman, trashman, and garbage man come down our alley, too.

The milkman with his horse comes down the *front* street. He has a white horse with pale gray circles all over. This horse knows the milk route so well he goes from house to house without the milkman telling him. Mostly the milkman comes early in the morning and I never see him, but sometimes the bottles rattling in the metal holder or the sound of the horse's hoofs wake me up and I'll sneak down to watch him from our front porch. This is only in the summer when it's light early in the morning.

In winter he comes in the dark. When it's really cold the cream freezes in the bottle so it pushes right up, lifting the cardboard lid with the little tab, like the lid on a Dixie cup. That frozen cream is *almost* ice cream, and it's delicious on cornflakes, shining slivers of ice tasting like cream.

The coal comes into the coal bin through a tiny window in front. We buy five tons a year. The coal truck is the same truck as the ice truck but two men drive it and they're not our iceman.

The coal comes in big burlap sacks and the truck has a long metal coal chute attached. They stick it through the window into our cellar. One man dumps sacks of coal onto the chute and the other keeps it sliding along with a big shovel. The coal is wet and makes a lot of noise; coal is cheaper if you buy it in the summer so that's what we do, even though the coalmen always break our snapdragons and tromp the grass flat.

One of my jobs is picking up the pieces of coal that fall on the lawn. I usually get half a bucket that way, and it keeps coal from getting caught in the lawn mower. I mow the lawn and trim edges in the summer. Trimming's the hard part, especially around the picket fence. Dad put up the picket fence to keep dogs out of our yard; kids too, I think.

The breadmen come by in front, but that's usually in the afternoon. There are two breadmen, Freihofer's and Bond. My mother buys Bond the same way we buy the *Bulletin* for a newspaper, not the *Ledger* or the *Inquirer*. I don't know why. There are so many things young kids are not supposed to know. I know we buy Abbott's milk, Bond bread, and the *Bulletin*. I also know we've never bought anything from J.I., not even light bulbs for three years and I *know* why we didn't.

Now Dad's back working for them I don't know if we'll start buying J.I. things again or not. J.I. stands for Jersey Industries. Dad told me it's not like a Jersey cow but Jersey like the state. We live in Philadelphia but Dad works for J.I. That's where the main plant is, New Jersey. I *still* don't understand why he went back working for them.

Also coming down the front street summers selling things is the ice-cream truck, and the man with the tiny merry-go-round for little kids.

One thing we have a lot of in our neighborhood is kids. There are almost more kids than there are dogs and cats. Most of the dogs and cats don't belong to anybody but usually the kids do.

I like the alley better than the front street. There's something secret about it, everything's so *real* back there. Nobody's putting out bird baths without water or planting flowers. It's just the way it is and I like it. The front porches are mostly all painted and some people even have enclosed front porches. We have one of the only trees on our street. It's actually in the middle of the lawn we share with the Robins next door. The Reynolds on our other side have a tree, too, they share with the Fennimores next to them; it's not quite as tall as our tree. These trees are the kind that grow up straight; they're the tallest things around our neighborhood. Taller than the telly poles, even. Any other kind of tree, like the kind that sends out side branches, wouldn't find any space. Everything's jammed in awfully tight around us in Stonehurst.

The highest part of the hill we're on, starts up at Clifton Road, which is on the high side of Radbourne Road. Then, after Radbourne, it's Clover Lane, below us is Greenwood Avenue. The other side of Greenwood Avenue opens up on a big open lot where we look for snakes, break bottles, burn Christmas trees, those kinds of things.

The street that actually goes down the hill, just five houses toward Long Lane from our house, is Copely Road. It's the best sledding hill close by. For real sledding, we go over to the golf course by Upper Darby Junior High School. There are some good hills there. But Copely Road's fine for ordinary sledding. When the snow's packed hard you can go all the way from Clifton Road alley way down past the end of the vacant lot, almost to where Copely Road turns up toward Guilford Road and out to Long Lane again. Long Lane is where most of the stores are; that is, except for the Little Store.

Not everybody in our neighborhood has cars, so a lot of the garages are empty. Some people use them to store extra stuff and some men have workshops in them. The Hershafts built the Little Store in their garage. It's one of the only places you can buy food or milk with only a piece of paper you sign and no real money.

But you have to live in the neighborhood for Mrs. Hershaft to let you do that. My mother says everything is always more expensive at the Little Store, but a lot of times we buy food there, especially things like milk or soap or cans of soup or sugar. It's a place my mother can send Laurel or me to buy something and not worry.

My mom worries a lot, that's the way she is.

We do the real shopping up on Long Lane in the A & P or the American Store. Saturdays we go to the Giant Tiger on Baltimore Pike, when Dad drives us over there.

My father has a car. It's a car that was in a crash and wasn't running. Mr. Carlson sold it to him for five dollars. He worked on it in our garage and got it running again. He cut off the crushed back, made it into a kind of truck, and painted it gray with some of our porch paint. It's a Ford Model A car but it doesn't look like any ordinary car. We use it to haul the wood for building porches.

My father and I build porches on weekends to pay off our back rent. For a long time Dad didn't have any job because of the Depression. When the Depression came, J.I. laid off *everybody*, with only two weeks' notice, including my father. There was nothing he could do about it. Most of the people on our street didn't have jobs either. Everybody was on relief or working for the WPA.

During that Depression time, we got three years behind in our rent. Mr. Marsden, who collects the rents, let us stay on in the house because there was nobody with any money to move in if we left. If a house is left empty in our neighborhood, all the windows get broken and even the front-porch railings get stolen for firewood. Some people move out in the night without paying the back rent.

When somebody moves, everybody helps. They'll have an old truck or a bunch of cars and they'll move away all the furniture in the dark. A lot of people have their electricity and gas cut off because they can't pay those either, so they can't live in the house any more.

My dad helped people like the O'Haras across the street and the Sullivans move. Even if anybody knew where these people moved to, they wouldn't say, so Mr. Marsden wouldn't find out. I don't know what the police could do to those people if they did catch them. Nobody has much money except rich people, and you can't throw *everybody* in jail.

* * *

It was a couple years ago when my dad got the idea of
building a new porch on our place. Mom was scared to
go out on our old little rotten wooden porch to hang our
clothes. Dad got the Reynolds next door to pay for the
wood, by promising he'd do the work himself. Mr. Reynolds works in a drugstore. We call him a pharmacist because it's a nice idea to think you live next door to a real
pharmacist, but he only works in a store in Media selling
things like lipstick and corn plasters. But he has a job.

Dad built one straight porch across our two places,
without any steps. It was a regular deck like the deck of a
ship. He put down new posts to hold it up further out
than the old posts but it still didn't go as far out into the
alley as the old steps did. This new porch is ten times
bigger than the old one. It's almost's big as the front
porch and has sun on it in the morning. On our side of
the street there's never any sun on our front porch, even
in summer.

Now, with our big porch, Mom isn't afraid when she
hangs out clothes; and we go downstairs through the cellar.

She and Mrs. Reynolds made Dad put wire on the
railing so nobody could fall off. Little Jimmy Reynolds is
only three and Mrs. Reynolds can have him out there in
the sun and watch him from the kitchen while she's cooking and washing dishes.

Of course, Dad had to get Mr. Marsden's permission
so he could build this porch, but since the old one was
falling apart anyway he said O.K.

When Mr. Marsden saw it finished, he asked Dad how
much it would cost to have porches like that one built on
other houses. I was right there. I'd never seen Mr. Marsden before. He was driving a new Dodge car, and wore a
suit with a tie. I think it might be the first time I ever saw

anybody dressed like that in the daytime, except in the movies.

Dad looked up at the porch, then at me. He said to Mr. Marsden, "I can build a porch like this, materials included, for sixteen dollars."

Mr. Marsden looked at the porch again.

"I'll tell you what, Mr. Kettleson. I'll knock twenty dollars off your back rent for every porch you build me."

The materials cost less than seven dollars, so Dad could make thirteen dollars' profit for every porch he built. Our rent is twenty-eight dollars a month so he could pay off our back rent pretty fast building porches on Saturdays. Only, somehow, we had to save that seven dollars for the wood, nails, and paint.

Dad explained all this to me afterward because he wanted me to help him. I'd *watched* him build the first porch but I didn't help.

This is the way we'd do it. First, we'd buy our wood at the big lumber yard on Marshall Road. Dad'd buy enough at one time to build three porches. Mom wasn't too happy because he was using the emergency money they'd saved for doctor bills, but Dad wanted to get that back rent paid; it really bothered him, owing money.

Then, we'd go down in the cellar. Dad had all the measurements for everything, even the railings. I'd mark the wood from his measurements and hold the long ends while he cut the lumber to length. We could do all the cutting for a porch at once; usually on Friday nights. At first I used to worry I'd mark something wrong and ruin valuable wood but then I got good at it.

Somehow, Dad found out about gray paint for battleships on sale, cheap, at the Navy yard. He went down there and bought four barrels of that gray paint. They were big as ashcans and we stored them in the cellar on the other side from the furnaces, at the bottom of the steps under our dart board. All the porches we built we painted with this gray paint. Then, early Saturday mornings, unless it was raining hard or too cold, we'd go out.

First we'd tear down the old porch. We have crowbars for this and Dad showed me how to start at the top so nothing fell down on us. The last thing to go would be the rickety old steps; there were sixteen of them. Then we'd chop and saw the old steps and posts into pieces and stack them in back of our car, where we'd carried the new wood for the new porch. The new lumber we'd have laid in the alley in a certain way so I can hand each piece to Dad as he needs it. He has it all worked out.

He has his tools lined up in a wooden box with a place for each tool. My dad has good tools from the days when he was a carpenter with *his* dad. There are two saws, one rip and one cross; two hammers, both Stanley, one carpenter, one mason; a level, chisels, everything you need to build. He has another wooden box he built for nails. Eight sections for different-sized nails, from four- to sixteen-penny with and without heads.

The old wood we'd take home at the end of the day and store in our cellar. We'd burn this in the furnace to save on coal during winter.

Next, Dad would bolt the wooden beam called a plate onto the wall. He'd stand on our ladder while I'd hold the bottom and hand things up to him. After that, we'd set in the cut-off-pyramid-shaped concrete foundation blocks to hold the posts for the new porch. These had bolts sticking straight up from the top where they were cut off. We'd set the posts up and Dad would stand up high on the ladder, with me holding it, so he could pound in the framing for the deck.

After that, we'd be up there, working from above, nailing down deckboards and putting on railings. About then, I'd start painting. Dad would nail along fast and we'd usually end up at about the same time. From start to finish we could put up a porch in under five hours.

* * *

At first, I hated losing my Saturdays, especially when it was school time. We worked Saturdays almost as long as a school day, and the only free day I'd have left would be Sunday. Sunday mornings are ruined by getting dressed, going to church, then having a big breakfast afterward. It's eleven o'clock before I can even change into play clothes.

But I didn't say anything. Then, gradually, I learned to like working with my dad. Not many kids have time alone with their dads.

He'd try to tell me the little important things about building, how to hold the hammer and swing from my wrist. You let the head of the hammer do the work. He showed me how to bear down with the saw only on the down stroke and just pull it back, letting the saw glide. He taught me how to load a brush with paint, how to hold it in my hands so I wouldn't get blisters, and how to tip the handle in the direction I pulled the brush, stroking with the grain of the boards.

We'd talk about other things, too. He's always asking about school, what I'm learning, if I like it. I don't lie to him; I tell him how I hate school and don't think I'm learning much, how I'm bored all the time.

Dad only went to eighth grade and keeps telling me over and over how there's no chance if you don't have a college education. As far as I'm concerned, eighth grade seems about right, only four more years not counting this one. By then, I could probably make enough money just building porches.

Dad put up a chart in the cellar and marked on it every month's rent we were behind. When we started, there were thirty-five squares, seven across and five down. When we'd come in from work he'd cross one off. Once a month he didn't; that was for the month we were living in.

Mr. Marsden was the one who told us which porches

to build. It was always the porches of people who were paid up with their rent. It wasn't very fair; most of the worst porches were people who didn't have any money. When some of those'd start to sag or fall down, we'd stop on the way to or back from a job and Dad would put a brace here, or a few nails there, to help hold them up. He did this for nothing. Lots of times people didn't even know who'd fixed their porch.

After a while, you could walk down those alleys and tell from the new gray porches without stairs, the ones we built, just who were the people with jobs. Anybody selling things from door to door would be smart to walk down the alleys first and look to see who had any money.

During two years, from the time I was eight till now, we built more than seventy porches. Sometimes in the summer we'd do two porches in one Saturday. Those days we wouldn't get finished until it was almost dark. We'd take our lunch and only come home for supper. Mom didn't like us to do two but we were proud of ourselves.

We got *all* that back rent paid up. I remember the day we came back and Dad crossed the last box off. He gave me his paper chart, which was brown and marked with paint now. One of the thumbtacks was always falling out so there were a hundred thumbtack holes across the top of the paper. It was a used piece of butcher paper he pulled out of the trashcan and it had meat marks on the other side.

"Here, Dickie, throw this in the furnace; we're finished. From now on we'll be getting *ahead* of the game."

He stood there, wiping paint off his hands with some turpentine while I pulled open the furnace door and threw the paper in. It went up with a quick puff of light. That was just before this summer.

We kept working, building porches over the summer till we were a whole year ahead in rent. We finished just before school started. That last night when we came in,

Dad stored his tools under his bench instead of setting them on top where he usually did.

"This whole year is like money in the bank, Dickie. In a certain way, for a whole year this house is *really* ours. But we aren't going to work any more Saturdays while school's on; you can have your Saturdays for yourself, now. Maybe next summer we'll go back to work if we have to."

He stopped, smiled, pulled the straps of his white carpenter's overalls down over his shoulders. He had regular clothes on under his overalls. It was summer but it was cold and wet that day. It wasn't raining but it was wet enough so it was hard to make the paint stick. He was wearing his old sweater with the holes in the elbows and all raveled at the cuffs.

"You remember this, Dickie. No matter how much you earn in your life you haven't made one dime if you haven't put some little bit aside. If you only earn it and spend it right off, you get nothing for your days, you're just a working machine, working for somebody else. The money you save is work you did for yourself, and the only thing really worth buying is your own time. You remember that."

By this time, Dad had gotten the letter from J.I. saying they were opening again and there was a job for him. They were going to pay him $37.50 a week. That's more than twice as much as he got with the WPA. Waxing floors in banks all night he made $22, at the most.

I was there when he opened that letter. It'd come in the morning but Dad had already gone to sleep after coming home from the waxing job. He'd get up when we came home from school for lunch and we'd all eat together, then he'd go back to work after we had dinner.

Lunch in our house is usually just tomato soup, pepper pot, or Scotch broth and sandwiches but it was fun having Dad there. He'd always have some funny story to tell about waxing the bank floors. His favorite was how he'd push the machine, waxing away, and keeping his eyes open in case somebody had dropped a little bit of all that money on the floor during the day. He'd tell the story going along as if he'd really found some money, but it would always turn out to be a Wrigley gum wrapper, or somebody's handkerchief, or, one time, it was an empty pencil box. I know if Dad did find money he'd give it back to the bank, but it was fun listening to those stories; it was the *way* he told them.

His other stories were about the waxing machine breaking down. These machines were old and I think only my father could really keep them going. He worked with three other men but they didn't know anything about machines, not even the boss, Roy Kerlin.

But this day, at lunch, Mom gave Dad the letter that came in the mail. She was all excited. Dad sat down and broke pieces of bread into his tomato soup; he put the letter on the table beside him and just looked at it, breaking bread into his soup. Mother couldn't sit down and was leaning over his shoulder. It was one of those envelopes with a little cellophane window in it so you could see my father's name and our address, 7066 Clover Lane, Upper Darby. It didn't say anything about Stonehurst Hills.

"Come on, Dick. Open it, I've been waiting on pins and needles all morning for you to wake up. Come on, open it. Don't just stare at it like that."

Dad looked up at Mom, put his hand over her hand on his shoulder. "I can't think of anything J.I. could have to say to me I'm really ready to hear, Laura. Even if they say they're sorry they shut down the place just because they weren't making enough profit, laying everybody off, even somebody like me, with nine years' seniority. I don't really think I'd be interested even in that."

But he used his knife to slit open the envelope; there was still some margarine on it. Then he read it out. He leaned back in his chair, speaking slowly like a priest reading the Gospel. He read how there was work and a position was open for him at the same bench and the salary was thirty-seven dollars and fifty cents a week. There was a lot of other stuff, too, about when and where he was to report and everything, but that was the main part.

Mom squeezed Dad around the neck from behind while he still held on to the letter. His bread was sinking into his soup. I looked over at Laurel; she wasn't paying much attention. I couldn't look at Mom or Dad, maybe she couldn't either.

"Thirty-seven dollars a week! But, Dick, that's wonderful. You could stop working nights and wouldn't have to spend all your Saturdays building porches any more. Aren't you excited?"

Dad stared at the letter. He glanced up at me, then back at the letter.

"I don't mind building porches, Laura. We have a good time out there in the alleys, don't we, Dickie?"

I nodded my head but I couldn't smile. I was hoping he wouldn't take the job. Going back to J.I. would be like saying "uncle" in a fight.

It was a Wednesday when Dad got that letter. He was supposed to report at the main plant on Monday. It was all Mom and Dad talked about for the rest of that week. I tried to listen whenever I could, but a lot of the talking they did in their bedroom, and Laurel and I aren't allowed in there unless we're invited. Mom wanted Dad to take the job because it was such good money and it was hard to get jobs. Dad didn't want to work there because of the way they fired him. One time coming down the stairs on Friday, he said, "But I hate that place, Laura. I hate everything about it. I don't like the people I work with and I don't like the work; it's dirty, hard, and dangerous. The whole building is dark and damp; they even

have the windows painted blue so we can't see out. It's
like a jail. I'll bet they get Sanderson back as foreman,
too. I can't stand that guy."

Saturday night at dinner he said he was going to take the
job. He said he had a responsibility to all of us. He said
we'd have enough money for things we needed and Mom
wouldn't have to worry so much. He promised us we'd go
to Wildwood in the summer when he had two weeks'
vacation. It'd been four years since we'd been to the
shore. I hardly even remembered it.

I still didn't want him to work for J.I. and I was
ashamed, but I couldn't get myself to say anything.

"But I told your mother, and I'm telling you kids right
now; I'm going back there to start a union if there isn't
one, or join one if there is. A union is the only tool the
working man has to fight back with."

I know this doesn't mean anything to Laurel, but I can
tell it scares Mom. I don't know why he has to tell us.
Then, and right now, there are big fights between the
companies and the unions. I guess the Depression made a
lot of the men like Dad mad. It makes me feel better
knowing Dad is going to fight J.I. even if he is going
back, so I guess that's why he told us, he was really
telling *me*.

But I'd rather be building porches. We could build
porches for other people than Mr. Marsden. Then Dad'd
be his own boss and I could work for him. Maybe I could
even get out of going to school.

There *was* a workers' union at J.I. The United Electrical
Workers, called the UEW. Dad joined it right away and
before long he was elected shop steward. This means he
represents all the men on his floor to the bosses. He's a
kind of boss against bosses.

One night about a month after that, Dad came home late.
The dinner was in the oven and Mom wouldn't let us eat

even though it was past seven o'clock, and usually we eat at five-thirty. Dad came in and one whole side of his face was swollen, with his lip cut and his shirt ripped. Mom almost went crazy.

Dad climbed upstairs to the bathroom and Mom ran right up behind him. When he came down he had some Mercurochrome and bandages on his face and a bandage on one finger that was bent back. He'd been beaten up just outside the gates of J.I. by some men the company hired to beat up union men, especially shop stewards like Dad. Dad ate his dinner quietly, grunting once in a while when he forgot and chewed on the wrong side; Mom kept crying.

After that, Dad starts meeting with other men and they go to work and come home together. Dad begins carrying a monkey wrench in his pocket, both to work and home again. He calls the people who beat him up "company goons." In Popeye comics, there's a character called Alice the Goon. She has a tiny head with no hair, a big body with thick arms and huge hairy feet. I keep thinking the company goons are something like Alice. Maybe Mom's right; I'm probably too young to be afraid enough.

I start going up to meet Dad where he gets out of the car he rides in to work with the other men. It's at the corner of Radbourne Road; Hershafts' Little Store is right there.

I meet Dad outside the Little Store and walk home with him. Lots of times he stops in and buys me some candy or bubble gum or sometimes Tastykake cupcakes. He always says the same thing.

"Share this with Laurel and don't eat any of it until after dinner. You know what Mother would say."

When he comes home, even when he isn't beaten up, he's always white-faced, tired, and dirty. He told me there are showers and a place to change clothes at work but he wants to get home early and he likes to start with clean work clothes every morning.

We have an old washing machine and hand wringer in the cellar. Dad found that old washing machine in the dump and fixed it up. He rewired the motor. Dad can fix almost anything. Mom fills that washer with his clothes every Saturday and washes them separately; they're too dirty to put in with other clothes.

Dad always comes home through the alley and in the cellar door. He takes off his shoes down there and scrapes the black grease off them, leaving them by the furnace to dry. Whatever he does at work I don't know, but it makes his shoes oily and wet. I know he's working on big circuit breakers but that doesn't mean anything to me. They're being built for a giant dam in Russia somewhere. Dad told me that. It makes him proud to work on something that's going all the way to Russia.

Then Dad goes upstairs and takes a bath. I've watched him scrub his hands with a brush and 23 Skiddoo hand cleaner till he almost wore the skin off. When he comes down to dinner he's always fresh in a white shirt with his sleeves turned up two turns to hide the frayed cuffs, but he looks clean and you'd never know he does such dirty work. The only thing that shows is he always has broken fingernails and bandages or a finger or thumb that's been hurt. He usually has at least one finger black and the nail working its way off, too.

About that same time is also when I found Mr. Harding. Mr. Harding lived at 7048 Clover Lane, the same side of the street we live on, next to the areaway. Mr. Harding used to have a good job selling Four Roses whiskey. He was a salesman and sold Four Roses to bars and restaurants, but he lost his job when the Depression came.

My mother said he lost it because he drank too much. Every bar or restaurant would give him a drink when he came in, and then he'd get drunk and couldn't sell anything. Four Roses wanted him to sell whiskey but not drink it, I guess.

Anyway, Mr. Harding was on relief like about half the people in our neighborhood but he never looked for work. His wife got a job as a waitress at a bar up on Westchester Pike called the Sail Inn. Dad said you sailed in and staggered out. She ran away with the bartender there, at least that's what the kids in the neighborhood say.

One Saturday morning, early, I was meandering down the alley looking for things on trash day. Even with everybody so poor, there is always something worthwhile in the trash. If you wait until it gets to the dump, most of the best stuff's already been picked over by the guys on the truck, so you need to go out before seven and look before they come.

It was the beginning of that summer when we were building those last porches, but we didn't work early Saturday mornings because that's the day when Dad and Mom sleep late.

One morning I found a perfectly good Sunbeam toaster worth twelve dollars new. My dad fixed it in about an hour. It's the kind that makes a ticking sound like a clock while it's toasting the bread, then pops up the toast when it's finished.

I also found an old portable Victrola in a black leather case like a suitcase. It's one of those ones you wind up. Dad fixed that, too, and I keep it in the cellar to play sometimes in the evenings when I've finished homework or in summer when it's too hot outside. I play old records Aunt Sophia gave me. They have great titles like "Just Like Washington Crossed the Delaware, General Pershing Will Cross the Rhine," and "It's the Japanese Sandman."

So I'm going down the alley rummaging through trashcans and sometimes peeking into a garage when I look into Mr. Harding's garage and see him sitting all alone in his car in the garage. He looks blue and fat but I just think he's drunk, maybe drove home, then fell asleep in his car before he could get out and go upstairs.

I go on down the alley and then back up the other side. When I get to Mr. Harding's garage, I peek in and he's still there. It doesn't look as if he's even moved. I'm still thinking he's only drunk when I go into the garage. But then I see his eyes are open, staring through the windshield, and his tongue is purple and swollen, sticking out of his mouth. His thick hands are wrapped tight on the steering wheel.

I'm sure he's dead when I see the vacuum-cleaner hose attached to the tail pipe and going in the back window. It's the first dead person I've ever seen except for my grandmother, my mother's mother, and Aunt Emmaline. But they were different, in white coffins, and with flowers all around.

I run out of the garage, leaving the two comic books and a torn-in-half *Little Orphan Annie* Big Little Book I'd found on the Greenwood side at the end of the alley. I run home trying not to cry and trying at the same time to get my breath. I've never fainted but I think I'm almost doing it.

As I go in the cellar door, I first begin thinking how I'm going to tell Mom; and how I can keep from telling Laurel. I stand there and think of waiting till Dad comes home and telling him, I also think of going across the street, at the corner, on the other side of Clover Lane, and telling Mr. Fitzgerald. He's a policeman. But then I think how it might be a murder and they might think *I* did it. So by the time I get to the top of the cellar stairs I'm already yelling for Mom and crying.

She's washing dishes in her dressing gown and comes running, thinking I'm hurt or something. She drops to her knees the way she always does when she wants to really look at me and see if something's wrong, although now, when she does that, my head's higher than hers. "Mr. Harding's in his car in his garage and he's dead."

"What do you mean he's dead?"

She's still not believing me. She doesn't look scared.

"He's sitting in his car and he's blue and his eyes are open. He's not drunk. He has the tube of his vacuum cleaner going from the back window to the tail pipe where the poison gas comes out. I think he's dead, Mom."

I'm shaking now and can hardly talk. Dead people look so alive and at the same time so dead. Mom stands up. She's not looking at me now. She grabs her dark reddish hair by both sides over her ears and stares at me with her wide green-gray eyes. Sometimes her eyes look like the green stuff that grows on the creek in summer, they're that green; now they're more white green.

"Oh my God! Are you sure?"

She knows I'm sure. She grabs hold of me, gives me a short hug, then dashes out from the kitchen, through the dining room, the living room and out our front door over to the Guinans' to telephone the police.

It turned out he was dead all right. They drove an ambulance and police cars right up our alley. My mom made me stay home through it all, but Doug Zigenfus saw it and said Mr. Harding was so stiff they couldn't straighten him out to put him on the stretcher, so he was on his back with his knees and hands out in front of him as if he was still sitting in his car, driving up a steep hill or a wall; driving straight up to heaven, maybe.

The police came and asked me a lot of questions. They wanted to know what exact time I found him but I didn't know; I don't have a watch. They made me guess and I said about seven o'clock. They wanted to know why I went into the garage and I told them about seeing Mr. Harding sitting in there alone and about thinking he might be drunk.

They even wanted to know what I was doing walking around the alley that early in the morning. I didn't want to tell them I was taking things from trashcans because that might be stealing so I said I was looking at some of the porches my dad and I had built. That wasn't a lie because I was doing that, too. I like looking at those porches; it makes me think I'm doing something like a grown person, even though Dad does most of the work.

Then they left us alone.

There was just a tiny bit in the *Bulletin* and the *Ledger*. The *Inquirer* didn't even mention it. But the little paper, our Upper Darby paper, had a whole column on the first page, with a picture of Mr. Harding dressed up in a suit, looking younger. They even mentioned my name as finding him. I was a kind of hero for several weeks there. Then Elizabeth Zane from down the street got run over by an automobile at the corner of Clover Lane and Copely. She was almost killed so she spent more than a month in the hospital. After that, everybody pretty much forgot about Mr. Harding; but I didn't.

It was then I really started thinking about being dead and what it was to die. It didn't look as if Mr. Harding had gone to hell even though he had committed suicide and was condemned. He just looked as if he'd swollen up and turned blue.

When school started this year I was still thinking about Mr. Harding a lot. I couldn't get him out of my mind. I even dreamed about him and I hardly even knew Mr. Harding. I cut his lawn a couple times for a dime but that's all.

Sister Anastasia is our fifth-grade teacher. As I said, I hate school and one of the ways I get through some days is daydreaming. I don't do it on purpose. My mind just goes off on its own, dreaming, thinking about things. One morning, I'm thinking about Mr. Harding during religion class. We have religion first thing and it's the most boring of all because all we do is memorize parts of the Catechism. We don't really talk about religion at all, like, What's being alive all about? What's it like to be dead? We're only memorizing and I hate that.

We're studying the seven capital sins, Pride, Covetousness, Lust, Anger, Gluttony, Envy, and Sloth. I'm still not sure what covetousness and sloth are. Coveting is also part of two of the Ten Commandments. It has something to do with wanting something you can't have, but how's that different from Envy?

We're all taking turns standing up and saying the answer to the Catechism question Sister Anastasia asks each of us. She asks each person the same question each time, although we all know what the question's going to be. We have to stand up and wait while she asks that same dumb question. I sit in the first row and I've already answered, so I know I have time for myself; that's when my mind takes off.

The desks we sit in have slanted tops and the seats are hooked to them with curved metal tubes. The slanted part opens and there's a place inside where you can put your books. At the very top of the desk is a narrow, flat part with a little dent for holding a pencil or a pen and there's a hole with a bottle of ink sunk in it with a black Bakelite top and a black Bakelite cover that slides back and forth to open a hole into the bottle part where the ink is.

These inkwells are for when we write with ink. We're never allowed to use fountain pens; we have to use these awful pens they sold us. There's a pen holder and little pen points which fit into them. Mostly we only do Palmer Method. Once in a while we have to write a composition with those pens, but mostly it's Palmer Method.

I can never write a composition without making big spraying blots. The points of these pens are very pointy and are split into two thin parts tight together with a hole for holding ink between them. My pen always gets stuck in the paper and then sprays over everything; or sometimes all the ink just rolls out of the pen and makes a big solid blot.

The Palmer Method is where you go across the page making up and down lines between the lines on the paper, or round and round things, where if you do it right it looks like a tunnel you could see through. But I can never do it. You're supposed to roll on the ball of your palm, holding the pen lightly in your fingers, gliding your little finger on the paper, and that way you get a nice smooth movement.

But it's not the way I write. I hold a pen hard in my fingers, then move my fingers to write with. The way I do Palmer Method when nobody's watching is turn the paper sideways and make those up and down lines and circles from top to bottom. That way I can do it, almost. But it isn't Palmer Method; I don't even use my palm.

The worst part is dipping that pointy pen in the glass inkwell. It scrapes against the bottom; hairs rise on the back of my neck, and my ears feel empty. Everybody in the class jams those pens in the inkwells hard, on purpose, but they can all do Palmer Method.

We aren't allowed to open our slanted desks unless we're told to. Usually the nun will say, "Now let's open our desks and take out our reading books" or our civics books, or something. That's one of the most interesting things that happens all day. At least there's something new to see: the inside of the desk. One of the ways my mind wanders is trying to remember everything inside the desk and where it is. I want just one time to put this picture in my mind and then look in the desk and find everything the way it is in my head.

This morning, during religion class, the first thing I know an eraser has hit me smack on the forehead. It's a blackboard eraser and isn't hard. It doesn't hurt but it's filled with chalk dust; so, chalk dust, like smoke, flies around my head. The whole class is giggling and laughing. Sister Anastasia, who's a fat nun, is standing up behind her desk in her dark blue habit with the white bib. She has some other stiff white stuff wrapped close around her face holding in the fat sides. There's a dark blue veil over that too. She's wearing the most shiny glasses I've ever seen, no metal around them, just thick glass. You can hardly see her eyes.

"All right, Kettleson. Are you deaf?"

"No, Sister."

"Then answer the question."

Of course I figure she's asking about those seven capital sins again. I start out.

"The seven capital sins are Pride . . ."

I stop. The whole class is giggling. Sister Anastasia comes out from behind the desk. She has her "signal" in her hand. I've already been hit on the hands with that thing for not paying attention, and it's only the second week of school. It's wooden and has a hard knob at the end. There's a rubber band or something in the handle, and Sister can make a clicking noise with it when she wants things quiet; but mostly I think it's for hitting kids with, at least that's the way Sister Anastasia uses it. I'm ready for another knock on the knuckles.

"Pick up that eraser and put it on the chalk rail here, young man."

She points at the chalk rail behind her. I lean down and find the eraser under Mary Jane Donahue's desk. It bounced against her, too, and there's a white mark on the side of her uniform, but she's keeping her hands crossed on the desk with her thumbs overlapped the way we're supposed to do when we're not writing. The thumbs crossed over each other like that are supposed to make a real cross and be a way of praying to God.

I carry that eraser to the front of the room and put it on the chalk rail.

"Now put your hand out."

I put it out and she gives me three good raps with her "signal." She's strong for a fat woman. The tears are coming into my eyes and I'm so mad I almost just run out the door, only I start back to my desk. The whole class is trying not to look at me, but I can hear them laughing inside. I don't blame them; there isn't much to laugh about in school. But I'm mad.

I go back to my desk and Sister Anastasia tells me to stand up again. "Kettleson, just what was it you were thinking about when you should've been listening to your Catechism?"

Before I can say anything, she starts up again.

"Children, this is a perfect example of the sin of Pride. Kettleson thinks he knows *more* than God's word. Catechism is God's word made easy for young people. If you don't pay attention to God's word then you're guilty of the first capital sin, Pride. Now, what were you thinking about instead of listening to God?"

I don't want to lie. I especially don't want to lie to a nun, even if it is Sister Anastasia.

"I was thinking about what it is to be dead, Sister."

She stares at me, shining circles in her glasses. Nobody moves in the class.

"Just what do you mean by that, young man?"

"I don't know, Sister. That's what I was thinking: how it must feel being dead."

"If you'd pay attention to your Catechism you'd know. You'd either be in Heaven with God, in Purgatory working out your salvation or in Hell burning for all eternity."

She pauses, turning her head to take in all the class.

"And I don't have much doubt as to where you're headed, Kettleson."

I stand there. What's there to say? I'm wondering if there's much difference between what she's just said and saying "Damn you" to somebody.

"Kettleson, I think for the good of your soul you

should come up here, kiss this crucifix and pray for God's forgiveness."

She motions me to the front of the room again. The rooms have scrubbed wooden floors and they're laid so they lead up and down the room. I walk up toward her with my head down, trying to walk on a single board and trying not to cry. When I get close to her, I smell the smell of a nun, the smell of baby powder and ironed clothes. She pushes me down onto my knees and holds out her large crucifix at the end of the giant-sized rosary wrapped around her waist. All the nuns in this school have rosaries like this around their waists. On the thin ones, it hangs practically to the ground, but with Sister Anastasia it comes to just below her belly, just about where my face is when she's pushed me onto my knees. I kiss the crucifix and wipe my mouth. Then, I spit on the floor.

It's something I do automatically; it isn't meant as an insult or anything. The taste of metal in my mouth always makes me want to spit. When I'm working with Dad he keeps nails in his mouth so they're handy, but when I've tried it, I drool around them and have to keep taking them out of my mouth to spit. It's the same way with toy whistles, anything metal in my mouth makes spit spring up. Also, I'm nervous and not thinking.

Sister Anastasia grabs me by the hair and yanks me to my feet. She's dragging me out of the room and I'm too scared to listen to what she's saying except she's taking me down to Father Lanshee because I've committed a sacrilege, spitting at the crucifix and spitting at a nun. I guess she believes that's what happened. I try not to yell, not to cry, but she's twisting my hair in her hands so it hurts and she's pulling hair out.

We need to go outside the school to get to the rectory and she stands at the door, rings the bell. We don't talk at all while we wait for the housekeeper to open it.

Father Lanshee finally comes himself and tells Sister to

let go of my hair. Father Lanshee is young and short with tight curly hair. He's the one you go see when it's even more important than going to see Mother Superior. Sister Anastasia tells him what happened, that is, from the way she sees it.

Father Lanshee looks at me.

"And what do you have to say for yourself? Why have you done a thing like this, one of our youngest and finest altar boys?"

Father Lanshee is from Ireland and has an accent. He's the one who taught me to be an altar boy when I was in fourth grade. I learned the Latin fast enough so during the summer I was the only fourth grader to serve mass.

"I didn't mean it, Father. It was only the metal on my lips."

"Are you trying to tell me Sister Anastasia is lying to me or maybe she's seeing things? She says you spit on the crucifix and at her. Is that true?"

It's in his voice. He believes her and he's mad.

"I only spit on the floor, Father, I didn't mean it."

He looks over at Sister Anastasia. Then I look over at her, too. She's standing with her arms folded across her fat stomach so the bib is pushed up almost like a table under her face. Father hits me hard on the side of my head with the back of his hand. It feels as if my ear is burning off and I know this is only the beginning.

"There must be a devil in you to do a thing like that, Kettleson, spit on the crucifix and spit at a nun!"

He has his face down next to mine and it's getting red. He's red all the way up into his curly hair. I can't turn my mind off from seeing things like that even when I'm probably about to be killed.

He grabs me by the other ear with his finger and thumb. He starts dragging me with him through the rectory and out the back door, the one that opens into the church. I'm learning not to say anything; there's nothing to say anyway.

He takes me into the church, leads me down the aisle, opens the gate in the altar rail and pushes me down to my knees again at the foot of the steps to the altar. Sister Anastasia isn't with us. I peek back under my arm and she's kneeling at the altar rail with her hands praying and her eyes watching me behind those shiny glasses, through the silver circles.

Father Lanshee, with his arms folded, is standing between me and the tabernacle. "You stay there and pray to God for your immortal soul. Sister Anastasia, you pray for him, too. I think he must be possessed."

He goes into the sacristy and comes out with the censer, filling it with incense. He also has the round gold thing with a handle they use to sprinkle holy water. I'm scared and I'm crying but I'm trying to pray. Father Lanshee puts his stole around his neck. This makes him a priest, officially. He kisses it before he slips it over his head. I look up at the altar with the Gospel on one side and the Missal on the other. I almost didn't get to be an altar boy because I couldn't reach up and lift that Gospel high enough to move it to the other side without scraping and making the altar cloth crooked. I needed to strain up on my tiptoes to do it. Then, carrying it down the steps and genuflecting when you can't see past it is another hard thing; and that Gospel's heavy. Besides, you have on a surplice so you can easily trip. I practiced moving the Gospel a lot before I got good enough to say a mass; it's much harder than learning the Latin, by a long shot. Father Lanshee must be reading my mind.

"There's got to be a devil in you, boy. That's what really did it and we're going to pull him right on out. What have you been doing lately which could let a devil take hold of you?"

He's waiting for me to answer. I think of all the things I've done that might be devil's work but the only thing that comes out is about Mr. Harding.

"Father, this summer there was a dead man, a dead

man who killed himself in his garage. I was the one who found him. I was thinking about that when I was supposed to be studying my Catechism."

Father Lanshee looks at me. He has the censer lit now and it's smoking. He has the holy-water shaker in his other hand.

"Yes, I heard about that. He wasn't Catholic, was he?"

"No, Father. He was just Mr. Harding; I think he was a Protestant."

"There could easily have been devils around a place where a man knew such despair so as to take his own life. That could be it."

He comes to the step just over me. I put down my head. The smell of incense makes me sneeze but I'm holding it in.

"You pray hard, Kettleson. I'm going to chase that devil straight on out of you. You'll feel better after you've been exorcised."

He's praying loud now and swinging the censer over one of my shoulders then the other. He does this while I say eight Our Fathers, three Hail Marys, and make an Act of Contrition. I'm just starting with a "Glory be" when he begins sprinkling me with holy water and praying louder. I'm so scared, black clouds keep coming down over my eyes. I'm expecting a devil to float in smoke out of my mouth or split its way out of my chest or my back the way it is in holy pictures. But nothing happens.

Father Lanshee stops. He puts the censer and the holy water on the altar. Then he comes down, tucks his hand under my chin and lifts me up.

"Let's pray that did it. But first you must apologize to Sister Anastasia."

He turns my head with his hand. She's still kneeling at the altar rail, shining-eyed.

"Do you think the devil's been exorcised, Father?"

"We can't be sure, Sister. But he should apologize to you first."

He leads me back down to the altar rail, where Sister Anastasia's still kneeling. He pushes me down on my knees. She looks at me, glinting, her lips all pulled together, almost as if she's trying to keep from smiling.

"Well, what do you have to say for yourself, Kettleson?"

"I'm sorry, Sister. I didn't mean it. I don't know what got into me."

"I think it must be the devil himself made you do a thing like that, Kettleson. If I were you I'd stay here in church and pray for the rest of the morning."

Father Lanshee is standing slightly behind me.

"That's a fine idea, Sister. Also, I don't think he should serve mass again until we're certain he's himself. What do you think of that, boy?"

"Yes, Father."

I'm supposed to serve at nine-o'clock mass that next Sunday. It's the mass all the kids go to; they sit in the center aisles, girls on the left side, boys on the right, with the little kids up front and the eighth grade in back. My parents know I'm serving this mass and will be there. How can I ever tell them that? I don't know how I can tell them how I've been exercised either. The trouble is, I don't even feel tired; that devil's got to be in there still.

Father Lanshee and Sister Anastasia leave me alone in the church all morning. I'm supposed to say five rosaries with all the mysteries, and when I'm finished, keep saying the ejaculation "My Jesus mercy—my Jesus mercy." Father Lanshee lends me his rosary. It's small, black, wooden beads, and he kisses the crucifix on it before he gives it to me. When the lunch bell rings, I can go home.

Sister Anastasia doesn't tell anybody, at least any of the kids, about my being exercised and I don't tell anybody either, not even Laurel. She's too little to understand. I keep hoping God knows I didn't mean it; that's all that counts. He must know about how I am with metal in my mouth; the sisters tell us God knows everything, even some things we don't know ourselves. After school I give Father Lanshee back his rosary. I hope maybe he'll let me back in the altar boys, at least let me serve that nine-o'clock mass, but he doesn't say anything.

Sunday when I'm supposed to be serving, I sneak off to Mr. Harding's garage and that's where I find the kittens.

There are all kinds of alley cats in our alleys and packs of dogs, too. The kids around our way are awful mean to the cats. They don't do much against dogs because some of them bite. But the cats mostly only run away. I used to think alley cats had shorter legs than most cats but they only look short because they're always crouched ready to spring away if you come near. They have little hollow places behind their heads and between the tops of their legs on the back when they're hunched down like that. When a cat's all set to spring there's almost no way you can catch it.

But Billy O'Connell showed me how you can always catch a cat if you just keep running long enough. They're fast but they get tired out soon. Maybe they don't get enough to eat from eating only garbage. Sure enough, though, he'd keep running after a cat in the alley where they had no place to go and he'd run them down finally. Usually, at the end, the cat would run into an empty garage, where Billy'd shut the door and corner them.

What Billy O'Connell likes to do with cats is climb up on somebody's porch, one of the old ones with the steps still on them, and throw the cat through the air. He throws them any which way, and they spin right around and land with their legs spread out, then run off. He tells me he threw one out his bedroom window and it was the same thing. He wants to throw one from a roof someday. O'Connell has the idea cats can practically fly. He'd like to throw one out from an airplane sometime to see what happens.

You have to be careful with these cats because they all have fleas. It's the fleas Mom worries about more than the cats, it's the same with frogs and warts.

Sometimes the kids'd catch two cats and tie them together by the tails. Those cats would swing around in circles yowling, pulling against each other. I never did anything like that myself but I've watched. There are some mean kids around our way, all right, but probably they're the same everywhere.

One of the worst things they do is pour gasoline on a cat's tail and then light it. A kid up on Radbourne Road was doing that and burned himself so bad he had to go to the hospital; he almost died and now he has shiny wrinkled scars on his arm so he can't open his elbow all the way.

When you light a cat's tail, it screams even worse than they do at night when they're fighting and making babies, only there's no purring or cat baby-crying mixed in, it's all just yowling and screaming. Most times the cat dies and somebody will find it in the back corner of a garage or under a porch when it starts to stink. But I've seen a few live. Gradually the black burnt bones that are left fall off a piece at a time until there's only a tiny stump of a tail left. Usually fur grows over this part so those cats look like a cross between a cat and a rabbit.

That Sunday, I go off as if I'm going to church. I'd been awake practically all night, trying to get up nerve to tell my folks I've been thrown off the altar boys. But I couldn't do it. So instead I go over to Mr. Harding's garage. They'd moved all his furniture from his house and his wife drove his car away but they didn't clean out the garage. There are boxes filled with old clothes and old blankets. Burlap bags, moldy cloths, and clothes are strewn around. I don't know why I went back. I'd only

been back once since I found him; that was when
Zigenfus told me the car had been taken out by Mrs.
Harding, and I wanted to check for sure.

When I walk into the garage, the first thing besides
car-grease smell is the smell of molding rags. One of the
garage windows has been broken already. Unless somebody else moves into the house soon, it won't be long
before they'll all be broken. Kids, even some grownups,
like breaking windows. There are some houses on our
block with more broken windows than ones with glass in
them. That's one reason Mr. Marsden let us stay in our
house even when we couldn't pay the rent; at least we
keep it clean and painted; the windows aren't all broken
out.

Once I threw a stone and broke one of Mr. Coughlin's
windows. He caught me and dragged me home. I was
only about seven then. My dad told Mr. Coughlin we'd
get it fixed. He was mad but he didn't holler or anything.
But that Saturday he made me go over with a folding
measure and write down the measurements of Mr.
Coughlin's window. Then we walked to the hardware
store, where they cut a piece of glass just that size. The
glass and putty and some little nails cost thirty-two cents.
Then we went over to Mr. Coughlin's house and fitted in
that piece of glass. Dad didn't say anything all this time
but showed me how to do it, and after he nailed in the
little nails, he made me put in all the putty. It's really
hard to do right. It took me two hours, doing it over and
over again until I got it all smooth and even. When I was
finished I was crying. Dad put the tools away, and took
me by the hand and led me home.

"Dickie, I just wanted you to know something. Any
fool can break a window but very few people can put one
back in."

The second thing I smell is the smell of that gas Mr.
Harding killed himself with. That's a smell that doesn't

go away fast. The door's open so I let myself just inside. I'm afraid to go all the way into this garage. I don't believe in ghosts, but Father Lanshee might be right about devils.

I'm standing there, thinking how Mr. Harding looked and trying not to think about Mom and Dad looking for me on the altar, when I see something move in the back corner of the garage in the middle of a bunch of old clothes. I step sideways to get a better view and lean forward a few steps. There's a green-eyed cat, eyes almost green as my mom's, and shining there in that back corner.

She's hunched the way cats get when they're about ready to run. Her eyes stay on me without blinking and I'm looking to see if she's hurt or anything. Lots of times cats get hit by cars then crawl into these garages to die. But she looks healthy, healthy that is for an alley cat.

I'm starting to back out the door when she dashes past me and scrambles up the inside of that garage door and out the broken window. I'd left the door open so there was no reason for her to go out that way.

She moves so fast she scares me and I push myself against the garage door that isn't open. These garages have two doors that swing like regular doors; they don't swing up the way they do in the movies.

I'm about ready to go out the door when I hear some sounds coming from where that cat was. I know right away what it is and I want to see them. I tiptoe back carefully and there, tucked in the cloth, are five baby kittens. They're so small their eyes are still closed; they can't stand up. I reach in and lift them one at a time. The mother was a striped tiger cat, standard alley-cat color, sort of greenish gray and black stripes. Two of these kittens look like that. Another is black and white, one is black, and the other is a brownish color with dim blackish stripes. This last one is strange because it doesn't have a tail and it's too young for anybody to have burnt it off.

I'm not sure if the mother had a tail but I think she did. Maybe the father was one of those cats who got his tail burnt off and this kitten inherited it. It *is* dark brown as if it's already been burnt. Maybe this one is a devil cat, come straight out from H-E-L-L.

After playing with the kittens for a while and listening to them, I decide to see if I can help them stay alive. Most of the kittens in these alleys get killed by dogs, boys, or other cats. A lot of times there just isn't enough to eat.

So, before everybody comes home, I go in, open the icebox, and take two pinches out of the hamburger in its brown paper. Mom is going to make meat loaf with it. I pat the meat back into shape so it looks the same. To make up, I'll eat a little less myself; I don't particularly like meat loaf much anyway. I pour milk into a cup without any handle I had in the cellar for my turtle before he disappeared. I take both these, a piece of broken broomstick, and some wire back to Mr. Harding's garage. I put the milk and the hamburger beside the kittens.

The mother cat isn't there. I figure she's out looking for something to eat.

I don't have much time before everybody comes home, so I go out and push the broom handle through the latches on the door and wire it shut. This will keep other kids out, and so long as the only way to get in is through that window, no dog or anything can get at them. When I finish, I feel better; I feel almost as if I have a little family of my own. I'm ready to tell Mom and Dad about being thrown out of the altar boys.

It isn't as bad as I thought it would be. Mom gets all excited at first but then settles down. Dad asks me to explain and I tell about the eraser and Mr. Harding and the taste of the crucifix and my spitting, the exercising; the whole thing. It sounds even crazier when I'm saying it than it did when it was all happening. While I'm talking, my scrambled eggs and bacon are getting cold. We always have scrambled eggs and bacon on Sunday morning. It's the only time we have bacon because it's so expensive. We each get two slices.

"And after that Father Lanshee threw you out of the altar boys, is that right?"

"That's right. I think he doesn't want to take a chance of letting someone who might have a devil inside him get on the altar."

That's when Dad starts laughing and I know it's going to be all right.

"Don't you worry, Dickie; you don't have any devils in you. Don't you worry about it.

"You know, your grandfather, my father, has the same trouble with nails in his mouth. They'd get so wet they'd almost be rusty before he could drive them into the wood, and there would be a little puddle of spit around the top of each nail when it was pounded in."

I stare at him, hoping he'll go on. I love to hear stories about my grandfather.

"You eat your egg and bacon now, Dickie. I guess there isn't much chance of your going to communion anyhow. But you'd better get to that eleven-o'clock mass. It's going to be a high mass and could last almost two hours. I guess that'll pay off to God for you missing the nine-o'clock today."

He pushes the last of his egg into his mouth, takes the final crust of his bread and scoops out his plate; pushes the bread into the side of his mouth.

"One thing, Dickie. Don't ever let anyone, I don't care who it is, throw any erasers or anything at you again. You just walk out of there and when I come home, you tell *me*. I'll take care of it. In fact I'm half tempted to go in and talk to that Sister Anastasia and Father Lanshee myself right now, but I've already got enough trouble to think about."

* * *

Over the next week I go every day to see the kittens. I never see the mother again. The third day I go, there are only four kittens; the black-and-white one is gone. All that's left is one ear, the little paws with tiny claws and most of the tail.

I figure a tomcat came in and ate it. Or maybe it could even be the mother. Jimmy Malony told me once how when cats are born in May the mother will eat them sometimes, but this is September. I can't think of a way to keep tomcats out without keeping the mother away too.

I start sitting across the alley in the areaway to see if I can catch the mother going in or out so I'll know she's feeding them, but she must only go in at night or during the day, when I'm at school. Or maybe she sees me hiding across the way and won't go in while I'm there.

Two days later, one of the striped cats is gone, all except two paws. The other kittens are starting to get their eyes open. This is the day Dad came home beaten up by goons the second time.

He'd had to work overtime and they were waiting for him. Luckily he had his monkey wrench because he broke away, ran, got on a trolley car, where they couldn't get to him.

This time my mom is really crying. She wants Dad to stop being shop steward, to just do his job.

Dad's white and his hands shake while he's reading the newspaper. He keeps making knots in his jaw, tight, the way he does when he chews, but he isn't eating.

I want to ask about the kittens disappearing and what I can do, but I'm afraid. He looks so strange. I don't think of my father as somebody who gets scared, and it scares *me* seeing him this way.

It's Thursday of the second week after I found my kittens, when I go in and there's only one left, the little brown one without a tail. I watch all the weekend, even eating lunch out there in the alley, but I never do see the mother cat go through that broken window; no other cat climbs through either.

When I go in the garage he's nuzzling in the mess at the bottom of the nest. By now, all the cloths are blood-soaked and there are pieces of kitten smashed into the cloth. As soon as that kitten sees me, he rears up on his hind legs and backs into the corner of the garage behind the nest. He's standing up there with his claws out and his eyes fastened on me like a lion or a bear. I sit down on the garage floor in a part where there isn't any grease and watch him. I also get to really *look* at him.

He's definitely like a burnt tiger except for not having a tail. There are darker stripes coming down between his ears, across his forehead, and between his eyes. There are also stripes going out from each of his eyes, almost like a raccoon, and there are dark drips coming down from the inside of his eyes right next to his nose. I can't tell for sure if these are real marks or only something like sleep that gets caught in the corner of your eyes.

His nose is pink on the end mostly but with some black parts on the top and outside. The bottom of his nose has a little slit in it to match his mouth and he has no lips. Whenever I move too fast, he opens his jaws wide and makes a hissing sound.

I keep calling this cat "him" but I don't really know. The kids in the neighborhood say it's hard to tell a boy cat from a girl cat till they're grown up; then it's easy. The tomcats have big nuts and the females a round pink hole under the tail.

This one has little sharp, white teeth and the inside of his mouth is pink in the front, the way you would expect, then it gets darker, almost blue or purple at the back of his tongue. When he opens his mouth to snarl, he tucks his tongue back away from his teeth; I never noticed that about cats before. But then I never really noticed much about cats; I don't think I even really like cats. I know they eat rats and mice but they also catch all the pigeons and sparrows. There are practically no birds in the alleys, only at the front, and then it's mostly starlings.

But I'm beginning to like this cat and I'm becoming more and more convinced he *ate* his brothers and sisters. I figure he'd wait till they were all asleep then kill one by biting it on the neck or something and draining the blood. Probably the other kittens, when they were still alive, helped him eat them, too. Four would eat one, then three ate one, then two ate one, then this one ate the last other kitten, the black one that's only one paw and a tail now. It must have been awful to see. I wonder if they ate the meat and milk I brought or some other cat came in and ate it. I don't know for sure whether it's true he ate his brothers and sisters but I decide to name him Cannibal.

I sit there a long time, watching, not thinking much, and then he begins to fall down. He isn't coming down on his four feet, he's falling over sideways. He does this twice, then just lies there on his side, his thin stomach going in and out. His eyes are closed so I can sneak up on him. I wonder if I could pick him up now without getting bitten. Actually I've been too afraid to put my hand near him the last week, even though he isn't much bigger than a mouse. He's really like a miniature wildcat, not like a kitten at all, except he's so tiny. I don't think he's actually grown much since the first time I saw him. Only he's opened his eyes, learned to growl and stand up. I haven't ever seen him walk. He just huddles in that bloody, messy nest or rears up in the corner behind it.

So, carefully, I put my hand under his tiny body and pick him up. He's limp and doesn't move. I see he's unconscious and I get scared. I tuck him against my stomach and run out from the garage, up the alley to our place.

I go in the cellar and make a little bed for him with one

of my dad's clean paint rags, then sneak up the stairs. Mom must be upstairs in the bedrooms and I don't see Laurel. I open the icebox and get some milk. I pour this from the bottle into the lid of a mayonnaise jar Mom has stored under the sink, then I add a bit of water to the milk bottle and put it back. I dash down into the cellar.

He's still breathing but sort of shudders at the end of each breath. His eyes are still closed.

There he was, standing up, trying to fight me, and dying right in front of my eyes. I hold him over the mayonnaise jar lid and try sticking his pink nose into the milk. He doesn't open his mouth, doesn't try to lick the milk. What happens is he breathes in some of it with his nostrils and sneezes. He shakes his head, sneezes again, but doesn't brush off his face the way cats do.

Now he's limp in my hand again. I keep trying but he's too far gone to drink. He's dying for sure. After all his struggle trying to stay alive, he's going to die anyway.

I put him down on the cloth again and tuck him in behind the small bucket-a-day furnace so he'll be warm. I hear Mom walking around upstairs. I go out the cellar door, run down the alley, up Copely Road, then along Clover Lane and into our house from the front. I come in as if I've been playing outside in the street with the other kids. Mom's busy cleaning house so she doesn't notice me much. I run upstairs quietly and go into our bathroom. What I need is there. It's the only place I can think to find one. I used to have one in my chemistry set but it got broken.

I lift the Argyrol out of our medicine cabinet and unscrew the top. It has a rubber squeezer and an eye dropper that goes into the bottle. I put the Argyrol bottle back in the medicine cabinet and squeeze the rubber, washing the inside of the eye dropper, until it isn't brown any more.

When I'm sure it's clean, I dash downstairs, out the front door, around through the alley, and back in the cellar door. I'm afraid the kitten'll be dead by the time I get there; but if I go right through the house, past Mom, she's liable to ask me what I'm doing, where I'm going, and I don't want to tell any lies. If there really is a devil in me, he'd just love to have me lying to my parents, especially about a cannibal cat. That's the first time I begin to think that this cat might be a devil himself. I read one time in a book about Halloween how witches' cats had the devil in them. It'd explain a lot of things about this cat, Mr. Harding, and me.

When I get there in the cellar, down on my knees, I pull Cannibal out from behind the bucket-a-day, half convinced he'll be dead, but he's still breathing. I hold him in my hand, fill the eye dropper with milk and start squeezing it into his mouth.

First I try putting the point of the eye dropper right in the center under that slit in his nose, but the milk only comes flowing out and gets his chin all wet. Then I figure how to slip the point into the side corner of his mouth and squeeze it slowly. I begin to feel him swallowing and it all goes in if I do it very carefully. I sit there for a long time, slowly dripping in milk while he swallows. He still doesn't open his eyes. I slide him under the paint cloth and push the cloth back behind the bucket-a-day again. I've used all the milk.

I go upstairs directly this time. Mom is going shopping and tells me to watch Laurel till she gets back. Laurel's jumping rope with some girls on the walk in front of our house. I tell Laurel to stay there till I come back.

This time I warm the milk in a pan, then go back into the cellar. It was hard getting the milk just warm enough and not too hot. I put a few drops of it on my tongue and it felt fine. I'm hoping old Cannibal is still alive.

When I slide him out, he opens his eyes at me but doesn't try to get up. His eyes look almost as if they've been crying but it could be only all the milk I spilled on him. I try wiping him off, but it's hard wiping off kitten fur, it's so soft.

I pick him up without any trouble and begin putting some of the warm milk in his mouth the same way. This time he begins sucking on the end of the eye dropper and it goes fast. He drinks down that whole second batch in about five minutes. I run back upstairs again. Mom still isn't home. I look out the front door while the new milk is heating. Laurel's fine, still jumping rope across the street. I dash back into the kitchen, the milk's too hot so I add some cold milk till it's just right. I'm using so much milk now Mom's going to notice. If I add any more water it won't taste like milk.

I decide I'll tell her I drank some. She'll like that because she's always trying to make me drink more milk to build strong bones and teeth, but I don't like it much, unless it's cold and with chocolate.

I drink a quarter glass so I won't be lying and leave it unwashed in the kitchen sink as proof. I wash out the pan I've been cooking in and put it back into the pot-storage part of the stove.

In the cellar, when I reach in back of the bucket-a-day for Cannibal, he takes a bite at my finger. I pull my hand away fast. He's worked his way up onto his stomach, still not standing but staring out at me with his yellow-green eyes. He has his mouth open again. I put the milk down just in front of his nose and sit back to watch. It's the same; he won't drink while I'm there.

I run upstairs to check Laurel and see if Mom's come home from shopping yet. It's all O.K. When I come back down Cannibal hasn't touched the milk.

I don't know what to do. I try waving one hand in front of him and then reaching back to grab him with the other, but he's too quick for that and I get another nip on the finger. He doesn't reach out to scratch me, the way you'd expect; he takes quick snaps with those sharp teeth. Maybe Devil would be a better name than Cannibal. No, it's like Dad said about me; there's no devil in there. He only seems that way because there's something I don't understand.

Then I get another idea.

I go upstairs and pinch off a piece of hamburger again. Most of the meat we eat is hamburger, except on Sundays. Then we usually have chicken. I do the same thing, pinching off a few bits, packing it together again and closing the paper the way it was.

I run down the cellar steps. I'm beginning to feel guilty about stealing milk and meat; our family needs it. I'll need to tell this in confession. I'll make sure not to go to Father Lanshee; he'd recognize me for sure. I'll go to Father Stevens or Father O'Shea. Father O'Shea never pays much attention to what you say anyway; he sort of half sleeps in there with a book, then always gives the same penance, five Hail Marys, five Our Fathers and a good Act of Contrition. He almost always slides the door shut before you're half finished with the Act of Contrition. I'll go to him.

There's no problem with the meat. Soon as I put it on the cloth in front of Cannibal's face, he starts gulping it down, chewing it back and forth the way a grown cat would do. He's a Cannibal all right.

By the time he's finished, he's up on his front feet. It's amazing how fast cats seem able to recover from almost anything. Everybody in our neighborhood, the kids that is, believe cats have nine lives. I've had some of the alley cats pointed out to me that everybody swears were killed by a car or something and there they are, alive.

I think it's only because cats can live through almost anything that happens to them, then most people think a particular cat's had another life.

The other thing everybody around here believes is if a black cat crosses your path you'll have bad luck. Once, I watched Joe Hennessy, who's a big guy and can beat up almost anybody at school, and does, lots of times, walk all the way around to Clinton Road when a black cat crossed in front of him. I wonder if Cannibal could be thought of as a black cat. Actually he's dark brown but somebody could easily make a mistake and see him as black.

Now I have to figure where I can keep Cannibal. If he keeps improving the way he is, he'll be wandering all over the cellar and he's sure to start making cat noises, meowing or growling or yowling or maybe purring. He'll also start making messes, the way cats always do. I still haven't heard him make any noise except the hissing he made at me when he was dying on his feet; but he could start making noises if he gets better. My mom would die if she knew I had an alley cat in our cellar. I haven't even thought about the flea part. I wonder if I already have fleas.

I rig up a place for Cannibal behind the big furnace. It's almost impossible to see back there and the furnace gets so hot you can't touch the sides so nobody's going to sneak back there. We just started the furnace last week when it began getting colder and we bank it down at night.

Last year, Dad taught me how to bank down our furnace, getting it to burn slowly and not use up much coal. This was after I learned how to sieve out the clinkers. In the morning, it's my job now, before school, to start up the furnace again. First, I shake down the ashes with a handle on the side, then I put in one shovelful of real coal. Over top of that, I spread a half shovelful of my clinkers. That way it gets started fast and then slows down as it gets to the clinkers. Sometimes I think I might be saving the same clinkers over and over, but there's no way to know.

One thing I do know is I've got to tell my parents about Cannibal. I want to keep him if he lives through everything, but I can't do it if they won't let me. When you're ten years old you can only do what your parents will let you.

I want to have an excuse to stay down in the cellar, so I decide to shine shoes even though it isn't Saturday. My dad's made a little portable shoebox you can sit on. It has a lid so when you open it, there's a place to put a shoe on, with little twist things on each side that are adjustable to hold the shoe tight.

My dad made this box when he was fired from J.I. and couldn't get any job, not even with the WPA. We were on relief but all we got was cornmeal, rice, and once some Spam. We ate an awful lot of cornmeal muffins.

Dad made this box and went down outside the train station at Sixty-ninth Street and sometimes at Sixty-third Street to shine shoes. He told me he never made more than two dollars any day and sometimes he'd only be able to charge a nickel a shine. There were a lot of other men trying to shine shoes around there, and sometimes they'd get into fights about customers. Sometimes the police would come down from the municipal building up the hill and chase them all away.

But then Dad got a job working with the WPA. He'd walk to a place past Sixty-ninth Street, up on Westchester Pike where they were fixing the streets. He'd walk all the way there and all the way back. He used to cut out cardboard or wooden soles for his shoes and tie them on to save shoe leather, also to keep his feet warm. Dad told me it was the coldest winter he remembers. I was too young to know; all I remember is the blankets we got from relief. We called them Indian blankets like Indian givers.

When I was seven, my dad showed me how to shine shoes. After that, shining shoes on Saturday for church Sunday morning was my job. Even when we were building porches, after we came in I'd do the shoes. Sometimes Dad would stay on to help me when he wasn't too tired.

Laurel's are easy. They're Mary Janes, patent leather, and I just brush them off, then rub Vaseline in to make them shine. Mom's are white and brown in summer. They're hard; you have to whiten the white part and shine the brown part. Now it's getting colder, she only wears brown shoes with high heels. I have to do the heel, too. I know it's about time Dad put on new heels; the bottom part on her shoes, that is, because it's beginning to wear along the edge of the side where I shine them.

Dad wears cordovan shoes with a straight-across tip. He's had these same shoes more than four years I know of; I guess all the way from back when he worked for J.I. before. He wears an old beat-up pair for working. The leather's all cracked and you can see his socks through the top, but the bottoms are perfect.

Dad repairs all our shoes. Part of his work bench is a regular shoemaker's bench. He has the right glue and the tiny square nails. He's always saving a piece of leather from some trash or other. He cuts the soles out of this leather with a real shoemaker's curved knife. I love to watch him when he fixes shoes; it smells good, too. I know I'm never going to be a man like my father; I don't think I care enough about things.

My shoes have sharkskin tips so the more you wear them, the more they're supposed to shine, but I wear holes right through the sharkskin as if it was nothing. Even so, I have to shine the rest of the shoe.

I go upstairs and gather the shoes. I line them up on the cellar floor. The floor of our cellar is always a little bit wet, even with the furnace going in the winter. Dad says the floor sweats.

I open the shoebox. I peek over at Cannibal; he's still asleep. I take out some Griffin's shoe polish and the Vaseline. I take out the shoe brush and the cloth for spreading polish. I've tried some others but I like Griffin's best. I like the song they sing on the radio, too. I sing it to myself, keeping half an eye on Cannibal while I work on the shoes.

The sun shines east
The sun shines west.
But Griffin's polish
Shines the best.

Some folks are not particular
How they look around the feet.
If they wore shoes upon their head
They'd make sure they looked neat.

So keep your shoes shined
With Griffin's all the time.
Griffin's time is the time to shine.
When you hear that familiar chime:
Ding-dong-dong-ding.
It's time to shine.
Everybody get set—
It's time to shine.

I decide to tell Laurel. I show her Cannibal behind the furnace; this is before Mom gets home from shopping. Laurel wants to keep Cannibal as much as I do but she's sure Mom and Dad won't let me. She wants to hold Cannibal but I tell her he's still too sick. Actually, I'm afraid he might eat off one of her fingers. Laurel's a very nice person even though she's only six. She's my best friend.

That night at dinner, before we finish dessert, when Dad is starting his coffee and Mom is coming in from the kitchen with her tea, I decide it's the time. Usually if we want, now, we can get up from the table and go out to play.

"Mom, Dad, I have something to ask."

I look over at Laurel. She's playing with her fruit cocktail, fishing out the cherries. She saves them for me. Dad looks at me over his cup, eyes gray, tired; he blows so the steam flashes out from his face the way I thought that devil was going to come out of my mouth.

"O.K., Dickie, what is it this time? Have they thrown you out of the choir now?"

He smiles and I know he's kidding. He looks over at Mom. She's watching me. Mom's better than Dad at knowing when something's wrong. She *always* knows.

"I have an alley cat in the cellar. Actually it's only an alley kitten. It's the smallest kitten I've ever seen."

Dad takes a sip of his coffee. Mom puts the back of her hand against her mouth. I'm trying not to talk too fast. When I'm excited about something I talk so fast nobody can understand me.

I start by telling how I found the kittens in Mr. Harding's garage, the day I didn't say mass. I tell how they've all disappeared except for one. I don't tell about how I think Cannibal ate his brothers and sisters. I don't even tell them his name is Cannibal.

I tell about how this kitten was dying and still trying to fight me off, standing in the corner with his paws up and his mouth open. I tell how I took him home and tried to feed him and now I have him behind the furnace to keep warm.

I stop and look at both their faces and try not to cry. Nobody says anything. Dad takes another sip of his coffee. Mom pours more tea in her cup.

"You're probably covered with fleas, Dickie. If we have to shave your head and sprinkle you with flea powder you won't be so happy about *that.*"

She says it but she isn't mad. She's even smiling at me and I don't quite understand. Dad puts his cup down, wipes his mouth with a paper napkin.

"O.K., let's go see this tiger cat of yours. He could already be dead. From what you say, I don't know how you can keep him alive."

We go downstairs into the cellar. I go first with Dad behind me, then Laurel and Mom. I reach carefully behind the furnace and Cannibal is asleep but he's still alive. I slide out the cloth with him on it before he knows too much what's happening.

I still haven't told about stealing the milk and hamburger. I'm feeling once they see Cannibal it will be easier. When I get him out from behind the furnace, he rolls onto his stomach, looks at all of us, then rears up into his bear-lion position ready to fight our whole crowd. He looks even tinier than I remember. He's rocking back and forth the way he did before and I'm afraid he's going to fall over. Dad gets down squatting beside me.

"My goodness, Dickie, I think you've got yourself a miniature tiger or a lion here, all right."

He puts out his finger and Cannibal strikes out at it with his pointy teeth. Dad just lets him bite and pulls him out of the paint rag *by* his teeth and holds him in his other hand. Dad's hands are so hard with calluses, cuts and bruises, he doesn't seem to even notice a little kitten biting him.

"You're a fierce little fellow, aren't you there? Dickie, this is the smallest living cat I've ever seen. He must be some kind of runt in that litter."

"He's the only one who stayed alive, Dad, even if he is a runt. I've never met anybody who wants to stay alive so much. I think *he* might have some kind of little devil in him."

"Does he or it have a name yet?"

"Cannibal."

He looks at me quickly, smiles, looks up at Mom.

Dad runs his other finger over Cannibal's head while Cannibal holds with his little teeth on to Dad's finger desperately, feebly; rocking his head back and forth, sinking his teeth deeper into that hard flesh. I turn around to look at Mom. She's standing with her arm around Laurel in our dark cellar and only one bare light bulb up in the rafters. "Can I keep him, Mom, please? I'll do anything you say."

She's looking at the top of the Argyrol bottle and the

lid to the mayonnaise jar beside the paint cloth; I forgot all about them.

"I'm sorry, Mom. I took some milk and even some little pinches of hamburger. He was starving to death and you weren't home to ask."

I'm lying with the second part. The devil in me made me do that. But I'm wanting so much for her to let me keep Cannibal, not to get excited and start saying no before she can think too much about it. She stoops down beside Dad. She touches the back of Cannibal lightly as if she's afraid fleas will climb up her arm.

"Why, Dick, this cat doesn't have a tail. It doesn't look like a cat at all."

"Dearest, I'm not even sure it *is* a cat. Have you ever seen anything so tiny? And look at this color. I've never seen a cat this color, have you?"

And that's the way it happened. That's the way I got to keep Cannibal. Mom insisted I buy flea powder and rub it into the fur. Dad said I could get some cat food and he'd take it out of my "salary" when we started building porches again. He turned to Mom.

"This is one of the things we can afford now I'm back working with J.I. But, Dickie, I have to tell you, I don't think this tiny thing can live very long. Be prepared for him to die."

The rule is Cannibal must stay in the cellar and under no circumstances come upstairs. When he makes messes I'm to clean them up. The first time Mom smells cat in the cellar, out Cannibal goes with the other alley cats in the alley. Dad says he'll make a sandbox; he tells me where there's some sand at a construction site on the other side of Long Lane.

I'm so happy I can keep him I have a hard time re-membering all the things I'm supposed to do and not do. Dad passes Cannibal into Laurel's hand and works his finger out of Cannibal's mouth. Cannibal looks up into

Laurel's eyes and I'm afraid he's going to spring for her jugular vein. But he sits quietly there, crouching, ready to spring. If he springs he'll only fall off onto the cellar floor. I guess he has that figured out already because he doesn't do anything, only keeps his eyes open, shifting from side to side and hissing if one of us makes any kind of fast move.

Dad and Mom go back upstairs. Laurel and I stay down with Cannibal. I know we'll have great times playing with him. I only hope Dad isn't right and that Cannibal *will* live. I know if there's anything I can do to keep him alive, I will.

PART 2

STURE Modig was born in 1896 to Swedish immigrant parents on a 320-acre dairy farm in Wisconsin. His parents had worked fifteen years as domestics and saved $2,000, with which they'd bought their farmland. The land cost $20,000. They took a $10,000 first mortgage and an $8,000 second.

They soon had a team of horses, three brood sows, and forty milking cows. They were living in a waterless, toiletless frame house when Sture was born. Sture's father had first built the barn for his animals while he lived with his bride in a combination hut-tent. Then he built the house so they could have children before it was too late.

Sture's parents had married in their mid-thirties after

the long thrifty years in service. Sture was born when his mother was forty. She almost died in childbirth, so he was an only child.

Sture was the sole luxury in his parents' lives, and from the beginning it was apparent he was truly an exceptional person.

Sture Modig was one of those few people who live up to their names. Modig in Swedish means "brave," and if there is one word to describe Sture both as child and man it's "brave"; he did not seem subject to the normal fears with which all of us are assailed. He was also "brave" in the German sense of the word, *brav,* that is: well-behaved, willing.

Sture walked unaided at nine months and seemed to have an unnatural ability for converting sound into language. He was speaking words at eighteen months and could converse clearly at two years. Soon, he could also imitate, and seem to converse with, most of the animals around which he lived.

At four, he could settle a frisky calf or cow using only sounds he made with his mouth. He spoke with the barn cats and the farmhouse dog; with the pigs. He could imitate the sounds and call to him most birds, including domestic chickens and ducks.

Sture liked helping his parents. By five he was helping with household tasks such as dusting, sweeping, straightening; hauling water from the well. He was so small he carried the water in a quart milk pail. He'd go the fifty yards to the well four times as often as his mother, but in the end he'd fill the large water container in the kitchen.

At first, his mother allowed Sture to help only to keep the child busy, but soon realized his value. He was a consistent, quiet worker and his "play" seemed to be what everyone else would consider drudgery.

Already, at that young age, Sture wanted to be of some good. It might be claimed this was because his parents were older and they doted on him, spoiled him in some way, expected too much of him; but it became more apparent with time this was not the case.

Sture was somehow unique in our world. His failing might have been that he didn't know how to express love. He admired, respected his parents, but he was never overtly affectionate. This could come from the traditional Scandinavian impassiveness: neither of his parents easily expressed their feelings, either.

It could also come from their years of servitude. They transferred their servile allegiance to their animals and even more so to Sture. He grew up feeling a guilt for the service, the love, the admiration he received, the joy they took in him. He reciprocated, in a sense, defended himself, by serving *them,* devotedly, to the best of his ability. It was a battle of goodness, of kindness, but there wasn't really much of natural spontaneous love.

Sture learned to milk a cow before he was seven. His small hands could just get around an extended teat but his strength, his will, and his communion with animals more than made up for this minor deficiency. The cows seemed to *give* him the milk. Sture could get more milk from a cow than his father or mother. At first, Sture's father let him work around the barn with the animals only to give him something to do, but he, too, became increasingly dependent upon him.

Nothing was too hard, too dirty, too monotonous for Sture. He mucked out the pigpens with a miniature shovel, singing. He broke up bales of hay and carried fodder down from the granary in the largest armfuls he could manage. And, all the time, he talked to the animals, seemed to keep up a running conversation with them.

By the time he was seven, both his parents were worried about Sture. He was *too* good; in some strange way he made *them* feel guilty. He was so happy all the time, so helpful, so willing. It wasn't natural. He wasn't in any way like a normal seven-year-old. But there was no one else to talk with about this problem; their farm was isolated and the nearest communities were French-speaking.

Mr. and Mrs. Modig spoke only English with Sture. They wanted him to be a real American, to have the advantages of a native born. However, they spoke Swedish between themselves. They thought of it as their private language.

Meanwhile, Sture learned to speak *both* Swedish and English; he spoke Swedish to his parents the way he spoke cow to the cows or dog to the dogs.

Even more amazing, his English was less accented than that of his parents. As a very young boy, he was already learning to *read* English on his own from the pictures in the catalogues his father tore up to be used in the outhouse. He learned how to read by himself because reading was not high on the scale of sensible skills in the eyes of his parents.

Sture didn't go to school until he was eight years old. By that time, he was doing about half the chores around the house: wood hauling, chopping, water carrying, sweeping, scrubbing floors. He was the first out of bed every day, starting a fire in the kitchen range or the pot-bellied stove in the sitting room. After this, he'd go out to the barn and join his father in the milking and other animal chores.

At calving time he'd often sneak away in the night to check that everything was all right. Twice he saved the lives of valuable milking cows in birthing by "knowing" something was wrong even before his father was aware of it. The animals confided in him and he could "read" their every movement as well as interpret their sounds.

His parents were glad when it came time for Sture to go off for school. They were concerned about his "unnaturalness." At the same time, they were sorry to lose him, not to have his cheerful smile, his singing, talking to the animals, and especially his continual helping hand. The day he dressed for school the first time, wearing his only pair of shoes, his father spoke to him.

"Sture, I know you'll be a good boy at school."

Sture nodded his head and smiled. It never occurred to him to be anything else, he could probably not even conceive of an alternative, but he listened.

Among other things, Sture was a good listener. He listened to everything and everybody. He listened to the grasses blowing, the insects buzzing. He could lie in a field and listen to the different sounds and tell without looking whether there were gnats, fleas, beetles, crickets, ants, or grasshoppers chewing the grass beside him, flies, wasps, or bees buzzing around his head.

He listened to anyone as if he really wanted to hear what was said. When he listened, one knew he not only heard the words said but understood their meaning and the feelings behind them. One felt Sture also heard a person's voice as a thing separate, a personal music, not even heard by the speaker, but heard by Sture when he listened.

Sture's dad continued: "I know you can already read better than your mother or I, but don't 'stick out' in the class. Everything is so easy for you the other children might be jealous and treat you mean. You understand?"

Of course Sture understood; he also understood all the things his father was not saying, all his father's fears and his pride.

"Father, I shall be good. I want to know everything. I know I will be happy in school and I want everybody else happy, too."

So Sture went off. As soon as he was over the first hill, out of sight from the house, he took off his shoes and shirt. He wrapped them carefully and started to run. It was five miles to the school and Sture ran the entire way. Sture liked to run; it made him feel close to the other animals. Because there was so much to be done on the farm, he never had enough time to run, but now was his chance for running: to and from school every day. He'd taken off his shirt and shoes so he wouldn't scuff his shoes or soil his shirt.

Before he reached school, Sture put on his shirt and shoes. He went inside and sat in a chair with the other young children and listened. It was a one-room schoolhouse and some of the students in front were as old as seventeen or eighteen.

The teacher was a local girl who had gone to the high school in Manawa. She was nineteen and not especially intelligent or well trained, but she was kind. She was teaching until the man she wanted to marry could find his own piece of land to farm.

At first, she did not notice the new little tow-headed boy in back. She was busy trying to manage some of the older children. She gave Sture a primer to look at because there were pictures. She also gave Sture and the two other children about his age each a piece of paper and a pencil.

"See if you can draw a picture from this book. Can you make your drawings pretty as these?"

She smiled. Sture smiled his disarming smile back at her. At first he did not know what she meant "to draw a picture." He knew what it was to "draw water," or for a horse to "draw" a cart or to "draw" a breath, or how to "draw" the small bow he'd made. He knew his father talked about the chimney "drawing" but he didn't know about "drawing a picture."

He read through the simple primer several times and looked around to see the other young pupils working with their pencils and looking back and forth at the pictures in the book. Then he knew. Drawing was like making the sound of a cow by listening to the cow, only on paper, with a pencil.

Sture proceeded to make almost perfect drawings, one

after another, of the pictures. Sture thought this was a wonderful idea. School was going to be even more fun than he thought. His drawings were actually superior to those in the book because most of the stories in the primer were about animals and so were the illustrations. Sture "drew" upon his constant observations of the animals to "draw" his pictures. The other little children soon saw what he was doing and stopped to watch. It was like magic the way Sture drew. He drew without hesitation as if there were some kind of invisible image already on the paper that he was tracing, copying.

When the teacher saw that the younger pupils weren't working but only staring open-mouthed at Sture, she came back to see what he was doing.

So began the schooling of Sture Modig.

The teacher quickly discovered he could do, easily, almost any task in reading or reckoning she could set. He asked to borrow several books reserved for pupils in the twelve- to fifteen-year-old range, and she willingly, but with some trepidation, agreed. Sture ran home that afternoon, barefooted, barebacked, with the books wrapped, along with his shoes, inside the rough shirt his mother had made for him. The shirt didn't get dirty because his shoes had scarcely touched the ground.

Sture immediately went out to help his father with the milking. He showed his parents the books he had been given, and since neither of them could read English well, they thought it was only natural and were glad that at last Sture was doing something normal just like any other child.

That evening after dinner, after helping his mother with the dishes, then helping his father sharpen posts for a new fence they were putting across one of the fields, Sture read his new books. He read each of them twice. One was about Ancient Greece and the conflict between Sparta and Athens. Sture was not sure with which side he felt the more sympathy. He liked the Athenians for their love of learning, but the austerity and efficiency of the Spartans appealed to him more.

The other book was an algebra book. The intricate beauty of the equations delighted him. It made him think of his feelings about how everything in nature seemed to fit.

At school, Sture quickly became assistant to the teacher. In reality, he became the teacher. He had natural patience and could help the students understand. He possessed a sixth sense for their individual minds, much like that he had for the cows and other animals.

Although he was always smiling and pleasant, even to the slowest of the students, some of the older boys became resentful. This was what Sture's father had tried to warn him about. The warning was not very necessary.

When the older boys tried to gang up on Sture in the schoolyard, they learned something new about Sture Modig. First, he was truly *modig,* brave. None of them spoke Swedish and could therefore not know this. They found out how Sture, without seeming to try, smiling all the time, could dodge like a rabbit, butt like a goat, run like a deer. If cornered he could squirm like a snake, scratch like a cat, and kick like a mule. There was no way to hurt this peculiar eight-year-old little blond boy. After a while they learned to leave him alone.

Then, in time, they joined the younger students in admiring and respecting him. It's hard to hate or hurt anyone with a smile like the young Sture Modig's. It radiated from him, let you know he saw you, knew you, felt for all your feelings.

In the classroom, before the year was out, Sture was helping even the oldest of the students. He seemed to have a special skill in finding the stumbling blocks to learning for each individual and making the problem clear.

Miss Henderson, his teacher, stayed on. Her beau had

found a proper piece of land, had bought it, and was building a barn on it, but she decided to stay another year at the school, mostly to see what would happen with Sture. She decided she'd wait until her fiancé had built the house and it was furnished.

At home, Sture became more and more interested in mechanical things. He managed to rig a crude pump run by a simple windmill to bring water from the well up to the kitchen. He worked out a system of gate latches between fields that were easily opened by a man but could not be budged by a cow. Earlier, they had only used a piece of wire wrapped around the posts. This took time to unwind, open, then rewind.

In the barn, he built a primitive forge and began making simple utensils and tools for the farm. It was there he designed the plow that made it possible for him to do plowing despite his light weight.

The plow his father used was pulled by a horse or mule and was an ordinary plowshare cutting into the ground and turning it over on the moldboard. It was attached to a pair of handles. This plow took considerable strength and skill to manage. It had to be forced into the ground, using the animal's strength to pull it through, and at the same time had to be kept straight. Sture had previously tried many times to plow so he could help his father with this most strenuous work, but it was impossible.

On his forge in the barn, he fashioned and tempered a new kind of blade. It was shaped like an upside-down T, a winged blade. The crossbar of the T was so angled it cut naturally into the earth by the pulling force of a mule or horse. Once down there, it tended to stay down and turned the earth up in two natural easy curls.

Sture then designed and carved plow handles, modeled on his father's but to his own size and longer to give him more leverage.

When he attached this new plow to a mule, it worked perfectly. With a minimum of downward pressure he got the blade into the soil, then, leaning on the handles and with the help of the winged blade under the earth, he could keep it down and at the same time it had less tendency to tip or turn.

Sture's father couldn't believe his eyes when one Saturday morning he woke to find the upper part of the south pasture already plowed. Sture had wakened at three in the morning and gone out to plow so he could surprise his father with the new invention. Sture was twelve years old now, and though not particularly large, was very strong for his age.

Sture next enlarged and improved his windmill to generate electricity. None of the other farms outside Manawa had electricity. Sture pounded out his vanes on his tiny forge, then read electricity manuals until he could wind a small electric generator with copper wire. It was enough to provide a dim, flickering light in the barn and in the kitchen. He gave this to his mother and father as a birthday gift to them on his own thirteenth birthday.

At about this time, Miss Henderson, Sture's teacher, realized there was nothing more for Sture to learn from her. She applied for his admission to the high school, where she herself had gone, in Manawa, fifteen miles away. She included samples of his work and, despite his age, Sture was accepted.

It was a hard decision for Sture's parents. They were so dependent upon him for everything, not only his incredible skills and willingness, joy in work, but his light spirit. However, they knew it would be a terrible waste not to give Sture every opportunity to be part of the great American dream; he had to go to *gymnasium*, high school. It was something beyond their wildest imaginings for themselves.

Sture insisted he could go to the high school and not miss more than an hour's work each day on the farm. His only request was for a bicycle. His parents couldn't refuse this. The farm was so much more prosperous owing to his constant contribution and effort, they must afford it.

Sture walked the more than thirty miles to Oshkosh, on Lake Winnebago, where there would be a chance to buy a bicycle.

This is the year 1908, and in Oshkosh, Sture sees his first automobile. He chases it down the street just to hear it, see it, smell it. The miracle of its running by itself, without a cow, mule, or horse pulling it, fascinates him. He's heard about automobiles but never seen one.

He also finds a bicycle shop. He spends all the afternoon watching bicycles being repaired, seeing the various types, different kinds of tires, steering systems. The men who run the shop begin to be a bit annoyed by this young boy standing around, watching their every move.

One of them goes over to Sture.

"Hey, you kid! What're you hangin' aroun' here for? What d'ya want, anyhow? You've been moping outside this shop all day. This ain't no circus, ya know."

Sture smiles his all-caring smile at him. He's tried to be careful but he knows that, just like any animal, a man, if he's watched too long, too closely, will become skittish.

"I would like to buy a bicycle but I want to look and see what kinds there are to buy."

"You know we're not giving them away, young fella. These bicycles cost a lot of money."

"Yes, I know. But I think I can pay. I only want to learn about them *before* I buy."

"You see that bicycle there?"

The man points to a black two-wheel, wheels-same-size, chain-driven-rear-wheel, pneumatic-tire bike leaning against the wall. It isn't new but has been recently repaired and refurbished.

"That there bicycle costs twelve dollars. You wanna buy it, kid?"

Sture walks over to the bicycle and looks carefully at

the machine. He fingers the chain, pushes on the rubber of the tires, takes hold of the handlebars, and shakes to check the rigidity of the frame.

The man has gotten the attention of his fellow workers. It's late summer and they're mostly in sleeveless undershirts, stained with sweat and grease. He nods his head and winks at the other workers.

"But, kid, if you got the cash, I think we could let you have that there bicycle for only eleven dollars and fifty cents!"

The man is convinced the boy only wants to hang around as so many boys do.

Sture is examining that bicycle as if it's a cow or a sick calf. With his fingers he's running all over it, checking the bolted and welded joints, sighting down the length of it for any torque or warp.

"May I try riding this bicycle?"

"You know how to ride one, young fella?"

"No, but I need it for riding to school."

Now all the workers are watching. This is going to be fun, something to break the monotony of their hard days.

"Look, kid. If you can ride that bike outta here and down the street without falling off, I'll sell it to you for only *ten* dollars."

He looks back over his shoulder at the other workers. They've all stopped working. They stand with their hands on their hips or holding tools. One straddles the bicycle on which he's working, lifts the cap from his bald head.

Sture rolls the bike by hand outside the shop. The men follow him out to watch. Sture has studied the machine carefully enough to know that in order to get it going and moving, he must start it rolling as fast as possible, as soon as possible, or it will tilt over. He also sees it has no brakes. No bicycles at that time had effective brakes. The only way to stop was to jump off or run your hand against the wheel. The trick was to somehow avoid the rapidly turning pedals. There were no free-turning wheels, no hand brakes, no coaster brakes.

Sture checks to see if his legs are long enough to reach the ground when he's straddled the center support bar. They aren't. The only way he can stop the bicycle will be to vault off, holding on to the handlebars and pulling the bicycle up on its back wheel. Sture has ridden many a cow in from the field and performed essentially the same kind of jump, so he's not afraid.

He works the pedal into position and pushes off. After a few yards of wobbling he's on his way down the street. His strong legs, incredible agility, and astounding sense of balance make it easy for him. He might have been the youngest person in Oshkosh to ride a bicycle. Bicycles at that time were for adults, definitely not toys for young boys.

Sture has some difficulty turning at the end of the street but learns to tilt his body in the direction of the turn and masters it. He starts pumping hard up the slight hill back to the shop. All the shop men are out in the street watching him. They're ready to catch him when he tries to stop. But Sture does his quick leap off one side of the bike, holding the handlebars tight so the bike rears up like a horse when its bridle is pulled back hard.

There's a moment's silence, then the shop men break out in applause. The head of the shop comes over and tousles Sture's head.

"You're really a wise guy there, ain't you, buddy. I was fooled sure enough and thought you didn't know from nothin' about a bicycle, but you must work in some circus or somethin'. I never seed nobody get off a fast bike that way; I was sure you was gonna break your fool neck."

Sture only smiles into his eyes, his own eyes sparkling from the pleasure of the ride. The separation from the earth, the speed, the sense of control and leverage on space, exhilarate him.

"Yes sir. If it's all right with you, I do want to buy this bicycle. I'll be back with the money in just five minutes."

Sture dashes off and the men laugh. None of them has any idea Sture is actually going to buy the bicycle, and they're amused at how the head of the shop got fooled into giving this fresh kid a free ride.

They go back to work. Sture has gone around the corner to get money out from the lining of his jacket where he's sewn it. He has fifteen silver dollars.

He pulls out ten of them, then quickly sews back the remaining five. Since he was seven, Sture has repaired all his own clothes. He's enjoyed long evenings quilting with his mother. He can sew with almost the adeptness and precision of a tailor. He bites off the thread and puts the needle back into the collar of his jacket, where he keeps it. He slides on a small piece of wood bark to cover the point. A needle is a precious object to Sture.

Then Sture runs back to the shop with his ten dollars clutched tightly in his hand. He walks up to the shop boss.

"So you're back again, you little tyke. What do you want, another free ride? I'm almost tempted to give you one just to see if you can pull off that trick you did there."

"I've come to pay for the bicycle. Is that all right? You said if I could ride it without falling you'd sell it to me for ten dollars."

The shop boss leans back looking down over his long handlebar mustache and beer belly at this little sinewy, blond boy.

"I did say that, didn't I?"

He looks around at the rest of the men in the shop smiling. They've all stopped working again.

"Well, I'll tell you, young feller, if you can get up that ten dollars in the next five minutes I'll give you back fifty cents of it right here. How's that? And then you'd better get out of here because we're not getting any work done what with watching your shenanigans."

He folds his muscular arms. Sture opens his hand with the ten silver dollars. The shop boss leans forward, his mouth open, his hands gradually falling to his sides in bewilderment.

"Sir, if you'll put out your hand I'll count the ten dollars into it. But you don't have to give me back the fifty cents because it wouldn't be fair. You didn't know I already had the money."

Sture starts counting the money into the shop boss's hand. The whole shop crowds around.

"Hey, boss, you'd better take a bite of that there money; it could be just tin or somethin'."

But the shop boss knows these are real honest-to-God U.S. mint dollars. Sture continues counting, trying to make sure the man is paying attention.

"There they are, ten of them, sir. Would you write me a letter of receipt so no one will say I stole this bicycle?"

At first, no one moves. Then the entire shop breaks out laughing. They slap themselves on the knees and each other on the back. The shop boss stands staring at his hand.

"How do I know you didn't steal this *money?*"

Sture gives him his open, blank, but deeply meaningful stare.

"Because I tell you, sir. I earned that money with my parents, working on the farm, and this is the first thing I've ever bought and I think I shall be most happy with my bicycle."

Sture walks over and holds the handlebars possessively. He's waiting.

"Sir, I'd appreciate it if you'd write that receipt so I can get home before it gets dark. I wouldn't want to hurt this wonderful bicycle by hitting a bump and bending a wheel or breaking the frame."

"Just where do you come from, kid, and how in hell

did some hick milk farmers get ten dollars together to buy a first-class quality bicycle like this? That's what I want to know. You tell me and I'll give you that fifty cents, one of the best deals you'll ever make in your life even if it is the first one."

"I live near Manawa and we got the money by working hard and being careful."

"How in hell did you get all the way from Manawa to Oshkosh anyway? That's over thirty goddamned miles."

Sture smiles another of his magic smiles with a slight shadow of frown built into it. How else could he have gotten here? He wouldn't saddle up a horse for such a short trip, he hadn't had his bicycle yet, and he surely didn't have one of those automobiles.

"I walked, sir. That's not true, actually, I ran most of the way. I wanted to see what a bicycle really looks like and find out all about them and I have no place to stay here so I must get back today, there was no other way."

"What time did you start, then?"

"About an hour before sunup."

"But you were here just about time we ate lunch. You mean you went thirty miles in only seven hours?"

"I guess so. I run fast, sir. May I please have the receipt so I can go home? My mother will worry if I'm out too long past dark. With the bicycle I should go faster but I must leave now."

"Well, I'll be hornswoggled!"

One of the men yells out from between the spokes of a bicycle:

"You were, Pat. Now give the kid his four bits and his receipt so he can pedal that bicycle thirty miles home. Probably he'll make it in about four hours and be there for late supper."

So, that's the way it ended. Sture got his bicycle and pedaled it at maximum speed over the dirt roads and back paths all the way home. He was home at ten o'clock, just as the last light was leaving the sky. Sture felt bad because he'd missed both milkings, but his bicycle was everything he desired. He rolled it directly into the kitchen for his mother and father to see. They were in their night clothes. Sture got out an old cloth and a bucket of water to wash off the spatters of mud and the coat of thick dust, so they could enjoy it with him as he'd first seen it.

"Dad, I go so fast not even mosquitoes can catch me. I went the whole way and not one bite, see?"

He holds out his thin, bare, but not fragile arms.

"Up high like that, Mom, you can see everything and I think I got home in half the time it took me running down there. Think of it: half the time."

That September, Sture began high school. He'd do the morning milking early with his father then start out on his bicycle. Most of the country roundabout was fairly flat, but it was a slow, long uphill pump to school. Sture would wear his farm clothes directly from milking and tie his school clothes on his back with his lunch.

At school, after he'd locked his bicycle, he'd go into the boys' room and change. He kept his farm clothes cached in a cubbyhole out of sight over the toilet. The high school was large, with inside toilets.

Sture quickly settled into his studies. At first, most of the other pupils thought he was only a child visiting. Sture was not particularly small but he was thirteen years old, two years younger than any of the other students. Within a few weeks, however, the other students knew about him. His class participation, questions, his first test and examination results set him apart. The teachers, originally apprehensive about so young a student, soon began to delight in his learning ability. His algebra teacher couldn't believe Sture's competence; it was unnatural the ease with which he handled the more complicated algebra usually reserved for the most advanced students. His

Latin teacher insisted he must have studied Latin before; no one could absorb and use so much of a new language without previous experience. Sture didn't know it, but by Christmas there had been several teachers' meetings devoted almost exclusively to him.

Sture enjoyed his school work, but because he had to leave immediately after the last bell, there was no time for socializing. He used the short lunch period to nibble on a piece of home-baked black bread and hard Cheddar. The school library was a place of wonder to him, and it was there he went for lunch. He quickly learned one was not allowed to eat in the library, so he started cutting his bread and cheese into bite-size pieces and stashing them in his pockets to be eaten surreptitiously.

Sture's mind was still mostly captivated by his bicycle. He'd bought a lock and chain so he could secure it to a post near the school gate. He was working on a way to pedal up the hill to school faster and more easily and at the same time not use all his energy going home by holding back on the pedals. After much experimentation he developed two different shanks to attach the pedals to the sprocket. One set was very short, only about four inches, and the other long, long as he could make them without his pedals touching the ground. When he went to school he used the long shank and could pump up the hills much more easily. He'd carry the short shanks with his school clothes, books, and lunch. Then, on the way home, he'd substitute the short shanks on the pedals and could pedal at great speed, getting home easily in time to milk the cows. In fact, on that bicycle, coming down that hill from school, he was probably the fastest-traveling human being within a hundred miles of Oshkosh. He started getting home too early for milking and began staying on an extra half hour to work in the library, where it was quiet and there was good, steady electric light.

* * *

Sture went through his high-school years, pedaling from home to school every day. Winters he tied rope around the wheels of his bicycle so he could get a grip in ice and snow. Even on days when snowdrifts were up to the second story of his house he snowshoed to school. Twice he was the only pupil to show up in his classes.

At the farm, they'd increased the herd by ten cows and that meant more milking, so Sture's time at school was soon limited to class time. He read almost every book in the school library. It was as if he ate books. In the evenings, he read everything he could, on the pretext he was doing homework for school. He actually could do all his required assignments during lunchtime at the library.

The world interested Sture. He began to want to travel and see some of it. He worked ever harder at the farm but he knew it was not where he wanted to be all his life.

He graduated from high school at sixteen with every prize and honor, but there was no way for him to go on to a college or university.

He helped his father build an extension to the barn, and together they installed an indoor toilet and bathtub. Sture's father and mother lived in a constant amazement at their son, and at the same time worried about him. He didn't seem to smile as much. He didn't talk with the animals any more. All he did was read books.

He wanted them to buy a tractor. He mailed away and got catalogues of tractors, showing them to his mother and father, trying to explain the work they could do with one, how the farm would prosper. But there wasn't enough money for that, and their simple, saving Swedish minds couldn't allow for borrowing any more money; already the mortgage payments were hard enough to make.

There were no girls in Sture's life. He didn't go to any of the social events at school, partly because he was too young, too small; but mostly because in his experience the unpredictability of girls made them unpleasant to him. Sture liked things to proceed with some understandable logic and direction. He could understand most things, but the things he could not understand he avoided. He tried to avoid illness, art, music, and girls. This was another weakness of Sture's. He valued consistency and predictability far more than change and chance.

His greatest interest was still in machinery of any kind. Man designed machines, therefore they were understandable by another man. It was like mathematics. If he took his time and paid careful attention, he felt he could understand any machine or any equation that someone else could invent. He also felt he could invent either machines or mathematics.

He invented many machines; one was a machine for washing clothes. It was run by his windmill and turned paddles back and forth in a large tub. The problem was he could never get his mother to use it; she was afraid of it, or any machine. Sture became the one who washed clothes on the farm. He was also working on a mechanical system for milking cows. He was trying to do it with vacuum pumps, also run by his windmill, but couldn't get the pressure valves regulated and the milk kept running up into his vacuum lines instead of out and into the milk pail.

He managed to build a small crystal radio set with which they could hear music from Oshkosh. This was a machine his mother *did* like. For her it was what reading was to Sture, a way to go away without leaving the farm.

When World War I started, Sture took a great interest in its progress. This horrendous conflict between men, in which thousands were dying, seemed incredibly illogical to him. He could not conceive of any other animal participating in such a crazy orgy of killing, maiming, and destruction. He would buy the daily newspaper in Manawa every day and pedal home with it quickly. It became part of his reading program. There was hardly a book in the high school and public library there he had not read, so the newspaper filled a gap in his reading time and a gap in his worldly knowledge.

In 1917, Sture was twenty-one years old and one of the first in his area to be drafted into the army. He had mixed feelings. He hated leaving the farm in the hands of his, to him, aging parents. They were at this time sixty years old. He also did not want to be killed.

But the chance to travel, to see what the rest of the world was really like, and to find for himself the nature of this seeming carnage going on in Europe, had its fascination. When Sture boarded the train going to training camp in Fort Benning, Georgia, he still had not been any farther from home than Oshkosh and he still hadn't kissed a girl, or even held hands with one.

His parents kissed him tearfully goodbye and assured him they would keep the farm in good order while he was away. They were frightened for him, at the same time proud. It was part of his being a *real* American, going away to fight for his country.

PART 3

*T*HE way they let us out at our school is exactly as if they were letting us out of some prison. We're all lined up in twos, girls in one line, boys in the other. The little first graders get to go first and then it's each grade till the eighth graders, who're last. We have to march with our schoolbags almost like in step at a parade. Anybody who goes to a Catholic school is all ready for the army; they only need to teach you how to shoot a gun.

I've been thinking about Cannibal all day, even during religion. He still bites at my finger when I put it near him but it isn't as if he wants to hurt me; he's only holding on. He's also started wrapping his little body around my hand, holding tight with his paws. Sometimes he forgets to pull in his claws so I've got scratches on the backs of my hands. I try not to let Mom see them and she hasn't said anything yet.

In our school we have what are called safeties. The top four kids in every class from fourth through eighth grade get to wear a white belt with a white shoulder strap and a badge. These safeties are supposed to help us cross streets so we won't get killed by automobiles going past our school. Most of the time there aren't any cars, so it isn't much of a job. I almost got to be a safety once but the sixty I got in religion kept me out.

After we get past where the safeties are, we cut loose like wild animals down Lewis Avenue all the way to Long Lane. There's a lot shorter way for getting to our house than going straight down Lewis but we're not allowed to go that way.

Old man Stringle is at Long Lane, where Lewis comes in, and he's supposed to help us across. There are some cars on Long Lane, practically traffic, almost, but I cross it all the time and I've never been killed.

Mr. Stringle is so old he can hardly see and lots of times, especially in the afternoons, he's so drunk he can just barely stand up. He walks out in front of cars, without looking, smiling, laughing, and waving us across. He's big, fat, with fat fingers and flat feet. I think he spends the time between lunch and the time school gets out at the Triangle Café, right up the street.

When I get across Long Lane, I'm supposed to wait for Laurel. Usually she's behind me, even though she got out first; the little ones can't keep up with us when we make the mad dash down Lewis Avenue. It's actually amazing the first and second graders don't get smashed into the ground.

Once, John Williamson stepped off a curb running with us and broke his collarbone. I didn't even know there was a bone to hang collars on; maybe that's how big businessmen and people in the movies keep their collars so clean and straight. My collar and necktie always gets wrinkled and sweaty, also the tie works its way around my neck. Maybe I don't have a collarbone. It'd help explain things.

I don't mind waiting for Laurel. We don't usually talk much walking home but it's nice walking with her. Laurel and I fight sometimes but mostly we keep each other company and play together a lot. I taught her to read and she could read the first-grade book when she was only four. I don't know what she's doing in first grade now where all the other kids are learning to read. She's probably as bored as I am. The Catholic school doesn't have a kindergarten; that's at the public school. So we have one year more freedom than the Protestants.

We're walking together along Long Lane when a really gigantic, shiny, fancy car pulls up beside us. It has a running board covered with black clean rubber, almost as if nobody ever stepped on it. There are great extra wheels in metal holders on the running boards set in the front fenders, and it has a slanted windshield. We both stop to look at this car; we don't usually see anything like this in our neighborhood.

There are four men in the car. They're all wearing suits and they look sweaty even though it isn't very hot. Of course, I'm hot from running, but that's natural. The man in the front seat rolls down his window and leans out. He has a wide space between his teeth and he has red eyelids.

"Hey, kid! You Dickie Kettleson?"

I nod my head. Laurel gets behind me.

"Remember, Dickie, Mother says we're not to talk with strange men or get in other people's cars."

Sure I remember. I'm already thinking of running. The man holds something out in his hand. It looks like an envelope.

"Here, kid. You take this. Give it to your old man and say some friends of his gave it to you."

I reach over and take the envelope. No sooner do I have it in my hand than he rolls up his window and that car speeds off down Long Lane, through the stores, and over the little hill to Marshall Road. I don't think I ever saw a car go that fast down Long Lane.

Laurel and I look at each other, then start running home. We speed past Mr. Marsden's office and up our street fast as we can. We go in through our alley the way we usually do, and I stop in the cellar to see how Cannibal's doing. I've already begun to think Cannibal isn't a he but is a she. I don't have any real reason for thinking this, but every day I'm becoming more sure.

"Come on, Dickie, you can't play with the kitten now. You've got to give that letter to Mom."

Laurel sometimes calls Cannibal a kitten, but to me it's been a cat from the beginning. There's nothing of a kitten there; it might be a he or a she, and it's tiny, but it definitely is *not a* kitten. She's asleep and looks fine.

We go upstairs and Mom's in the kitchen. I tell her about the man stopping. Rather, we both tell her, Laurel interrupting me and me interrupting her, then both of us talking at the same time. Mom doesn't like confusion. She looks from one of us to the other but she's smiling.

"I can't tell hide nor hair from what you're saying. What man, what car, what envelope?"

I hold the envelope out to her and she opens it right there in the kitchen.

I'm already sitting down to our lunch spread out on the table: tomato soup and cheese sandwiches again. Laurel's sitting on the other side. I look up. Mom's face is turning white and she's running her hands through her hair.

Then she sort of half screams and starts crying. She runs out of the kitchen into the living room and locks the front door. Then she runs upstairs.

Laurel and I look at each other. We only have half an hour for lunch, so we eat. The radio's on and they're playing that Helen Trent song, "Just a little love, a little kiss . . ." Before we leave, Mom comes down again and locks the kitchen door; then goes downstairs and locks the cellar door. I can hear the lock click. Then she comes back up and sits at the table. She leans close and gives each of us a big hug, so hard it hurts. You don't think of Mom as strong, but adults, even small ladies, are strong compared to kids.

She's crying. She has a hard time talking. She still has that envelope and the letter in her hands getting wet with sweat and, I guess, tears. The letter looks strange. It isn't written or even typed but somebody's cut out different-size letters from magazines and pasted them all over the paper. It's like something in the movies. Maybe Laurel and I are going to be kidnaped the way they did the Lindbergh baby. No, that's dumb; we're not worth anything.

Mom looks me straight in the eye; I'm finishing the last spoonfuls of soup, tipping the bowl. The clock on our wall says we still have almost fifteen minutes before school starts. We're having a test in arithmetic but that'll be easy. It's easy but boring.

"Tell me everything again, Dickie. Where did the car stop you? What did the man look like? Tell me everything."

I tell her everything I can remember and so does Laurel. That's when Mom says we're to stay in the house and not go back to school. I try telling her about my arithmetic test but it doesn't make any difference. I'll get to play with Cannibal so it's O.K. with me, only Laurel begins crying. I think she's just crying because Mom's crying. She can't really want to go back to school as bad as that.

So all afternoon I stay in the cellar playing with Cannibal. It's almost as if I'm sick or it's Saturday. Laurel plays with her paper dolls and we try to stay out of the way. Mom keeps coming down to the cellar and asking if we're all right. Of course we're all right; we're in our own cellar. She even checks the lock on the cellar door. I don't think we've locked the cellar door in the daytime, ever.

We're all down there, in the cellar, waiting, when Dad comes home. Mom wouldn't even let me go meet Dad; in fact, she started crying again when I asked if I could.

Dad comes in and Mom falls into his arms. Laurel and I are sitting on the floor beside Cannibal. We have some old newspapers under us. Neither of us can figure what's going on. Mom pushes away from Dad and hands him the piece of paper with the cutout letters. She's been carrying it around in her hand the whole day, so it's all wrinkled.

Dad looks over her shoulder at us, especially at me. He puts down his work jacket and lunch pail on his bench. He holds on to Mom while he reads the piece of paper, holding it in one hand. He has his work cap tipped back on his head, his blue one with the brim like a baseball player's cap. As he reads, he lets go of Mom and holds the paper in both hands. His hands start shaking.

"What is this? Where did this come from?"

He looks at Mom, at Laurel, at me. I try to tell him what happened, about the man, the car, and all but I'm getting scared myself. I've never seen Dad so scared-looking and mad at the same time; he looks cut in half; his lips are quivering and tears are coming into his eyes. He turns away from us and faces the dart board.

"Oh my God! Don't let this happen."

Then he holds on to Mom again, the two of them in the center of our cellar. Laurel gets up, goes over, and grabs Dad by his leg. It's what I want to do myself but can't. Mom's crying hard, shaking against Dad.

"You've *got* to quit, Dick; we'll just move away from here. Nothing's worth this; my nerves can't stand it. I've been so afraid for you, now it's all of us. Please, why can't you just do your job like everybody else and get out of all this union business?"

Dad puts his arms around Mom again with the note in his hand. I can see it flat against her back. The letters are big and clear, though some of them are crooked, but it's easy to read. It says:

LITTLE KIDS SHOULD STAY HOME AND NOT WALK AROUND IN STREETS. SOMETHING BAD MIGHT HAPPEN

A FRIEND

We don't go to school for the next two days. Mom won't let us out of the house but Dad goes off to work. It's like when we had the chicken pox and were quarantined but there's no yellow sticker on our door.

When he comes home Friday night, Dad looks smaller, more than tired—worn down. He hasn't been eating much at dinner and I can hear them talking all night in the bedroom. They talk about police and my father's having borrowed a gun from Uncle Joe, his brother. Uncle Joe brought it home from the war. Mom's afraid of the gun. I don't mind missing school at all and I'm getting to play a lot with Cannibal; Mom even lets me play with Cannibal upstairs sometimes, but she still has to sleep in the cellar.

Cannibal's learning to use the sandbox; it's as if she *knows* that's the place to do her mess. She doesn't have any mother to teach her and I don't teach her at all. She just starts going over there and scratching around when she has to go. It's terrific to see because she's still so little. It's hard to describe how tiny she is and still how much she's a real cat, not a kitten.

I've made a little house for her out of a Borden cheese box Dad always used to keep extra screws in. He told me I could have it and showed me how to make a nice little carrying box from it, with a handle. Those boxes are something beautiful. All the corners dovetail cuts and glued. Dad says the cheese is worth buying just for the box. They used to make the same kind of box for scrapple in the old days, Dad says, but now they only use a cardboard box. I like the song they sing on the radio about Philadelphia scrapple. It's one of those songs I can't get out of my mind. It goes:

> Listen to this, friends of mine,
> Philadelphia scrapple's fine.
> Try it once and you'll agree
> It's the thing for you and me.

Some people say scrapple's made from dead horses, cats, and dogs but I like it anyway. In our family we all like fried scrapple with our eggs; it's almost's good as bacon and a lot cheaper. It's one thing that's good with ketchup on it.

The top of Cannibal's cage slides in little grooves and Dad drills small holes all around the sides so Cannibal can see out. I get down low next to the box and peek in at her through the holes; it's like looking at a tiger or a lion at a zoo or in a circus. And Cannibal doesn't mind being in the box at all; in fact, she seems to like it. I think she feels safe in there, and it's hard for Cannibal to feel safe.

Saturday morning at breakfast Dad tells us we're going to Wildwood! *Nobody* goes to Wildwood during school time. I look over at Mom but she won't look back. I look over at Laurel, and she's as mixed up as I am. She puts her spoon into her cereal.

"But, Dad, Sister Carmelina will get mad at me if I don't go. She must already be awful mad because I've been absent two days and I'm not even sick."

"Don't worry, Laurie. I'll fix it up with Sister. You, too, Dickie. I'll explain everything at school. You don't have anything to worry about; I'll even get your lessons and homework for you. In fact, I'm going to the convent now; then we'll start on our trip."

I can't believe it. I'm not going to mind missing school but it's all so strange. I begin to think we're going into hiding or something, the way they do in a cops-and-robbers movie; maybe we're hiding from Alice the Goon.

Dad's so serious, sad, and choked-up mad. Mom is just white, her freckles standing out like dark brown spots on her face against her deep red hair. Her eyes are the same pale green as Cannibal's now. Everything's so uncomfortable in the house I'll be glad to go anywhere just for a chance to get away.

Mom has us ready and Dad comes back with our lessons for the next week. He doesn't tell us anything about what Sister Anastasia or Sister Carmelina said. We pack the car and, just like that, we drive off and leave our house. Dad had gone around locking all the doors and windows while Mom vacuumed and dusted. It's the closest thing to actually moving I can remember. When we moved into this house I was too little, so I have no idea what it really is to move, to leave the place you live in. Laurel gets to bring along two dolls and I can bring Cannibal and a deck of cards. Maybe if Dad isn't working we'll have time to play some Euchre. That's one card game I really like, and sometimes I can even beat Dad.

Dad's put the back seat in our car again. When he uses our car as a truck he keeps this seat in the garage. The car's open to the air in back of us but that's where Dad has put our two suitcases and tied them in so there's no way we can fall out. He's bolted the seats onto the floor again, too. The wind blows around some so it's like a rumble seat; if we tip our heads back we can look right up at the sky. We've never ridden in a rainstorm so I don't know if water would get in on us or not if it rained.

Both Laurel and I are leaning way out the car when we go over the Delaware River Bridge. I never knew there was anything so big. Alongside the bridge, they have an advertisement for Whitman chocolates. There's a little man with a cap on and he's outlined in different lights so the lights make him look as if he's running with a big box of chocolates under his arm. I hold Cannibal up so she can see all this but she only looks at me. I don't think she wants to look out the window of a car when it's moving. I'm so happy seeing all these new things I'm hoping we don't ever go home again.

Dad's face is still white except behind his ears, which are red with the morning light shining through them. He has his hands gripped on the steering wheel so hard I think he might break it.

We have to pay twenty-five cents' toll on the other side of the bridge. Most of the cars in the lines at the toll booths are newer than ours but I don't think any of them is practically handmade by one man the way ours is.

Then we get on the Whitehorse Pike or the Blackhorse Pike, I'm not sure which. Laurel keeps looking out the window. I want to play Fish with her but she says she wants to see the horse first.

Mom is sitting quietly and tries talking to Dad once in a while, but he only hunches over tight, hard-driving the car, staring out the windshield, saying nothing. Finally, that is, after I explain how there won't be any horse, that it's only the name of this road, Laurel and I get to playing Fish.

Laurel never *tries* to cheat but lots of times she forgets she has a card or sometimes it gets hidden behind another card because her hands are too little to spread the cards right. So we get into a big argument when she asks for my three jacks after I've asked her for the same thing and she's told me to go fish.

Cannibal is on the seat beside me in her box sleeping. I keep hoping she won't do her business before we get to Wildwood. Dad'd said he'd stop a couple times on the way down but maybe he's forgotten. I guess I'm scared about that, because I never should've started arguing and fighting with Laurel about three jacks. They don't mean anything; it's only a game we're playing while we drive to

Wildwood and she's little, and maybe she just fished that jack. But I do it. She gets so mad she messes up the whole fish pile and pushes them onto the floor. That's when I get mad and slap her hand, then she cries.

Dad turns around and starts hitting at both of us, keeping his other hand tight on the steering wheel.

"God damn it! You kids stop it. How can anybody expect me to drive with you two fighting all the time."

He doesn't even look back at us and he's slapping left and right, hard. My dad's strong and we both slip down off the seat into the foot space with the cards. Normally, Dad *never* hits us. Mom always says he's going to if we're not good, but he never does. Mom's holding on to Dad's arm.

"Stop it, Dick! For heaven's sake, don't take it out on them. They're only playing. It's not their fault. Stop it now!"

And Mom starts crying. Dad stops swinging his arm, turns, looks at Mom as if he could kill her, too, then holds on to the steering wheel even harder than before. The bump in his cheek is going in and out faster, deeper than I've ever seen. There's a line of muscle like a string going up inside his cheek almost to where his eye is, and it's sticking out and disappearing every time the bump does. I see this by looking in the rear-view mirror from on the floor because he's staring out at the road, not looking back.

Mom gets up on her knees and turns around to face us in the back seat. We're still on the floor and I'm trying to pick up all the cards. Cannibal fell off the seat when I slid down and she's on the floor with me. Laurel's crying and I think I am, too; not because Daddy hit us, even though he does hit hard, but because it's all so awful, everybody crying and even Dad practically crying, too.

"Look, you two, get those cards all picked up and sit back on that seat. Laurel, you stay on your side and, Dickie, you stay on yours. It's hard enough for your father driving all this way without you two fighting and taking his mind off the road."

We both slide back onto the seat. We're afraid to look at each other. I'm trying not to look at Mom. I don't like to hear or see her cry and she's been crying so much the last days. Everything seems so terrible, and I wish Dad was waxing floors at night and we could go back to building porches together. It's that stinking, rotten J.I. job that's made everything go wrong. I'm almost afraid to talk to my own mother, but I do.

"Mom, Daddy said we'd stop so Cannibal could go to the toilet. She hasn't done anything yet but I'm afraid she might."

Mom, still up on her knees, looks over at Dad. He looks at me in the rear-view mirror; his eyes almost smile.

"O.K., Dickie. We'll stop at the next pull-over place. Maybe we can buy fresh fruit and vegetables. New Jersey grows some of the best tomatoes and corn in the world. It's probably too late in the season but we might just be able to get some if one of these roadside stands is still open."

Mom leans close, kisses Dad on the side of the head just behind the ear, and slides down on her seat, not against the door where she's been all the time before on this trip, but near to him, where she usually sits when we drive anywhere.

Laurel and I look at each other; it's so good having Daddy talk again. I don't even worry much if he forgets and we don't stop for Cannibal. But we do. Daddy sees a stand on the other side of the road. There's practically no traffic, and he pulls across the road and parks on the dirt.

It's a stand with a canvas top and they have all kinds of fruits and vegetables. Mom and Dad go over to buy stuff with Laurel while I go around in back to let Cannibal out. After she's sniffed for a few minutes and fought two leaves, she does her business behind a tree, scratching away with her tiny paws and claws. When she's finished, I pee too, then walk back to the car.

After they buy the fruit and things, Laurel and Mom go around behind the stand, on the other side, while Dad comes back to the car. He puts the bags in with our suitcases. He opens one up and takes out two beautiful pears. He gives one to me and bites into the other himself. It's so juicy, juice runs over his hand and down his arm. He wipes it with the red bandana he always keeps in his back pocket. My grandfather keeps a red bandana in his back pocket like that, too. Sometime, when I've grown up, I'll get a bandana and I'll never go anywhere without it. I tell Dad how Cannibal did her business without any trouble at all.

"I don't particularly like cats, Dickie, but that's a smart one all right. Come on now, eat your pear. I'm sorry I took some whacks at you and Laurel like that. I'm just all mixed up right now about my job with J.I. and all the union business; then there's that letter and all, O.K.?"

I can't talk so I nod my head. I bite into the pear. I like pears actually but some of them have a grainy feeling. This one is smooth and delicious.

Dad climbs up into the front seat. We see Mom and Laurel coming out of the trees. Laurel's running and Mom's walking the way she does, as if she's still a high-school girl and not a mother at all. Nobody else's mother I know of walks like that.

We don't have any trouble at all finding a place to stay in Wildwood. The place my parents finally decide on is built around a court and is only two squares from the beach. Our room is big, big as our living room and dining room at home put together, and is on the second floor. It opens out onto a little balcony, which goes around the inside of the court. We have our own sink in one corner of the room near the big bed where Mom and Dad will sleep, and there's a toilet just at the corner of our floor, opening onto the balcony. The beds are metal and painted a creamy white. There are rugs on the floor. Laurel and I have separate beds next to each other at the other end of the room near the door you come in.

It's such fun thinking of sleeping in a different bed in a different house in a different place. Mrs. Sykes says we aren't supposed to cook in the room because of fire regulations, but then she winks at Mom and says something about it being O.K. to warm up some soup or hot milk for us kids.

Gee, I hope Mom doesn't warm up any hot milk. I don't like milk much anyway, but hot milk can make me sick; it brings out the smell of cows even stronger.

It's fun unpacking, and each of us has two drawers to store our clothes. Dad and Mom are more fun and not so serious. I let Cannibal out and she decides to fight everything that hangs or moves, like the covers on the bed and a ball of dust in one of the corners.

I'm wishing we could stay here forever. Maybe Dad and I could get to building porches around Wildwood and make a good living. We'd never tell anybody I was here so they wouldn't make me go to school. Even in this one place I see plenty of porch work that needs to be done. There are at least four boards on the balcony that're cracked and need replacing, and I'm sure most of the posts holding up the balcony are rotting at the bottom because the floor of the balcony leans out and some of the railings are wobbly.

Later, down at the shower, under the toilet, I find that most of the wood is rotting from all the water. There must be at least a hundred places like this in Wildwood where we could fix things up. Dad doesn't need that darned J.I. for anything. We can be free. We'd just go back, pick up his tools, then live here. Those company goons could never find us.

We get unpacked and eat lunch. We eat apples and

pears while Mom cooks some of the corn on a little hot plate in a pot we brought with us. Dad keeps feeling the wires to see if the hot plate is going to overheat them but it's O.K. After he's convinced the wires aren't getting hot, he goes out to the fuse box on the porch near the bathroom, unscrews one of the fuses, the one with the number of our room on it, and puts a penny down in the bottom of the hole, then screws the fuse back over it.

"That's not a very safe thing to do, usually, Dickie, but now we won't blow any fuses and those wires are heavy enough to hold any current we use. We'll have to cook here because we can't be going out to restaurants all the time, you know."

I know. I've never even been to a restaurant; neither has Laurel. When I see movies of people at restaurants I try to figure it out. Somebody you don't see seems to do the cooking and then people all dressed up bring you the food and nobody ever does the dishes.

The corn is delicious; Mom even has plates, butter, and salt to go with it. We eat more fruit for dessert. We put the extra fruit back in the paper bag they gave us at the fruit stand and slide it far under the bed. Cannibal goes under to see what it is, maybe some kind of monster she can fight, but I squeeze under and pull her out.

It's sure hard catching a cat when it doesn't have a tail. She's still just as liable as not to bite my hand when I put it under her body pulling her away from something she wants to investigate.

After lunch, Dad goes out the door with his bathing suit over his shoulder.

"I'm going down to that shower and put on my suit. Who knows how many nice days like this we'll get. You people change up here, and when I come back I want everybody ready to jump into that big old ocean out there with me."

Mom stops putting the eating things away and jams her hands on her hips.

"Don't be in such a hurry, Dick. Try to relax, enjoy yourself."

"That's just what I'm going to do, honey, in that soft blue ocean: relax. You guys better be ready if you want to come with me."

With that he's gone. I'm already slipping my shirt over my head. I know where my bathing suit is. I turn my back on Mom and Laurel and slip it on. I must have grown since summer because it's hard getting the straps over my shoulders.

When I turn around, Mom and Laurel are practically ready, too. Mom's wearing a bathing suit but she won't go in the ocean. For some reason she's always been afraid of the water, even little ponds or Morton pool.

"Put your clothes away, Dickie. If we're all going to live in this one room you've got to put your things away before they get spread all over the place."

Laurel's already folding and putting her things in her drawer. She's like that even at home. It must be discouraging for my folks having a boy; I never think of putting things away, and even when I do, I usually forget again before I do it.

I put Cannibal in her box. She seems to like it in there; lots of times she crawls in herself when she wants to sleep. I think she'd even slide the top on if she could, just to feel safe.

"Can I take Cannibal with me, Mom?"

"What, take a cat to the beach? Oh, I guess so. But you ask your father."

Just then, Dad comes to the door. He has his clothes over one arm and his towel on the other. He's wet and his hair's dripping as if he's already been in the ocean but I think he only took a shower. He's wearing his bathing suit with holes in the sides and the big K Mom's sewn on each of our suits. We all have black suits with big white

K's sewn on them. Mom says it's so she can find us on any crowded beach or at any pool but I think it has something to do with her idea of being a family. Maybe it's my idea of being part of our family, too. I know I really like having a big K sewn on like that. It's as if our family is a varsity football team.

Dad doesn't come in the room except to lay his clothes on the chair just inside the door. He says I can take Cannibal with me if I want. Mom has the key and locks up after us. We're really going to walk down this little street and see the ocean. It's been so long for me I can hardly remember what it looks like, except it's big. Laurel says she doesn't remember the ocean at all.

We've both been swimming at League Island in Philadelphia summertimes but there's more people than water there. We've also gone out to Morton pool on some really hot days in summer, but that's almost the same thing, it's so crowded, and it's expensive; League Island's free.

Dad's put his arm around Mom's shoulders. She's holding on to Laurel's hand with her other hand and I'm behind with a towel in one hand and Cannibal in the other. I wonder what a tiny cat like Cannibal will think of a whole ocean. I'll bet the sand on that beach will seem like the biggest sandbox in the world. That might not be so good.

Dad lets go of Mom and spins around to see if I'm coming along. I smile. He smiles back. It's so great to see him smiling. He points at my chest then at the K on his own.

"Boy, Dickie, we look like the original members of those crazy Ku Klux Klan people in the South. Some niggers around here are liable to pull out knives and cut off our ears."

Mom looks back, waiting up for me.

"At least I can always find all of you; you know how nervous I get when I don't know where you are."

Dad turns, puts his arm around Mom again, kisses her on the shoulder.

"We won't have any trouble with crowds this time of year. We might even have that whole ocean to ourselves."

"Well, I give my part of the ocean to you, Dick. If I'm going to drown, at least I want warm water."

"Laura, I'll bet the water will be warmer than it's been any day in August. That ocean's been soaking up sun all summer and it's out there waiting for us. This visit to the shore might be the best thing that ever happened."

. He musses Mom's hair gently, slips his arm around her again. I look back.

At least there's practically nobody around to see them acting like lovers in some kind of lovey movie with John Boles and Greta Garbo.

"Don't worry about drowning, Laura honey. So far's I know there's never been a case yet of anybody drowning on the beach in the sand."

"Please don't try to teach me swimming again, Dick, please! Let's just enjoy ourselves."

"O.K., O.K. But you don't know what you're missing. Those kids of ours will be swimming circles around you and probably me too before this week is out."

And Dad means it. He shows me how to reach out from my dog paddle I learned at the Morton pool and actually swing my arms over my head as if I'm really swimming. He makes me kick my legs hard, too, all the way from the hips, not just from the knees. I swim to him every time and he catches me.

"Now, Dickie, if you get a mouthful of water, the important thing is to be expecting it and spit it out like this."

He ducks his head under water and spits a long stream of water in the air like a whale or a horse in the street, pissing upside down.

"Now you stay here and practice. I want to get Laurie swimming this year; she's big enough now."

He strides in to where Laurie is playing at the edge of the water, running in and out as the waves chase her. Mom's just above the water's edge with our towels. I wave and she waves back. I know she's watching me every minute; there's no way I could ever drown, with her watching and Dad swimming the way he does; it's better than ten lifeguards. There aren't any real lifeguards at all; I guess they don't have them this time of year.

I try my new swimming a few more times. It isn't as much fun as it is swimming to Dad because I can't tell how far I've swum; the ocean is so big my little bit of swimming doesn't matter much; but still it's fun and I even learn to spit water the way Dad showed me. I see what Dad means. I'm beginning to feel how I'm going to enjoy the ocean all my life.

Dad holds Laurie under the stomach and is pulling her along, telling her how to kick and swing her arms. Most of the time he holds her almost completely out of the water, but sometimes he lets her down in some so she gets water over her face.

"Just float, Laurie, don't struggle so. Honest, the water will hold you up if you only relax. Try just lying out on the water."

"Promise you won't let me go. Promise!"

"Don't worry. I promise."

He supports her, moving her along some more, while she pulls her thin arms through the water and flutters her legs. She keeps pushing her hair back with her hands. I take another swim trying to make it ten strokes before I bring my feet down to the bottom. I'm always afraid I'll bring my feet down and there won't be any bottom there, and then I'll drown.

"See, Dickie; I'm swimming. I'm only six years old and I can swim already."

"Yeah, that's great. But try it once without Daddy. You'll see. It's not so easy."

I hate myself almost before I'm finished saying that. I guess I'm jealous, jealous over nothing. Dad looks at me quickly and there's some of the old sadness on his face.

"You kids go up on the beach with Mom awhile. Both of you are getting blue around the lips. I'm going to take a little swim myself. You take care of Mom."

Dad stands there, moving slowly out into the deeper water, twisting, turning back, watching till we're out on the sand. I turn around and watch him. He dives under a wave and seems to disappear, then comes up, his arms stroking sharp, strong cuts through the water, almost as if he's flying. I know I'll never be able to swim like that. I don't think he even cares if there's a bottom to the ocean anywhere. He doesn't seem to worry about anything.

"What the hell do you mean you're quittin', Kettleson? You can't quit; you're the best shop steward we've got."

"Four of them in a car handed this to one of my kids, Mr. Fabrizio. Look at it! Remember, I got a family. Find some young guy without any family for the job. My wife's goin' crazy an' I can't take these kind of chances."

"God damn! Them dirty bastards! Now don't let 'em scare you, Kettleson. They ain't gonna be hurting no kids. They're just bluffin'. I know them SOBs."

"I'm not sure, Mr. Fabrizio. They weren't bluffing when they beat me up twice; and now Jim Morris is gonna be in the hospital for a month and miss three months' work with that broken leg they gave him."

"Don't you worry none about that, Kettleson. We're takin' care of Morris, his hospital bills, his family, and everything."

"Don't get me wrong, Mr. Fabrizio. I'm not quittin' the union or anything like that. I'm behind the whole idea, but I can't be shop steward, that's all."

"You can't *quit, Kettleson. That's just what they want.*

It'll be a real black eye for the whole union. The guys on the floor would sure think you're lettin' 'em down."

"You gotta understand, Mr. Fabrizio. This is my family! These are my kids! Those goons don't care about anything, kids, wives, anything, just as long as they get paid for it. I can't take the chance."

"Kettleson, you never know what the guys on the floor will do. You know they really look up to you. I hate to think what might happen if they feel you went yellow on 'em."

"Maybe I'll have to quit this whole job, quit J.I. I'm not stuck on J.I. or the union, either, for that matter. I can start somewhere else. I hear Westinghouse is hiring."

"You'll find it harder to get a job than you think, Kettleson. We don't forget a thing like this. Think it over. Think about your family. All this crap will blow over, but eleven years' seniority along with the pension fund and medical benefits we're working for, you could relax the rest of your life. If you quit, besides letting everybody else down, you'd be letting your family down and letting yourself down, too. Remember that."

"If it was just me . . ."

"Listen, Kettleson. I know the company's been thinking of making you foreman. That's what we need, somebody going from shop steward to shop foreman. That'd make the union really look strong, give the young ones someone a look up to. I'm telling you this in private, but it's the God's truth.

"Now, if you quit as shop steward and they make you foreman how'll that look, huh? The guys'll figure you've turned into a company man. Your life wouldn't be worth dirt out on that floor, Kettleson. Think about that."

"I've been thinking about it. But I can't take the risk with my kids. Foreman's job, shop steward, the whole works; none of it's worth having my kids get hurt."

"Listen here, Kettleson. You're just all excited. You're not thinking clear. You got some vacation time comin'; I'll

*work it out so you can take a whole week off, right now.
Don't worry, I'll arrange it, and with full pay; give this
thing a chance to cool off. You disappear for a while. Then
come back to me afterwards and we'll talk about it. Just
let me work on this."*

I stand at the edge of the water and watch. Dad's swum
straight into the ocean, almost out of sight. Then I see
him roll over on his back. Mom's come up beside me and
put her warm hand on my shoulder; her hand is shaking.
We stand there watching as Dad disappears, seems to go
deep down into the water and not come up. I'm holding
my breath for him.

Then, just when I'm about to cry, he comes springing,
flying up out of the water like a whale or a big hunting
fish, splashing white way out there. He goes ducking under a few more times like a real fish, then begins stroking
back toward us on the beach.

I look up and Mom's crying. She turns away and goes
back to our blanket on the sand. I stand there at the edge
of the water but Dad walks right past me without looking. He walks past Laurel, who's building sand castles
just where the sand is wet enough but not too wet. He
flops down in the sand next to the blanket Mom brought.

I go over and kneel beside Laurel. I start building a
moat in front of her castle to stop the water when it
comes in, and so we have soft sand for making turrets
and steeples by dripping. I hear Mom even though I try
not to.

"Dick, why do you do things like that?"

Dad doesn't say anything. I peek over and he's rolled
over on his back. He's taking fistfuls of sand and pouring
them over his face, over his eyes. He's all coated with
sand. Then he starts lifting his arms and pouring sand so
he's covering his whole body. He's gradually disappearing. Laurel looks up, then dashes back before I can stop

her. She runs and jumps on Dad's sand-covered stomach, straddling him in the sand as if he were a horse.

"Come on, Daddy. Help us build a sand castle. Dickie and me are working on one but I know you can really make a beautiful castle, a palace. You can build anything."

I really think for a minute he might kill her. I don't know what he'll do. What he does is sit up, shake all that sand from his eyes and hair, then brush it off his chest. He carefully dumps Laurel onto the sand beside him. Then he rolls over onto his hands and knees and shakes some more like a dog shaking water out of its fur. He begins slowly crawling along the beach ahead of Laurel, down to where we're building the castle. He crawls right past me into the waves, still on his hands and knees, out deeper into the water.

Big waves break over him. He turns back and dog paddles in, crawling again in the surf, back up the beach slant and onto the sand. Laurel's jumping up and down laughing. Dad shakes himself and water flies around exactly the way it does off a dog.

"Come on, you two. Let's build a castle for Cannibal. We'll call it Cannibal Castle."

Dad starts digging in the wet sand with his hands, piling large loads of sand in the center while he continues my moat all around a large space.

"Laurie, you go get your sand bucket and shovel from Mother."

Laurel runs up the beach, screeching as she goes. She comes back with the bucket in one hand and the other hand wobbling the shovel over her head.

In no time, Dad has a huge pile of sand surrounded by a deep moat; the moat's so deep you can hardly touch bottom, and it fills with water seeping in from the ocean. He shows Laurel and me how to make the castle walls, patting the sides with our shovel and using the shovel top to make windows. On the corners he builds towers, using

Laurel's buckets. He packs the buckets so full and hard he can put one on top of the other without the sand collapsing. On top of the towers and around the walls we build places where you could shoot arrows through if you lived in this castle. It looks great. I run up and get Cannibal, who's asleep on one of the towels. I bring her down in her box but don't put her too close to the water. She climbs out and sits there, watching, sometimes dashing forward to swing a paw at somebody's hand or at some sand that flies near her. We're working fast but carefully.

Dad builds a door opening in the castle wall and a bridge over the moat. He puts towers for guards at each opening of the door. Then, inside the walls, in the middle, he builds a tower higher than the outside towers; he calls this a "keep." He says it's where the king and queen and all their friends go when they're attacked. The soldiers would stand along the outside walls to shoot the enemy or pour boiling oil on them. It's so real-looking, and Dad tells the way it is so seriously, I can almost see it. On top of the keep Dad jams a Popsicle stick for a flag.

I get so busy helping, putting my head down on the sand to see the castle as if it's really big, that I forget all about Cannibal. When I remember and look up, she's down by the water. She's rearing up on her back paws in her fighting pose, fighting waves. The waves are coming up over her feet, but she's swinging away and hitting at the foam on the edge of the ripples. Cannibal must be the fightingest cat in the world, fighting a whole ocean.

When we've finished the castle, it's smooth and beautiful, I don't think there was ever a more beautiful castle built in the sand anywhere. Dad could probably be the best *architect* in the world if he'd only had a chance to go to school.

I'd love to live in our castle. First I'd change my name from Dickie to Richard. That's my real name and it's a good king name. I don't like being called Dickie anyway, and I don't want to be Dick Junior either because everybody starts calling you Junior. What I'd like to be called is Rich but I don't know how to start people doing it.

Dad's squatting and Laurie's nestled herself between his legs. She has two fingers in her mouth sucking on them; I don't know how she can do it with all the sand. Dad gently pulls her fingers out of her mouth. He reaches across to me.

"Dickie, now put our queen in her castle. Let's see how she likes it."

I don't know how Dad knows Cannibal's a she. It stops me for a minute. Maybe he heard me calling her "her." I pull Cannibal away from the war of the waves and put her in her box without its lid. Then I carefully lower the box into our castle courtyard just inside the doorway with its guard towers. We sit back and watch.

For the first minutes, Cannibal only looks up at us from her box. Then she climbs out and walks around the keep and back to her box. She looks out at us again. We're squatting around the castle and I think she's wondering what she's supposed to do. Then I expect she thinks it's a sandbox because she starts scratching on the courtyard floor and goes pee-pee.

Dad laughs so hard he falls back on his hands. After this, Cannibal walks around to the other side of the keep and lifts her front paws up onto the wall to look out. She knocks off two of the square bumps you're supposed to shoot arrows through, then gets down again and walks around to the front. Carefully, she looks out our door, past the guard posts and across the drawbridge. When you have your head down on the sand looking at her through the door she looks monstrous, big as a lion or maybe even an elephant.

Then she tucks her head back in and climbs up on her box and from there jumps onto the top of the keep. Some edges of sand slide off but the keep stays up O.K. Cannibal knocks down the Popsicle stick and then, because she's so small, settles herself down and makes herself comfortable right on top there. She tucks her little paws under her body and looks from one to the other of us. I know she's wanting to be good, to do what we want her to do, only she doesn't know what it is.

Dad's been chuckling and laughing all this time, and Laurie's jumping up and down or running around the castle, or getting so close she almost scares Cannibal.

Dad takes Laurie in his lap. I haven't sat on my dad's lap since we started building porches together. That's one of the sad parts about growing up. And I'm too big to sit on Mom's. Sometimes she pulls me next to her and runs her hands through my hair, puts her arms around me, but I don't get to sit on her lap. Those things seemed to stop, to end, without my hardly noticing them. I might never sit on anybody's lap again the rest of my life.

Finally Dad reaches over and picks up Cannibal. She doesn't even swing her paw at him. He puts her in the box and strokes with his big thumb between her ears. Already, after only one day not working, his hands look better, not all beaten up, maybe it's because of the water in the ocean and then scraping them in the sand.

Anyway, they look more like hands and not so much like animal paws. He's wearing the gold ring with his initials Mom gave him before they were married. He can't wear it at work because it might get caught in one of the big machines.

I look at the castle. Water has twice come all the way up and run into the moat.

"Gosh, Dad, the ocean's going to wash all this away."

"That's right, Dickie, the tide's coming in."

"Can't we build a sand wall and hold it back, save it somehow?"

"There's no way to hold back the ocean, Dickie. Our castle was fun building; we had a good time. Maybe if it stays we won't build one again but if it gets washed away by the ocean we can build another tomorrow, even better, with secret dungeons."

Dad carries Laurie back up to Mom, swinging her back and forth as he goes, so she gets "tickle tummy" and laughs. I remember how that used to feel. Dad knows that when Laurie sucks her fingers she's usually tired, so he puts her on a towel and wraps a blanket around her. The sun is bright and it isn't cold but it's not the kind of sun you would get sunburnt by. I never heard of anybody getting sunburnt in October, but I never knew anybody who ever went to the shore in October, either.

I can't believe all the other kids are actually in school with that awful smell of floor wax, chalk, pencil wood, nuns, and damp wool. The back closets in those classrooms have sliding doors. Inside they smell of wet clothes and galoshes that are stored in there all winter long. It even smells that way at the beginning of a year *before* it gets cold and wet. That smell stays on in there right through the summer.

I do my homework *mostly* to be in the front of our class, away from those closets. The nuns sit the boys on the door side and girls by the window. The ones with the best report cards sit up front, except for John McGee and Joe Guerney, who always have to sit up front even though they get the worst report cards because they're so bad and dumb, too.

I wonder if anybody ever told *them* they have devils inside them?

In second grade, Sister Bernadette used to punish us by making us go in those back closets, and she'd close the sliding doors. I got shut in there once for making a paper airplane that I didn't even throw, and I vomited all over everything. That's the kind of smell it is.

I think these thoughts about school and squat in the sand watching the ocean licking our castle. Then I remember the other kids aren't in school anyway; it's Saturday.

I decide not to do anything to help the Cannibal Castle, not even fix it up when parts get washed over. I watch the front wall with the guard posts fall into the front moat and then the bottom of the keep gets washed out and the tower falls in. The sides of the moat begin collapsing, and then one giant wave comes up and goes over the whole works, splashing around and sliding back, leaving the castle as if it were a real castle and a thousand years old, ruined, washed over by sand and desert winds. I don't know why I enjoy watching things get ruined like that; it's almost like burning cats' tails. Maybe I do have some devil in me after all.

When I go back up to the family, Mom's sitting looking out at the ocean. Dad's on his stomach on a towel.

I put Cannibal down in her box and she doesn't come out; she has her eyes closed. I guess all that wave fighting and castle exploring wore her out. In her box, I put a small piece of liver I brought with me. Even the smell of that doesn't wake her up. I think Mom is beginning to like Cannibal because she smiles while I'm trying to feed her.

"Are you having a good time, Dickie? Isn't the ocean beautiful? I've never been to the shore when it wasn't hot, muggy, and too crowded. Now I can sit right out here in the sun without worrying about getting freckles."

I walk around in back of her, and, as I'm going past Dad, he reaches out and grabs me by one of my feet.

"O.K., come on, Buster, let's you and me wrestle. I'll show you some of my old Jim Landon wrestling holds; you'll be the terror of the block when we get back."

I'm scared at first. I can never remember wrestling with Dad; in fact I've hardly ever wrestled with anybody. I hate that stuff at school and most of the other kids leave me alone. If you're either bigger than everybody or smaller, then you need to fight all the time, but if you're just in the middle, like me, sort of skinny and ordinary-sized, you don't have much trouble. You only have to stay away from certain kids who like to hurt.

Now, Dad's up on his knees. He still has a hold on my leg.

He lets me go and spreads his arms out like a bear coming toward me, still on his knees.

"O.K. now, Dickie, see if you can take me down. See if you can pin me."

"I can't, Daddy. You're too strong."

"Come on, try. I won't hurt you and we'll have fun."

I put my arms out like Dad and try working my way behind him, but he keeps turning and keeping his eyes on me. I'm glad I'm not one of those company goons trying to fight with him. Finally, I just dash straight in and try putting a headlock on. He has his arms around my chest but he's only holding me, not squeezing. I struggle to hold his neck under my arms and tighten my hold; that's what the kids at school always do, then throw you on the ground over their hip; Joe Guerney did it to me once.

But Dad's neck is so thick, his head so hard; I pull tight and he falls over backward, not the way I was pulling at all. I fall on top of him.

"O.K., now, Dickie, see if you can put a half nelson on me. Put your arm over my shoulder like this and under my neck, then grab my other shoulder hard."

He shows me with his hands but my arms aren't long enough. I can't hold on to his hairy shoulder.

"O.K., now jack me up. Put your hand under my leg in the crotch like this and use your knee to lift me up onto my shoulders. That way you can pin me easy."

I try but I can hardly reach down that far and keep my arm around his neck, also I feel funny about putting my hand under his crotch. I never knew wrestling was that way. Dad arches up on his head and his feet as I'm lying across trying to pin him with my half nelson and crotch hold.

"See, Dickie, I'm bridging now. It's a way for me to keep my back off the ground so you can't pin me. See?"

I didn't know anybody could do what he's doing. All his weight and mine, too, across his body, is on his neck. I push down but he really is like a bridge.

"Now watch, Dickie. Just hold on, I won't hurt you."

Slowly he turns, twisting on his head and holding on to my arm so he comes out on top of me. He puts a half nelson on me lightly and lifts me up by the backside so my neck is bent on the sand. I don't know whether to cry or not. He isn't hurting me but it's awful to realize how much stronger and bigger he is than I am, how terribly he could really hurt if he ever wanted to. I know I'll never grow up to be the way he is. He lets loose of me some.

"Now try to bridge, Dickie. Push your head down hard as you can, and get your back off the ground. That's it."

I know I'm not really doing it. He's mostly lifting me but I get the feeling. The trouble is, my neck is about as big around as his arm, the *bottom* part of his arm. I could never really hold myself up. I know I'm not very strong compared to my father. In fact, I know I'm not strong at all, but I never knew how much difference there really is. This is supposed to be fun but it's more scary than anything. I know Dad isn't going to hurt me but I'm scared inside.

"O.K., Dickie, see if you can turn and break my hold now. Just twist suddenly, see if you can catch me by surprise."

I put all my strengh in it and turn away from him. I get on my stomach but I know he let me do it. Just that effort has taken all the wind out of me. Dad's hovering over my body like a police dog standing over some kind of little poodle dog.

"Now we'll get in the wrestler's position. I'm going to hold your arm like this."

He's kneeling beside me and holds my left arm, just where the muscle should be, with his big left hand. He has his other arm over my back. We're both on our knees.

"Now see if you can get away from me, or get on top of me. I'll give you a hint. Hook my arm that's over your back with your arm then roll away from me, holding tight on to that arm and my hand under you, right here. You'll have all the leverage on your side."

He shows me what he means at the same time. I know if I do it he's going to fall on top of me and crush me into the sand, but I want to do what he says; a part of me likes wrestling with him, playing this kind of puppy-dog play. I roll and Dad goes over me onto his back in the sand. He lies there smiling up at me.

"See, it worked. See how easy it is if you know how? It's like carpentry, all a question of getting the right leverage. Now get me in that half nelson and the crotch hold again; see if you can pin me."

I really grab hold this time and lean my chin on his chest to help hold him down. He pretends to twist this way and that, starting to bridge and then falling back. Finally he just lies there.

"O.K., Buster, you pinned me. I give up."

I climb onto his chest and sit on him. I look over at Cannibal; she's awake and watching. I thump my hands on my chest and give a Tarzan yell. Dad lifts me up by putting his hands on my sides and holds me up in the air over his head.

"Straighten out your feet, Dickie. See if you can arch your back."

I try but it's hard and he lets me down on the sand beside him. Laurel's awake and jumps on Daddy's chest.

"He didn't really beat you, did he, Daddy? You just let him."

"Oh yeah? You want to wrestle with your old daddy, too?"

Laurel tries to hold Dad's arms down by pushing on his muscles and holding his hands. He pretends she's really pinning him. I go and pick up Cannibal; she gives me a little soft bite on the finger and I wish we could live here on the beach at Wildwood forever.

I move over and sit beside Mom. She's watching Laurel and Dad roll around in the sand.

"Did you have fun, honey?"

"Yeah. Daddy's really strong, you know."

"Yes, I know."

"You know he smells like a lion when you wrestle with him. He smells like the lions smell in the zoo."

Mom looks at me closely; there are almost tears in her eyes. But then she's looking into the sun going down and her eyes are very sensitive to light.

"Yes, I know, Dickie. Your father *is* a lion in some ways. Always remember that, no matter what happens."

Later on, with the bathing suits hanging on the ends of the beds to dry, along with the towels, and after we've all taken a shower to get the sand off, I'm playing on the floor with Cannibal and Laurel. I have a marble and I'll roll it to Laurel, and Cannibal will chase it. Then Laurel'll get it just before Cannibal catches it and roll it to me. Sometimes Cannibal only stands in the middle and watches it go back and forth and sometimes she'll strike out with her paw and give the marble a good push. I think she likes playing with us, too.

Mom and Dad are in their bed. They're talking quietly and sometimes giggling or laughing and they seem really happy. From the way they're jumping around I think maybe Dad's teaching Mom how to wrestle, too. Dad gets up on one elbow. He isn't wearing any shirt but then under the blankets it would be warm. Mom is wearing what she calls a chemise; it's pink and has shiny material with lace around the bottom. Dad reaches for his wallet on the table beside their bed and opens it.

"How would you kids like to go down on the boardwalk and have a little fun? Here, Dickie. I'll give you a dollar and you can buy a half pound of salt-water taffy. Get some of the ones with spearmint or cinnamon or peppermint for me and some walnut and honey ones for Mom; the rest you can choose for yourselves."

He holds out the dollar bill and I take it. It's a real dollar all right. I don't think I've ever had a whole dollar to spend.

"Whatever's left you can use to go on a few rides. But be careful not to lose the money or waste it on things you don't really like. Look around at all the rides before you choose."

Mom's up on her elbow, too. One of the straps of her chemise has fallen off her shoulder and she pulls it back up.

"Now, be careful. Don't talk to any strange people, and stay where all the lights are. And, Laurel, you stay right with Dickie; I don't want either of you getting lost."

"Oh, we won't get lost, Mom. The boardwalk's right there and if you go the wrong way you walk right into the ocean. Our street is Baltic and I know where this court is and our apartment is number sixteen. How can we get lost?"

Dad lies back on the bed; he runs his hands through Mom's hair, which is all loose.

"She only wants you to be careful, kids. We're going to take a little nap, so don't come back too soon. There are all kinds of things to see."

Mom's still sitting up and smiling, wiggling, almost as if Dad's tickling her.

"But be sure and be back before dark. We'll eat here, then we'll all walk down on the boardwalk together this evening before we go to bed. You be good now."

Mom lets herself back and snuggles down inside the

covers. Dad puts his arm across her. Laurel and I put on our sweaters and I decide to take Cannibal with us. Laurel wants me to take Cannibal along, too.

We have no trouble at all going to the boardwalk. There's one big street we have to cross but there's a red light and there's no more traffic than there is on Long Lane. Where we come up on the boardwalk there aren't many things to see but it's only about ten streets away where it starts.

First we hunt around for a place to buy salt-water taffy. There are lots of different places but we want to buy the biggest box with the most different flavors for the least money. We finally pick a store. We buy a whole pound and it costs fifty-nine cents. Laurel says she'll carry it because I've got Cannibal.

I've opened the top on Cannibal's box so she can look out. The only danger I have to watch for is dogs. When Cannibal sees a dog, no matter how big it is, she wants to jump out and kill it. Thank goodness we only see two dogs and I see them first so I can close the box before she springs.

There are colored lights everywhere, and even though a couple places are closed down because it isn't summer any more, some places are still open. There's a merry-go-round running and it costs ten cents. We both decide that's something we want to do, so we buy our tickets and go on it. There are only two other people on the whole merry-go-round; they're a boy and girl, practically grownups.

On the outside, the seats are the kind of animals that slide up and down on golden poles; Laurel and I each choose one of those. I have a black horse with red trim and Laurel's on a giraffe. The man helps Laurel get her feet in the holders but I get mine in O.K. and balance Cannibal while I buckle myself on. The man buckles Laurel in. She's just behind me.

I open Cannibal's box a bit so she can stick her nose

out and see. I'm afraid she might want to jump out and try killing all the animals on the merry-go-round. But it's O.K., I don't think she likes to see the world going around. It makes *me* a little bit dizzy and I *know* what's happening; a little cat like Cannibal might just get sick.

The man really gives us a long ride. There's nobody else waiting for a turn so he lets us go on and on. He lights a cigarette when he starts the motor and we keep going around all the time he's smoking that cigarette until he throws it on the ground and stomps it out. I think the other people on the merry-go-round might be friends of his because he keeps talking to them every time they come around. The girl is sitting on an elephant and she has both her legs sticking off the merry-go-round. Her skirt blows in the wind and she's wearing white shoes.

I keep looking back at Laurel; she's smiling and staring all around, turning her head. She's holding tight on to the strap but lets go sometimes to wave at me. The music is loud and I don't recognize the tune. I thought it might be the one about the music going round and round whoh-ho-ho-ho-ho-ho, but it isn't.

When we get off, we're both dizzy. I'm thinking also I ought to take Cannibal out of her box and give her a chance to do her business. We find a stairway onto the beach and go down there. The sun is starting to set and the sky's turning red. Cannibal jumps up and down, spins around as if she has a tail to chase, then moves away from us a little bit and really does her business, both kinds. Laurel won't look but I don't mind.

Laurel wants to start home because she's afraid it's getting too dark. I talk her into going just a little bit farther, past the pier, then we'll hurry on back. I figure we have at least half an hour before it'll be really dark; we'll give Mom and Dad a chance for a nice long nap.

We go up on the boardwalk again and walk through the center of all the amusements, past Hunt's Pier, and at the end we see another even bigger merry-go-round. Laurel wants to keep on to see that but then I spot something more interesting.

When I point it out to Laurel she's as interested as I am. Right there on the boardwalk is a cage with a *real* lion in it. He's sitting up looking out at the crowd, his eyes open, following people as they walk along.

Laurel and I go close as we can. I've seen lions at the zoo in Philadelphia but never so close as this, and there's something special about this lion. He seems lonesome, as if he'd like to be friends. He's like the lion in *The Wizard of Oz*. When we're close he's definitely watching us. One time he opens his mouth and takes a good deep yawn. I never knew a lion's mouth could open so wide. It's big enough to take my whole head off in one bite. And the teeth are long, sharp, and more yellow than I thought they'd be. His teeth are almost as yellow as his eyes, and those eyes are really yellow-brown, not green, not like Cannibal's and Mom's.

I pull back the top of Cannibal's box a few inches so she can stick her head out. As soon as she sees that lion she backs into her box so only her nose and eyes and one paw show over the edge. It's the first time I've seen Cannibal afraid of *anything;* that is, she isn't willing to jump out and attack; she looks as though she's thinking it over. She wasn't afraid of the ocean but this lion is altogether another thing. He sure scares me and he scares Laurel so much she's pulling on my sleeve to stay away from the cage.

There's a big sign beside the cage. The top of the sign has lights blinking on and off saying WALL OF DEATH. There are pictures showing a woman on a motorcycle with a lion in a sidecar and they're hanging sideways, sticking right off a wall. At first, I thought they'd put the picture up wrong but you can see they really are hanging sideways up on the wall. They can't have glue on the wheels so there must be some kind of track the wheels of the motorcycle fit into to keep it up there. There are yellowed newspaper clippings framed in glass, with pictures of the motorcycles, the people, and the lion. It looks as if they've been riding that lion up the side of a wall all over the country. There are also pictures of racing cars.

Laurel's pulling on my sleeve again as I'm trying to read this. She's holding the salt-water taffy close against her chest with one arm and pulling at me with the other. Then she points. There's a little stage. A lady comes out on it wearing a purple, shining costume and with bare legs. She has on high-heeled shoes and wears a sort of glittering crown on her head.

After her come two men pushing motorcycles. They push them up a little ramp onto the stage and sit on them. Other people are stopping to look, but we're right up front. I look back and it's beginning to get darker. But now even Laurel's so interested she doesn't notice.

The lady stands in front of a microphone. First the microphone clatters, then squeaks and howls a few times so the lion growls back. Then she begins talking into it. She tells how these men are going to ride on the WALL OF DEATH; do death-defying acts while hanging from the wall. She tells how the lion will ride on the wall. She tells how he's a full-grown African lion and how this is the only act of its kind in the whole world.

Just then, one of the men, a young one with a black leather jacket and slicked-back hair, kicks down so his motorcycle starts. He rolls it, pushing with both feet in big leather boots until the motorcycle is sitting on rollers. The rollers look like the rollers on Mom's washing machine, the wringer part where you squeeze out water.

Mom got her fingers caught once and they swelled and turned blue, one fingernail fell off. That was two years ago. Since then, Dad insists she save all the wringing-out for him. So Mom washes on Sundays after lunch and Dad wrings so she can hang them Monday morning with everybody else. She hangs out his work clothes at the same time, the ones she washed Saturday afternoon.

These rollers are the same, set close together, but there are two sets of them, one set for the back wheel, one for the front; they're bigger and they're black shining metal.

The man starts his motorcycle running on those rollers and they roll but his motorcycle stays there, the wheels spinning fast no matter how loud he turns up the motor. He tilts back and forth and stares out at the crowd while he makes noises with his motorcycle. I look back and there's a crowd of people but it's really dark now. This time *I* pull on the sleeve of Laurel's dress; she's as interested as I am and there's so much noise she could never hear me say anything. I point out past the people behind us at the sky. There's just a little bit of light still left out there over the ocean. Laurel looks at me with her mouth open and we start sliding our way out through the crowd.

When we get back to our room, Laurel's almost crying, both because she was afraid we'd get lost in the dark and because Mom will be mad. But, when we come in, Mom and Dad are still in bed and I think we wake them up coming in the door. Dad swings his feet over the edge of the bed. He looks at the alarm clock we brought with us.

"My goodness, it's late. Did you kids have a good time?"

Laurel goes over and gives Dad the salt-water taffy.

"We saw a real lion, Daddy, didn't we, Dickie?"

"We sure did and they have him trained to ride in a motorcycle on the side of a wall. I don't know how they can get a motorcycle to stick on the side of a wall like that."

Mom's up on her elbows now. She's not wearing her chemise and holds the covers up to her shoulders.

"Did you two just get in? I thought I told you to be home before it got dark. You should know better, Dickie."

"Gee, Mom, It got dark so fast and we were so interested watching the motorcycles and the lion we just didn't notice."

I go over to Dad. He's pulling on his pants.

"The salt-water taffy cost fifty-nine cents and we both went on the merry-go-round for ten cents each, so that leaves twenty-one cents."

"You keep it, Dickie. The two of you might want to take another ride. So you had fun, did you?"

"The man on the merry-go-round let us stay on for a real long ride. He smoked a whole cigarette while we went around. We were both on the outside and had the kind that go up and down."

Mom's sliding out the other side of the bed. She pulls her chemise on over her head.

"Well, I figure it's about time I put together something for us to eat. I have hamburger and beans, how's that sound?"

Dad leans over, kisses Mom on the bare shoulder.

"Sounds wonderful to me, love; and we can have salt-water taffy for dessert. Did you kids get the kinds of flavors I said, peppermint, cinnamon, spearmint, walnut and honey?"

"We got everything, Dad, just the kind you said."

PART 4

S TURE Modig was overwhelmed by his first few days in the army. He was paraded naked from one place to another. His head was shorn; he received shots in both arms till he couldn't bend his elbows, then was given new clothing, most of which didn't fit.

Sture felt as if somehow he had lost everything that mattered in life: his animals, the farm, his mother, his father; and nobody seemed to care.

He was assigned a bunk of woven canvas straps covered by a straw mattress perched high on top of another bunk. He sat there with his needle and thread, carefully tailoring and adjusting his new clothes to fit. He shined his high boots till they glowed, while his arms ached and he daydreamed of the farm. He worked on those boots with the heels of his hands so they wouldn't pinch his feet. Without knowing it, Sture was well on his way to becoming the ideal soldier.

He quickly grew accustomed to the six-o'clock wake-up, late for Sture. He enjoyed the food about which others complained. He began to be proud of his smart appearance in a military uniform.

On the field and at the rifle range he far outstripped his fellow draftees. He became expert with the rifle and 30-caliber machine gun; he qualified as a sniper. He was tireless on marches, spurring his fellow draftees on. By the end of the first month he was marked by his superiors for non-commissioned grade.

Because of its predictability, its very mundane demands, military life was ideal for Sture Modig. He enjoyed taking his rifle apart, cleaning it; here was a machine he could appreciate. The reality of ballistics appealed to him. Here was a true Spartan life.

At the end of basic training, he was called into the company commander's office. By now, Sture knew all the rigid formality of military bearing and actually liked that, too. He snapped to attention in front of the company commander. This captain had been a Greek-literature major at Princeton, had asked for and received his commission automatically. He was assigned as captain to an infantry company, but still hadn't qualified with his pistol.

"Private Modig, your sergeant, Sergeant Meek, has recommended you be promoted to corporal as his assistant squad leader. You will receive your notification of promotion in the next week but you may sew on your stripes now. Congratulations."

"Thank you, sir."

Sture knew he deserved it. He deserved to be company commander far more than this pale, stubble-bearded man in front of him, a man who spent his evenings in town dancing, or drinking at the officers' club.

Sture waited for the mandatory salute ending the discussion. Almost as if he'd forgotten, Captain Fitzgerald gave his salute so Private, soon Corporal, Modig could return it, spin on his heel, and leave the orderly room.

Sture climbed up on his bunk. He pulled out the corporal stripes he'd already bought and proceeded to sew them on the sleeves of all his shirts with neat, tight lock stitches.

Sture was soon shipped overseas with the 32nd Infantry Division.

Before his outfit was shipped, however, Sture Modig made platoon sergeant. He was the only draftee in his regiment promoted so fast to such rank.

His outfit was one of the first American divisions actually to participate in the fighting. They were attached to a French command and took a terrible beating with staggering casualties. They fought bravely, starting August 1 along the banks of the Vesle, Aisne, and Ourcq, attacking northward. They captured Fismes, east of Verdun, on August 1–2. Although General Pershing had thought first of breaking up this division of the Wisconsin National Guard, it soon became known as the Powerhouse Division. On August 30 they captured Jovigny, and overran the plateau around Terny.

On the evening of the first attack, his platoon lieutenant was killed and Captain Fitzgerald just disappeared. For two weeks, in the midst of combat, while replacements were being awaited, Sture Modig served as acting platoon leader. One of the other platoon lieutenants filled in for the missing Captain Fitzgerald.

In early September, 1918, Sture Modig was commissioned a second lieutenant of infantry, one of the first field commissions awarded to an American in this particular war.

War was something at which Sture was good. His men, most older than he was, respected him. His benevolent smile and innate confidence inspired confidence in others. His lack of fear in danger, his adept decision-making, justified, verified this confidence. At Terny, he was awarded the bronze star for bravery, also his first purple heart for a shrapnel wound received during a heavy bombardment. He spent three hours in the hospital tent while his wound was dressed. He then, without permission, worked his way back to his outfit.

There was a cheer heard through that section of trenches when he showed up, his hand bandaged and his arm in a sling. He smiled his enigmatic smile and passed among his troops, enjoying their adulation but looking for any sloppiness in their weapons, or lack of safety in their positions.

It was in the St.-Mihiel offensive in mid-September that the regiment took its most serious casualties. There was rumor of armistice but the war went on. A minor skirmish developed almost on its own as a sort of *coup de grâce* by the Americans, an *auto-da-fé* for the Germans facing them.

In the process of this raging battle, the captain of Sture's company was seriously wounded. He later lost a leg, then his life.

Sture Modig was by acclaim and natural authority company commander. He became Cap Modig to all, despite the fact that Lieutenant Burns, as executive officer, outranked him. Lieutenant Burns had been a history major at Harvard when he managed to arrange a commission with the help of his lawyer father in Boston. He could keep company records, manage the company roster, but recognized his own ineptitude as line commander. He willingly ceded field command to Modig. After two captains lost in a few months, the job did not hold much appeal for Lieutenant Burns. Sture was promoted to first lieutenant.

It was the last days of September. The weather had turned unseasonably cold but still the men were plagued by mosquitoes. Two of Cap Modig's men, one of them Sergeant Meek of the second squad, his old squad, were caught out in a shell hole under enemy fire. It was in a gas-filled blind alley called by the Germans *Stumpflager*. Clouds of yellowish-brown smoke began billowing toward them from the German lines, clinging close to the ground. It was chlorine gas mixed with phosgene and mustard gas. This was not the first time Sture and his men had experienced this sickening, all-pervading virulent weapon: droplets that stung, burned, and ate out the lungs. But they'd always managed to retreat in time. Gas masks, promised, never arrived and, even when used, were not effective.

Sture ordered his company back to the next line of trenches, then started working his way out to the shell hole. He found his old sergeant, Sergeant Meek, dead, a piece of shrapnel buried in his temple, blood coming out of his nose and mouth from some other serious internal injury, his eyes open and empty in the burning gas. But the second soldier, though unconscious, was still alive. Sture hoisted him over his shoulder and started running back through the suffocating, brownish-yellow, blowing clouds of gas. The gas clung to the ground and there was no way to avoid it. He tried to hold his breath, not suck in the burning, destroying, fetid clouds. But he couldn't. He gasped in agony and struggled on with his heavy load through the slippery mud. He felt a hard thud in his upper leg, which knocked him sideways and over onto the wet ground. He struggled back to his feet again, lifting the wounded man onto his shoulder, and staggered on with blood streaming down his leg into his boot. He was practically unconscious, his throat, eyes, lungs, nose burning so he could scarcely breathe. He fell down the parapet into the arms of his men.

"Get back! Get back farther! Come on, let's go!"

He tried to stand but fell unconscious. His men hurried him and the man he'd carried onto a makeshift litter, and they all retreated before the billowing, sickening droplets of death.

Cap Modig woke in a bed. His eyes were bandaged. When he tried to breathe he couldn't suppress the scream. A hand out of nowhere held on to his. He struggled. He felt as if he were drowning.

"That's all right, lieutenant. Just try to relax. You'll be all right."

It was a woman's voice. He felt the hypodermic needle slip into his arm and then a muffling thickness surrounded him until the fire in his chest quieted and he went to sleep again.

It was two weeks before Cap could stay awake more than two or three hours without morphine. But something in him knew he had to live with the pain; the soft rubbery weakness of the drug wasn't life as he wanted it. He gritted against the searing pains of breathing, suffered through the agony of fighting back coughing fits; often surrendering to the racking, rending pain when he couldn't stop himself from hollering out.

And he was still in the dark, a red-black haze, frightening because it wasn't the way he remembered things to have been when he simply closed his eyes. This was more: a wet, thick darkness, not restful, a blinding red of dark with spots of light like fireflies drifting or sparking across his eyes.

He lay there, day after day, losing some days to the needle, holding on to others. They never put him out unless he screamed. He felt gently with his arms and found a tube attached to one arm; there was another tube in his penis. He felt like one of the cows on his failed milking machines, or a tomato plant held up with stakes and strings.

Sture didn't have will enough to lift the tight bandages over his eyes. Twice he knew the bandages had been changed while he was asleep because the smell decreased. Complaint never occurred to Sture Modig. He knew this is the way life is; sometimes it's hard and you must wait, be patient, till you find out what's happening.

It was almost a month later when he knew there was someone standing beside him, talking to him.

"Lieutenant Modig!" He said the first part like the mo in eeny, meeny, miney, *mo,* rather than like the moo of a cow. "I'm going to take the bandages off your eyes. I want you to tell me how much you can see. Can you talk at all?"

Cap nodded his head. He hadn't tried talking because he didn't want to start coughing, but he'd screamed so he must be able to talk.

Slowly, with much unwrapping and clipping of scissors, the bandages were unwound from his head. At the end there were only gauze pads left over each eye. Carefully, the doctor lifted one pad and Cap opened his eye slowly until he felt a blinding pain. He closed his eye and then slowly squinted it open again. He could see blurs of light, couldn't focus, couldn't recognize anything.

"Can you see, lieutenant?"

"Blurs."

Cap exhaled the word softly, quietly, delicately.

"That's good, you've still got some sight in that eye anyway."

Cap for the first time realized how serious the chance of his being blind was. So many things he couldn't do if he were blind: couldn't ride a bicycle, couldn't help much on the farm, couldn't see the beautiful world. Tears started burning in the corners of his eyes as a new gauze patch was adjusted over the eye he'd opened.

The doctor started slowly lifting the other patch. There

were areas of pussy mucus sticking the pad to the eyelids
and to the lashes; he gently separated them.

"Now try this one, lieutenant. Can you open it?"

Cap was feeling a strong need to cough, to bring up
another glob of thickness gathering in his throat. He held
back. He opened his eye slowly to avoid pain from the
light. There was no pain this time. Again he saw blurs,
light movements, but it was not as bright as with the first
eye. He didn't know the doctor'd had the shade drawn by
one of the nurses.

Cap thought he might be even more blind in this eye.
The doctor was flashing what seemed like a red light on
his eyeball, pushing the lid up and away so the skin
cracked. He closed it again, slipped the pad into place.

"Nurse, you can wrap him up again but less tightly
this time. We'll have those bandages off in another week."

"Well, lieutenant, you're lucky; you'll see, you might
even see as well as you did before."

Cap only nodded, trying to hold back the burning tears
and the choking need to cough. He felt terribly alone. He
wondered, as he had so often during the past weeks,
what'd happened to his company, if any more had been
killed, if they'd taken back the territory they'd fled before
the gas, who was the new company commander?

"Well, you have two things to celebrate, lieutenant.
You will see again, and the war's over. The armistice was
signed three weeks ago. When you get out of the hospital
you can go home. The Huns got themselves licked,
thanks to brave men like you."

Cap stayed quiet. He tried to smile, to bring forth one
of his glowing smiles, but it wasn't there. He felt as if
he'd missed the end of the party. He was glad the war
was finally over, that no more soldiers would be killed,
but he hated not being there with his good friends, his
company.

Cap Sture Modig was sent to a hospital in France near
a town called Contrexéville. It was a hospital specializing

in seriously gassed patients. They were given curative waters, encouraged to eat much fruit and lie out in the sun when it wasn't too cold.

It was several months before he could breathe without pain and months more before he could do even the lightest exercise without bringing on spasms of coughing and retching. His eyes gradually improved until he had full vision, but this took almost nine months. Cap did eye exercises he'd devised himself, focusing near, then far, shifting his eyes from side to side, concentrating on making the fuzziness go away. The doctors were amazed. They didn't actually expect anyone with the degree of eye injury Sture suffered to totally regain sight.

Cap's gums had also been affected by the gas, so he lost most of his teeth except for four on top in front and six on the bottom. The roots had turned blue-purple and rotted out. He was fitted for a full mouth plate so he could chew food properly.

Also the bulk of his thick blond hair had fallen out, leaving only a thin, fuzzy coating over top of his head. The doctors were not sure if real hair would ever grow back. Cap's scalp was rubbed each morning and evening with hot oil to try stimulating some growth, but nothing helped.

He was truly Captain Sture Modig now. He'd been promoted to that field rank in recognition of his service. He was also issued a second purple heart and a distinguished service cross. He mailed both back to his parents in Wisconsin along with simply written explanations as to why he still was not home. He did not tell them the extent of his injuries. Cap Modig had learned to lie by omission.

He was twenty-two years old and was growing up the hard way. He was also growing restless in the hospital. The handsome, blond, blue-eyed youth with so much promise was now a sallow, sad, unsmiling man who'd lost confidence in promises.

Finally, just a year after he was wounded, in late 1919, he was discharged. He was declared seventy percent disabled on a permanent basis. For the rest of his life he would receive a monthly disability check from the U.S. government.

His parents cried when they saw him. It was almost impossible to recognize him as the smiling, always helpful, almost saintly boy who had gone away. He was no longer innocent. In his heart he felt a deep, unresolvable guilt. Cap suffered from what in those days was called shell shock, a combination of a sense of loss for the comradeship he'd known in the midst of battle and a guilt for still being alive.

The farm was in deep trouble. The prices of milk, butter, grain were so low his parents couldn't meet the mortgage payments on their acreage. During the years, they'd paid off the second mortgage by hard work, but now had loans on the $10,000 first mortgage. The combination of interest payments owed on the mortgage at $3.60 per acre and taxes of $1.90 per acre were greater than could be earned. Sture's father was fast becoming a renter farmer, with an insurance company holding the loan on his property; he was in grave danger of losing his equity on the whole farm, a lifetime of hard labor. This was happening at that time to farmers all over the region: Minnesota, Idaho, Wisconsin, the Dakotas.

Sture decided he could make the farm pay if he invested in a tractor. He had all his back disability money and pay from the time he was in the hospital as well as his discharge bonus. He put it into an International Harvester tractor.

This tractor became the joy of Sture's life. He had reason to live again. He'd work it all day in the field, breaking virgin territory into meadows, pulling stumps, plowing. Then, at night, he'd work on it in the barn, taking it apart, learning all its mechanical secrets, designing improvements. Often, he'd stay awake all night, breaking down, studying, analyzing the function of his machine. He began to regain something of his innate confidence in life, in living.

But the farm still couldn't make enough money. Cap was fighting something beyond him, an economic tragedy in the making that finally disintegrated into the Great Depression. Sture was also beginning to be restless on the farm.

Cap, who now wore a cap all the time to hide his premature baldness, wanted to be around motors. He was convinced he could get a job as a mechanic in Detroit, then send home money to help his mom and dad hold on to the farm. There was good money to be made in Detroit if one had mechanical skills, and Cap was convinced he was as good as anybody could be with machines, almost as good as he was with animals.

His parents were not happy, but they knew it was the only way they could keep the farm, their life dream of being independent. They also saw that Sture was not himself any more. He didn't get the same joy from animals. He rushed through milking to tinker with his tractor. He was a grown man and had to make his own life.

Cap walked to Detroit from the farm. He carried extra socks, two extra shirts, extra underwear, and a second pair of pants, all wrapped in a large red bandana at the end of a stick. He looked like a hobo in a comic strip. He also carried a small leather satchel with his tools. Cap didn't see anything funny in it; this was the way he could carry his things with the least bother; it was like carrying a rifle and an ammo case.

It didn't take Cap long to get a job in Detroit. It had become a center for manufacturing automobiles. Cap quickly was recognized as a natural. This bland-faced bald man knew machines as if he'd invented them.

Within the year, Cap was picked as mechanic by a racing team racing competitively all over America.

The great boom in auto racing, especially board-track racing, was just then coming to the fore. Cap worked with a team racing the durable and popular Dusenbergs.

Cap began to travel with them. He went to the two-mile oval board track in Maywood near Chicago. It was here he first had a chance actually to drive one of the cars in a tryout. He was electrified by the experience. Here was a chance for speed in which his damaged lungs and bum leg didn't hinder him. Cap had tried running at the farm, slogging up hills, drifting down, coughing all the way, struggling for air. Even a mile run was more than he could manage, with his shrapnel-damaged leg.

Next they raced at Omaha, a mile-and-a-quarter track. Cap began to get a reputation as a mechanic who could also drive. The drivers and other mechanics watched how his natural quickness, his fearlessness, his ability to think under stress gave him control of cars at high speeds. Cap began to enjoy his double reputation as mechanic and potential driver.

It was at Des Moines, a one-mile track with steep bankings, some steep as forty-five degrees, where Cap got his chance. The driver of the second car was too drunk on the day of the race to drive. The decision was to let Cap try it.

This car was a "blown job," a souped-up 1922 model. Cap took his qualifying heat and then came in second in the main event. The main event was twenty-five laps, and there were sixteen cars running. Cap pushed his high-powered job to the maximum but it wasn't the best car. Cap was the best driver, but he came in second.

From then on, Cap was a major driver. He made more money each year. In three years he'd paid off the mortgage on the farm. But he wasn't ready to go back milking cows. The speed, the superlative design of these machines had him captivated. He began to learn that, even more than in the war, here his fearlessness was exceptional. It was what he had to sell.

Cap raced in Kansas City, Tacoma, Playa Del Rey, Indianapolis, Omaha, Santa Monica road races, the Atlantic City Speedway board track. He won on boards at Sheepshead Bay in Brooklyn, and came back to Detroit to win again on the tiny half-mile track there.

After that race he took off two weeks to go visit with his parents at the farm. This wild-eyed man with the tight-set jaw was even more unfamiliar to them than the hurt and wounded boy who'd come back from the war. Cap's mother and father didn't know how to treat him. To them, he was still Sture, although he hadn't been called that in over three years. He wore a leather cap now with a short bill. He turned it around on his head when he raced; the bill protected his neck from flying splinters on the board tracks. Because of this habit, his racing name was Cap, as much from his headgear as from his former military rank.

While he was home, Cap helped with the milking and plowing. He took his beloved tractor completely down and rebuilt it. His father watched over his shoulder, shaking his head in amazement. What kind of a son did they have?

He left the tractor in better shape than when he'd bought it new. He'd added yet more improvements: bored out the cylinders, put in oversize pistons, improved the carburetion, and installed an electro-start, battery, and generator. He left the tractor in great condition, but he also left farming. The excitement and challenges of race driving now occupied completely the forefront of his mind.

Four years later, after many races, Cap was in California. He was racing with another team, a more important team, a team that raced all the major tracks throughout the nation.

America was in the midst of a grand party, an hysterical party, an ongoing celebration of war's end, of seeming new prosperity. It was totally unrelated to the grinding, constantly losing battle his mother and father were waging on the farm. It was impossible for Sture to put the two worlds together in his mind, so he didn't. He was addicted to, fascinated by, the speed of these new machines, the competition, his own skills virtually unmatched, the adulation he received from every side as he won more and more prizes.

He was staying at the Coronado Hotel right on the beach outside San Diego and had just driven a successful race in which he'd barely missed first place. It was evening, he'd eaten dinner in his hotel room, and was bored. So, he decided to go down by the waterfront.

He borrowed one of his team's spare cars to drive into the area where sailors hung out.

San Diego was then primarily a sailors' town. Sture was yearning for people of his own background, simple people who knew how to work with their hands. He was, more and more, as a famous auto racer, surrounded by the idle rich, the bored wealthy, looking for cheap thrills; using Sture as a way to obtain them. There were women who wanted him as a plaything, but Sture didn't want to play or be played with. He was still leery of women.

Sture went into a bar. It was noisy, smoke-filled, crowded, just what Sture was looking for, a place where he could sit and watch, feel part of things.

He had been there perhaps an hour or more when a small, compact sailor came in the door. He had a burlap sack under his arm, and slung it onto the bar.

"Hey, anybody here wanna buy a lion? The skipper won't let me ship this one on and we're heading out for Lima tonight."

Cap, always interested in animals, drifts over. Judging from his voice and loud bravado, the sailor had apparently been to other bars before he hit this one. Cap moves close to the lion cub. It lies bewildered, close to dying, thin, bedraggled, its fur matted and sticking in tufts from its thin body.

Cap reaches out for it, pulling the stinking burlap away. "O.K. if I hold this feller for a minute, sailor? He looks pretty tuckered out."

The sailor leans over to look at Cap. He's been getting free drinks all along the waterfront walking into bars with the lion cub. He's about decided just to drown the animal when the evening's over. He's tired of cleaning up filthy, stinking messes, trying to feed it with a milk bottle, then pushing down its throat handfuls of scrap meat he begged from the cook on ship. He'd bought two cubs in Mombasa and the other had died after two days at sea. There'd been a lot of complaining in the locker from his mates about the one cub that was left, and now he had to get rid of it.

"You wanna buy this little lion, matey? I'll sell it cheap."

He shouts this out, clamoring for attention. He gets it. So far he's gotten it wherever he's gone. It was for this he'd kept the poor critter alive, thinking of when he got shore leave, how he'd be the center of things with a real lion.

"No, I don't know what I'd do with it. I'm on the move all the time myself."

Cap splays the cub out on the bar. He picks at where the milk and meat have clotted around the cub's muzzle and pulls some running sleep from the corners of its eyes. The cub looks as if it doesn't have much longer to go; it'll probably be dead before morning.

Cap lifts the cub, holds it against his chest. The cub wraps its huge soft front paws around his neck. The rest of the bar has huddled closer. The cub almost tilts off

Cap's cap to expose his bald head. Cap reaches up quickly to hold it in place. He's still embarrassed by his baldness.

Cap is surprised how light the cub is: it's literally only skin—loose skin—and bone. Cap pulls his head back to look into the cub's eyes and sees they're half closed, lusterless. There is a bluish cast over them.

"How much you asking, anyway?"

"How much'll you give me, mate?"

Cap looks into the cub's eyes again. He's sure the poor dumb animal is dying.

"I don't really know what I'd do with a dead lion cub. He's too little to make a lionskin rug in my den where I could seduce Theda Bara or somebody like that."

Cap is playing to the crowd, too, now. He's trying not to show his anger at the condition of the helpless cub.

"You saying I'm mistreating this lion, mate; that whatjur sayin'?"

Most of the merchant sailors in any bar are looking for a fight, not necessarily one they'd get mixed up in themselves, but something to watch. Still, some of them are *really* looking for a fight, especially those about to ship out. They want a few cuts, black and blue marks, a black eye, maybe some loose teeth to share with their mates at sea, something to nurse during a long cruise; something to back up the wild stories they'll tell about shore leave. If you can't take a woman with you, the next best thing is the remnant of a tough fight.

Cap realizes this. He doesn't want to get involved in any rough stuff. He's getting all the competition he needs driving cars. He's low on aggression, hostility, desire to prove anything. He hasn't much to waste on lonely sailors.

"Nope, but he does look pretty well done in. I'll bet it's hard keeping a cub like this on a boat; lions aren't exactly seagoing animals."

The sailor leans over even closer to look at Cap. The

sailor's unsteady on his feet. He has vomit and the smell of sick cat on his uniform. Cap stares levelly. He hopes he doesn't have to fight a more than half-drunk sailor for a dying baby lion.

The sailor leans back, swills down his drink.

"All right. You look like an O.K. guy. What'll you give me for him, anyway?"

"How's twenty bucks sound?"

"Like plain robbery, that's how it sounds."

The sailor reaches over and takes the cub from Cap's arms. He grabs him from underneath behind the front paws just below the shoulder joints and holds him up in the air with one hand.

"This bastard's offered me twenty dollars for my lion cub. Anybody here willing to give me more than that?"

There's quiet up and down the bar. The bartender moves along the bar toward the sailor. Cap stares up at the cub; there are some dark marks across his muzzle as if he's been hit or scratched. Cap holds out his hand for the cub.

"O.K. I'll make it twenty-five, but that's it."

The sailor yanks the cub away. Cap reaches into his pocket and pulls out his wallet. He has most of his prize money stashed at the hotel but he has forty dollars in his pocket. He pulls out two tens and a five, spreads them like a poker hand, looks the half-drunk sailor in the eye, then shifts them to the eyes of the cub. This lion is so sick, so tired, he looks more like a newborn calf than anything. The sailor lowers the cub onto the bar again, looks at Cap aggressively.

"Hell, this critter's worth at least a hundred dollars to any zoo. He's a valuable animal. I paid fifty dollars for two of them and had to pay the coxswain another ten to let me keep them on ship. Lost the other just out of that crummy African port. This one's worth more than a lousy twenty-five bucks, I can tell you that."

He orders another drink. Cap spreads and leaves his

money on the bar. He's beginning to wonder what he's doing. He knows he's not drunk, but what in hell will he do with a baby lion cub? He knows he's thinking the cub will die in a few days at the most, but even so, how'll he smuggle it up into his hotel room? What'll he do with it during the days? He can't possibly travel across the country in a car with a lion cub.

There's a moment's pause and the sailor sweeps Cap's money off the bar.

"O.K., matey. You drive a hard bargain but this here lion's yours now. He needs a couple bottles of milk a day and he's started eating meat. Here's the bottle and some nipples."

He reaches into the shore bag at his feet. "Try to keep him warm nights; he comes from a hot place. I tell you he's gentle as a kitten but watch out for them claws; he's not careful sometimes and they're sharp."

He pulls up the sleeve of one arm and shows long raked scars down the length of it. The sailors at the bar laugh. They all figure this landlubber with the leather hat's been taken to the cleaners. Who the hell wants a lion cub anyway? He's not much different from some alley cat, only bigger.

The sailor pulls down his sleeve.

"Here, mate, have a drink, on me."

Cap joins in, glugs down his drink. He has the cub against his chest; from its breathing he can tell it's asleep. Its thin stomach rises and falls. Cap is surprised at how long the cub's body is, even though it's young. When the cub breathes out he can see the vault of his ribs; there are soft folds of skin over his empty belly. Cap wants to get out fast, buy some milk, some meat, a brush, and take the cub back to his hotel.

Cap leaves to the cheers and jeers of sailors. He buys the things he needs at a little market by the waterfront, one he knows is open till midnight. It's where he buys soda crackers and ginger ale to nibble on in the hotel when he can't sleep. The old man in the store can't believe Cap has a real live lion cub in his arms. He's sympathetic but scared. It's the first time Cap runs up against the almost universal fear of large cats.

Cap manages to smuggle the cub into his room by going up the back way. He puts some milk in the bottle with a nipple the sailor gave him. The cub's so sleepy, or maybe in the process of dying, Cap has a hard time getting him to start sucking, but once he starts the cub empties the bottle twice. Then Cap opens up the pound package of ground round he's bought and puts it on the floor. He lowers the cub to the rug; the cub collapses onto its side. He's so weak he can't stand.

So Cap takes pieces of meat and pushes them into the cub's mouth. When he gets it past the milk teeth and onto the tongue, the cub gulps and swallows. Cap gets half his meat into the cub's mouth before it falls asleep.

By now, it's almost two in the morning and Cap is tired himself, but he puts the cub on his bed and, using the hairbrush he bought at the store, starts currying the cub's fur, pulling out knots, straightening all the snarled hairs until the cub begins to look presentable. Presentable for death, Cap thinks. He turns out the light and goes to sleep.

Cap is wakened in the morning by a rough licking on his cheek. It's the lion cub and it's standing shakily next to Cap in the bed. His eyes, although still covered by the bluish haze, are open, awake, aware. He's standing, a bit wobbly on the shifting bed, but standing.

Cap reaches up and pulls on the cub's ears.

"Hey there, feller. You're supposed to be dead. What you doin' standing up on my bed, getting ready to eat me, huh?"

Cap rolls out of bed and pours more milk into the bottle. The cub sucks at it voraciously, pulling on the nipple so it almost tears, pushing hard against Cap's hand. He's obviously been starved.

"You really are a tough one, feller. That's what I think I'll call you, Tuffy; if you live long enough."

Cap's beginning to feel he might very well be the owner of a live, more or less healthy, growing lion cub. It's something he hadn't bargained for. He puts the rest of the hamburger Tuffy didn't eat the night before on the floor and Tuffy snuffles it down. He looks up at Cap, strolls around the bed.

Cap sees where he's made a mess in one corner.

"Oh, boy, just what I need."

Cap cleans up after Tuffy, showers and dresses as the cub follows him around the room. He knows he has to buy more food and some kind of collar and leash for the cub. Cap's supposed to race the next day up on the Beverly Hills board track. He needs to join the team and help pack up the cars, all the equipment.

Cap goes out the back way again, puts Tuffy in the car he borrowed, and goes around front to pay his bill. He shops on the way and buys three more pounds of meat with two bottles of milk. He'll have to win more races just to feed this cub.

At Beverly Hills, on the board track, Cap does win. It's his first win in five races, so he considers Tuffy his lucky omen. He introduces Tuffy to the rest of the racing team. They aren't too enthusiastic about a lion cub being around, but after somebody's driven and won a major race you don't argue much. The lion is Cap's problem anyway. Cap doesn't seem to have anything for women so maybe he's got something special for lions.

The next weeks Cap drives in an open car, cross-country to a race at Maywood, near Chicago. Tuffy is in the front seat beside him. Cap stops every hour or two to feed the cub, curry his fur, or give him a chance to do his business. Tuffy, by now, is beginning to act like a real lion, that is, sleeps most of the time. But, when he isn't sleeping, he's sitting up on the passenger's seat staring out the front windshield or out the side as the landscape passes by. There isn't too much traffic but Tuffy carefully observes passengers in cars that pass and they in turn look carefully at him.

The road is mostly paved but Cap has three flat tires, about right for the trip on those roads.

Sometimes while Cap is driving, the cub puts one of his heavy paws on Cap's arm almost as if he's helping. By the end of the trip, Tuffy's hair is beginning to shine.

Cap has no fear of Tuffy; that's one of Cap's troubles; he doesn't know when to be afraid. Tuffy doesn't seem to fear Cap either.

At Maywood, Cap wins again. He knows how, in a certain way, he's driving for Tuffy; trying to make things right between them, even though Tuffy is locked up in a cabin outside town.

Cap knows better than to go into a hotel with the rest of the driving team. They'd go crazy if he walked in with a lion cub. Somehow, Cap feels that having a lion as a pet is right for him. It fits with everything he feels about his own life. Tuffy is a perfect blend of his love for animals and his need for risk, his attraction to danger.

Then, gradually, Cap begins to think about what will happen to Tuffy if he crashes, is hurt or killed. The team would probably take him to the SPCA or a zoo. The careless ease, lack of fear, he's always known dissipates. The team, the other drivers, can't understand what's happening and Cap can't tell them.

Three months later, in Atlantic City, he has the crash that was coming; his combination of fear and bravado catches up with him. He wakes in a hospital having suffered several fractured ribs, a scalp cut, and a broken collarbone.

Cap senses he's finished as a major racing driver. He's lost his nerve. Whatever it was that kept him concentrated on the task at hand, whether farming, fighting, playing, fighting war, whatever it was, is gone. He knows fear, the prospect of death, injury, the same as everyone else. His imagination has in some strange way been set free.

While in the hospital, partially drugged by morphine, suffering from shock, pain, Cap keeps asking for someone to go take care of Tuffy. Tuffy is locked in a cheap cabin at a lodge, inland three miles from the beach. It was the only place Cap could be sure of keeping him. Tuffy is now six months old, larger than a large dog, and frightens almost everyone who sees him.

The nurses and doctors in the hospital are convinced Cap's delirious as he keeps talking about his lion and how somebody must feed it. Cap doesn't know what to do.

There is a young woman who was in the stands at the race. She works as an operator for the telephone company and came to the race only because the girls with whom she works dragged her there. Her name is Sally.

Sally is a quiet, simple girl with notions. She bobs her hair and has it dyed a light blond color. She wears lipstick and heavy eye makeup. Her idols are Jean Harlow and Carole Lombard. She buys movie magazines, song sheets, *True Confessions,* and, daring for those times, smokes cigarettes. She's a hopeless, childlike romantic.

When Cap crashes, she's terrified and wonders what's happened to him. She telephones the hospital from her board at work and finds he is seriously but not mortally injured. She talks to the nurse and discovers no one has come to see him except for a few visits by members of his racing team.

She decides to dress in her newest outfit and go visit. She wears a cloche hat, long beads, and her new button-down-front dress. They can only throw her out. She has a simple-minded adulation of the notorious, and Cap Modig is notorious in his field.

* * *

When Sally comes to visit him, Cap is mortified, scared. Not since he was a little boy has he been in bed while a woman was in the same room. He still has his irrational mistrust of the ambiguous, unpredictable: art, music, sickness, and especially women. Here are two of them stalking him at the same time.

Sture's head is bandaged to cover burns and minor abrasions as well as the eight stitches just above what would normally be his hairline. Sally does not know he is bald. She thinks him incredibly handsome for an older man. Cap is thirty-two, Sally twenty.

Cap is very concerned about getting someone to feed Tuffy. After accepting Sally's consolations, and after being embarrassed by her obvious adulation of him as driver—adulation he feels he doesn't deserve at all, when in his heart he knows he's finished—he finally gets around to it.

"Miss, would you do me a big favor? I hate to ask but there's no one else and it's something that must be done. I've been worried crazy about it all the time I've been here."

Sally looks at him, so pale in the bed: his head, all his chest, his arm in bandages and one arm in a sling. "I'd like to help however I can, Mr. Modig."

Cap looks at her. Almost before he starts, he realizes how crazy it will sound, how he can't expect a young, glamorous woman to do what he wants done.

"I don't know how to ask this. You see, I have a lion cub in a cabin outside town. It isn't far from here, not more than three miles, and there's a bus that goes right by. It's called Shore Lodge. He's there in the cabin and is probably starving. I haven't been able to get any food to him for three days."

Cap stops as Sally puts her hands over her mouth, her eyes open. Tears start springing into her eyes.

"I'm sorry, miss. I only thought I'd ask. I'll have to

figure some other way. Maybe one of the team will come
visit again and he can go feed him."

"Oh no, Mr. Modig; I'll do it. Do you mean you have a
real lion here in Atlantic City? How long can he go without food and stay alive? Maybe he's dead!"

"I hope not. Grown lions can go a long time without
food and he's almost six months old now. But he must be
hungry. He wouldn't ever hurt anybody. He hasn't
learned to hunt or anything. To be perfectly honest, he's
probably my closest friend in the world, except for my
parents."

Sally stares at him. She hadn't thought of a race driver
as someone with parents, and she'd thought he'd have
many friends. She thought he was like a movie star, an
artificial sort of person, more or less unreal, made up in
magazines, living a separate life, nothing like everybody
else.

"What does he eat? Tell me exactly what to do."

She looks Cap straight in the eye for the first time. She
sees him. She sees the shy farm boy who has only just
learned to love—his first love a lion cub.

And Cap sees her. He sees past the bob, the peroxide-
bleached hair, the eye makeup. He sees the little girl playing grownup.

"Over there in that closet are my clothes. In my jacket
is a wallet. Go over and take out the wallet."

Sally does as she's told. She feels as if she's entering
into something very intimate; she's never gone through
the pockets of a man's clothes. She has no brother and
her father died when she was fourteen. She carries back
the wallet, formed to fit in the back pocket of a pair of
pants as Cap usually wears it, sweat-stained.

"Now open it up. In the back part you'll find money.
Take out five dollars."

Sally opens the wallet, takes out money. She closes the
wallet. She goes to the closet, puts the wallet back in his

pocket. She stands with the five dollars in her hands, looks at Cap.

"You don't need to give me money, Mr. Modig. I have money. I have a good job with the telephone company."

"That's no reason you should pay for Tuffy's food. Tuffy's my lion. I think you'll like him; he's very loving and kind."

Cap stops.

"I'm still not sure I should let you do this."

"Is it dangerous? Will he try to eat me up?"

Her question is so obviously sincere Cap smiles, then laughs. It hurts his head, his shoulder and ribs. He coughs.

"No, he's perfectly safe. It's just he might be so excited he'd break past the door and escape. Even though he's young, he's very strong."

"I promise I'll do my best, Mr. Modig. We had a big dog once and I took him for walks. I could hold him when nobody else could. I'm stronger than I look."

"I'll bet you're strong. By the way would you call me Cap or Sture, please? You make me feel old calling me Mr. Modig."

Sally looks down at the five dollars in her hand. She looks up, shifting from one foot to the other.

"Would you stop calling me Miss, too, Mr. Modig, I mean Cap? It makes me feel I'm talking to you on the switchboard and I don't feel that way at all. Please call me Sally, that's my name."

A blush comes over her face, and she turns her whole body away from Cap. He, in turn, feels a sweat rising on his forehead under the bandages.

"O.K., Sally. First go buy five pounds of hamburger. You don't have a motorcar, do you?"

Sally smiles and shakes her head.

"Not on what they pay a telephone operator I don't."

"Do you know how to drive?"

"How can I drive if I don't own a motorcar?"

They both smile at each other. It's a brief moment of ridiculous joy. Cap has a hard time getting back to the subject: his starving lion, Tuffy.

"O.K., then. I guess you'll need to take that bus, it's the bus going out the Blackhorse Pike."

"I know the one, the number twelve. I've taken it out to a place where there's dancing and music, a place in a big elephant. Do you know it?"

"No, I'm sorry I don't. I don't know how to dance, anyway."

"Maybe someday I can teach you. It's fun. But first you need to get better and out of bed."

Cap looks at her. She's so shy in some ways and then so direct in others. She's like a good animal.

"Yes, but first we must feed Tuffy; that is, you'll have to feed him. I forgot; you'll need the key."

Cap points to the closet again. "In my right pants pocket you'll find a key attached to a piece of wood. It has the number of my cabin on it; I think it's thirteen."

"No wonder you had bad luck and crashed. You know you *were* winning before you had that terrible crash. I was so excited and proud of you. You were so brave."

Cap is blushingly embarrassed. Sally goes to the closet. Reaching into his pants pocket is even more adventurous, more intimate. She feels the hard round wood of the key holder and pulls it out. She holds it up for Cap to see. "Is this it? It's number thirteen."

"That's it. When you get to the cabin, open the package of meat *before* you open the door. Then, holding tight on to the doorknob, slip the package into the door and close it quickly.

"Listen on the outside to hear if Tuffy comes and eats; that is, if he's still alive or still in there. He might have made so much noise because he was hungry the owner could've called the SPCA and they might've hauled him off.

"If he's there you'll *hear* him eat; he makes a lot of

grunting and snuffling sounds, you can't miss it. If you don't hear anything, open the door carefully again and listen, then look to see if he's there. If he's there and isn't moving don't go into the room, just come back to me here and I'll call the SPCA.

"You never know with a lion; he could only be asleep and when he sees you, you might not know what he's doing. I don't think he'd ever hurt anybody, but then he hasn't been hungry like this since he was a little cub."

Sally is listening with her eyes open.

"What do I do if he *isn't* there?"

"Then go to the owner of the lodge and telephone the SPCA. You can explain what's happened."

"Will I be arrested?"

"No, just tell them I sent you. I'm sure Tuffy will be there, though. He'll be hungry and restless. Also he's probably lonely. He's never been alone by himself so long in his life."

"He really is your best friend, isn't he?"

"Yes. I find it hard making friends. I have a lot of people I like and I think they like me but we don't become friends, or maybe we are friends and I don't know it."

"I'm your friend, Sture."

Cap stares. It's a long time since anyone's called him Sture. He looks away. He's wishing he could escape from the bed; he's scared and at the same time inside he's churning, the way he does on a tight turn, wheel to wheel with another car.

"I guess you are, Sally. And if you can rescue Tuffy, I'll never forget it."

With that, Sally turns and leaves the room. Cap settles back in his bed and tries pulling himself together. He's feeling more shaken by the last half hour than he was when the car spun out and burst into flames. He feels he has fallen into some kind of new life, starting with Tuffy and now this young girl.

* * *

Sally finds number thirteen at the lodge without trouble. No one at the lodge office seems to notice her. The cabin is one of the farthest back, against the pine barrens so common in that part of New Jersey.

She listens carefully at the door but hears nothing. After unwrapping the hamburger as Sture has told her, she slowly turns the key in the lock. She pushes the door in and Tuffy the lion shoves his muzzle into the space. Sally is frightened, shocked, surprised so she almost lets go of the door. She forces herself to put the meat on the ground at the threshold and shoves it in with her foot. Tuffy pounces on the hamburger immediately, gulping and swallowing with grunts and groans of contentment. He looks up at her twice while eating. Each time Sally is prepared to pull the door shut but Tuffy continues to concentrate on his food.

Finally, with his large, rough tongue he's licking the last bits of meat from the package. His yellow, round eyes look up at Sally. Then he quickly forces his face through the opening in the door and leans so hard she can't hold back. As the door swings farther open, Tuffy can apply his full strength and wrenches the doorknob from her hand.

Sally stands with her fists against her mouth as Tuffy comes out, stalks around her, and begins rubbing his face, his body, against her so hard he almost knocks her over. He's behaving exactly the way any domestic cat would, except he weighs almost a hundred pounds.

Sally pulls herself together and goes into the room. Tuffy follows her. She closes the door behind him. He isn't trying to escape, he's only wanting company; as Cap has foretold, he's almost more lonely than hungry.

The room smells. Sally sees where Tuffy has made his messes. She takes a newspaper from the table beside the bed and scoops them up, flushes them down the toilet. She opens a window slightly from the top to air the room.

Tuffy stays close to her rubbing hard against her whenever she stoops or stops. When she's finished, she sits on the side of the bed. Here she is in the cabin of a man she hardly knows, feeding and cleaning up after his lion. She's between crying and laughing. What would the nuns say? This is even more of an adventure than a Gloria Swanson movie.

Tuffy comes up and rests his large head across her lap on the bed. It's such a natural thing for a dog but seems wrong for a large cat. Sally pushes his head away and Tuffy starts prowling around the room.

Sally finds some milk in the wooden icebox in the kitchenette. The ice has long ago melted, so it's warm but not sour. She pulls the melted ice-water pan out into the middle of the floor, pours milk into another pan, and puts it beside the water. While Tuffy drinks, she carefully edges her way to the door, opens it quickly, and goes out. She locks it behind her and walks surreptitiously past the office of the lodge keeper. It's the kind of lodge where casual visitors to guests' rooms are tolerated, even expected.

Back at the hospital, Sally tells Cap all that she's done. She tells him she has to work the next day but she'll go out in the evening after work and feed Tuffy. She'll come visit Sture, too.

"I can't thank you enough, Sally. Looks as if I'm going to be in this hospital when the team leaves for Langhorne. I'll need to catch up later. You'll never know how much I appreciate all you're doing; not many people are brave enough to go into a room with Tuffy alone."

"But he's so gentle. He loves to be loved. He's like a big pussy cat."

"He probably thinks you're part of our pride. I'm really glad he took to you like that."

"What do you mean 'pride'?"

"A lion's family is called his pride. Since I got Tuffy

I've been reading all the books on lions I can find. Mostly they talk about lions in zoos and the diseases they get; there isn't much about how lions actually live in the wild. I wish I could take Tuffy back to Africa and set him free with other lions."

Sally smiles. "I like being part of Tuffy's pride."

During the week Sture is in the hospital, he and Sally start confiding about their past lives. Sally feeds Tuffy, then comes to visit Sture until visiting hours are over. Sture tells about his boyhood on the farm, about his bicycle, about being in the war and getting wounded. He tells her about his lost hair and lost teeth, about his lungs, about his hurt leg.

Sally tells about her poor family, about having a sister who died of galloping consumption at thirteen, about her father dying of the same deadly disease, contracted while trying to nurse her sister. She tells how she quit school in sixth grade and was lucky to get a job with the telephone company. She'd always wanted to be an actress but now knew she'd never be one, just work at the telephone company until she met somebody at one of the dances who would want to marry her.

"I'd think anybody who'd ever met you would want to marry you, Sally."

Cap says it before he knows it's coming; it's what he feels. He still can't believe that this lovely woman, in many ways only a girl, is still unmarried, still not taken. The women he's met so far in his life, except his mother, have all been so hard and grasping, so easy to read and yet so hard to know.

He feels Sally is almost like the sister he'd always wished he had. He likes the way they can talk together, laugh together, and enjoy long private silences, looking into each other's eyes quickly, looking away.

"Would you want to marry me, Sture? You act as if you're afraid of me, afraid to be a friend. Would you go to a dance with me before you leave for Pennsylvania? I'd like that. That's the way you could pay me back for helping with Tuffy."

She looks straight into Cap's eyes, not looking away this time. Cap tries to look back into hers but is so confused he needs to look away. He raises his good arm and puts the back of his hand across his face. He tries to keep his voice in control as he speaks, his hand turned backward over his eyes. He thinks of how he was almost blind, how he fought for his sight.

"Sally, I'm too old for you. I'm too old even for myself. I'm not sure I'll ever be able to drive a racing car again. I've lost something inside, a way of believing everything would always turn out all right, that nothing could really hurt me. I'm beginning to be afraid, Sally. If you're going to race cars, you can't be afraid or you'll get hurt.

"That's how I had this crash. I was afraid and trying to make myself think I wasn't. I took stupid chances at the wrong time because I wasn't in tune with myself.

"You'd best forget you ever knew me. I'm an outsider, a wanderer, and I guess I'll always be one. You'll make a good wife to some real man, and a fine mother to beautiful babies. That's what you need, not a vagrant type like me. God, I'm old enough to be your father. How old are you, anyway?"

"I'm twenty, Sture. And I'm old enough not to believe what you're saying. You only say those things because you're discouraged here in the hospital. You'll be yourself when you get out, get driving again."

Cap looks at her. She's saying what he'd like to believe, but he knows it isn't true. Still, he's glad to hear her say it.

When Cap finally is out of the hospital, Sally comes regularly to see him. She goes on long walks with Tuffy and Cap in the pine barrens. They talk about all the things they'd never talked about to anyone else before. Cap tells how he loved the animals on his parents' farm, how he talked to them, how much he enjoyed school.

Sally tells how she hated school, couldn't do the work; always wanted to run away to Hollywood. Sally tells how she's bored with her job at the telephone company, how she hardly gets breaks even to go to the bathroom; how the other operators are coarse and mean.

Cap discovers that Sally smokes cigarettes. He embarrassedly tells her how his lungs are burned out and he can't be around cigarette smoke. Sally snuffs out the cigarette she's smoking and says she's been looking for an excuse to quit, that it's a filthy and expensive habit and she only started because her friends at the telephone company smoke.

Here, walking in the woods with a young lion we have two people. One looking like the classic flapper, giving the appearance of being fast, as loose as the women she's imitating; yet actually, naive, inexperienced, scared. And the other, our Cap, brave beyond reason, gifted above all, man among men, however also scared, unprepared for the hard life he can see looming before him. They fall into each other, both feeling they've found the perfect blend of humanity and an ideal of the opposite sex they wanted but of which they were afraid.

Sally starts coming directly from work to Sture. Cap sends a telegram to the racing team saying he'll meet them in Detroit, that he isn't well enough to race yet.

When they first sleep together in Sture's cabin, they're both virgins. They come to the end of play-acting against the wall of physical reality. Their unsuccessful efforts only increase the mental, spiritual bonding between them as they laugh uncontrolledly at their mutual ineptitude.

They'd locked Tuffy in the small bathroom, and, after laughing, they cry together, then sleep together, wrapped in each other's arms, legs, knowing the end of aloneness. Sture's whole life, his reasons for living are changed.

* * *

When Cap goes to Detroit, Sally quits her job and goes with him. Cap insists they get married but Sally puts him off. She finally agrees to a civil marriage before a justice of the peace in Elkton, Maryland. Her only concern is that she not get pregnant. Sally is willing to be married but not ready to be a mother. Sture represents love, affection, passion; a chance to get away from the boredom of her life, but she still clings to her aspiration of being something on her own.

They're now comfortable with each other sexually and blossom in the joy of discovering their long-suppressed sensuality.

Tuffy rides cramped in the back seat of the motorcar. He's accepted Sally easily into the pride but is perhaps feeling somewhat displaced by her in Cap's affection.

The drive from Atlantic City to Detroit is a marvel to Sally. She's never been farther than Philadelphia and rarely has ridden in a motorcar. The entire experience makes her glad she's left her job. She feels guilty not being able to send the five dollars from her pay check home to her mother, but Cap says he'll make that up. Since they're married, that seems all right to Sally.

At Detroit, Cap drives on a dirt half-mile track, difficult and dangerous driving. He finds he not only can't pull away from the pack, take the lead, he can barely keep up with it. The team figures he is still suffering from his last accident and needs a few races under his belt to get his nerve again. But Cap knows otherwise. He knows he'll never be willing to take the kinds of risks he's always taken without thinking. Now he's thinking *too* much. He's thinking of Tuffy, of Sally, of himself. He's no longer just a comfortable, natural animal.

He races twice more, first at Omaha on a mile track and then at Altoona, Pennsylvania. He's scheduled next to race in Laurel, Maryland. In both races he's had the same problem. It's as if he's forgotten how to do something perfectly simple, like walking or milking a cow. He knows what he has to do but he can't get himself to do it.

The worst thing is he doesn't even *want* to force himself to it any more. He not only *can't* drive competitively, he doesn't *want* to. In Altoona, Cap and Sally stay with Tuffy in a lodge outside town.

Sally cuddles against Sture, puts her arms across his chest, whispers in his ear.

"Don't talk like that, Sture. You know you're the best driver around, as good as De Palo or Shaw or Bill Cummings or any of them."

"Yeah, maybe I'm good as Frank Lockhardt and look what happened to him. I was there. And I don't really think I was ever as good as those guys. I'm a lot better mechanic than any of them but I'm just not crazy-mad enough to be an outstanding driver. Sometimes they drive almost as if they *want* to be killed."

"Please, don't say those things, Sture. It scares me."

"Well, it scares me, too, Sally. It's what I'm trying to tell you, I'm scared.

"Look, Sally, honest, I know you came off with me because you thought I was a big-shot automobile racer and now you find out I'm so scared I can hardly get myself to ride a kiddy car. If you want to go home I'll give you the money and you can just forget you ever knew me. It'd be the best thing. We could get a quick divorce, and since you feel we've never really been married, since it wasn't in the church, you can go to confession and start out fresh again."

There's a long silence. Sally lifts herself with her elbows on Sture's chest. "Is that what you really think of me, Cap? Do you think I ran away with you just because you're an automobile driver? Do you really think that?"

"What I really think, Sally, is I want you to feel married to me and stay with me. But I also want you to know what I can and can't do. I don't want you to be sorry afterward."

So they make love again, the *most* complete and somehow *least* complete of all communications. The next day, Sture tells Sally his plan.

"Listen, Sally, I have just over ten thousand dollars in the bank right now. I know if I keep racing I'll only get worse, and I'm sure to get hurt or killed. I'm a menace now to the other drivers as well as myself.

"I thought of buying a garage and running that, but I'm still not ready to settle down and I don't think you are either. So tell me what you think of this idea."

Cap looks at Sally. They're having coffee in their cabin. Tuffy has been fed and is asleep under the table with his chin on Cap's foot.

"I know of a car for sale. It's a 1930 Model T Ford Miller 91 with a Fronty overhead valve conversion. It's narrow, light, and I know some things I can do to make it a perfect sprint car. Then, instead of racing in this crazy race scene with international and top-flight drivers I can race the dirt tracks, the county fairs. With this car I could win easily and beat out the local cowboys with their souped-up jobs. I can buy the car and a Ford truck in good condition with a trailer to haul it with and we could be off. What'd'ya think of the idea, Sal?"

"Is that what you want, Sture? I want you to be happy and I don't want you to get hurt."

"It sounds fine to me and we could take Tuffy along in the truck. I could probably fix him a place to live in there; it's big enough. The team's getting nervous about Tuffy anyway and I hate leaving him alone all the time when I race. He's liable to break out from one of these cabins, then some idiot of a sheriff will most likely shoot him."

"It sounds wonderful, Sture. We could go from one county fairground to the other and it wouldn't be so dangerous, would it?"

"Safer than driving on the road. I think we could have a good time all the way. There's all kinds of betting at those county fairs, and we can make more money that way, too, with you doing the betting and me doing the driving. We'd make out great. I think anybody'd be glad losing money to a pretty girl like you."

Sture bought his Ford Model T Miller converted Fronty and a truck to pull it. He paid $5,000 for the entire rig, half of his capital. At that time, a good job paid $25 a week; $5,000 was four years' hard work.

Sture tinkered with that car for a month, making the conversions and adaptations he thought would turn it into the ideal "sprint car," a car that could get going fast and maneuver easily. Sture knew his car wouldn't have much of a chance in big-time racing, because there's nothing more obsolete than last year's car, but it could be a winner on dirt-track sprinting.

And he was right. Cap Modig became the terror of county fairs. With his jackrabbit car he'd get off fast and hold his lead for the short runs.

The typical race would have four qualifying laps to shake out all the cars not fast enough for racing. Then there'd be a trophy dash to determine the fastest four cars. These four cars would then compete in the main event. The main event would usually be twenty-five or fifty laps on a half-mile track.

Cap won more than his share. Sally did the betting, and even at short odds would usually more than equal the prize money Cap won.

The most dangerous part for Sture was that the tracks were so short he'd have to lap some of the worst drivers before the end. Some of these cowboys wouldn't pull over to let him by. He wasn't afraid so much for himself as he was for the car: half of his capital was tied up in it.

* * *

He kept working on the car after every race, tinkering, tuning up, making minor improvements. It was a good life for the two of them. They bought a tent and they'd usually camp near the fairground, but not too near because of Tuffy.

Cap and Sally lived this roving life for three years, moving with the seasons. Tuffy was developing into a full-grown lion. He could already pull off a roar, and his mane was thickening and darkening. He was still playful and would wrestle with Cap evenings. When Cap wrestled with Tuffy, sometimes the local people would come out to where he was staying and watch. Cap could probably make as much money wrestling Tuffy as they were making on the track.

The meat bills for Tuffy were a major factor in the budget. Sally, partly out of jealousy, partly fear, and partly resentment at the cost, kept encouraging Cap to sell Tuffy or give him to a zoo.

Cap knew he'd have to do something, sooner or later, with Tuffy, before an accident happened; but he couldn't think of Tuffy in a cage all the time with no company and he knew that something of his own sense of security, his deepest joy, was invested in Tuffy. It was a fine thing for a man like Cap owning an honest-to-goodness full-maned lion, especially since Sally still didn't want to have children. She said it would be impossible being on the road all the time. She was young; they could wait till they settled down.

Cap would buy his meat for Tuffy from local butchers and sometimes at horse-slaughtering houses. Tuffy needed about ten pounds of meat a day. He used his teeth to pull the last meat off a bone, and his jaws were so strong he could crunch down and splinter a horse or cow thigh bone to get at the marrow. But his favorites were the cheapest meats: the kidneys, lungs, and intestines.

Cap loved to watch Tuffy eat. The lion's claws would

actually dig into the bone as he held it to gnaw off the meat. Cap could almost understand why people were afraid of lions. Meanwhile, Sally was getting less and less comfortable around Tuffy. She told Cap it scared her when he stared at her as if he could wish her away.

One of Cap's favorite positions was lying with his head on Tuffy's chest, snuggled under his forelegs. Sometimes when Cap tried to get up, Tuffy loosened his top leg and flopped it across Cap's face without unleashing his claws. The claws were now each more than an inch long, and sharp. A vet near Kalamazoo, Michigan, one Cap took Tuffy to when he had a cold, said Tuffy should be declawed, but Cap wouldn't have it done.

Cap even liked the smell of Tuffy, especially just after he'd been brushed. He had the smell of the first sweat on a man before the air gets to it and turns it sour, not nervous sweat, but honest, hard-work sweat. But Tuffy's smell couldn't be from hard work; lions are among the laziest creatures in the world. If they're fed they'll sleep most of the time or just lie around.

In New Jersey, at a small county-fair track not far from Asbury Park, Sally and Cap are walking down the midway of a traveling carnival that has set up beside the track. Sometimes a race meeting lasts four or five days and carnivals like this take advantage of the crowds. They pitch their tents and set up equipment: small Ferris wheels, merry-go-rounds, various rides, sideshows, and other acts.

It is in the evening after the last day of racing. Cap has won two races. He and Sally are walking down the midway of the carnival, late, after most of the crowds have gone.

There are booths for pitching baseballs against metal milk bottles, or popping balloons with darts, or banging a sledgehammer on a scale to ring a bell—all the sucker traps that make carnivals fun.

At the end, closing off the runway, are two interesting setups. One is a boxing ring with a really beat-up-looking pug sitting on a small ring stool. The ropes of the ring are covered with red velvet. The manager of the act, a bald-headed, middle-aged, well-pouched man, is sitting on the edge of the ring at the feet of his fighter. The fighter has heavy eye ridges from many poundings, and both ears are cauliflowered. There are thickened scars on his brows and on his cheeks. He's sitting with his back to the ring, his arms looped over the ropes, his gloves on his hands, but the laces loosened. He looks to Cap like somebody who's really been through the mill, someone, like himself, who has too many scars. The promoter yells over to Cap.

"Hey there, feller, you look tough. Why not give my boy a workout? There's nobody around to bet so it'll only cost you ten bucks; if you can stay in there with him for three rounds it's worth a hundred to you. What d'ya think, make a big impression on your pretty girlfriend there?"

It's only a half-serious proposition; he doesn't even stand up. Cap strolls over, shakes hands with the promoter, with the fighter. The fighter pulls off his glove and shakes with his bandaged hand. Cap sees the fighter is slow, standing up shakily, somewhat back on his heels, rocking above them, looking down, practically expressionless, a slight smile revealing missing teeth in front, probably has just about as many teeth left as Sture. But Cap feels this man, even fighting on instinct, would be deadly close in, past his prime but still out of any ordinary person's class, just as Cap now is as a driver.

"Nope. I wouldn't have a chance with the champ there. I drive cars, couldn't punch my way out of an empty apple box."

The manager cocks his head, birdlike, looks closer at Cap.

"Hey, you're the guy won that race today, ain't you,

the one people say has a full-grown lion with him somewhere, that right?"

"That's right."

"Ya know, I was thinking about that lion when I heard
about it. We could have him declawed and he could fight
my boy here the way they do with kangaroos. It'd be an
act nobody could resist; we could go big time with an act
like that, a boxer fighting a lion. He don't bite or nothin',
does he?"

Cap smiles, looks at Sally. Her eyes are wide open,
listening, watching. She still hasn't had much experience
with carny folks, their wild ideas, their dreams, impossible propositions. Cap smiles at the promoter.

"Naw, he's not for sale. And besides, even with his
claws pulled, he'd knock your boy right out of the ring,
probably break his neck. A full-grown lion can snap the
back of a mature horse or buffalo with one swipe; they've
got power in the shoulders you wouldn't believe. They
make Jim Thorpe look like a marshmallow."

"Well, just thought I'd ask. Could you tell me why
you're keeping that lion anyway; going to teach him to
drive a car or something like that? He must cost a fortune
just to feed."

"No, he's a friend, a pet. I bought him down in San
Diego when he was a cub, in a bar there. I don't actually
know what I'll do with him in the end. Maybe give him
to a zoo someday. I hate to think of it."

They talk a few minutes more then move over to another attraction next door that's been interesting Cap
since they set it up. It's one of those "Wall of Death"
acts. They've put up a huge wooden bowl twenty-five feet
high or so, with straight wooden sides. These sides are
held together by wide metal straps screwed tight on the
outside of the wall. There are steps up to a catwalk
around the top from which people can look down inside
to see the act.

There's also a platform in front of this Wall of Death where the performers do tricks to attract crowds.

Into the platform are built rollers. The performers ride their motorcycles on those rollers.

Cap'd gone by before and seen the riders dipping and doing tricks, running the bikes on the rollers. They'd made a lot of noise and done some impressive tricks such as standing on the seats of the motorcycles. Once Cap saw one of them stand on his hands using the handles of the motorcycle. He wondered what they did on the inside, if they did any of the tricks in there they did on the rollers. It had to be like some of those high-banked fast curves at Des Moines. If you got out of your car there, you could hardly stand on the track.

Two guys are on the platform out front. They've got one of the motorcycles, an Indian, broken down and are working on it. The mechanic in Cap, as well as the driver, is fascinated. It looks as if they're trying to adjust the timing. He stops and watches; one of them looks up, smiles, then looks again. He turns to the other driver, working on the other bike.

"Hey, Jimmy. Here's the guy who drove that Ford Fronty job and won today."

They both turn back to Cap.

"Boy, those rubes didn't know what hit them; they didn't have a chance against that machine and you really drove them into the ground. Hey, you're Cap Modig, ain't you? Holy cow! I didn't recognize you today. You've always been one of my big heroes, one of the *real* drivers, one who came out of the garage; a mechanic, not just some rich playboy.

"Gees, I thought you got killed in a crash in Atlantic City or something!"

"Not quite; just banged up some. But it finished me for big-time racing. Maybe that's why you thought I was dead. I raced a couple more times but I'd lost it."

The two young men are standing. For them it's like

looking at the ghost of Valentino or Caruso or even Frank Lockhardt. They're both young, strong, full of life, greasy-shirted, greasy-handed, nails and cuticles packed with black dirt the way it is for anyone who works all the time with machines.

They make Cap feel old. They're both under thirty and the younger one probably a long way from thirty, maybe under twenty. The younger one swings his leg up over the machine he's been working on, another Indian; he rolls it off the kick stand and pushes it over the rollers.

"Ever try one of these, Mr. Modig? It's the greatest thrill in the world, almost like flying."

He looks over at Sally, who's leaning on Cap's arm, taking it all in, fascinated.

"Honest, Mr. Modig, you ought to try. We've got these bikes specially geared for that wall in there. You got to get up fast or you're dead; a driver like you would love it."

He's playing to Sally. She leans tighter against Sture and he puts his hand over hers.

"I drove one of those Indians once, but I've never raced one. I only borrowed a machine and took a few short trips. That damned engine scared me, I must admit, all that power between my legs. But it's a thrill all right."

The young one kicks his engine over and guns it a few times. The boxer and his manager look across. Then the young driver strips off his undershirt in the cool evening air. He has an eagle astride a motorcycle tattooed on the top of his left shoulder. His body is tight, muscular, a gymnast's build. He's short, not more than five feet seven, not much taller than Sally, and he's wearing high-heeled boots.

He begins by larking and dipping, his own speed keeping him up as with a gyroscope. He stands on the seat, first holding on to the handlebars then letting go. He's locked the accelerator cable so the engine keeps up its speed. He stretches out his arms, then swivels his hips so the motorcycle tips left and right, synchronized with his swivel. He smiles, bright, wild-eyed, cocky. He knows he's good and keeps his eye on Sally.

Cap thinks it's hard not to wish he'd get down before he hurts himself. Cap knows it's only carny corn and he and Sally are probably more in danger themselves standing there. That motorcycle might catch or turn and swing off the platform at them, but something in him won't flinch. He moves himself slightly in front of Sally to protect her in case something does happen. Finally, the young fellow lowers himself back onto the seat, unhooks the accelerator throttle, shifts down, and leaves the motor purring on the rollers, wheels stilled.

"Come on, try it, Mr. Modig. It's the real thing."

Cap knows he's being egged on but it's the kind of temptation he can't resist. Almost any machine, any risk situation, has a strong attraction for him. If it weren't for this personality flaw he wouldn't't've wound up riding cars at county fairs trailing around a grown lion. If it isn't hard, it isn't interesting to Cap Modig.

Cap springs onto the platform, playing young, slightly pulling his hurt leg by hurdling with a one-handed vault. He takes the handlebars from the kid and swings his good leg over the bike. It's a wide, comfortable seat. Cap checks all the controls, accelerator, brakes, gears, revs it a few times with his feet still flat on the platform.

He shifts carefully into first and lets out the clutch. The wheels start, and as the gyroscopic effect comes on, he slowly lifts his feet and hooks them into the foot pegs. It's a strange feeling having the back wheels turning and the bike going nowhere. The bike's taken on life, but there's no pull of acceleration. He shifts up one more gear, gives it more gas, adjusts the magneto a fraction for more spark. Then, gently at first, he starts dipping as if he's going into and out of curves. He finds it really is a good feeling, some of the thrill in driving without all the fear. You're not going to run into anything and nothing can run into you.

But Sture finds the old devil is still there inside, urging him to stand up on that seat, show up the young bastard making eyes at Sally. But, at the same time, he knows he's liable to break his neck and it wouldn't prove anything anyway, so he lets up on the accelerator, comes to a halt, switches off the motor, rolls the machine back off its rollers, and swings down the kick stand.

This time he lifts his bad leg up high over the seat trying not to wince. There's still a piece of shrapnel dug into his femur high on the inside of his leg near the hip joint. The doctors at Metz said it wasn't worth taking out, they'd do more harm than good just cutting through muscle to get at it.

Two days later, while Cap is strapping his car up onto the truck, the older of those two with the motorcycles comes over. Cap and Sally are ready to take off for a track just about fifteen miles away in Wall township. It's another dirt track on a county fairground.

The young fellow stands around watching. Cap figures he has something on his mind. Tuffy is tied under the truck and stays quiet, looking out. Cap's trained him to stay under there to keep from scaring people half to death. Cap looks up and smiles at this guy, who smiles back, lights a cigarette, offers him one. Cap refuses. He couldn't smoke. With the little bit of lung he has left after his gassing, just being around someone smoking is almost impossible. Sal has kept her promise and hasn't smoked since they got married.

The young guy rocks back and forth on his boots.

"Hey, you wouldn't be interested in a trade, would you?"

Cap stands up. He doesn't understand what this is about. He looks under the truck at Tuffy. Does he want to trade something for Tuffy? Maybe he wants to trade something for Sally; maybe the young guy put him up to it.

"Look, I'll trade my whole rig over there, wall, bikes, truck, the whole thing, for your car and that truck. You can keep the lion."

He peeks again at Tuffy, who's asleep. He stamps out his just-lit cigarette.

Cap's reaction is that this man must be crazy. It's like asking somebody if they want to trade *lives*.

Cap pulls hard on one of the straps holding his car in place and looks to see if there's anything serious here. It's a crazy idea, but he's half interested. He knows sooner or later some fool's going to crash into him or he's liable to do something dumb himself. He stops and puts his hands on his hips, listening.

"I tell you there's a good living to be made with that wall. You have to travel most of the year but you're already doing that. I know getting a bike up on the wall and doing a few little stunts would be nothing for a real classy race driver like you.

"If you want, I know Jimmy'll stay around and do most of the stunt stuff for you, anyway. He's absolutely crazy to go up there and put on his act. I give him fifteen dollars a week and found; he really earns it. He's a hard worker putting up and taking down that wall, too. That's the worst part, getting the damned thing up and taking it down again each time. I talked to Jimmy about it and he'll stay with the act if you decide you want to trade. But we ain't got no contract or nothin', you can just dump him if you want."

Cap's thinking. Do they really want to live the carny life? He knows if something happens to his car he'll wind up a grease monkey in a garage somewhere working for somebody else. He's not ready. He's not sure he could take the gaff he'd have to put up with just staying alive, keeping a job.

Running a motorcycle around a wall is one hell of a

long way from being a war hero and race driver, but then he knows he's not a race driver any more, no hero either. He's already halfway to being a carny man without even knowing it. Next thing he'll be one of the geeks eating raw chickens, stomping around naked with his bald head and bum leg for people to laugh at.

"Tell me, what's your typical daily or weekly take when you run that thing?"

The young motorcycle driver lights another cigarette, strikes the kitchen match from his pocket by running it down the side of his overalls.

"Depends. Depends on the place and time of year. If you can find a good summer concession in a place like Atlantic City or here in Asbury Park, something like that, you can really rake it in. Maybe, if you work up a good enough act, you could practically live the rest of the year on what you make summers.

"Little short gigs like this fair don't last long enough and there's not enough people; it's hardly worth putting the wall up and taking it down. Yesterday we only took in thirty-two dollars, but the day before it was almost fifty."

He stops, letting smoke curl across his face in the evening light. He looks over Cap's head, staring.

"I tell you one thing, though. It's what got me thinking about this whole idea of trading. You have a real ace-in-the-hole with this here lion of yours. If you could get that big cat to sit in a sidecar and let himself be driven around a wall, you'd have a regular gold mine. You'd scare people out of their wits with a full-grown lion roaring as he goes around and with no cage between him and them. I'll bet you'd make over a hundred dollars a day right on the boardwalk at Asbury. Or you could check other places like Wildwood, Atlantic City, or even Cape May. Being scared is what people come into this kind of act for; they want to be scared without taking any real risks. That's why they go to races and circuses, too, right?"

Cap knows it's true but hasn't thought about it much.

He's wondering just what he's doing with his life. Maybe he should go back and take over the farm. His dad's getting too old for the job and his mother's slowing down.

"O.K., but what's *your* angle? What is it you want out of this? If you've got such a good deal why give it up?"

"I want to race a really good car. All my life I've wanted to race but could never get up enough money for a honest fast job. If I can't win some with that one you've got there I'll never do it. It's sort of a last chance."

Cap thinks how, in a certain way, it's a last chance for each of them. They stroll over to the Wall of Death, half dismantled. Chuck, the owner, with whom he's been talking, shows Cap how it's done, how the whole thing can be put up or broken down in about four hours. Cap looks over the bikes and listens to the motors on each of them; the pistons on one sound sloppy but that would be easy to fix. Jimmy's standing around watching, something like a slave at a slave auction. In a sense, he's being sold with the rest of the chattel and isn't even sure if the new master will want him.

Cap takes his car off the truck and lets Chuck run it around the dirt track a few times. He gives him some hints about a slight pull to the left and how this pull can be used making tight turns on a counter-clockwise track. Sally stands beside Cap as they watch Chuck push the car around some turns. Cap sees this young feller might make a fair racer with experience but probably won't win much, even with the Fronty.

Sally holds on to his arm.

"Do you really think you'll do this, Cap?"

"What do *you* want, Sal? We can still back out of this whole thing you know, or we can keep on with the racing, or get into this carnival stuff."

Cap waves his free arm back at the carnival area. Most of the tents and trailers have pulled out. The boxing ring is dismantled and being stored on another truck.

"I want to do whatever you want, Cap! I'll be happy wherever you are, no matter what you're doing. But I hate to think of you riding a motorcycle around on that wooden wall; I'm afraid you'll get hurt. What keeps the motorcycle up there anyway? Is there some kind of trick?"

"No, it's just the speed of the motorcycle pushing out against the wall holds it up, the same way you can swing a pail of water around, have it upside down, and the water doesn't spill out, sticks there in the pail."

Sally smiles, reaches over, pulls Sture's head down close, and kisses him.

"Can you imagine? I've never swung a pail around in a circle. Does that show I'm not a farm girl?"

"Just means you haven't had a chance. I think you'd make a darned good farm girl myself."

Cap pulls her around in front of him, holds her out at arm's length, looks her up and down.

"You look kinda strong to me, lady, and feel those muscles."

He pretends to squeeze them as Sally pulls up her short cape sleeves and crooks her arm to make a muscle.

"I really do have muscles for a girl, don't I? Maybe it's from plugging in and taking out all those telephone lines."

"There *is* something else we can do, Sal, go back to the farm. I've been thinking I'd rather do that than be a mechanic if it comes right down to it. I'd like to go back to that farm and have a whole passel of kids."

"I'm not ready for anything like that yet, Sture. Give me some more growing time."

Sally comes close to Cap. He looks over her head. Chuck's stopped the motorcar and is walking around it. He comes up to them.

"Well, it's O.K. with me if it's O.K. with you."

Cap looks at Sally and she looks at him. She smiles. And so it was done. They traded lives.

PART 5

W E ate the dinner Mom cooked on our little cooker off dishes Mom had brought with us. The salt-water taffy was delicious. My favorite kinds were the one with peanut butter inside and one that tasted like strawberries. The kind Dad likes were too strong, like his horseradish. But Laurel liked those kind, the same as Dad, so it worked out fine. I don't remember ever having had salt-water taffy before.

Mom washed the dishes in the little hand sink while Laurel and I got to dry them. It was like playing house. Then, afterward, I crawled under my bed and played with Cannibal. We played at fighting, that's the game she likes most. I try to fool her and reach in so I can touch her nose without her being able to hit my hand with her

paw. She doesn't scratch me any more except by accident. I saved part of my hot dog and gave it to her, and I
think under that bed was the first time I ever heard her
try to purr. It sounded almost like something inside was
broken and couldn't get started. She purred the way
Mickey Saunders talks, and he stutters so he can hardly
answer any questions in class. I had my feet sticking out
from under the bed and then felt Dad's hand on my an-
kle. He softly tugged me out.

"What do you think of that, Dickie? How'd you like
going back up on the boardwalk to see what's going on
this late in the evening?"

I reach out fast, catch Cannibal, and put her in her
box. I squiggle out from under the bed till I can look up
at Dad. He's stretched out on the bed on his stomach
with his head hanging down so he looks upside down to
me looking up.

"Gee, Dad. That sounds great!"

I look around and Mom and Laurel are already in
their sweaters and standing at the door. I scramble to my
feet with Cannibal under my arm as Dad gets off the
other side of the bed and swings his coat over his shoulder. I think my dad carries a coat jacket that way—one
finger hooked under the neck part through the little loop
for hanging a coat, that coat hanging down his back—
more than he ever wears it. I think he only carries it
along in case he might get cold, but he never seems to.
My dad's hands and feet are always warm. Mom says
that's what makes him one of the nicest people in the
world to sleep with.

I pull on my sweater, push down my hair, turn up the
sleeves and the waist part.

"Is it all right if I take Cannibal along? I want her to
see that lion again."

Dad puts his hand on my shoulder, the hand he isn't
using to hold his coat.

The other thing is my dad never wears a hat. He has

curly, dark hair, really wavy not curls, and he hardly ever has to comb it. If I could have hair like that I'd never wear a hat either.

"Sure, Dickie. But maybe the lion will be asleep now or they'll be using him in that Wall of Death act."

"That's O.K. She'll love to see the lights and the merry-go-round."

So we start off. It isn't cold at all. It was much colder in Stonehurst Hills when we left, really beginning to feel like Halloween coming. But here it's warm. The air feels full of water, soft, but it's warm.

The first thing Dad does is buy more salt-water taffy. We know now what we like so he gets some of everybody's favorites. Mom is holding on to Dad's arm and leaning into him. They look like some of the high-school kids getting off the school bus. It's nice to see them that way; maybe they're that way a lot but I've never noticed it before. Dad's always working or tired and Mom's so worried and busy with the house they don't have much time just to be people.

We pass the merry-go-round and show them the animals we were riding on. It's more crowded now, with someone on almost all the outside animals. We watch and they only get about fifteen times around; I think we must have gone around thirty or more times.

"Do you kids want to take another turn?"

I look at Laurel and she shakes her head no, points down the boardwalk. We smile at each other. "Gee, Dad. There's another merry-go-round farther down the boardwalk, one we haven't tried yet. Could we go on that one?"

"Sure, kids, whatever you say."

We walk along some more. There are good smells. There's all the smells of the places selling candy, popcorn, hot dogs, salt-water taffy; but there's more: the smell of ocean, of sand and wood in the boardwalk. It all blends together.

We're getting near the Wall of Death when I begin hearing the motorcycles warming up, and then there's actually a roar from the lion. I look over at Dad. He runs his hand through my hair.

"I must say, Dickie, that sounds pretty impressive. We'll have to take a look at that, all right."

We start hurrying and there's a crowd around the little stage. By the time we get there, the older man is on his motorcycle, and he's standing up on the seat with his hands outstretched, balancing. The younger one is sitting back on his bike cleaning his teeth with his little finger-nail. The lady is still talking about "the most amazing act in show business." Mom doesn't want us getting too close; she's afraid the man will fall, or that motorcycle will just go flying out into the audience; but we get up close anyway. I can tell Dad likes it as much as we do.

But more than anything I want to go over to visit the lion again. When the motorcycles roar, he roars back. He roars then growls and coughs. They have a light in the back of his cage so you can see him and he's pacing back and forth as if he's nervous. I'd sure be nervous if anybody put me in a motorcycle sidecar and hung me on the side of a wall like in those pictures.

It turns out the Wall of Death is the big round thing behind the lion cage and this little stage. It looks like the gas tank down at Long Lane and Marshall Road, only not as big, and it's made out of wood. There's a staircase like a fire escape up the side and people who buy tickets from the lady with the microphone walk up there. We can see others up at the top walking around a little plat-form, where I guess they can see right down in.

I take Dad's hand and pull him over to see the lion while he's still out there. They're pushing the motorcy-cles back down the ramp and inside now. The lady stays out, selling tickets. Pretty soon, I guess, the lion will be gone inside.

We all go over and stand in front of the lion cage. Mom holds on to Dad with one arm and on to Laurel's hand with the other. I open Cannibal's cage a little bit so she can see, the same as last time, and she does the same thing, just sticks the top of her head out, her eyes peering over the edge of the box. That lion, pacing back and forth, is even more scary than he was sitting down. I never knew a lion was so long, that its tail was so thick. Dad's leaning forward looking hard.

"I think that poor creature's practically starving, Dickie. See his ribs and look how the skin's hanging under his stomach. I'll bet he needs about ten pounds of meat a day and these people probably don't make enough money to feed him properly."

I look and see Dad's right, the lion is hungry. I wonder if he knows we'd be good to eat.

Dad backs off a step, looks over at the board with all the pictures, at the lady alone, nobody buying any more tickets. "Well, who wants to go in and see this with me? I know twenty-five cents is a lot of money, but this looks like something special, the kind of thing we'll remember all our lives."

"Oh no, Dick! You aren't really going up there and watch them do this, are you? Somebody's liable to get killed."

"Oh, come on, Laura. They've been doing it all summer long and nobody's gotten killed. They know what they're doing, and I'll bet it's a great act. Besides, a little money from us might help fill that poor lion's stomach some."

It turns out I'm the only one who will go with him. I think for a minute Laurel wants to go, too, but then she decides to stay and keep Mom company. I leave Cannibal in her cage with the top closed and hand it to Laurel.

Dad just catches the lady with the tickets before she goes inside. He gives her the fifty cents.

"Hurry up, mister. They're about to begin the show."

Inside we can hear the motorcycles being started. We take the tickets and dash up the stairs. There's plenty of space up top when we go around to the other side. I don't know what I expected but I'm really surprised when I look over the edge down into the Wall of Death.

There are lights over the top hanging down and it's all bright in the bottom. We look right straight down on two motorcycles. The men are on them but only one has his motor running. The sides of the Wall of Death are black with splintered boards and skid marks from tires and what I guess is black from the motors. In a strange way, there's something about this "Wall of Death" reminds me of our alley, or maybe it's the garages with the deep spots of oil from drippings out of cars. It smells something like a garage, too, damp and the smell of motors. The smell of the car gas Mr. Harding killed himself with, the smell of old wood from the porches, a slight smell of rotting garbage, too, and the smell of the lion is almost like alley-cat smell.

Just as we get settled against the wall, leaning over, one motorcycle starts off running along the bottom in a circle fast, then up the side of the wall, going faster and faster till it's right out sideways, going around the inside of the round wall, making everything rattle. Sometimes he comes so close to the top edge where we are I can't stop myself from ducking. I look over and Dad's ducking, too.

He leans close to me and cups his hand around my ear.

"Now, this is what I really call *something*."

He smiles and we both stick our heads up carefully. The man riding the motorcycle is standing on the seat now, the way he did outside, but he keeps hold of the handlebars. If he lets go, then he'd sure as the devil fall all the way to the bottom and be killed. It's the young one with the slicked-back hair who's up on the wall. His hair just stays in place without getting mussed up, even though he's going fast, so he must have some Wildroot Cream Oil or Vaseline, or some other kind of stickum on it. Mom tries to make my cowlick stay down for church sometimes by combing my hair with stuff, and when it drips off the comb into my eyes, it stings and stinks. She always used to do this when I served mass but I don't have to worry about that any more. When you have stuff like that in your hair and it dries, then your hair feels like broom bristles, not like hair at all. It feels as if, when you bend it, it'll break.

Now he's up on the handlebars bending at his waist, with his feet sticking out in space. He's doing a handstand on those motorcycle handlebars sideways! I can't figure what keeps any of it up on the wall. I keep looking but I don't *see* any tracks and he goes all different angles so there *can't* be that many tracks.

Now, the older man, thicker, slower-moving, takes off his cap, and I can see he only has thin blond hair like fuzz on his head. He puts on a helmet and climbs onto his motorcycle, then starts it with a hard kick. The young one is sitting back on his motorcycle as he rides and twice goes right across the bottom and up the other side; you'd swear he'd fly clear off that wall; then he turns and gets going fast as the wind again. He's shouting down at the older man. We can just hear him as he shouts over the sound of the two motorcycles.

"Come on, old man! I'll race you twenty-five turns."

The other motorcycle comes up the wall fast, almost to the top, then they start crossing back and forth over and under each other. The whole wall is practically rocking now, so I'm afraid the boards will break or maybe the wall will just lift up and turn over. The little walkway we're on is shaking and wobbling.

They're racing around those walls and everybody starts counting as they go around: nine, ten, eleven, twelve. Dad and I are counting, too. Everybody's doing it, and it gets louder and louder. At first the older guy gets a good lead so he's almost half a length around the wall in front of the young one. Then gradually as we get close to twenty the young guy starts gaining. Then, just as we're counting the twenty-fifth turn, he passes the older guy and goes up into his handstand, crossing his legs in the air. He comes down and sits straight on the seat with his hands out and goes around a few extra times, no-handed, while the older guy goes down to the bottom and parks his motorcycle. The young one comes down and rolls his bike outside through the door. Everybody applauds. The lady from the stage comes in with a megaphone in her hand and the two men push in a sidecar. They start attaching it to the older guy's motorcycle.

The lady is shouting up at us through the megaphone. She turns around as she talks so we can all hear:

"Now, ladies and gentlemen. You are about to see the only full-grown male lion who can ride on the Wall of Death in a sidecar. Let me introduce Satan, the Dare-Devil Lion!"

She points over at the side with her hand and I see another door, one I didn't even notice before. It opens and there's a barred door that the older guy pulls up. He has a whip in his hand and snaps it a few times on the floor, making it really pop. The lady takes a jacket and helmet from the young one and puts them on. It looks as if *she's* going to ride that lion around the wall because she climbs on the motorcycle.

She only has those bare legs, or maybe she has silk stockings on, I can't really tell. With a lion it wouldn't make much difference, anyway.

Then we hear the lion roar and he comes to the opening of the door. He stands there with his paws on the edge and looks up at all of us around the edges on top. It's really scary seeing a lion without any bars between you and him. He looks up at the light, then at the older guy with the whip. The lion starts walking toward him.

He keeps popping the whip but doesn't pop it any-where near the lion. The lion moves over toward the side-car and stops. The other guy, the young one, who won the race, is standing against the wall, away from the door, holding a long pole with a pointed metal sticker on the end of it. He looks as scared of that lion as I am. I know I wouldn't like to be down in a wooden hole with a lion and nothing between me and those teeth but a long stick.

The older guy keeps snapping his whip and gradually gets the lion to climb into the sidecar and sit. That whole sidecar sags with the lion in it, he's so heavy. Then, the older guy runs his hands through the mane of the lion while the lion actually rubs his big hairy head against the man's shoulder. The older guy locks a bar across the lion's front legs, over his paws, and straps him in. The lady is sitting on the motorcycle seat staring straight ahead, not looking at the lion at all. Then the older one, with the whip, comes around and kicks the starter on the motorcycle so it coughs, then roars, ready to start.

He steps back and gives a snap of his whip in the air but I think that's just for show. The lady in the purple, shining costume waves her hand, the one away from the lion, up at all of us on the top, half smiles, then starts the motorcycle going around in circles. The man with the whip stays in the center of the pit, turning around as the motorcycle gains speed then starts going up the side of the wall. It really looks as if she'll never get going fast. That lion must weigh hundreds of pounds, at least twice as much as a human being.

Then she's really up on the wall. The whole wooden bowl begins rocking as she gets higher and higher. I man-age to keep my head up once when the motorcycle goes by just below us and the lion isn't more than five feet from my face; there's no bars or anything. I look at Dad and he's looking as scared as I am. It's hard to believe and I'm having an awful time keeping my head up, look-ing; after all, we did pay twenty-five cents. At least I ought to *look*. I'm beginning to wish she'd stop and go back down. It's not like on the merry-go-round at all when I wanted it to keep going. I'm so scared something bad will happen I want it to stop.

Finally, she begins to slow down and goes rolling onto the bottom of the pit. She sits still on the motorcycle while the older guy goes over to the lion and unhooks him. The younger one has moved toward the door opening into the lion cage; he's pulled back the wooden cover and pushed up the bars. He stands there with his pointed stick like a harpoon, still looking scared and trying not to let on.

The older guy helps the lion out of the motorcycle and holds him by the mane beside him. He doesn't seem afraid of that lion at all. But the lady gets off the motorcycle on the other side from the lion, takes off her helmet, and holds her hands up in the air, smiling a fake kind of smile and sneaking looks over at the older guy and the lion. She stays like that with her arms up and perfectly still while the older guy leads the lion toward the door out of the pit. Everybody is applauding. The lion gives a growl at the young one with the pointed stick but goes into the door without any trouble. Then, quickly, the young guy comes over when the lion's already halfway through the door and gives him a good hard punch with the pointed end of his stick. This makes the lion really roar, but he hurries through the tunnel and out to his cage.

I look at Dad. For some crazy reason I feel almost as if I'm going to cry and I don't really know why. It's probably all the excitement. Dad's face looks mad.

"There's no excuse for treating a lion that way, Dickie. He didn't have to poke him; he's just goading the poor thing. I really don't think that lion would hurt a soul; he's tame as a kitten. Cannibal's meaner than that lion by a long shot."

He puts his arm over my shoulder and we start toward the stairs with all the other people.

Mom and Laurel are waiting for us outside. Laurel has bought a little statue of Happy, one of the Seven Dwarfs. It cost twenty cents. I guess it's to help balance out the twenty-five cents I got to spend watching the Wall of Death.

Dad and I go over to look at the lion again. He's already settled down and is just sitting there staring out at the crowd as if all those things we saw inside hadn't happened at all.

Laurel is between Dad and Mom. She has hold of their hands.

"Gee, he looks so nice but he must be lonesome all by himself. Doesn't he have any family?"

Dad leans down and gives her a kiss on the top of her head between her braids.

"A lion's family is called its pride, Laurie. This lion was probably born in captivity; he's never had any family, any pride."

I turn away from watching the lion. I know he's looking right at Cannibal, and I'm sure he doesn't want to eat her or anything, he just wants to be friends.

"Is that pride like one of the capital sins, Dad? Can lions commit sins too, like people?"

"There's all kinds of pride, Dickie. There's real pride, like being proud of good work, like when we do a good job building a porch. Then there's false pride like when you think you're better than somebody else for no good reason; that's the sin one. Then there's the lion's pride, his family."

"Gee! I like the idea of a family being a pride. Let's call our family a pride. I'd be proud of our pride and I bet it wouldn't be a sin at all."

"Probably just the opposite of sin, Dickie. I hope we can always be proud of our family."

Now Laurel pulls on Dad's hand again.

"What's the opposite of a sin, Daddy? Even in first grade Sister Carmelina talks a lot about sins to us but nobody's ever said anything about the opposite of sin. Opposite means the other side, doesn't it?"

Dad looks over at Mom. He has a big smile on his face just at the edge of a laugh, but he knows Laurel's serious. Laurel's much more serious than I can ever be.

Mom straightens Laurel's collar over the top of her sweater.

"Laurel, don't you worry your head about sin. I think the opposite of sin is good deeds or maybe it's 'grace.' You can ask Sister Carmelina when we get back home."

She looks at Dad again and they don't smile. I think the idea of going back isn't something they're looking forward to either.

Really, we should just up and move here to Wildwood. Imagine living all your life next to an ocean. It'd make your life seem important. At home, there's nothing but streets, pavements, houses, and lawns; only the alleys are any fun. There's nothing big and natural. I've never even seen a mountain in my life except pictures in books. It's terrible not seeing lakes or mountains or oceans. The only thing big I ever get to see is the sky and that's big but it's not enough; you can't touch it. I grab hold of Dad's other hand. I have Cannibal in one hand and Dad's hand in the other. He gives my hand a little squeeze.

"Daddy, do you mean that lion there never lived in a jungle with other lions; he's always been by himself in a cage like Cannibal in her box?"

"I don't know, but probably. Lions don't live in jungles anyway, Dickie; they live on grassy plains called savannahs."

"In *Tarzan* they live in the jungle."

"That's only in movies. I think tigers live in jungles but not lions. I could be wrong, though."

PART 6

CAP decides to keep Jimmy on for a while, anyway, until he's learned how to put up the wall, take it down himself, mostly how to run a motorcycle up the wall and keep it there.

The next morning they remount the wall on the same spot. Chuck and Jimmy had been scheduled to go on to Point Pleasant, but Cap can't do that until he's mastered the wall. Cap and Chuck drive into Freehold and fill out the papers transferring ownership. When they come back, Chuck shakes hands with Jimmy, Cap, and Sally. Then he drives off with the truck and car.

It doesn't take Cap long to catch on to the skills necessary for riding a motorcycle on the wall. It's a question of getting up speed quickly and feeling for the relationship of gravity and centrifugal force. With Cap's skills and his sense of balance he is swinging around that first day. It takes some adjusting to the tilt, looking over his left shoulder and seeing the bottom of the pit below.

Cap soon finds out that you have to keep up the acceleration, and if for some reason you lose speed, you turn quickly toward the bottom. He takes a few spills but it's more like learning a new trick than taking real racing risks. It's just you and the wall; you don't have to depend on anyone else.

Jimmy shows him that about twenty of the two-by-six, tongue-in-groove timbers forming the wall are splintered and need replacing. Cap has had enough experience with board-track splinters racing, so he makes the investment and replaces the boards. But, even with that, the entire wall rattles and rocks under the weight of the motorcycles, especially when Jimmy and Cap are up on the wall together.

Cap first practices his stunts on the rollers in the platform before he tries them on the wall. He learns to stand on the seat and do the handlebar handstand while on the rollers, but can't quite manage it up on the wall. Jimmy gets a kick out of this and keeps egging him on.

In some ways Jimmy reminds Cap of himself at that age, before he went off to war. But Cap also feels there's something completely different. Jimmy has a deep mean streak in him: he likes to hurt; he'll do almost anything to dominate, get on top. He sees everything in competitive terms: life is one long battle for survival. For him, winning is all that counts, and he's a sore loser.

But worst of all he fears and hates Tuffy. From the very beginning he taunts him. For the first time, Tuffy manifests hostility to a human, strikes out at his tormentor. Cap's afraid something bad can happen.

Jimmy also keeps after Sally. He makes no bones about it; there's nothing subtle in his approach. He's accus-

tomed to taking what he wants and he has the male no-
tion that he can physically get a woman by constant
touching, rubbing, grabbing, pinching, stroking. Sally's
scared and wants Cap to fire Jimmy.

But Cap's beginning to realize he needs Jimmy—for a
while anyway. Together they work out an act where they
pretend to race on the wall. Cap takes an early lead and
Jimmy gradually catches him just before the end of the
race. Jimmy follows this up by doing a few laps, stunting,
standing on the seat, handstands, one-leg-stands on the
seat. Cap knows if he's going to fire Jimmy he has to get
Tuffy into the act somehow.

Jimmy is constantly trying to corner Sally, and she
sticks closer to Cap. Whenever Sally is there to watch
them practice, Jimmy goes through the wildest stunts,
hanging out sideways and slowing down until he's right
at the point of falling off, then shooting down at a sharp
angle to the bottom.

Everything has to be exciting for Jimmy and at the
same time he's basically afraid. He's superstitious, wears
a crucifix and an amulet he claims has rhinoceros-tusk
dust in it. He's deathly afraid of the dark. It's almost as if
he's afraid to close his eyes even to sleep. He's better than
a watchdog because he wakes at the slightest noise
around their camp.

He insists that what annoys him more about Tuffy than
anything is when Tuffy roars in the night, or even when
he gets up and paces, as lions sometimes do. Jimmy is
awake immediately, then can't sleep.

The only thing Cap gets out of Jimmy about his background is he grew up in the panhandle of Texas and ran
away from home at fourteen because his old man beat
him so bad. He won't tell his last name, so Cap figures
there must be something more to it than that. He never
reads, and Cap isn't sure Jimmy can write, even his

name. He's as close to a natural animal as you'll find inside civilization and outside jail or a mental institution.

Cap buys a sidecar near Uniontown and trains Tuffy to ride in it. He strengthens the shocks and springs so they can handle Tuffy's four hundred pounds.

It isn't easy getting Tuffy up on the wall. At first he's willing to sit in the sidecar and let himself be strapped in. He's even willing to let Cap ride him around on the level without making too much fuss. But when Cap tries him on the wall, mounting higher bit by bit, Tuffy struggles to free himself. He roars, coughs, and grunts. Cap tries to comfort him but it's months of training before Tuffy submits to this indignity.

The problem is a cat automatically twists to balance itself. It does this, using information piped into its brain by an internal gyroscope in the middle ear. At the same time, it uses its eyes to make adjustments in space. Poor Tuffy's getting two different sets of information. One, from his eyes, says, Twist, you're out there sideways and you have to land on your feet. The other, from his gyroscope, which is being fooled by the centrifugal effect of the motorcycle on the wall, is saying, You're O.K., the gravity pressures are all in the right direction, you don't have to do anything. So Tuffy is confused.

He never closes his eyes while he's in the sidecar. He's upset and roars all the way around, not looking down into the pit, but looking, staring up out of the bowl. It's all so unnatural, so hard for a simple lion to understand.

But Tuffy finally succumbs. He succumbs out of his love for Cap, who wants him to do it, and, probably something of his feelings for pride. This is what his pride seems to be doing now, riding sideways on walls.

Cap is lucky and gets a regular concession in Wildwood right on the boardwalk. This is mostly because the concessionnaire in charge of making these assignments is one of those people who live a war over and over again long after it's finished. He's a member of the American Legion, the Veterans of Foreign Wars. The aftermath and reconstruction of those brief months of involvement by the AEF have become the center of his life. From his reading he knows about the 32nd Division, "the Powerhouse Division," and also about Cap Modig, one of the few drafted enlisted men who reached the temporary rank of captain, who won a bronze star, a distinguished service cross, and two purple hearts.

It's one of those lucky breaks that make life. Cap takes advantage of it, immediately, though he refuses to join the Legion or the VFW. With this Wildwood concession alone, in normal times, they can make a living.

During the next three years, the act gradually changes. Cap finds it hard both to race Jimmy and ride the lion around in the sidecar. Sally, who's dressed in a purple sequined costume to show off her beautiful legs and her generally fine figure, has done only the announcing of the acts, the come-on spiel from the platform. She's now enlisted to ride Tuffy around on the motorcycle. For the act, they also change Tuffy's name. He becomes Satan, the Dare-Devil Lion.

She, like Tuffy, doesn't like it, but agrees. It takes a long time before she can get the motorcycle with the sidecar empty up on the wall. Finally after much practice, she can develop the speed to climb up the wall with Tuffy. Tuffy now weighs over four hundred pounds.

A part of the problem is Sally is scared of Tuffy. But she isn't scared of Jimmy any more. Jimmy's theory about women has been proven out for him once more. He's got her on her back, legs up, whenever he wants her.

The first time, it was rape. Jimmy trapped Sally in the pit while Cap was out buying meat for Tuffy. He closed and locked the trap door. There was no escape. Then he began pressing himself on her, first undressing himself, baring his hard, magnificent body, the ample evidence of his passion for her. He then pushed her against the blackened wall, violently ripping off her clothes, pressing his hand over her mouth, wrestling her down the tilted edge of the wall to the bottom of the pit, where she finally succumbed in unsummoned abandon.

Whenever, after that, she tried to refuse him, he threatened to tell Cap and she surrendered again. Then the surrendering became easier, until she realized, strangely enough, she enjoyed Jimmy's rough, eager ways. Something in her responded to being taken, without love, with violence, transported in torrents of animal passion. She began waiting for, anticipating, Jimmy's degrading attentions.

Sally feels guilty in her relationship to Cap; Cap with his gentleness, respect for her as a woman, as a person. She knows Cap loves her, needs her, feels deeply married to her, and she knows in some way she still loves him. Sally is up against another wall, another crossroads in the conflict between her basic goodness, sensitivity, awareness, and her yearning for excitement, anything to make the day-to-day, momentary quality of her life more meaningful, something left over in many humans from the millions of years lived before agriculture, cities, law, ethics.

And she withdraws from Cap more and more, not just physically, sexually, but in her mind. She begins to see him as the outside world perceives him, a broken-down ex-soldier, shell-shock victim, ex–race driver who's lost his nerve, a beaten man, playing nurse to a lion; a forty-year-old loser racing motorcycles around a wall. He's bald, crippled, and sometimes has trouble chewing because so many of his teeth are missing and his plate is loose.

Still, she loves him, knows she'll never be loved as totally, without reservations, as Cap loves her. Also Sally is feeling trapped. Here she is almost thirty with no children and no sign there ever will be any. Cap always takes care, just as he faithfully sends money to her mother every week, no matter how bad things have been. She feels guilty about that now. She also knows her mother considers her a whore for not getting married in the church. And Sally knows she can't really ever go back. She hasn't worked a switchboard for almost ten years and jobs are hard to find.

Cap is sensitive. He's known what's going on, almost since the beginning. Sally's starting to smoke again, at the beginning surreptitiously, then openly, first tipped him off. Jimmy smokes all the time. He knows Cap's vulnerability and blows smoke in his direction to start him coughing, then laughs, coughing himself in exaggeration.

But Cap's so in love with Sally, so dependent on her for meaning in what is beginning to look more and more like a meaningless life, he can't face up to it. So, as with many others before him, he reverts to the familiar formula: I love her; Jimmy seems to make her happy; if I love her then I want her to be happy. So let her have Jimmy if she wants.

But the difficulty is that something in Sally, something probably related to her convent years, and her basic honesty, goodness, can't let her have the same easy mental, personal, spiritual relationship with Cap they've always had. More and more she doesn't want to be with him, share with him. She feels guilty.

Cap is missing intensely this big part of his life, his closeness with Sally, his once-in-a-lifetime love. He depends heavily on Tuffy to fill the hole of loneliness he's found in the core of his being. Sally, irrationally, is jealous of Cap's time with, affection for, Tuffy.

The lion is now full-grown, practically aged; ten years old. He has a dark thick mane falling across his muzzle and over his shoulders. There's a long furrow between his eyes going down to his snout. His nose is black and shining. When he opens his mouth he shows an impressive set of strong, slightly yellow teeth with canines more than two inches long. Below his chin is a beard that blends with his mane.

When he stands and walks, muscles ripple over his entire body. Even with the slightest twist of his tail a wave of muscle writhes and twitches.

Often Cap goes into Tuffy's cage to play with him or lets him into the pit of the Wall when Sally and Jimmy aren't there. Cap rubs Tuffy's chest or digs his fingers up into the shoulder muscles behind the mane. Tuffy flops on his back and lets Cap rub his stomach. Sometimes they still wrestle, Tuffy entering into the game and trying to be tender, careful with his claws, teeth, great weight, and enormous strength.

Cap is confused, he doesn't know what to do. Sometimes he's tempted to talk it out with Sally, tell her the way he feels, but she senses this in him, is afraid, resists. Other times he wants to have it out with Jimmy. He knows he can't beat him up, Cap is still strong but because of his lungs has no endurance at all. Jimmy is young, knows his advantage. Cap is sure if he gets rid of Jimmy, Sally will leave, he's afraid Jimmy won't take care of her, protect her in any way.

Toward the end of summer, Cap discovers that the transmission on his truck is shot. It's the year 1938, and they're still in Wildwood. The truck is old; it's hard to find parts. The year has been a poor one as have been the past five years. People don't have much money to spend watching two men, a woman, and a lion spin around inside a wooden bowl. Most people are barely earning money enough to feed themselves.

So Cap finds himself with no money and the season over. They can go on the road, head south as they've done before and probably stay alive; make enough to eat and feed Tuffy. But although he's got the truck fixed, he needs to sock away money for gas and food until they can get down to Florida. Cap's already a month behind in Jimmy's salary. Jimmy's never going to quit, he really has no other place to go, but he keeps threatening.

Cap can't help but wonder if he has any control over his life. Maybe it's all some kind of crazy accident, slowly unfolding, in which everybody loses.

PART 7

*P*ROBABLY most of what Dick Kettleson thought about lions was wrong. At that time, in 1938, not much was known about the lives of lions in their natural state, at least, not by non-Africans. It is very difficult for us to observe lions in nature.

Because Tuffy is a major character in our tale, perhaps it would be best if we consider briefly the life he might have lived if he had not been taken at such an early age from his home environment. Since a lion is primarily an instinctual animal, some of the ensuing events will be better understood if we contrast the life he's living with the one he *should* have lived.

Apologies are hereby proffered in advance to readers in the twenty-first century for whom the material here presented might be both inaccurate and inadequate. That is, if there are any lions left then, in fact, if there's anything at all left.

Tuffy was one of two cubs born to a lioness, part of a small lion grouping, not a pride. She cubbed in a fissure of rock on the Serengeti Plain, about twenty kilometers from a pride territory and a hundred kilometers or so from the sea. She, the lioness, was killed by local hunters and the cubs brought to the port where they were sold to the sailor we've already met in the San Diego bar.

Lions in their natural habitat are no more dangerous to humans than automobiles. As with automobiles, they can be dangerous if you get in their way under the wrong conditions; but by nature, lions will avoid humans and do not consider them natural prey as they do, for example, the gazelle or giraffe.

As far as is known, there seem to have been ten races of lions, two of which are recently extinct. The bulk of the existing lion population now resides in Africa, although a small subculture remains in a limited part of India. Earlier, lions were spread over the entire Mediterranean basin. At one time, it's been calculated, there were as many lions as men on this planet, about six million of each. Man has gradually destroyed the lion population, while he himself has proliferated. Perhaps this explains lions' fear and avoidance of man. Man's irrational fear of lions is not so easily explained.

Usually, lions will tolerate coexistence with man in a prescribed area. For reasons not directly ascertainable, perhaps genetic, although man, unarmed, is easy prey for lions he is rarely hunted by them. However, older, failed, non-pride lions or lionesses might, when no longer capable of catching and killing ordinary prey, become man-eaters.

It is difficult to determine exactly, but probably less than fifty percent of lions and lionesses live in a pride.

The rest are "vagrant." Although these vagrant lions and lionesses might form groupings for social reasons—to hunt, or for reproduction and mutual protection against other lions or hyenas—they have no determined protected territory and therefore do not constitute a pride. This seemingly large percentage of vagrant lions could be the result of man's depredations on lion territory.

A true pride can include from as few as four to as many as forty lions, cubs, and lionesses. This pride inhabits territory that is defended.

Territory adequate to support a pride must have water and a sufficient supply of natural prey, resident or passing through it in migrations, to provide food. The life of a pride is relatively stable and stationary. This is especially true for the pride lionesses, who, along with the territory, are the heart of a pride.

Vagrant lions and lionesses follow or migrate with their food supply. Pride lions and lionesses *intercept* prey animals within the pride territory when they pass through. This is an enormous difference. The average life of a pride lion or lioness is considerably longer than that of the vagrant. Also, and perhaps more important, the survival rate into adulthood of cubs in a pride is vastly greater than that of vagrant cubs such as Tuffy.

Lions are the only social cat. Leopards, tigers, almost all the other large felines live alone, or, at most, come together for brief breeding periods. It is rare to find a lone lion, however, except for the ill or old lion close to death.

A lion or lioness comes into adulthood in its fourth year. A grown male lion can weigh four to five hundred pounds, a lioness somewhat less. Tuffy, as a grown male lion, is over four hundred pounds at the time of our story.

Some lions have been known, in captivity, to live twenty years, but in nature a ten-year-old lion such as Tuffy is rare. Pride lionesses, however, can survive much longer.

While hunting, a lion or lioness can knock down a six-hundred-pound zebra with a swipe of its paw, can jump across a thirty-foot gorge or leap vertically as high as ten feet. For short spurts, a lion or lioness is very fast. But it does not have much staying power. If its prey can keep running for a quarter mile without being injured or caught it can usually escape. Strangely enough, lions and lionesses fail more often than they succeed in their hunting attempts, especially when hunting alone or with a small grouping. Therefore, starvation is common in the lives of lions, especially the young and old. The pattern for lions and lionesses is feast or famine. When there is a large supply of meat, a hungry full-grown lion or lioness can consume as much as sixty pounds at one gorging.

Lions and lionesses sometimes hunt at night but rarely in full daylight. Although they mostly hunt at dusk or twilight, their eyes have round pupils such as with human eyes. They do not have the vertical-slit pupil of night-hunting animals such as the domestic cat and other felines.

A typical "kill" usually begins with knocking down the prey by a powerful swing of the paw. The actual killing is typically done by suffocation, either by taking the head of the victim into the mouth or by biting and closing the trachea. It is rare for a lion or lioness to kill by going for the jugular and causing death by bleeding.

When a lion eats its kill, the belly is ripped open first. The choice morsels of an animal are the viscera: liver, heart, kidneys, lungs. Even the intestines are eaten. The lion or lioness squeezes out the contents, then eats the intestines themselves.

According to hunting conditions, a lion or lioness will eat almost anything from a mouse to a hippopotamus. They will eat fresh-killed meat or carrion. They are great stealers of prey from other animals. Lions or lionesses, when hungry, constantly scan the sky for vultures and buzzards, knowing these birds signal prey, which they can steal without needing to hunt.

The lion family is notoriously lazy. A pride lion or lioness will rarely travel as much as four miles in a day. When well fed, they will sleep or lie about in social clumpings for up to twenty hours at a time. There seems little inclination on the part of lionesses to leave the center of the pride or the nursery area except to hunt, litter cubs, or breed. The male or males of the pride will sometimes circle the pride territory to establish boundaries by spraying a mixture of musk and urine. This is to define and declare the defended territory. Except for that, they rarely move about. A male lion in a pride does not often hunt; this is the work of the lionesses.

When a kill has been made, the lion will chase the lionesses away and gorge or take his preferred parts of the prey to another place and eat in peace. The lionesses get to eat what is left. The lionesses typically chase away the cubs until they themselves are satiated. For this reason, among others, even in a pride, many starve. Less than fifty percent of cubs reach adulthood.

Generally, there are from one to four males in charge of a pride. They are the *only* adult lions allowed in the pride; all young males are chased from the pride territory when they reach maturity. They are chased by the pride lion or lions and lionesses and are not allowed to return.

A team of pride males almost always comes from a single litter, direct brothers; or sometimes from one lioness but of different litters. The reign of a pride lion or team of lions is precarious at best. It may be as short as a few months or as long as an exceptional observed six years.

Any sign of weakness in the pride leader or leaders is picked up by other lions, either vagrants drifting along the edges of the pride or former pride members waiting for a chance to take over. There is no observed example of a lioness taking over a pride. Infrequently is there a fight to the death between lions, for a pride.

Dominance is mostly asserted by roaring. Showing

teeth is a defensive threat. There is much strutting and staring down. A lion rarely looks directly into the eyes of another lion unless he is determined to be threatening.

An uncertain or frightened lion turns his head to one side, sometimes all the way onto the shoulder, and then twists the body even farther back. This is a sign of surrender, yet a fight will take place if this acquiescence is not respected.

When fighting, lions grunt, moan, growl, meow, and roar. A lion cannot purr; no cat that roars can also purr.

Lions and lionesses can go as long as seventeen days without food. They drink water slowly, taking five to fifteen minutes to lap water into their mouths. They have no system for siphoning or sucking water up, so must form cups of their tongues and lap in a small bit at a time. In normal circumstances, they drink every day or two.

The members of a pride are seldom all together. Sometimes they are as much as ten miles from the pride center. Roaring is often used to communicate location and is a part of "prideness."

The lion pride society is complex, especially complex in regard to lionesses. Typically a pride will have from three to fifteen lionesses plus their cubs. All the lionesses will be related—mother, sisters, daughters, granddaughters, over several generations. They remain together for life in the pride, regardless of change of pride male or males heading the pride. With few exceptions, pride lionesses, as well as pride lions, will tolerate no vagrants in the pride territory. They will band to drive off wandering lions or groupings.

Lionesses come in heat every three weeks for a period of five days, unless pregnant. The lioness approaches the male and makes all the advances. Typically, during a courtship period a lioness will seduce away from the pride center the pride male, or, if there is more than one,

one of them. They will leave the central grouping for five days of ongoing sexual activity.

Copulation is quick and frequent. During copulation, the male bites the neck and shoulders of the lioness. Sometimes, in the fury of his orgiastic excitement, he will actually kill her. Copulation occurs every twenty minutes to half hour over those five days, virtually day and night. There is scarcely time taken to eat.

When one lioness comes into heat it tends to set off into heat any other lioness who isn't pregnant. This can be quite demanding on the pride lion or lions. Under such circumstances sometimes a vagrant lion can successfully invade a territory to fulfill the duty of the tired or busy pride leader or leaders.

The gestation period is three and a half months. As the time of birthing approaches, the lioness again separates herself from the center of the pride and, still within the boundaries of pride territory, searches out a hiding place where she can have her cubs in privacy and some security. Other lions and lionesses have been known to eat cubs, and there are always the wandering, voracious hyenas.

When the lioness has had her cubs, usually from one to four, she will keep them away from the pride, and the young will survive exclusively on her milk. She does not, despite some statements to the contrary, bring back food for the cubs.

The lactation period lasts from two to three months. Since the lioness is a social animal, there is always the danger during this time that she will join the central pride group for socializing or for a hunt and completely forget about, abandon, her cubs. Lionesses are *not* the best mothers in the world. The abandoned cubs will either starve or be eaten by other animals.

When the cubs have reached a certain age—between two and three months—the lioness will lead them to the center of the pride. There, the lioness will first make up to the others, rubbing her face against the muzzles of other lionesses and lions. She will then come back to her cubs and, one at a time, bring them to be introduced to the pride. These cubs will rub faces, be licked, stroked, and generally initiated to the group.

From this time on, their life changes significantly. Any responsibility of maternity the lioness might have possessed before is now distributed among all the other nursing lionesses.

Each lioness has four nipples. A lioness will accept any cub wanting to nurse until it has reached the age of about six months. They seem to play no favorites toward their own; perhaps they don't even recognize them any more. Because of the phenomenon whereby lionesses come into sympathetic heat with one another, there are usually several lionesses with cubs about the same age. Most of them are already pregnant again. These lionesses form a sort of nursery where the cubs can nurse almost at will.

The lionesses still hunt together, providing the pride lion with food and themselves with sustenance for milk.

As the cubs grow older, they try to follow the hunt. They develop a taste for meat and want to join in feasting on the prey. However, they are invariably chased away by the lionesses, including their own mothers.

The lion will frequently shoo off all the lionesses so the cubs can eat, or he will drag away some of the choice portions and allow the cubs to share with him. Except for this rather unusual behavior, many more of the cubs would die by starvation.

One mysterious element in this social life of lions is how some lionesses are selected to remain in the pride, replacing older lionesses, becoming part of this life-support system while others, when they reach maturity, are chased out along with the maturing young lions.

Some carefully trained observers, watching over many years, feel it's a question of how the young sub-lionesses approach the other members of the pride. If they act as if they belong—approach directly, rub faces frequently and with affection, lie about in the communal groups, participate in the hunt effectively—they have a better chance of acceptance. If, on the other hand, they act timid, sly, approach the other members of the pride too cautiously, behave suspiciously, and are contentious, or don't hunt well, they are likely to be expelled on reaching maturity along with the lions.

Since the difference between life for a lioness in a pride and life outside one is so tremendously different, these seemingly unimportant variations in deportment can mean life or death.

There is a difference between the roaring of a lion and of a lioness. A lion's roaring is typically more aggressive, more challenging. A lioness will often roar lightly or groan to call her cubs.

A lion's roar begins with a moan or two, then a series of earth-shaking roars followed by several harsh grunts. The series can last as long as a minute. A lion or lioness will roar from any position; standing, sitting, or lying down. Neither lions nor lionesses can roar before they're about two and a half years old, and a typical grown male lion will roar twenty or more times in a night.

An aggressive lion coughs when angry; he also growls. A snarling lion has his mouth open with his teeth exposed. However, in general, a visible lion or lioness is not a menace because, when a lion is hungry or hunting, it makes every effort to be invisible.

The life of vagrant wandering lions and lionesses is precarious. It is harder for the lionesses to bear and raise cubs. The chasing after migrating prey makes it difficult for her to come back to a fixed den or nest; abandonment of cubs is more frequent.

Since vagrant lions and lionesses live in unprotected territory, the cubs are more often prey themselves. There is usually no male lion to guarantee a source of meat to the cubs, so starvation is frequent. These are some of the reasons why the cubs of vagrant lionesses have so little chance of survival. The chances are great that Tuffy would not have survived in the natural state.

Lions and lionesses have excellent eyesight and hearing; a keen sense of smell. They are sensualists and enjoy physical contact. They bunch and spread themselves out over one another, piling up in groups for hours at a time, cubs playing with the tails of adults, wrestling with each other, adults resting heads across the backs of others, or spread out on their backs with feet in the air. They generally move away from the pride group only to excrete in private, to breed, cub, or hunt.

Cubs are constantly playing and wrestling. Playing for the sake of play seems to be a big part of lion life. Adults will put up with continual lunges at their tails or cubs embracing their legs or paws, jumping on their backs. Cub wrestling seems to have nothing to do with survival; a lion never wrestles with its prey; this is not its way of killing. When a lion kills it rarely leaps; it almost always keeps its back feet on the ground, providing a base for its tremendous power, striking out with its paws like a boxer delivering roundhouse punches.

In general, a lion needs ten to fifteen pounds of meat per day to stay healthy and comfortable.

So this is the life Tuffy never knew. It is most likely Tuffy considers Cap to be a member of his pride and the two of them pride leaders. Sally, as Cap's mate and because she started feeding Tuffy at an early age, is probably included in Tuffy's sense of pride and pride protection.

It's difficult to project Tuffy's attitude toward Jimmy. He's definitely a rival, perhaps as a juvenile within the pride or as a peripheral vagrant. In any case, there is no love lost between them.

It's very hard to know if a lion can make these kinds of

substitutions for his instinctual patterns, based on an unnatural situation. Some animals seem to do this, such as the ducks and geese in Konrad Lorenz's studies.

If this kind of substitution *is* possible it could help explain some of the following events.

PART 8

*I*T'S a beautiful early October morning in Wildwood, the sun only a glow over the ocean; a bluish brightening dusk fills the air. Just off the boardwalk, a hundred yards from the sea, behind a hotel called Broff's, a man is rooting in garbage cans. He has a half-filled burlap sack at his feet. The sack is damp and bulging. The man is wearing a cap. It's Cap Modig.

Behind him a police patrol wagon rolls up slowly. Two policemen step from a running board while the vehicle is still moving. One is heavy-set, in his mid-forties, the other young.

Cap glances over his shoulder, straightens up, puts his hands over his head in mock surrender.

"O.K., Murph, you caught me red-handed; slip on the cuffs."

Sergeant Murphy, the heavier, older policeman, strolls up behind Cap, his pistol on one hip, his night stick and handcuffs dangling from the other. He folds his arms across his chest.

"Cut it out, Cap. You know I got no choice."

"I don't have many choices left either, Murph. To be perfectly honest, this is *not* the way I enjoy starting off my day, grubbing through Broff's stinking garbage."

Cap slowly lowers his arms, wipes his wet and sticky hands on the top of his burlap sack. He peers into it.

"Boy, you can sure tell the Depression isn't exactly over *yet*. Even these millionaire types, eating at Broff's, are gnawing every piece of meat off their T-bone steaks. Poor Tuffy couldn't get those bones much cleaner with that big rough tongue of his, and it's designed for just this kind of work."

The young cop has come up behind the older one. He has his night stick in his hand. Murph is obviously embarrassed; he looks down at his feet, square-toed black shoes, well shined, classic cop shoes.

"Look, Cap, Broff's complained again. He doesn't want you grubbing through his garbage mornings. This is the fourth time I've caught you at it; next time I'll have to haul you in."

Cap tilts his cap back, puts his hands on his hips. He smiles, not the golden smile of his childhood, or even the manly, confident smile of the young infantry officer or the cocky race driver; it's a smile of acquiescence, of acceptance, on the border of resignation, defeat.

"Broff complains. You should hear poor Tuffy!"

"We *all* hear Tuffy, Cap. That's another thing. We're getting complaints from every direction. That lion roaring and coughing is keeping half of Wildwood up all night; everybody's nervous. You've got to *do* something."

The young cop moves closer. He looks into Cap's burlap bag, the open garbage pails; turns away in disgust;

holds his nose with his fingers. Murph puts his hand on Cap's shoulder.

"You know how it is, Cap. Broff's a big taxpayer around here and he's got important friends in politics. If he wants me to stop you from pawing through his garbage, I stop you. That's what I'm paid for. That's how I feed the wife and kids. I need my job just like everybody else and I'm only six years from retirement."

Cap looks down at his sack again, tilts his head, glances over at the fastidious young cop, then back at the sergeant.

"You know, Murph, I went to Broff, asked if he'd hold out the bones and things, put them in a special pail or a sack. I told him I'd pay. He chased me off, said he was going to call the cops, didn't want any bums hanging around his restaurant. You can thank me for something, anyway, at least I got out fast; saved you from having to charge over here again.

"What the hell am I going to feed him, Murph? A full-grown ten-year-old lion like Tuffy needs at least ten pounds of meat a day. I buy all the bones and guts at Simon's, the butcher's, but it's not enough.

"Besides, who's it hurting if I take some of Broff's crummy garbage? I don't get in anybody's way, I don't make any mess. I always put the lids back on the cans. I'm actually doing the taxpayers a favor."

The young policeman struts up, rocking back and forth in policeman fashion, advancing half a step with each swing, his club dangling between his legs as he comes forward.

"If I was you, I'd start off by feeding your lion that smart-ass bastard you got working for you. Now that's *real* garbage. The city'd probably pin another medal on you. Be doing *yourself* a big favor, too."

Cap looks into the young policeman's eyes, smiling a slightly twisted, yet vaguely menacing smile until the cop lowers his head, looks down at his club.

"What's the trouble? Jimmy been hustling some local talent again?"

Murph edges the young cop aside, pushes his face close to Cap's, whispers:

"Junior-high-school kid this time, Cap. Jesus! Comes from a good family, Dad's a doctor. That Jimmy takes her up to Atlantic City and keeps her there overnight, practically rapes her, she don't know from nothing. Father's got her in a hospital and shushed things up pretty good but I'd like to throw the goddamned book at that pervert. Nothing in a skirt is safe with a mean stud like that around town. He's gonna cause big trouble before he's finished. He's almost worse than your lion Tuffy, there."

Cap doesn't reply for a minute. He's thinking of Sally. Does she know? What does Jimmy tell her? Does he brag about it? He slowly reaches into one of the garbage cans, pulls out two pork bones with a little meat still left in the crotch of the cut.

"Yeah, that's bad. I know I've got to get rid of Jimmy sooner or later, but that kid sure rides a motorcycle on a wall, doesn't seem to have any nerves at all. The act wouldn't be much without him, Murph. People always like to see a young guy beat an old one like me in a race. Ever catch our act?"

"Yeah, I seed it a couple times with Mike, my oldest. He thinks that dirty, no-good punk's one of the heroes of our times. That's the trouble, he makes like Barney Oldfield up there on the wall and kids fall all over him, are convinced he's a bigshot."

Murph steps back. This is all hard for him to handle. He pulls a handkerchief out of his back pocket, lifts his cap from his head, and wipes his brow. It's still too chill in the early morning for him to be sweating.

"You listen to me, Modig. I don't want to make any trouble. I know about your war record and all; I respect you for that and I know you was once one of the best

auto racers in the business. But the commissioner himself
is after me on this. He's up there looking for city ordi-
nances about wild animals within city limits. He's under
pressure himself. So I'm warning you, you're in trouble.
Get out of this town fast, take that lion and that good-
for-nothing with you, then maybe things'll simmer down
by next summer. You got that?"

Cap twists and closes the top of his sack, puts the lids
back on the garbage cans, looks into the police sergeant's
eyes.

"Thanks, Murph. But, you know, Tuffy isn't going to
hurt anybody. I can't vouch for Jimmy, but Tuffy's mild
as a kitten. I got him when he was a mite of a tiny cub;
I'm the only family he's ever known. Sometimes I think
he thinks he's a human being; or maybe he thinks I'm a
small, crippled two-legged lion.

"A male lion like him, without a pride, is practically
helpless. Tuffy's never even *seen* another lion, never
hunted for his own food. Those teeth and claws are deco-
rations far as he's concerned."

The young cop has started walking back to the wagon.
He's disappointed they aren't going to make an arrest.
Murph adjusts his hat.

"I don't know about that, Cap. Your cat there looks
dangerous to me. I never knew lions came so big. I'd sure
as hell hate meeting him in a dark alley somewheres. All
I know is, the lieutenant told me to come over here and
vag you if you were into the garbage again. They'll attach
that wall of yours or impound it along with your lion and
the whole shooting match if you don't get out and soon."

"O.K., Murph, I promise. I'm off for Orlando in a
week. We stayed over a little too long, past the season.
The transmission in my old truck gave out and then I
couldn't find parts. It was quite a job breaking it down
and repairing it, but it's done. Now it's fixed. As soon as I
have gas money, we're off. Thanks for the word, I appreciate it. See you next year. Let's hope this damned De-

pression is really over by then and we aren't all mixed up in another war."

Cap wipes his hands off on his trousers, then pulls out a dark blue bandana, wipes his right hand more thoroughly. He reaches out and shakes with Murph. Murph's face breaks into a smile and he taps Cap lightly on the shoulder.

"You watch out for yourself, now, Cap. Next time Broff's liable to call the National Guard and you'll have to fight them off single-handed. I'll bet you could still do it, too. I tell you, that Broff's one gigantic pain in the ass."

He turns and walks away. He swings into the front seat of the patrol wagon beside the driver and they roll off.

Cap waits until they're out of sight, sighs, opens his bag again, lifts the lid off another garbage can, and goes back to shuffling through lettuce leaves, soggy vegetables, paper, pulling out bits of meat or bone and dropping them into his sack.

After another half hour has passed and as the sun comes up over the edge of the sea, Cap twists his sack closed again, hefts it for weight, then swings it over his shoulder. He starts limping along the ramp from behind Broff's onto the boardwalk.

He walks across to the far side facing the sea. He leans on the metal railing and puts his sack down again. The sun is about a hand's width above the horizon. There are still some fishing boats out. The sun makes a flickering silver path across the quiet, almost surfless water to the breaking, lapping foam at the edge of the beach.

There's been the usual morning offshore west wind blowing. Cap knows the water will be clear and cold but still not too cold for swimming, maybe 65 degrees. Already some early bathers are spreading themselves on the beach or walking along at the edge of the water. It's going to be a nice day; the late season has been exceptionally good this year; today'll be as warm as some days in

August. Cap just hopes this clear weather holds till next weekend. If they can only get in one more good weekend, break down the wall, and get moving on to Florida, then maybe everything will be O.K. Maybe he can even talk it out with Sally, get things straightened out, find what she really wants.

Cap swings his bag back on his shoulder and turns north toward the amusement-park area just past Hunt's Pier. His mind is spinning on the same old problems. No matter how often he goes over it, nothing seems to make it better and he doesn't know what to do.

By the time Cap gets back to the section of the boardwalk where his Wall of Death is set up, the sun's higher and it's beginning to warm up. Cap limps even more with the weight on his shoulder, and he's breathing hard. He shifts the sack to his other shoulder. There're a few other people out taking a walk in the beautiful early-morning light, but Cap isn't paying too much attention; he's lost in his own thoughts, talking to himself, indulging a habit he started as a boy on the farm, working with cows. The cows seemed to like hearing his voice.

"I'll feed Tuffy first, that'll give Sally and Jimmy time to break it up before I go into the pit. It's a damned shame we all have to sleep in that black, smelly hole but it's the only way we'll ever save any money these days with so little coming in. If we tried staying in a rooming house or something we'd never get ahead."

Tuffy has stood up on Cap's arrival. He paces back and forth, rubbing his muzzle against the bars of his cage, making low sounds of greeting. He lets out grunts as Cap sets the heavy burlap bag at his feet outside the cage. Cap reaches through the bars and rubs Tuffy's nose, reaches farther in and rubs under his ears.

"Hungry, huh, fellow? Well, this isn't much but it's better than nothing. Sorry it's only chewed-over cooked stuff but that's all I could get this morning. Tomorrow maybe I'll have some real gizzards and bones for you."

He reaches into his bag and begins pulling out pieces of meat. He puts the first ones into Tuffy's mouth. Tuffy takes it through the bars daintily.

"Try eating slowly, Tuf; make it last."

Piece by piece, Cap feeds the lion, waiting each time until Tuffy has chewed up and swallowed the last bit. Sometimes Tuffy drops a piece to the floor of the cage and tears at it with his claws and tongue. Cap is humming "You Must Have Been a Beautiful Baby" as he waits between morsels while Tuffy eats. Finally he's emptied the sack. Tuffy paces back and forth again when he sees Cap is leaving. He grunts, roars. Just then Sally comes out a door cut into the side of the wall.

She stretches, has a very languorous, satisfied air about her. Cap tries not thinking about it. After all, it's only a physical thing; he can't see how a wonderful woman like Sally could have any true deep feelings for a piece of trash like Jimmy.

"Did you get something for Tuffy, Cap?"

"Yeah. I raided Broff's garbage again. I've also got some innards and bones lined up from the butcher up on Atlantic at only five cents a pound. There's usually strips of meat on the bones Tuffy can lick off and you know how much he likes lungs. Where's Jimmy?"

"Oh, he's inside straightening things out. God, it was hard sleeping. Tuffy kept pacing back and forth, coughing, growling, and sometimes letting off real roars. Those roars sound so sad and each one practically shook the whole boardwalk."

"I know, Sal. The poor guy's almost starving and doesn't know what's wrong."

"What're you going to do, Cap? I lay awake last night in the dark listening to Tuffy and wondering how we're ever going to get out of here; we're barely making enough money to keep going."

"Don't worry. We'll get out. We've almost got what we need now. A good weekend and we're gone, off to Orlando, where it'll be warmer and maybe people will have more money."

Tuffy is following Cap with his eyes and with his body. Cap goes back, puts the sack in his cage for Tuffy to tear at, maybe get the last tastes of meat.

"That's all there is, Tuf. Sorry. Tomorrow I'll have those guts and butcher bones for you; you can have a feast."

Sally's standing back with her arms folded, watching, waiting for Cap to come inside with her.

"Honest, Cap. You talk to that lion as if he's a human being. People must think you're crazy."

She turns her back, walks through the small curved door into the pit; Cap follows.

Inside, Jimmy is rolling up blankets. Cap pulls together two orange crates. He places a board over top to make a table. Then he drags an apple box out as a chair while Sally gets one for herself. She goes over to another wooden box with a hasp lock, painted black, but splintered and worn. She takes out a loaf of bread, a bottle of milk, a bottle of beer, a small package of sliced Lebanon baloney, and a half-full bottle of ketchup.

Cap rolls up his sleeves and walks over to a corner where there's a bucket of water. He dips his hands in the bucket, rubs them together, then runs them over his face, scrubbing, pushing his fingers into his ears, his knuckles deep into his eye sockets. He finishes by taking off his cap and rubbing his wet hands vigorously across his practically bald scalp.

He pulls his cap back on and picks up a fragment of toweling from beside the bucket. He dries his hands but leaves his face wet. The towel is a dark color, even darker with dirt. He comes back; Sally is sitting at the table; Jimmy is standing behind her.

"O.K., Cap, so what are we going to do? Jimmy says he's quitting if he doesn't get paid."

Cap lights a big kitchen match, snapping it lit with one of his few real front teeth; then he lights a candle on the makeshift table.

"I tell you, Sal. I've got enough food for Tuffy tomorrow, then if the weather holds good another weekend so there are enough weekenders, we'll be off and running. I know it's hard but then I can pay Jimmy and we'll be hunky-dory."

"How much do you think we took in altogether this last weekend, Cap? We didn't even make fifty dollars. We're stuck here; we're *never* going to get out."

"Yeah, Sal, but it rained most of last weekend. This looks like good weather for a while. Sure we got stuck. But now I've got that transmission installed we'll be on our way. By living in the pit here and keeping our food bills down we'll be out and running in no time at all."

Jimmy's walked around behind Cap on his way to pick up another box for a chair. He does a derogatory imitation of an automobile racer, twisting an imaginary steering wheel, ducking in his head, tilting his body.

Sally looks down at the table.

"I don't know, Cap. I'm scared."

Jimmy sits down. His undershirt sleeves are rolled up over his shoulders to show the tattoo. He reaches out and takes two pieces of bread, puts them beside each other on the table. On one he folds two slices of baloney; the other he coats thickly with ketchup, spreading from edge to edge with a pocket knife. He licks the knife on both sides, puts the ketchup-covered one on top of the bread with the baloney and lifts the sandwich. He licks around its edges where the ketchup is leaking out.

He bites into the sandwich and ketchup drips on the table and slides across his hand. He licks his fingers. He isn't looking up at Cap or Sally; concentrating on his eating. He shifts his butt on the box, farts. It's done automatically as if part of some ritual. Cap looks across at Sally; she's daintily constructing a sandwich; he turns back to Jimmy.

"Gees, Jimmy, even if we have to live like animals let's not overdo it, huh?"

Jimmy takes a swig from the common beer bottle, glugs down about a third; wipes his mouth.

"Jesus! Eat nothin' but beans and crap like this all the time; anybody's gonna start fartin'. It's lucky I'm not pukin' all over the place."

In the background Tuffy is roaring, tapering off with a series of cough-like wheezes. Jimmy turns his head toward the lion cage and spits.

"It's for sure *that* SOB don't hold nothin' back. Piss, shit, fart, roar, whatever comes into his head, he just does. I hate that overgrown alley cat!"

Sally takes a small bite from her sandwich, chews it carefully, swallows. She looks at Cap.

"Honest, Cap; if Tuffy lets off another one of his stink bombs when we're up there on the wall the way he did last night, I'm liable to pass out and drive over the edge. It's really bad. And not only that, his breath smells like a sewer. When he turns toward me and gives off one of his roars, I swear I could light what comes out of his mouth. It's awful."

Cap doesn't say anything for several seconds. He looks at his hands, folds them on the board serving as a table.

"I guess if you were eating garbage you wouldn't smell so hot either."

Sally stands up quickly, knocking over her apple crate, brushing crumbs from her lap. She's dressed in dirty men's white coveralls pulled over a frayed sweater. She still has a slim yet full figure, but her face is set, marks of dissatisfaction, disappointment beginning to show. The peroxiding and heavy makeup have taken their toll on her fresh good looks.

"What d'ya think this stuff here is, Cap?"

She puts her sandwich on the table, her hands on either side. She stares down at herself, overalls, sweater, worn slippers. She pushes the ragged edges of her sweater sleeves up over her elbows.

"Me, ha! What a jerk. I run off from a good job with a hotshot race driver and now I wind up playing driver to a lousy, stinking lion. I gave up all that for this; if I'd've stayed on I'd be a supervisor by now, and I'm telling you, that's *good* money!"

Jimmy looks at Sally, a cool, rejecting, questioning look. He takes another bite of his sandwich, shoves it into the corner of his mouth, uses one finger to dislodge some bread caught in his teeth.

"Ya know, I don't wanna go to Florida anyway. I'm sick of your fart-face lion and this whole crappy setup. The guy who runs that gas station outside town says I can have a job there pumping gas into cars and fixing flat tires. I'm just gonna hole up here in Wildwood for the winter; maybe I'll join the act again when you come next summer. You can do without me, long's you have Tuffy. You'll be playing mostly in the sticks anyway down there; these rednecks don't know the difference. Satan, the Dare-Devil Lion, is good enough for them hicks."

Sally looks quickly over at Jimmy, then at Cap. She's confused, frightened.

"Don't do it, Jimmy. You can't quit us now; you *make* this show. Without you, it's nothing but an animal act, like seals or poodle dogs. Besides you'll never stick it out here. Wildwood's canned death in winter, ask anybody."

Cap's embarrassed by Sally's vehemence, her obvious fright, despair, at the idea of Jimmy leaving. He's even more convinced that if Jimmy leaves she'll take off, too. He spreads his hands on the table, lifts his palms, stands his hands on their fingertips.

"I'll tell you one thing, Jimmy; Murph isn't exactly one of your biggest fans. Do whatever you want; we'll make out somehow. But if I were you, I'd think twice before I stayed on here in Wildwood."

Jimmy shoves the last of his sandwich in his mouth. He stands up, stretches, yawns, forces another fart.

"The hell with Murphy! Just 'cause I banged some of the local jail bait, he's got me marked down as public enemy number one. Folks around here should pay me for keeping these little twits home, keep 'em from running away. I give what they want, a good bang, and it doesn't cost them a cent; best damned medicine in the world for a wild-assed, teenaged girl."

He picks up his knife, scrapes some ketchup off the table, and licks it again. Tuffy roars in the background. Jimmy turns toward the lion cage, plants his feet, throws his knife at the Wall of Death; it clatters to the floor of the pit. He shakes his fist.

"Shut up, bush face!!"

He turns back to Cap and Sally, still holding up his fist.

"You know, I'm gonna kill that yella-eyed tomcat if I stay around here much longer. It's him or me.

"Didja ever look into them eyes? He's waiting his chance. He'd like to rip all of us up, me first, turn us all into cat food. But, goddamn it, he sure as hell ain't gonna get me."

Jimmy walks over to pick up his knife. Cap starts clearing off the makeshift table. He carries the bread, the baloney wrapped in waxed paper, the milk, the knives over to the black box, stores them. He lifts the board and moves the boxes so he can open the trap door in the bottom of the pit. He lowers the boxes, including the black one, the board, everything, into the hole in the pit, then slides the trap door into place.

Sally is leaning against the wall, trying to pull herself together. She looks at Jimmy, then at Cap.

"Tuffy's beginning to really scare me, Cap. Last night, all the time we were up on the wall, and I was trying to keep speed, hold it straight, he kept looking at me. I could see him from the corner of my eyes. He'd look at me and then roar his stinking roar. I could smell him, not just his sewer mouth and his farts; I could smell the lion in him, a thick, deep, animal smell. I was afraid to look him in the eyes. He knows I'm afraid, Cap, and he's hungry. I think he's beginning to see me as food."

Cap's pulling off his garbage-gathering clothes and getting into the outfit he wears for the act, black leather trousers, a slightly stained wide-sleeved tight-cuffed silk shirt. Jimmy's doing the same thing on the other side of the room. They're getting ready to put on their demonstration out on the platform.

Cap stops a minute, looks at Sally. "It isn't your time of month, is it?"

Sally stares back at Cap, embarrassed, resistant, turns her head away.

"No, it isn't. That isn't it."

Cap is tightening the laces through the hooks at the top of his left boot, his good leg. He half mumbles to himself: "I'd be the last one around here to know."

Cap finishes dressing. He starts sweeping out the pit. Jimmy has pushed his motorcycle through the small door and up a ramp onto the outside stage opening to the boardwalk. Cap carefully sweeps where the curve of the pit bottom turns up onto the wall. It's here where there's the most danger of slipping. The wall is blackened from the skidding of tires and exhaust fumes.

"Well, Sally, maybe we'll have some takers today. Then, I'll fill Tuffy up with meat, that truck up with gas, and we'll be on our way."

Sally has turned her back on Cap. She has her arms spread out against the wall, her face to it. She's crying.

"Stop it, Cap! Stop kidding yourself. There's nobody here in Wildwood; it's October. We should've been gone a month ago. If we make another fifty bucks this whole week it'll be a miracle."

Cap doesn't say anything. He doesn't even look over at Sally. He grabs the handlebars of his motorcycle and starts pushing it up toward the door after Jimmy. Sally closes the door behind him.

Absent-mindedly, still sobbing, she strips off the overalls and her sweater. She's wearing her orchid spangled costume underneath. She rolls the sweater and overalls into a ball, slides them through the trap door. She goes to another small box in the corner. Out of it she takes a brush and mirror. The mirror is about six by eight inches with a small fold-down metal stand. She stands it on the floor of the pit. She fluffs out her hair, using a small hand mirror to see the back and sides.

Alone, in the dim light, she turns slowly, looking at herself from all angles. She runs each hand carefully over her hips, slaps them a few times, then slides her fingertips down the backs of her thighs. After several minutes, she puts her mirrors and brush back in the box, pushes it under the lip of the trap door and latches the trap tight.

She stands in the center of the surrounding walls, takes a deep breath, goes over, lifts a roll of tickets and a wrap-around-waist apron with pockets from a hook on the wall. She lifts the hook as well, puts it into the sagging pocket of the apron, then goes out the same door Jimmy and Cap used.

PART 9

*T*HE next morning I'm still asleep when I feel something rough rubbing my nose and cheek. I open my eyes and it's Cannibal. Somehow she got out of her box during the night, climbed up the side of my bed, and crawled on top of me. I rub my hand down her back, and she doesn't try to bite me. With both hands, I rub her under the ears. I'm wondering how long she's been out of the box and if she's made a mess anywhere. I hold her in my hand, slowly swing my legs out of bed, and put my feet on the linoleum floor. I look around everywhere, especially under the beds, but don't see anything. I don't smell anything either. Cannibal has her own special smell when she's up close to my face, but that's different. Her fur smell is like the inside of a drawer that's been closed a long time in a hot room.

She's wakened me so I can take her outside, I'm sure of it. We don't have a sandbox here for her; there was no way to carry it with us in the car. I slip on my bathing suit, a shirt, and sweater, then pull on my pants and decide not to wear shoes. I take the towel that's mine from where it's drying over the end of my bed. The sun is just coming up outside and shining through the window onto my pillow.

I think of waking Mom to tell her I'm taking Cannibal out to do her business, but she and Dad look so comfortable all curled around each other I don't want to wake them. I look over to see if Laurel's awake but she's asleep and sucking her fingers.

Gosh, I went down to the boardwalk alone, or almost alone, with Laurel last night. They can't mind too much if I go out so Cannibal won't make a mess.

I open the door and look back to see if it wakes anybody up. They all stay asleep. I hold Cannibal in her box in one hand and slowly close the door to see if anybody wakes up but there's nobody moving. I carefully go along the balcony and down the steps. I cross the courtyard and out into the street.

It's beautiful and quiet. It must be trash day because there are trash and garbage cans in front of all the houses, or maybe they collect trash every day here. I haven't seen any alleys in Wildwood yet; maybe there're some farther inland.

I walk toward the ocean, looking into trashcans as I go. I don't see anything, mostly only newspapers and garbage. There aren't any ashes. I decide to take Cannibal right down to the beach, where there's all the sand in the world.

I cross one big street and there isn't a car in sight. There are streetcar tracks but I don't see any streetcar either. Near the boardwalk, I see one man with a cap on, hunched over, going through trash barrels with a burlap sack between his legs. I guess the Depression's even hit here. Dad says, "Happy Days Are Here Again" and the Depression's over, but I'm not so sure. A lot of kids at school are still on relief or their dads are working for the WPA. Mrs. Loughlin's son, who's only eighteen, just went into the CCC, which is almost like going into jail.

I get to the beach and there's nobody there. It's empty and cold when I go under the boardwalk. On the other side, the sun's just coming over the ocean; it looks as if it's only about two feet above the water but it must be hundreds of miles actually; it's so far away. I keep Cannibal in the box until I get down to the ripples of the surf. I want to see if she'll fight waves again, and I want to feel the water on my feet.

I let Cannibal out and watch. There aren't many strong waves and Cannibal walks along the edge of the water, then up onto the dry sand, where she turns around about five times then squats and does her business. Such a smart cat. I dig a hole, push the mess in, and cover it up.

I walk backward and look at my footsteps in the sand. My shadow is long like a giant, at least five times as tall as I am. Then Cannibal notices her shadow and rears up to fight it. It's one of those mornings when shadows look very important, almost bluish or purplish against the sand color. Every bump from footsteps has a long shadow, too, so the sand looks like little mountains.

There are birds flying over the water, seagulls, and they're hollering at each other, sweeping down on the water trying to catch fish but missing every time. There are also some kind of long-legged birds running along the edges of the water.

They run fast with short steps and shoot in after each wave, ducking down to eat something just behind the water when it goes out. Cannibal sees these birds and decides to chase one of them. She chases it right out under one of the waves. Then when the bird dashes back in, as the wave comes up the beach, Cannibal can't run fast enough and a little wave crashes on her head, tumbling her over, and she's pulled by the undertow into the deeper water. I dash down and rescue her just before she gets drowned. She's sopping wet.

I dry her off with my towel as best I can. She's soaked. She keeps shaking her head to get the water out of her ears. I sit down in the dry sand and rub as much as possible, but the fur is soft and keeps sticking down. I didn't realize how skinny Cannibal is; the fur makes her look twice as big as she *really* is and that isn't much.

When I get her mostly dry, I put her back in her box and walk up away from the ocean toward the boardwalk. I want to go see that lion again. Mostly I want to give Cannibal a real chance to see it and maybe not be so afraid.

We walk up the steps onto the boardwalk. It's the same place where Laurel and I took Cannibal last night to go to the bathroom.

Up on the boardwalk, everything is empty. There's only one man going along with a stick and a nail in the stick picking up papers and putting them in a bag he has slung over his shoulder. I guess he gets paid for doing that but it doesn't seem like very hard work.

I walk along the boardwalk trying not to swing Cannibal too much in her cage and at the same time seeing how many boards I can step over, stepping far as I can. I can step eleven boards each time, without jumping, just stepping. I notice the whole boardwalk is made with two-by-fours. It's great having done carpenter work so you know these things. Boy, a carpenter could keep busy all year just replacing two-by-fours that get worn and splintery. You'd never be out of work.

When I get to his cage, the lion is awake, sitting comfortably up near the front so sun is shining on him. Without the bars he could almost be sitting in Africa, out on a grassy plain like Dad said, just enjoying the sunshine. I come close up from the side so I won't block his sun. He looks over at Cannibal and me but then turns his head back and stares at the sun some more. The light of that sun seems to go through his yellowish-brown eyes so they look as if you could see clean through them from one side to the other. His mane is well brushed so it sticks up and hangs over his face. There's a pink spot on his nose I hadn't noticed before. It's almost the same as Cannibal.

I carefully open Cannibal's cage. She's reaching back and trying to lick off all the salt water from the ocean. Her fur is still sticking down. I might have to give her a real bath to get out all the salt and sand. I carefully climb under the little fence in front of the cage and put the opening to Cannibal's box near the edge of the cage. The lion stares down at me and the box. Cannibal looks up and sees the lion.

This time she doesn't duck down but suddenly jumps right out of the box and *into* the lion's cage! She rears back in her fighting position and takes a swing at that lion's paw. I *can't* reach in and get her; I'm afraid of the lion! In fact, I'm scared to death, partly for me but mostly for Cannibal. She *really* looks like a mouse compared to that lion. The lion's paw is twice as high as Cannibal's head!

At first I try calling her quietly, holding out her box so she can see it, but she won't pay any attention. I'm almost crying; how could I be so dumb? The lion looks slowly down at this mouse of a cat between its paws.

I remember it's elephants who are supposed to be afraid of mice. Mike Conway said it's because they're afraid a mouse will climb up their trunks the same way ladies are afraid of mice because they're afraid they'll crawl into their whatsits.

Then the lion opens its mouth and closes his big paws close around Cannibal. Cannibal isn't paying any attention at all. She's still swinging away at the lion's leg with all her might. That lion sticks his tongue out and licks Cannibal so hard she's knocked right over on her back.

Then the lion licks her again on the stomach while she's still on her back.

The lion stops and looks at Cannibal. Cannibal looks up into that lion's big yellow eyes. I figure this is where Cannibal gets eaten all in one bite. That lion's tasted her and now he's ready to slurp her right in. Cannibal has one paw out ready to strike but isn't swinging. The lion gently licks the side of Cannibal's face. Even that almost pulls poor Cannibal's whiskers out and rolls her over on her side.

Cannibal isn't more than a foot inside the cage but I'm afraid to stick my hand in there. Maybe that lion will be nice with Cannibal because, in a way, they're both cats, but I'm not a cat; I'm the kind of meat lions like to eat. I'd probably just about make a reasonable-sized breakfast for a lion.

I can't get myself to stick my hand inside the cage, but I push Cannibal's little box between the bars and hope she'll crawl in so I can pull the cage back out with Cannibal in it; but Cannibal is enjoying being licked by a lion.

We kids always say we can lick each other, or our dads can lick each other, but this lion is really licking Cannibal and I *know* he can lick me for sure. But, when it comes to me, I think he'll do it with his long sharp teeth and claws, not with his tongue.

I need something to attract Cannibal's attention, to get her close enough so I can grab her quick. I look around for a piece of paper or string, anything, but that man with the nail on the end of a stick must have gotten it all; there's nothing.

Back on the side of the lion's cage I see something golden. That would attract Cannibal's attention for sure; she likes anything that shines. I run around that side of the cage but it's a padlock holding the cage closed. It's one of those kind of hasp things with the curved part of the lock sticking through a slit on the hasp. The lock's hooked in the loop to hold the cage closed but the lock isn't pushed tight.

At first I'm afraid, but I'm more scared for Cannibal. I pull out the lock carefully, testing to feel if the door will open by itself. I do this quietly so the lion won't hear me. The door seems to be stuck anyway with the loop through the hasp even without the lock. There's a small piece of wood on the ground and I push it through to hold the door shut till I can put the lock back in. Then I run around to the front of the cage. Now Cannibal is trying to climb up on the lion's leg; she doesn't seem to be fighting any more.

I call her name and dangle the lock. Cannibal turns around and walks toward me, balancing along the lion's arm to the end of his paw. She puts her own paws on the end of her box and I can almost reach her. I lean the lock in farther so she can strike at it. Suddenly, she swings at the lock, I drop it quickly, grab hold of her paw, pull her out of the cage and close her into the box.

Then I see how the lock has dropped in the cage about as far in as Cannibal was when I was trying to reach her. I set Cannibal down on the boardwalk in her box and go around to where the stick is stuck in the loop of the door. I pull it out and run around to use it for reaching in to pull the lock out from the lion's cage.

It's almost long enough, but not quite, unless I push my hand into the cage farther. I reach in quickly, but even *more* quickly, that lion swings at the stick and knocks it out of my hand. He also knocks the lock farther into the cage so it's right up against his chest.

I don't know what to do. I'm afraid to reach in and I probably couldn't reach in that far anyway, without the lion eating off my arm.

I stand there. I look around for someone to help, but there's no one on the boardwalk. I don't know what's happened to the man with the sack and the stick with the nail on the end. That stick would reach the lock just fine and I could pick it up with the nail part. I can't even find another stick to put inside the loop of the hasp to hold the door. I'm getting more scared by the minute, and at the same time the lion is pushing his face against the bars the same way Cannibal does when she wants me to pet her. I don't know why I do it, but I rub my fingers against his muzzle, above his whiskers and teeth. He closes his eyes and pushes harder against me. He wants to be friends; he's only lonely. I rub his face some more and try to convince myself that he's just a friendly old lion who wants to be petted; but the smell of him, the size, the force he uses to push his face against my hand scares me.

I decide to run home fast so I can tell Dad what's happened. He'll know what to do.

I run a long time along the boardwalk until I get to where I go down our street. On the way I see the older man in the lion act, the one with the whip. He has a filled dirty burlap sack over his shoulders. He might be the one I saw going through the garbage before. Now he's walking toward the lion cage.

I figure for sure he'll get there before the lion pushes against that door. He'll know how to get the lock out of the cage; probably he'll just walk in and pick it up. I'm convinced that lion wouldn't hurt a flea. If he wouldn't even hurt Cannibal who was *looking* for a fight, why should he hurt a human being? I decide not to tell Dad or Mom or even Laurel. It would cause such a ruckus; not even Dad would understand why I went under the fence put there to keep people away, just so Cannibal could meet a real lion.

Now it's happened and it's all over. But I'm still scared; I slow down to get my breath. Maybe I should tell the lion man about the lock being off the cage. I start to go back, after him. Then I decide just to run back to Dad and Mom. It'll be all right.

PART 10

*A*FTER the boy has left, Tuffy stands up. He pays no attention to the lock at his feet. It's getting later; he's hungry.

Cap is out gathering food. The butcher who's promised the meat said he could pick it up at seven o'clock so Cap's scrounging for garbage scraps, something to give Tuffy until the store opens.

Tuffy, in his usual way, his custom of years, goes around the cage, rubbing his sides against the wood and the bars; except for Cap, it's the closest thing to stroking he knows. When he pushes against the wall with the door, the door swings open.

Usually the door opening either means Cap coming in to clean the cage or time for Tuffy to get into the motorcycle sidecar with Jimmy prodding at him. He takes another tour around the cage before he sticks his head out. The attaching tunnel to the motordrome, Wall of Death, is pushed aside. For the first time in a long time, he's looking out into open space without bars.

On the right, beside the Wall of Death, is another boardwalk attraction. It's called Sammy, the Human Fish. Sammy is a man who lost both legs to an artillery shell in the World War. Sammy and Cap are friends; they were in different divisions but shared the knowledge of death. Sammy's act is to stay under water for from five to seven minutes, performing several tricks, such as pretending to sleep or smoke cigars; standing on his hands, his head. Sammy is about Cap's age and lives all the year round on the boardwalk. He has a tiny apartment attached to the back part of a small platform, level with the top of the pool in which he does his act.

A market nearby delivers food to Sammy and he has a small dolly-like flat car on rollers he uses to hand-push himself up and down the boardwalk. Sammy rarely, if ever, goes anywhere except along the boardwalk and then usually only off season when the weather isn't cold and there aren't too many people.

During the season, he's busy most of the time giving performances. He gives a performance every half hour, and each performance lasts about fifteen minutes, so that, in season, except for sleeping, really sleeping, Sammy is in the water almost as much as he is out.

Sammy is actually happier, more comfortable in the water. Owing to lack of exercise and also because of the enormous lung and diaphragm development he needs to stay under water so long, he's huge across the chest and stomach. He has arms stronger than most people's legs, from pushing himself along on his cart. Even without his flat car, the way he moves is to make fists of his hands, then rest his weight on his fists and swing, sliding the rest of his body along. He's baldheaded and looks more like an egg than a fish. If ever anyone wanted to make a film of Humpty-Dumpty, Sammy would be perfect.

Sammy is having his breakfast. He's dressed in a bathrobe cut off just below the waist, and is up on his platform. Behind him is the pool where he does his act. It's like a large aquarium, twenty feet across, with a glass panel fronting on the boardwalk. The tank is ten feet in depth and the water is also ten feet deep. On the bottom of this tank is specially built furniture: a table, a chair, dishes, a couch, all part of his act, special in that they're attached to the bottom of the tank and don't float.

Sammy is, at that moment, pouring some cornflakes into a bowl and has a small can of Sterno heating his coffee. He looks up to see Tuffy slowly padding up specially built stairs, each step wide enough for Sammy to place himself so he can lower his fists onto the next step and let himself down.

Sammy doesn't know how to react. He likes Tuffy. He's often talked about him with Cap, and Cap's always wanted Sammy to come into the cage with Tuffy to see how tame he is. But Sammy has never done it, not so much because he is afraid as because the smell of the lion's cage would get all over his clothes and hands. At least that's what he tells Sture.

Sammy hurriedly pours the milk for his cornflakes into a bowl and pushes it with his arm as far forward as possible.

"Here, Tuffy, here's some milk. Be a nice lion now, drink some milk." Tuffy continues to advance. He's curious. He wants to get next to Sammy, maybe be caressed, maybe be fed. Sammy is backing off, using his arms, keeping his eyes on Tuffy. Tuffy sniffs at the milk, the cornflakes, but doesn't drink or eat. He continues slowly, a slow step at a time toward Sammy. Sammy reaches the edge of his pool and lets himself fall over backward into the water.

Sammy is fighting off panic, trying to conserve his

breath, looking out his front glass onto the boardwalk for someone to help him, rolling on his back, looking up, seeing the lion, the paw of the lion in the water. He's quickly running out of breath, excitement, fear using his oxygen rapidly. Sammy comes up as far from Tuffy as possible. He gulps a breath of air, shouts, breathes deeply again, and goes under water just as Tuffy swings at him, fishing, playing, or hunting.

Sammy comes up twice more, each time shouting, then going under, pressing his face against the glass to see anyone who might be passing by on the boardwalk and be able to help.

Jimmy climbs out of the blankets, leaving Sally's slack arms. He stands up, slips on his underpants, a pair of work dungarees. He goes outside. He still hasn't heard Sammy. It might be what wakened him but all he knows is he needs to take a piss.

He goes outside the Wall of Death. He turns and pees against the side, tucks in, swings around, whirls, windmills his arms. He takes a few steps out onto the boardwalk, drops and does ten quick pushups, swings his arms again, starts back.

He sees Sammy in the tank, his mouth against the glass, his hands pounding on the glass to get Jimmy's attention. Jimmy walks slowly over.

"What'r'ya doin' down in there, Sam? There's nobody out here. What the hell."

Sammy is pointing up desperately. He's running out of air again. Jimmy looks up, sees nothing. It's impossible to see Tuffy on Sammy's platform from the boardwalk unless you look up through the aquarium. He goes closer. Sammy slides to the surface for another breath of air, comes down again. He tries to imitate a lion with his mouth, teeth bared, hands clenched like claws; he points again.

Jimmy looks up through the water, sees Tuffy.

"Holy shit! That bastard lion's out. Where the hell's Cap?"

He runs over, opens the door to the pit. He knows Cap isn't there. He spins around twice. He takes a few cautious steps up Sammy's staircase, sees Tuffy, tawny back to him, tail twitching, leaning over Sammy's pool. Jimmy eases himself down the steps again, dashes into the pit, shakes Sally awake.

"That goddamned lion's out. Where the hell's Cap? The son of a bitch is trying to kill Sammy! Get dressed, go get the cops, or find Cap, or something."

Sally stands up, naked, begins pulling clothes on.

"Oh my God! I always knew this would happen sometime. I'm afraid to go out, Jimmy. I'm afraid of Tuffy."

Jimmy grabs the goad. He's white with fear. "I'll hold him off. But for Christ's sake, hurry! That SOB hates me and I don't want to be eaten by no fart-faced lion."

Jimmy goes out. He stands outside the door until Sally appears behind him. Tuffy's nowhere in sight. Sally slips around the Wall of Death and runs off down the boardwalk.

Jimmy starts up the stairs again to look at Tuffy, the goad held in front of him. Tuffy turns and sees. Jimmy begins backing down the stairs.

Now Tuffy is stalking. He recognizes Jimmy, sees the goad, smells his fear. This is Tuffy's first experience with prey. He gets down on his stomach, legs tensed to spring, eyes fixed on Jimmy. He begins moving toward him, swinging short swipes at the tip of the goad, growling, coughing in anger.

Jimmy is transfixed at first, then backs slowly away, holding the goad out in front of him.

"You stay away from me, you bastard! God almighty, he's trying to kill me!"

Tuffy is tensed, snarling, teeth bared.

Jimmy backs down the stairs, the lion just behind him. He wants to get into the pit, but that's too far. He passes the lion cage and sees the door open. Tuffy's close enough to attack. Jimmy quickly jumps into the cage and pulls the door shut behind him, leaving the goad on the floor outside.

Tuffy stalks around the cage until he's in front of it. He looks in at Jimmy. He attacks the goad, knocking it around on the wooden floor. Then he stalks back and forth several times as Jimmy cowers at the back of the cage. Tuffy has his eyes fixed on Jimmy. He moves closer to the cage, gets up on his hind legs, reaches in with both paws, tries to swipe at Jimmy. He can't reach him.

Jimmy screams:

"Help! Help, somebody! I'm going to be killed. There's an escaped lion and he's trying to kill me. Help!"

Sally is running along the boardwalk and she sees Cap. She runs toward him hollering. Cap has stopped at the butcher's so now he has a good load of meat for Tuffy. He starts running toward Sally. There's no one else on the boardwalk.

"Sally, what is it? What's happened?"

"Tuffy's escaped. Sammy's in the water and Tuffy's trying to catch him."

Cap starts running, limping with his heavy sack. Sally runs after him. He turns his head.

"Where's Jimmy?"

"He's there. He told me to go get you or the cops. He has the goad and he's trying to keep Tuffy away from Sammy."

"Jesus!"

Cap runs hard, not moving fast. He rounds the corner of the Wall of Death and sees Tuffy squatted on his haunches in front of the cage. He stops.

"Tuffy! What on earth are you doing?"

Tuffy turns at Cap's voice. He cringes, turns his eyes, then his head to the side. He moves away from the cage toward the Wall of Death as Cap approaches. Cap puts down his sack of scraps. He moves toward Tuffy, expecting him to come docilely as usual.

But something has happened in Tuffy's internal world. He's more afraid of Cap than glad to see him. He has stalked one of the pride, tried to kill him. He's confused and dashes past Cap out onto the boardwalk and past Sally, who falls down in her fear, covering her head with her hands, expecting to be mauled, killed. But now Tuffy's fear is greater than his hunger or new-found hunting instinct. Also he likes Sally; she's fed him, she's a member of the original pride.

Cap starts running after Tuffy, then stops, comes back. Jimmy is still in the cage. He comes to the front, peers out. "That bitchin' lion tried to kill me. He was reaching in this cage trying to eat me. Where is he?"

"He wasn't trying to kill you, Jimmy. That lion wouldn't know how to kill a rabbit. But, God damn it, now he's running down the boardwalk. Somebody's going to see him and then we're really finished."

Sally comes around the Wall of Death. Her knees are skinned. She's scared, and she runs up to Cap.

"That lion's running loose; what're you going to do, Cap? We need help. I'm going for the police. Somebody can get hurt or killed. That lion's hungry and he's mad, too."

Cap starts pulling his motorcycle out from the pit.

"Come on, Jimmy, we can catch him and maneuver him back here into the pit or into the cage. Let's go."

Jimmy holds back a minute, looks over at Sally. He doesn't want to go but he can't let Cap show him up either.

"O.K., but after this I quit. I've had it."

He dashes in, pulls up his motorcycle. They both kick-start and rev up so they sound like lions up from the pit themselves. Cap leans toward Sally.

"Maybe you'd better go to the police, Sal. Talk to Murph; tell him what's happened. He'll try to help."

With that, Cap zooms off, Jimmy behind him. They roll fast down the boardwalk and spot Tuffy walking along nonchalantly, enjoying freedom, the first he's had since he was a cub. He turns when he hears the sound of the motorcycles; then he starts running.

As the motorcycles come close, he jumps over the side of the boardwalk down onto the beach, luckily a relatively unoccupied section; it's still early morning. Cap and Jimmy ride the bikes down a set of steps leading to the beach a little past where Tuffy went over the edge. They start trying to move themselves behind Tuffy, aiming him back up the beach to the Wall of Death. The dry sand is deep; the motorcycles twist and veer. Tuffy is running out toward the ocean. He runs into the surf, turns, and roars.

The cycles move better here down on the hard sand close to the water. Cap and Jimmy, Cap in front, start edging Tuffy back up the beach. Waves crack behind Tuffy. When one wave breaks over his back he turns, roars again, grunts, coughs. It's a new world to him. He's wet; his roar is almost lost in the roar of the ocean. The few people on the beach have run for cover, under and past the boardwalk.

Suddenly, Tuffy breaks back toward the boardwalk. Cap and Jimmy take off after him. Tuffy bounds up onto the boardwalk in one leap. Cap and Jimmy roar up another set of steps, barely gaining grip and standing on the footpegs to minimize the shock. At the top they take off after Tuffy.

Cap yells over his shoulder.

"I'll go on by to turn him back and into the pit. You stay up behind him. He can't keep running much longer. Lions tire fast. Don't get too close; just keep him in front of you."

Jimmy nods. Cap roars off past Tuffy, giving the lion plenty of room so he won't turn back again. He swings his bike to a stop on the boardwalk in front of Sammy's place. Sammy is over his pool on the catwalk from where he delivers his spiel to the people. He has a megaphone and starts giving directions to help Cap and Jimmy.

"O.K., Jimmy, don't go too fast, just putt along behind him slow, but gun your motor if he starts turning. That's right. Now, Cap, you stay there. He's turning in. O.K. now, I think he's in, both of you follow him on in. I think he's going into the pit. No, he's stopped. He's nuzzling at that bag of meat you brought, Cap. I think it's O.K. Cap, you come on in without the motorcycle and see if you can get him to go into either the cage or the pit. If he comes up here again, I can just drop into my tank."

Tuffy is waiting at the sack of food when Cap comes up. Jimmy guards the exit on his bike. Cap ruffles Tuffy behind the ear, Tuffy rubs his face against Cap. Everything's all right again. Cap reaches into the sack and gives Tuffy a half-eaten pork chop. Tuffy holds it in his mouth. Cap looks over at the cage, up at Sammy.

"Did you see the lock to the cage? I don't see it anywhere. I know I put it back on after I cleaned the cage this morning, but I don't find it anywhere.

"Well, we'll have to put him in the pit for now till I find that damned lock. It's got to be around here somewhere. How in hell did he get out of that cage anyway?"

Cap leads Tuffy by the mane into the pit. He closes and bolts the door behind him.

"I'm gonna head off Sally before she gets to the station. Maybe we can still work our way out of this without any real trouble."

Jimmy rolls his bike next to the Wall of Death. "Well, that's it. I've had all I'm going to take with that god-damned bush-faced bastard. I'm getting out of here right now and fast."

"O.K., Jimmy. I don't blame you. If what you say is true about Tuffy trying to kill you, *I'd* leave. But, before you go, would you feed Tuffy these things I bought him? Just go up on the catwalk and drop them down. He must be starving; he's had more exercise this morning than he's had in years. There're some scraps, also some liver and lungs and beef hearts I got at the butcher's; that should hold him. It'll only take a minute. I want to catch Sally before she gets to tell Murph. No sense having Murph all hot and bothered over nothing. I'll be back and settle out with you."

"O.K. But I wish that goddamned animal would start eating itself, beginning with its tail and pulling itself inside out."

Jimmy takes the sack distastefully, holding it away from his dungarees. Cap kickstarts his bike and zooms around the side of the Wall of Death and off out of sight.

Jimmy starts up the stairs to the catwalk, then comes back. He picks up the goad he dropped in his flight from Tuffy. The door to the cage is open, the lock in the back of the cage, unnoticed.

Jimmy smiles to himself and goes up the stairs two at a time, the sack in one hand and the goad held like a javelin over his head to clear the curves of the Wall of Death.

Jimmy opens the sack and pulls out a piece of beef lung. He spears it on the end of the goad, pushing it past the hook (actually, the goad is a grappling hook from a boat), then he lowers the goad over the edge with the meat on its end, dangling, caught behind the hook like a baited line for big-game fishing.

"O.K., furface, how'd you like a piece of meat, real meat for a change, not garbage?"

He dangles it in the middle of the pit. Tuffy looks up. He leaps to hook the meat with his paw, but Jimmy jabs the goad, pokes Tuffy in the face so he falls back onto his side.

"How'd you like that, you stinking son of a bitch? Come on now, be a nice pussy, jump on up and take a bite."

Tuffy, confused, circles the pit a few times, while Jimmy dangles the meat in the center, taunting him.

Tuffy springs again. Again, Jimmy jabs, catching Tuffy with a stiff poke just under the eye. Tuffy lands on his back, deflected in midspring and off balance.

"That's it, dummy, break your back. Those claws and those teeth won't do you no good now. Come on, try and get it. Get your teeth into some of this delicious meat, make hair grow on your chest."

Tuffy continues to leap, knocked down each time; Jimmy laughing, taunting Tuffy, circling on the catwalk between the lion's leaps. Bloody spots are appearing on Tuffy's muzzle; one eye is swollen. Tuffy is more than hungry now; he's angry, challenged. This is something he's never known, directed viciousness unmitigated. He circles the pit faster and faster, more cautious with his leaps now. Jimmy is exultant at the top of the pit, enjoying his revenge, circling faster to gain advantage over Tuffy.

Then, who knows by what combination of memory, learning, instinct, experience, desperation, Tuffy begins running faster, at a gallop, in a circle at the bottom of the pit, gaining acceleration, using this acceleration and the centrifugal force it generates to mount higher and higher on the sides of the wall until he's high enough to lunge, grapple, and scramble himself up onto the catwalk.

Jimmy stands transfixed. He holds on to the goad, tries to pull it up from over the edge of the pit to defend himself, but Tuffy is too quick.

He bounds the few yards to where Jimmy is standing, shocked, defenseless. He swings his mighty left paw at Jimmy's haunch, knocking him against the Wall of Death and probably breaking his spine with that first blow.

Then Tuffy is on top of Jimmy. The lion takes his victim's head into his mouth and bites down, virtually decapitating him but smothering him at the same time, stilling whatever life is left in Jimmy's now inert body.

Then, carefully, without hesitating, and also without haste, operating on latent instincts, Tuffy rips off Jimmy's clothes and disembowels him. He begins feeding cautiously, nuzzling gently at first, then more and more furiously. Tuffy eats between hurry and leisure, hunched over his victim, preying on his unnatural prey.

He empties the greater part of the thoracic cavity, and nudging, turning the body over in his ferocity, gnawing, worrying, rips large hunks from the haunches.

After the first ten minutes Tuffy subsides and almost gently strips off the large femoral triceps, revealing the glistening bone of the great trochanter of femur. Then, using his side teeth, he scissor-cuts one of Jimmy's muscular arms off at the shoulder. He holds this dripping in his mouth. When he does stand up, he's so bloated with food he can scarcely move. As with any lion, after gorging, he's interested in only one thing, sleep.

He slowly, awkwardly, walks across the common rafters of the Wall of Death and a curio shop beside it, on the opposite side from Sammy's platform. He slinks off into the darkness, into the attic of the shop, and settles his weight onto the floor, surrounded by cardboard boxes filled with trinkets and souvenirs sold in the shop below.

Sometime later, Sally and Cap arrive. Cap managed to intercept her before she got to the police. Sally is riding on the back of the motorcycle. Cap is anxious about Tuffy, concerned that the whole escapade might have changed their relationship. He stops to let Sally off, then goes over to park his motorcycle beside Jimmy's. Sammy leans down from his platform.

Sally looks up.

"How are you, Sammy? Did Tuffy hurt you?"

"Nothing but my feelings. I think I lost about two years' growth, too. But no hard feelings. He was probably only playing, but *I* couldn't tell the difference. After all, a cat does like to fish."

He laughs, slides himself closer to the edge.

"Where's Tuffy now? I heard some growling and rustling around over there just after you left but it's been quiet ever since."

Cap comes up beside Sally.

"Tuffy's in the pit. Jimmy was supposed to feed him, that's probably what you heard. You haven't seen Jimmy, have you?"

Sally looks around.

"He wouldn't be in the pit with Tuffy. He most likely took a walk or something. I imagine he wants some time to pull himself together after what's happened. I can't blame him."

Cap looks at Sally. He's wondering how she'll take it when she knows Jimmy's leaving, might even be gone already. He thinks again how it will be when Sally leaves. Maybe she's only been sticking around the last few years because of Jimmy. Cap hates to think of life without her. Love for him, late to come, is not easily given up.

"I'll look in the pit to see if Tuffy's O.K."

Cap opens the door to the pit carefully. He's not afraid, but he doesn't want Tuffy escaping again. He also wants to see if Jimmy has really fed him. It's fairly dark in the pit and Cap switches on the overhead lights.

When he discovers Tuffy is gone, he stands there a few seconds in bewilderment. He checks to see if Jimmy's things are there; they are. Now Cap's scared. He dashes out, leaving the lights on. He runs over and peers into the cage, an illogical last hope. It's then he sees the lock on the floor back in the cage. He reaches in, picks it up.

Sally's still talking with Sammy. She turns around and looks at Cap. "What's the matter?"

"Tuffy's gone!!"

"What do you mean he's gone? Where's Jimmy?"

"Tuffy's not in there where I left him. There's no meat on the floor and the sack isn't there either. He's just gone."

"Mother of God!"

Cap looks up at the catwalk. It doesn't make sense but it's the last possible place. It's where Jimmy was supposed to go. He starts in a dash up the steps with Sally behind him, her concern for Jimmy overwhelming her fear of Tuffy.

Cap starts running around the catwalk clockwise. A quarter of the way around he comes on the remains of Jimmy, the filled burlap sack beside him.

Jimmy is such a torn mess, the blood so all-encompassing, and Cap is so confused, frightened, he doesn't realize at first what's happened. If you don't believe something will happen, it's hard to see it, even when it's before your eyes.

Sally runs past Cap. She falls to her knees in front of Cap beside Jimmy. She sees one of his arms ripped from the carcass, twisted backward across his torso, so the tattoo of the eagle riding a motorcycle, smeared with blood, is just visible.

"Mother of God! Jesus, Mary, and Joseph! Oh, please don't let this be. Oh, Jimmy! Jimmy! Jimmy!"

She's not expecting an answer, only trying to call him back, asserting her right to him.

Cap drops to his knees beside her. He stares, the blood drains from his face, and he vomits. He vomits on Sally's feet. He stands up and starts vomiting over the edge of the railing into the pit. He vomits until he's retched dry and is crying.

Sally stands up, her back to Cap. She's hunched over sobbing, sobbing so hard now she can't talk. She turns, looks down at her shoes. She looks up at Cap, who is standing there, vomit on his chin, across his shirt. Sally swings back her arm and slaps Cap hard across the face. He stands without moving. She swings with the other arm, full swing, and slaps him again. She's hurt her hand and tucks it against her breast, holding it with her other hand. Cap takes a step forward, his arms out to hold her, to comfort her; he staggers. When he gets close, Sally begins pounding on his chest, his face, with her fists. Cap tries to hold her in his arms; she kicks at his legs.

"You wanted it to happen. Jimmy *knew* it; he told me so. He knew he was going to get killed by Tuffy and it'd be your fault. Oh, God! I hate a coward."

"You're talking crazy, Sally. Come on, let's go; we've got to *do* something."

Cap starts running, pulling Sally with him. She follows unwillingly, looking back at Jimmy. Cap pulls her behind him down the stairs. When they round the side of the Wall of Death he yells.

"Sammy!! Sammy!! Tuffy's escaped again and he's killed Jimmy up there. I'll report to the police, then look for Tuffy. I'm taking Sally with me."

Sammy's face appears over the edge of his platform.

"He's killed Jimmy? Are you sure?"

Cap is trying to kickstart his motorcycle. Sally awkwardly, reluctantly climbs on the back. It takes four kicks to turn the motor over. Cap shouts up to Sammy as he keeps kicking, adjusting the magneto:

"I'm sure. Jimmy's dead. Tuffy could be around somewhere, so stay close to your pool. Warn everybody away with your megaphone. If you see him just jump in the tank."

Cap gets his bike started. He pulls out, around the Wall of Death and off to the police. Sammy watches them go, then looks carefully all around him. He slides over to where he can keep an eye on the boardwalk. He settles down there, turning his head over his shoulder now and again, half expecting to see Tuffy stalking him, maybe only trying to be friendly, or maybe wanting to kill again.

PART 11

"COME on, Dickie. No lion's going to catch us way out here; lions are afraid of water."

Dad has the fishing poles we rented and he's ahead of me. We're walking out on a rickety old pier with boards missing so we can look right down into the water.

Two days have passed since the lion escaped and killed that man in the motorcycle act. It's been in all the newspapers, even the Philadelphia papers, the *Inquirer,* the *Bulletin,* and the *Ledger.* The lady at our place where we're living says the radio told everybody to stay at home if they could, except for emergencies, until the lion was either caught or killed.

But after two days in our room, while I'm having an awful time keeping from crying or sometimes from just coming right out and telling Mom and Dad how I let the lion escape, Dad says he isn't going to waste his vacation mooning around and anybody who wants to go fishing with him can come.

I want to do anything, just to think about something else, so I say I'll come. Mom and Laurel decide to stay inside but say they'll go out with us in the afternoon to the beach, especially if the lion gets caught. I leave Cannibal with Laurel.

So we're walking out on this old pier with thick pilings, thicker than telephone poles, holding it up all crooked and coated with black shells and green seaweed. The whole thing sags and tilts back and forth. Boards are missing everywhere, and it all shakes when the waves break against it. We walk past a sign saying FISHING PROHIBITED ON PIER. It took me a long time to learn that prohibited meant you couldn't do it. *Prohibited* sounds an awful lot like *permitted* to me. It looks like *permitted,* too.

But Dad walks right past that sign. He says it's only put up there so if anything happens to us it's our own fault and we can't sue anybody; he's fished lots of times from this pier and he's always caught good fish.

I follow along behind him. I try not looking between the boards when there are two or three in a row missing; some of the boards look as if they might break if you step on them, too.

I know Dad's taking me out here partly because he feels something's wrong. Both Mom and Dad have some mysterious way of knowing if I've done something bad and I don't know how to hide it from them.

But I can *never* confess about letting that lion out; they'd probably have to tell the police. Then everybody'd *know* I have some kind of devil in me for sure. Who else but a devil would let a lion loose so he could kill somebody? The way it happened, I didn't even know I was doing it; but now, in my mind, I can almost believe I did it on purpose with some help from Cannibal and the lion. That lion *is* called Satan, the Dare-Devil Lion. That must mean something.

I'm wishing I had Cannibal with me here but she'd have to stay in her box all day. Laurel's getting really good at playing with Cannibal, and I think Cannibal likes her. Cannibal acts more like a kitten and less like a cat every day. I'm not so sure I like her as much this way.

Dad's stopped and has our fishing poles leaning in a crotch where two huge posts stick up higher than the pier. He's down on his knees opening up the waxed paper full of cut-up squid we bought for bait on our way.

It was still dark when we bought the bait and rented the poles. I was looking out our car window into the salt marshes and under all those little wooden bridges, hunting for the lion. If I could only help find him it might make things not so bad.

Now Dad's tying the hooks and sinkers onto the leader. Dad took me fishing before once, when I was real little, little as Laurel, but I've never caught anything. Dad puts some bait on each of the hooks. He's tied two hooks on the line, three feet apart.

"We're going to catch some fish today, Dickie. I feel it in my bones. Once, in this very spot, I caught eleven kingfish and two flounder, all of them at least two pounds each. Boy, were they ever good. I don't even mind cleaning fish like that. We'll clean anything we catch out here so we can bring the fish home all cleaned and ready to eat. That's the way Mom likes it."

He's still watching me. As he untangles his line and swings his pole over his shoulder to cast, he takes another look at me, and just before he whips off his cast he gives me a wink.

My father *never* winks. He can't *know*, can he? If he did know, he wouldn't wink, would he? Winking that way he looks like Brian Donlevy or some other actor in a suit.

His cast is perfect, arching up high and dropping a long way out there just at the right time. My dad can really fish. He puts on the ratchet and reels back in slowly until his line is straight. I take the other pole and swing my line with the bait on it back and forth, getting it clear of things. I take off the ratchet but keep my thumb lightly on the reel so the line can go out but it won't backlash. Backlash is usually what happens when I cast.

But this time it goes out pretty far, for me; at least it doesn't get all snarled. I don't think I jerked the bait off either. Dad sits down on the edge with his feet hanging over the side of the pier. I'm a little bit afraid but I sit beside him. He wouldn't let me fall in, and if a really big fish bites on my line I can pull back hard and hold on to the post beside me so I won't get pulled into the water.

The waves are crashing into the pilings under us. They smash, and foam crashes up high or sometimes the waves just roll on by, creeping up the side of the pilings, then rolling on toward shore while the shells and seaweed on the pilings drip water and hiss after they're gone.

I like fishing more for watching the water than catching fish. I peek over at Dad a few times but he's looking out across the water, watching his line. He has one finger pushing against his line above his reel to feel for any bites, and he has his ratchet on so every once in a while it clicks. I put on my ratchet and push my finger on the line the same way; I'd forgotten all about that part.

I stare some more down into the water and think about the lion. The water's something like a lion; awfully strong so nothing can stop it. But the ocean isn't in a cage, it's free; now the lion is too. I wonder if he's happier this way. I guess an ocean is one of the freest things you can think of except the sky. I look over at Dad again; he's looking at me and smiles.

"What in heaven's name are you thinking about, Dickie? You look as if you have the weight of the world on your shoulders. You worrying about me and J.I?"

I don't know what to say. Nobody except Sister Anastasia that time in Religion ever asked me what I was thinking about. I don't think anybody ever even cared what I thought. It's a peculiar thing to feel somebody wants to know what's inside your head. I don't know how to answer. I don't want to lie but I could never tell Dad the truth about the lion, not now anyway, maybe some other time, after they've caught the lion. I wonder if I'll need to tell about letting that lion out when I go to confession. Which one of the capital sins is Mistake?

If I tell, I know darn well Father Lanshee will squeal to my parents. Even Father O'Shea might. But I'd never tell about it in confession anyway. I'm ready to live with this lie, even go to communion without telling it. Letting out a lion to kill somebody is a bigger thing than confession and communion can do anything about. I'm like one of the old pagan Romans putting Christians in to be eaten by lions. I wonder if the motorcycle driver the lion ate was a Catholic.

"I was thinking about that a little bit; but mostly I was thinking about how strong the ocean is, how it keeps doing the same thing over and over but it isn't monotonous like a clock."

"Dickie, they say each seventh wave is supposed to be bigger than the other ones. I watch every time I've come down here to the ocean but I don't think that's so. People just make up those kinds of ideas."

We're quiet some more. I try to think about school things or about Cannibal or even about Dad and J.I. and the union, anything except about that lion; so if he asks me again what I'm thinking I won't have to lie. I wonder what *he's* thinking. I wonder what he'd say if I asked him.

Just then, something strikes so hard on my line it almost cuts my finger. There's a sucking pull, then a strong jerk so my pole bends. I grab the pole with both hands; the line starts reeling out fast and I can't catch the handle.

"Holy smokes, Dickie! You've really caught into something there! Try to slow it down before your line runs out."

I try again to catch the handle but it's spinning too hard, too fast. Dad jumps up, wedges his pole between two boards, and reaches over to me, fast. He's already breathing hard.

"Here, let me give you a hand with that. You must've caught into a whale or something. My goodness. We're liable to lose the pole and everything."

Dad takes the pole from me, braces the end against his knees held tight together, and manages to slow down the line going out. He can't stop it but he slows it and starts trying to pump the pole up and down the way you do when you're pulling in a big fish, but he can't do it; the pole is practically bent in half. It looks as if it's going to break, and then we'll have to pay for it. Dad's concentrating and sweat is coming on his forehead.

I'm scared. It reminds me of the lock inside the lion's cage. It's something so scary and you're caught into it and there doesn't seem to be any way out.

The line out there starts pulling sideways toward the end of the pier, where there are practically no boards. We can see the fishing line cutting against the water. Then the line begins slackening and Dad reels in as fast as he can. He's slowly working his way out to the end of the pier at the same time. I'm afraid to follow him; sometimes there are as many as four or five boards missing and you have to jump over empty places. Dad's a good swimmer so he could swim in, but I'd have to hold on to one of those big pilings with that strong water and I'd probably get all cut to smithereens.

Just when it looks as if that fish is going to go completely around the pier and get everything all tangled up, he turns back to where he started. Dad's letting out a bit now but pulling in whenever he can. The pole still looks as if it's going to break.

"Watch, Dickie. The important thing is never to let the pole flat down or the fish can break your line for sure. You've got to keep as much drag on him with the pole and pumping as you go without breaking anything and at the same time keep trying to bring him in close. This is some kind of a monster fish and I think he's about ready to make another run. If he goes too far, we run out of line and I'll lose him. We can only hope he'll tire out first. I've never had such a big fish on a line before. Isn't it exciting?"

It's *too* exciting for me. What'll we do if it's a shark and it jumps right up out of that water and eats us because it's mad. I don't know whether to mention my idea of a shark; Dad doesn't like it when I say sissy things like that. He's pretty good, usually, that way, hardly ever makes fun of me, but sometimes when he's excited like this he forgets.

"Gee, Dad! What do you think it is?"

"It's probably some kind of sand shark. Whatever it is it can sure swim fast. Oh oh! There she goes again."

The line starts spinning out fast. The ratchet's practically screaming! Dad's trying to slow it with his thumb because he can't hold on to the handle any more. There starts to be blood on the fishing line from his thumb burning and rubbing against it. Dad doesn't seem to notice. He's so concentrated on that fish there's nothing else.

Then when there's only a little bit left on the reel so we can see the metal part underneath, the fish starts swimming toward us again. Dad reels in as fast as he can; the line is slack in the water. If the fish changes direction suddenly now he can break the line for sure. Dad's leaning over the pole, with the pole almost straight up to absorb the shock if the fish starts going out again. He's still turning the handle as fast as he can.

"Dad, I think I just saw something. It looked big as a whale but it was a sort of pinkish brown. See, there it is again."

I lie down on the boards so I can lean over without falling. Sweat's dripping from Dad's forehead now. Then, suddenly, the line goes tight. Dad holds it for a few minutes but the pole's bent almost to breaking and he lets go of the handle, puts his thumb on the reel again.

This time the fish only runs about twenty yards then slows down. Dad begins reeling him in, lowering the pole, then pulling back, then lowering, reeling in and pulling back. The fish seems to have tired out or given up, or maybe that's what he wants us to think. I'm afraid of what's going to come out of that deep green under the pier, but I'm interested at the same time.

"We should be seeing it soon now, Dickie. Too bad we don't have a gaff. There's no way we can get this fellow in without breaking our line. It's about to break now and he'll be three times as heavy at least when we try lifting him out of the water. If it's a really good fish, something we might win a contest or fish pool with, I'll try holding him while you run back to that house down there near the beach and see if you can borrow a gaff, or maybe I can walk along the pier pulling it with me and beach it. I did that with a giant sea turtle once, but this is no turtle."

Just then we see it. There's a pointed nose like a shark and white on the underneath turning to pink and then brown on the back. I can see its eyes and its mouth, with sharp needles for teeth. The fishing line's coming out between those teeth. Then I see it has wings. It's a gigantic ocean bird, flapping wings that are wider across than my dad's arms when he spreads them out. I didn't know there were bird fish swimming in the bottom of the ocean.

"Gadzooks, Dickie!! It's a stingray. First I thought it was a skate but this is too big. This is one of the biggest stingrays I've ever seen or even heard of. It must weigh over two hundred pounds."

He reels it in a little closer so the snout of this stingray is resting against the rounded skirt of shells on the bottom of the piling. The eyes are looking at us; fierce, mad eyes. That fish is tired but he hasn't given up yet.

"Do stingrays eat people like sharks?"

"No. But he has a long tail, and on the end of his tail is a stinger that'll kill you quicker than you can say 'Jack Robinson.'"

I look down into the water. He's almost the same color as the lion only not so yellow. But the lion had nice eyes; these eyes are different—cold, wet, ocean eyes.

"What'll we do, Dad? Do you want me to run for a gaff so we can bring him in?"

"No sir, Dickie. We're not about to be on the same pier with this fellow. He's no good to eat, and in a certain way he's too beautiful to kill. Think what it must be like swimming around in that ocean with those big, strong, muscular wings."

Dad wedges my pole into a place where two pilings cross. He motions me over and puts my hand on the pole. He's tied the line through a crack in the piling to hold it so there's no danger that stingray can pull me or the fishing pole into the water.

"You hold on to the pole, Dickie. I'm going to see if I can save our sinker and our other hook. He's taken the bottom hook but I hate to lose the whole rig. Besides, he'll have a better chance to recover if he doesn't have a sinker and hook trailing after him."

Dad goes over the edge of the pier, holding on to the boards. He lowers himself into a place where there's a crossing of poles for support. He slides down the support right close to where the stingray is. Then it happens. Just as he gets his knife out of his mouth and lowers it below the second hook to cut the line, that monster starts thrashing. I see his tail whipping in the water and once actually coming up out in an arch over his back.

But Dad cuts quickly and the stingray settles slowly

into the water. He stays there a few minutes looking up at Dad. He seems to be deciding whether to attack or not, then slowly turns and swims away, going deeper, with the thin parts of the backs of his wings fluttering like curtains in the water.

Dad twists around and shimmies back up the pole until he can get hold of the edge, then he pulls himself up onto his stomach and swings his legs back up onto the pier. I never knew my dad could do a thing like that. I've watched him do some pretty scary climbing when we were building porches but never anything like that, and there wasn't an ocean under with a mad stingray swimming around in it, just a hard alley. I'm glad when he stands up.

"Well," he says, "that was a real adventure. This is something you can tell your grandchildren. I'll bet that's the biggest stingray in the Atlantic Ocean. Up close I could actually see into his eyes. The devil himself must have eyes like that. I don't think that creature likes anybody, not even himself. If he could've reached up and pulled me into the water I'll bet he would've. I'll tell you I was scared when I reached out to cut the line and he started thrashing around. Did you see that stinger?"

I nod my head yes. I'm still too excited to talk.

Dad undoes his own pole and starts reeling it in. The bait on one hook is gone. He puts the pole down and opens his fishing box, a box he usually uses at home for tools, and pulls out a hook. His hands are shaking but he's smiling.

I reel in my own line, what's left of it. Dad takes hold of the end.

"A number six should be about right. Maybe you can catch something a little more reasonable-sized this time."

I watch him tie on the hook. I wonder how Dad learned to do all those things.

"Dad, is that stingray really dangerous?"

"He sure is."

"Is he more dangerous than a lion?"

"Don't you worry your head about that lion. I told you he's probably miles from here now. A lion can't live long on his own in country like this. He'll come out and they'll catch him. Don't you worry."

"Sure, but everybody's so scared and wondering how he escaped, but we just let a stingray go. He must be as dangerous as a lion. He can kill anybody who goes swimming."

When we were holding that stingray there and Dad was trying to cut the line I almost decided I was never going to swim in the ocean again. There must be thousands of sharks and stingrays and things like octopuses in the ocean. No wonder Mom doesn't like to swim.

"Now don't fret about that, Dickie. This feller we just saw, and just about every wild creature, will stay away from a human; they're afraid of us. It's only when they're captured like that lion, or hooked the way we had this stingray, that they're dangerous. People are the same way."

He has my pole ready again and new bait on it. I know I'm going to fish the rest of the day hoping nothing bites on my line. I make a cast and it backlashes a little bit and I only get the line out about half as far as the last time, but it's O.K. with me. I pull out the line from the reel and Dad helps me wind it on the reel straight again.

Then Dad goes over and reels in his line. The bait on both hooks is gone.

"I think I'm just feeding crabs."

He kneels down and cuts more bait for his hooks.

"You know, Dickie, sometimes *people* can be more dangerous than any other animal. There are sharks and lions and stingrays in the hearts of some people. You have to learn to recognize them and stay clear so you won't get hurt."

"You mean like the J.I. people and the union people?"

"Yeah, I guess that's a pretty good example. J.I. didn't

want to hurt me, Dick Kettleson, personally, they're just trying to scare the shop steward, to chase out the union, and I got in the way. They're business people. They want to make a good profit with their factory the same way that lion or that stingray wants to eat. It's their nature. If I get in the way I could get eaten and they'd hardly notice. It's the same way with the unions. It's like lions fighting tigers or sharks fighting stingrays. They both want to win, and if somebody tries to stop them, they can get hurt."

We sit down on the edge of the pier again. Dad takes out some sandwiches Mom packed for us before we left. My sandwiches are peanut butter and jelly. Dad's are Lebanon baloney. He has them packed in the lunch pail he takes to work, and there's a Thermos bottle. Mom's put hot cocoa in it. He pours some out for me in the top, and drinks from the bottle himself. It's still steaming hot.

"But everybody isn't like that, are they, Dad? Everybody isn't just trying to beat everybody else, are they?"

"The way I see it, there are three kinds of people, Dickie. There are the *'get by'* people, who won't do anything unless you make them do it. They don't care about anything or anybody except themselves, to me they're the lower-lower class. Then there are the *'get along'* people. They get along with others and they want the job to get along, too; they want to get it done right. That's the upper-lower class. That's what we are.

"The last bunch is the *'get ahead'* people. They're almost worse than the *'get by'* people. They only look out for themselves, and they don't care about the job any more than the *'get-byers';* just so long as they come out ahead and make more money. They're all the rest of the classes.

"But don't you worry about it. Just stay away from *'get-byers'* and *'get-aheaders'* whenever you can."

"You aren't doing it, Dad. You're working at J.I. and

you're a steward with the union. Why do you stay with these people if they're so bad?"

Just as I'm saying this, Dad casts his line. He doesn't wink this time. He shoots that sinker and those hooks straight up and out way over the water. It keeps sailing until it hits almost twice as far as he threw it the first time. He tilts his reel to show me there's almost no line left. He's smiling a really big smile.

"Boy, I almost outdid myself. That must be the longest cast I've ever made." He reels in the slack, sits down, takes another bite of his sandwich.

"You're right, Dickie. But there are other things to think about. We've got our family and we've got to live. With the Depression and all, we got behind; we couldn't pull our own weight and fell into debt for the rent and things. Then, J.I. offered me all that money and it was hard to resist. I got back my seniority, too, nine years of it. That means they have to fire other people before they can fire me and I make more money than if I was just starting on the job. I had to think about all that."

I know he's looking at me while he's talking but I can't look back. This is partly because I still think he was wrong going back to J.I. and partly, too, because my mind has run off again and is thinking about that darned lion.

One part of me feels guilty because a man got killed but another part is glad the lion is free and I'm hoping they don't catch him, even if he freezes or starves to death; it'd be better than putting him back in a cage.

"Do you understand me, Dickie? I *had* to go back. I joined the union because I thought I could fight against J.I. that way and be a little bit free from them, but that didn't work. The union people are only more bosses, *'get-aheaders.'* You see, your Daddy makes mistakes, too."

"Why don't we stay here in Wildwood, Dad? It'd be like vacation all the time. There are plenty of broken porches I see everywhere. You and I could go around fixing them up and just take the money from the people and never worry about anything."

Dad pulls suddenly as if he has a bite, then reels in slowly. I wonder if he might have something on his line.

"Nothing but a crab nibbling again. They'll steal your bait every time.

"Dickie, it's not that simple. During this last while at J.I., what with our rent already paid, we've been able to put the money we used for the porches back into our emergency fund and some extra besides. It won't be long before we'll be able to buy a better car."

Now Dad's looking out over the water. Maybe he's only feeling if he really has a bite or it's just crabs again. I think I get a bite but I don't pull too hard. If some fish wants to bite itself onto my hook that's O.K. but I'm not going to hook any fish on purpose.

"A married man has to think about security. And, I don't think anybody gets any security without giving up some freedom. Sure we'd all like more freedom. I'd love working for myself, being my own boss, but then I wouldn't have any security at all. We can't afford that. Mom would worry all the time and I'd worry, too."

"Sure, Dad. But some people do, don't they? How about Mr. Greene, the paperhanger? He doesn't work for anybody and he pays his rent all the time; we even built a porch for him. He doesn't work for any J.I. or anything and I'll bet he doesn't belong to any union either. Why can't we be like him?"

"You're right, Dickie. Maybe I just don't have what it takes to step out on my own. When I was a kid, I watched my dad lose his farm, then his store. He tried contracting and building houses with us boys helping, but he lost all that in the Depression. It's hard not to get scared."

I knew most of those things about Granddad. I never thought about how my dad felt about them. I don't think enough.

I start looking out over the ocean some more myself. It's getting to be warmer and warmer. It's going to be a good day for the beach. I hope Mom and Laurel will want to go, too. Dad starts reeling his line in fast. At first I think he's caught something, but his pole isn't bending so he's just reeling in to check his bait.

"Let's call it off for the day, Dickie. I don't think we're going to catch anything more after that stingray. He was enough to last the whole season for me, maybe my whole life."

I begin reeling in. It's only then I realize I do have a fish on my line. I'm not sure, but it's pulling and swirling back and forth that way. I won't say anything until I'm sure. Dad pulls his line in; the bait's still on each hook so the crabs didn't get it.

"One more idea. The union bosses at the meetings keep talking about the class war, about the working class and all that. Most of the people I work with aren't workers. They just do something, anything, for money, and they don't care what they do or how well they do it. They get no pride at all from doing something right. They wouldn't do a lick if somebody didn't watch them. It makes me discouraged working with them, locked in that grease-smelling brick cage of a building all day.

"I *like* to work, even in that stinking, rotten J.I., and I feel good when I've done something the way it ought to be done."

I pull in my line and there *is* a fish on it. Dad's all excited. He wiggles it off the hook. It's a kingfish, about a two-pounder.

"Hey, there, Dickie, you're quite a fisherman. We can all have a nice little fish dinner from this fellow."

Dad takes out his knife, scrapes off the scales, cuts off the head, pulls out the insides, and throws all that stuff over the side. Cut up like this, the fish doesn't look very big, but Dad hefts it in his hand and hands it to me.

"Feel that, Dickie. That pays our rental fees for the

poles and for the bait. We got a whole morning's fun fishing for nothing. That fish'd cost at least fifty cents in a market."

I hold it a minute. It feels wet and cold. Dad takes it back, wraps it in one of the sandwich wrappers, the baloney one, and slides it into his lunch box.

"Another thing, Dickie. Most of the people who get to be bosses, whether it's with the company or with the union, are people who *don't* like to work. Now they want me to be shop foreman at J.I. That's what the union people are worried about. If I quit the union it'll look as if I'm going over with the company people. To be honest, I don't think I'd even *like* being a foreman, telling other people what to do."

"You tell *me* what to do when we're working on the porches. That's a little bit like being a foreman, isn't it?"

"It's not the same, Dickie. You *like* working the same as I do. We got satisfaction out of building those porches fast and right, getting ahead of the game with our own hands. These people I'd have to boss around wouldn't be that way. They'd always be trying to duck out of work and I'd be a kind of policeman and slavedriver forcing them to do what has to be done. But we were a team, right?"

He puts his hand on my shoulder from the front not around the back of the neck the way you do with a little boy. He puts his hand on my shoulder the way a king does when he makes a regular soldier into a knight.

"Dad, I still think we could make a better living working for ourselves. We could do all kinds of things. You can fix anything. We could put papers under everybody's doors telling them about our fix-it business and put an ad in the Upper Darby newspaper. We could call it Kettleson's Fix-it Shop."

"But we'd have to have a phone then; that'd cost money."

"Sure, Mom could take all the messages and keep the

bills straight and everything. I could help you and pick up or deliver all the things that are close by. There are hundreds of things that need fixing, and people wouldn't be throwing so much stuff away in the trash. I could even go around picking through the trash early in the morning and find things for you to fix up and sell. That'd be fun."

Dad's got everything packed up. We're walking back along the pier. I'm just behind him. I'm so interested in talking about Kettleson's Fix-it Shop I'm not even afraid of the holes. The water's not as far in as it was when we first went out. I think Dad's even listening to me.

"It'd be fun all right, Dickie. I could fix up the truck to go around and fix things right in people's homes. I'd have our Kettleson's Fix-it Shop sign painted on both sides. How'd you like that?"

"That'd be terrific. We could cruise around in the truck looking for work and I'd carry your tools. I could even learn to help, little things at first."

"Yeah, but how about school? If you don't go to school you'll never amount to anything."

"Oh, come on, Dad. I hate school. I'm not learning much there. I learn more out fishing with you or fixing porches than I ever learn at school. Do you think Sister Anastasia knows about stingrays or unions or *'get-byers'*? She doesn't teach us anything except religion and civics and diagramming sentences. Those things don't mean anything to me."

"Maybe not; but you have to go to school. You could help me weekends and after school if you want."

Heck, I knew I'd have to go to school. My dad and mom have this idea that your whole life will be different if you only go to school. What'll happen is I'll probably just get to be another one of those *"get-aheaders."* They don't think about that.

PART 12

*T*UFFY wakes and rolls over on his back. It's dark and warm in the attic. He gnaws awhile on the untattooed arm he's dragged with him. He's thirsty, but not thirsty enough to go looking for water. There are probably two factors involved in his lack of mobility. One, he's lived in a cage most of his life; moving around searching for food or water is not part of his normal experience. His tendency is to wait until Cap brings him what he needs. Tuffy is probably not totally aware he isn't in a cage. Secondly, a lion's natural state when it's satiated is inertia. Tuffy has moved only twice in the two days since he killed and ate Jimmy, each time to excrete in another corner of the attic. This was at night so no one heard him or was aware of his heavy, muffled movements.

Tuffy falls asleep on his back, his legs spread, his paws cocked loosely outward. He is feeling no threat at all, perfectly comfortable in the quiet darkness.

Cap Modig has been booked and released without bail to aid in the search for and capture of the lion. At Cap's insistence, Sally was not charged but told to be available as a witness. Cap has been accused of criminal negligence for harboring a dangerous animal in an urban area.

When they get back to the Wall of Death, Cap tapes on his New Jersey license plates and mounts the headlight to make his motorcycle legal on the road; Sally starts packing, throwing her clothes into a battered brown suitcase. There is quiet in the darkened pit. Except for the necessary conversation at the police station, she has not spoken to Cap, nor he to her.

"Aw, come on, please, Sal; you aren't going to leave me now. Besides Murph says you have to stay until I'm arraigned before the judge. I'll plead guilty, then you can go."

"I'm getting out of here. I should've left a long time ago. This whole act is ruined now, anyhow, with Jimmy gone and Tuffy run off. What're you going to do, train Sammy to ride in the sidecar?"

"I wish you wouldn't go, Sal. I'll do whatever you say."

Cap pulls out one of the apple boxes, collapses onto it. He's feeling the quiet, no Tuffy in the background, grunting, padding back and forth, coughing, growling. He turns his head. The smell of Tuffy is still there but then it would be; the smell of a lion in captivity is strong and he's only been gone two days. Cap can't know that Tuffy is less than fifty yards from where he's sitting.

Cap reaches in the black box, takes out his locked metal coffer, where they keep the money. He pulls out a roll of bills, starts peeling off some of them, then stops, snaps the rubber band back around the entire roll. "Here,

Sal, take it. You're going to need money wherever you go. This will help you get started again."

Sally doesn't turn around. She has her knee on her overfilled bag, trying to get the snaps to hold; the other side bulges open. Cap goes over to help. She pushes him away with her arm, her hip.

"Go away! I don't need your help and I don't want any of your blood money either. I'll make out O.K. Good operators are hard to find and now the Depression's not so bad I can get a job. You don't have to worry about me; you never did anyhow."

"Don't say that, Sal. I love you. I've loved you from the first day you came to the hospital."

"That's what you say. How long has it been since we let that little J.P. in Elkton pretend to marry us, and what good did it do? I'll tell you, almost ten years now. Jimmy says I was just some kind of a whore to you; all you ever really loved was that damned lion. Now look what's happened and Jimmy's dead."

She starts crying. She sits down on her sprung suitcase, jams her elbows on her knees, her face in her hands. Cap gets down on his knees beside her.

"I didn't have anything against Jimmy. I knew about you two all the time, but I *loved* you, I wanted you to be happy. That's what love is, isn't it, Sal, wanting the other person to be happy?

"I know I'm too old for you, I tried to tell you that. I think somewhere along the way we got to be more like father and daughter. I don't know how it happened, it just did. But that doesn't mean I don't love you; I do; you're the only woman I'll ever love."

There's a long silence broken by sobbing. Cap, whose leg hurts where he kneels, struggles up on one knee. Sally's face is still buried in her hands and she's not looking at him.

"Listen, Sal. I know it's dumb and all and I know you really ought to just pick up and go, get out of here.

You're young, you have your whole life ahead of you. But, before you go, I want to say something. I want to say it and maybe it'll help you know Jimmy's wrong. I love you truly and always will."

There's a long pause as Cap lowers his head, his baldness shining in the bluish-gray light coming down into the black pit.

"Sally, I'd be the happiest man in the world if you'd marry me in your church before a real priest as soon as possible. I don't know what the police will want of me, if I'll have to go to prison for this or what. We still don't know what else Tuffy might do before they catch him, but I'm asking you to think about it.

"Will you marry me, Sal?"

Sally slowly lifts her face from her hands. She looks at Cap in that dim light. "No, Cap. I don't think I love you any more. You really are a fine man and you've always been good to me, but I don't want to live this kind of life. I'm all done in."

"I'm finished with it too, Sal. I'm ready to settle down. I can probably get something for the Wall and the bikes. Just this concession is worth a lot and we have three more years left on it. I can sell all this and we could take off out of here, in the truck."

Sally buries her face in her hands again but continues shaking her head back and forth sadly. Her sobs have subsided but she's crying freely now, tears running through her fingers.

"Look, Sal, I have my motorcycle fixed up for the road. I can put the sidecar on and take you to a hotel. You can stretch out there, take a bath and everything; get cleaned up, and enjoy a good rest. That's what you need. Or, if you want, I can take you over in the truck; it'd just take longer because I have to go all the way out to the garage and pick it up. What do you say? I know you don't want to stay here, but let me help you. God, I owe you at least that. I don't mean I owe you, I *want* to help you."

Cap stops. He's trying to stand now, pushing himself up painfully on his good leg. He has his cap in his left hand. He puts it on his head and stands limply, his hands at his sides.

"I don't know what to say, Sal. I only want to help. I love you and I want everything to be the best for you."

Sally speaks through her hands, through her fingers, through her crying.

"Oh, Cap, I'm so down in the dumps. I can't get anything straight in my head. I don't know what to do, where to go, what I really want."

Cap reaches out tentatively, takes her hands from her face, pulls her slowly to her feet.

"First, at least, let me help you with that suitcase."

Sally stands, hunched over, her head bent, her hair disheveled, while Cap puts his weight on the suitcase and manages to get both snaps tight. He stands it on end.

"Here, Sal, sit on this or on that box while I hook my sidecar to the motorcycle; I think that'll be the best way. Then, after I get you safe in a hotel, I can go help look for Tuffy. If I find him he'll get in the sidecar and I can take him back to the cage. If he's hiding somewhere near and he hears the motorcycle, I know he'll come out to me."

Sally continues standing, her hands clasped in front of her. She's wearing a dress, the dress she wore to the police station, her only dress now. Cap stares at her a minute, then hustles outside, pushing the sidecar with him.

"I'll be right back, you just stay there, O.K.?"

Sally nods her head slightly; Cap leaves. She settles onto her suitcase again. She picks up her handbag from where it was on the floor of the pit beside her. She opens it, takes out a compact, wipes away her tears. She runs her fingers under her eyes to even out the smear of her mascara. She pulls out a small handkerchief and blows her nose, then takes a powder puff from the compact and powders her nose and cheeks. She puts the compact away and pulls out a brush, with which she smooths her hair, brushing her blond bob to the shape of her head. Then she reaches into her purse again and pulls out a lipstick, turns it up and carefully applies the deep red to her upper lip, presses the upper lip against the lower with practiced swiftness, turns the lipstick down again, caps it, and puts it into her purse. She continues to hold her compact in her other hand, checks her hair again and wipes once more the moist mascara under her eyes. She's still crying.

Cap comes to the door of the pit, she stands, he moves and picks up her bag.

"O.K., Sal? I'll take you over to the Brighton, where you'll be safe and comfortable."

He starts to turn, not sure if she's coming. He doesn't seem to notice that she's freshened up. Cap is worried, so anxious for Sally and for Tuffy he isn't noticing much of anything. His hands are slightly greasy from attaching the sidecar to the motorcycle. Sally follows him.

Cap helps Sally into the sidecar and puts the suitcase across her lap.

"It won't be a long trip and that suitcase will help break the wind. I'm sure there will be a room this time of year. It's the only place I could think of that'd still be open off-season like this."

Sally looks at Cap as he concentrates on setting the magneto, priming the choke, getting the bike in neutral, and kicking over the engine. He looks at her before he engages gears, and she gives him a quick wisp of a smile.

"Cap, I really do love you, but I'm all mixed up inside. Just give me some time to get over this, please."

Cap looks at Sally then turns gently, slowly off onto the boardwalk as if he's transporting an invalid, a case of eggs, rather than the woman who has, herself, driven this motorcycle on a wall with a four-hundred-pound lion in it beside her.

* * *

After Cap has left Sally at the hotel, promising he'll come back to tell her what's happening every day, he takes off for the police station. One condition of his release is that he's to check in there every two hours. This is fine with Cap; it's his only way of finding out if anybody's spotted Tuffy anywhere and to keep up with what's being done in terms of a search party. He doesn't want anybody to get hurt and also he doesn't want anything happening to Tuffy. He parks his bike outside and goes inside. Murph is at the sergeant's desk. He's on the phone. He motions Cap to sit down on one wooden bench across from him.

"That's right, sir. We've got everybody out looking for the lion: our local police, the state Guard and fifty members of the CCC who were working at the recreation park.

"Yes sir. We're doing everything we can. We're hoping to have that lion behind bars again by the end of the day.

"Yes sir."

Murph hangs up, looking at the phone, unhappily, as he lowers it onto the hook. He glances over at Cap. Cap gets up and comes to Murph's desk. Murph lights a cigarette.

"That was the commissioner. He's really up a creek. He wants us to shoot Tuffy on sight, not take any chances. If you want to save that lion, Cap, you'd better find him yourself. There are an awful lot of scared-to-death, trigger-happy cowboys out there, with guns, who want to be the local hero who kills a real man-eating lion."

Cap looks down at the floor, then up at Murph. "I'd like to say he wouldn't hurt anybody. I've known that lion well as I know you, Murph, but after what's happened, I can understand if nobody believes me. God, I feel awful about all this. I just never expected it. Jimmy must really have done something terrible for Tuffy to do a thing like that."

Murph looks at Cap through the smoke of his cigarette.

"I'll tell you, Cap, if it'd been anybody else got killed we'd've probably booked you for involuntary manslaughter and you wouldn't be walking the streets. That guy wasn't even worth being called human far as I'm concerned."

"Oh, Jimmy was O.K. He was only a mixed-up, scared kid. I don't think he was much more than twenty-six or twenty-seven. He might've straightened out."

"My guess is he might've straightened out behind bars somewhere; straightened up into a hardened criminal."

Murph pulls over some papers and goes through them. "You're sure you don't even know his last name? How can you live with somebody for ten years and not even know their last name?"

"I told you. He just never talked. I know he comes from Texas somewhere and that's all. I don't even know if Jimmy's his real name."

"Well, identification's going to be a big problem. We got two fingers from that pile of meat we brought in. There wasn't enough left of his face to even do a proper mug shot at the morgue, nothing we could hang on a post-office wall, anyway. If it were up to me, and we can just get Tuffy back safe in a cage again, I'd as soon forget the whole damned thing.

"The little bastard just didn't exist far as I'm concerned. Filling up Tuffy's stomach is probably the best thing he ever did in his life."

Cap's uncomfortable. He knows Murph's trying to make him feel better, make him feel less guilty, but he feels even more guilty talking about Jimmy. "Has anything come in at all, Murph? Has anybody heard or seen anything?"

"Just the usual crap, same people who are always seeing burglars or having people peeping in their windows. We have a regular file on them. About half of them have already called in, hearing snarling sounds in the night or roaring in the distance, shadows in the next-door garden. One daffy old dame on E Street is even convinced her dog was bitten by the lion. I tried explaining to her how if that lion had taken a bite of her dog, he'd have eaten the whole animal. Some flea probably bit it."

"Still, Murph, if Tuffy does attack anything it could be a dog. Normally, lions stay away from humans. I'll never know why he went for Jimmy. Jimmy would always give him an extra poke with the goad, things like that, because he was afraid of Tuffy, hated him, probably because he was afraid; but I still can't understand Tuffy killing him and actually eating him like that."

"Don't worry about it, Cap. You just go out and get that lion locked up and we'll hope for the best."

"I have the motorcycle with the sidecar he's always driven in. If he hears that motorcycle and is in hiding I know he'll come out. And that way I can put him right in the sidecar and carry him home with no trouble."

"Well, you'd better get out there and start cruising. I sure hope you're the first to find him and also that none of those trigger-happy morons out there start shooting at each other the way they do during hunting season up in Pennsylvania. I'm staying here partly to be on the phone and take any messages but mostly to stay out of the way of those private safari hunting posses. I don't think I'm as afraid of Tuffy as I am of those guys."

"O.K., Murph, and thanks a lot. I'll keep checking back just in case there's a sighting of some kind. I can't imagine where Tuffy would go, but it can't be too far. A lion, after he's eaten like that, doesn't usually go running around much. He's probably sleeping it off somewhere like a drunk."

Cap starts toward the door.

"Don't know how to thank you, Murph. If Tuffy's got any chance at all it's because of you."

"Come on, Cap, get out here. Go get that big cat of yours and put him in a cage where he belongs."

Cap goes out the door, jumps on his motorcycle, kicks it into life. He says to himself:

"That's the trouble. Behind bars, in a cage, is just where he *doesn't* belong."

Cap first goes along as close as he can stay to the board-walk all the way into South Wildwood. He leaves his engine running as he looks under the boardwalk, through the marsh grass which grows high here where the board-walk ends and sand piles in drifts against the boards. He goes along whistling his usual signal for Tuffy and calling his name. There's no one else around; this is a deserted part of the city. But no Tuffy.

Cap mounts again and cruises inland to where there are salt marshes. He looks under each of the small bridges passing over the salt-water runoffs to the sea. These marshes fill and empty with the tides. Twice he sees groups of men with rifles, searching. He manages to avoid contact with them. If they see anything of Tuffy they'll phone in to Murph at police headquarters or they'd've blown Tuffy to kingdom come.

Every two hours throughout that day and through most of the night, Cap checks back at headquarters but there's nothing. Murph's replacement at the sergeant's desk isn't sympathetic and makes it clear he thinks the whole business is Cap's fault. There've been more call-ins about sightings but each proved to be nothing when checked out.

Finally, at about three in the morning, Cap drives back to the pit. He needs sleep. He'll wake at dawn and start hunting again. From what he's read, lions tend to hunt at first light and at twilight, but he isn't sure. They might also hunt in the night but he can't go any longer. He needs sleep desperately. He falls asleep spread-eagled on the floor of the pit.

Just as Cap's falling asleep, Tuffy rouses himself. He uses his strong side teeth to rip off some of the last meat from Jimmy's arm. He still isn't particularly hungry. He moves softly across the rafters and out onto the catwalk.

He walks slowly down the stairs and jumps lightly into his cage. The door is still open. He sits in the cage for several minutes, then paces slowly back and forth.

Then he jumps lightly down from the cage and goes up the wide stairs to the platform of Sammy's pool. Sammy's asleep in his apartment, the door locked and barred. He doesn't hear anything as Tuffy leans far over and laps up water from his pool for the five to ten minutes it takes a large cat to drink. After he drinks, Tuffy, who can smell Cap inside the pit, rubs against the door, but doesn't grunt, growl, or roar.

He pads softly up the stairs to the catwalk and across the rafters to his lair. He circles twice then settles back to sleep.

PART 13

WE ate that fish I caught for lunch. There was more than I thought there would be and it was delicious. Mom cooked it up in a little pot with some milk and butter. We dipped bread into the juice and that was delicious, too.

It was a good feeling to know I'd caught food for our lunch. Dad gave a description of me catching that fish so it sounded as if I was the one catching the stingray, too. While he was telling it, he winked at me again. I'll *never* get used to my father winking.

I saved some little parts without any bone and gave them to Cannibal. She really liked it and for the first time meowed to get some more. It's the only sound she's made except for growling and that one try at a purr under the bed. I forgot; she also hisses like a snake when she growls.

Mom isn't too happy about the idea of going to the beach. She's still afraid of the lion. Dad puts his arm around her shoulder and kisses the side of her neck so she bends her head away as if she's being tickled. Dad hasn't shaved since we left Stonehurst Hills, so in some ways he looks like one of the bums hanging around down at the dump, and in other ways he looks tough. I guess that's why Mom ducked away; those bristles can be like sand-paper.

One of the favorite things my grandfather likes to do is rub his bristles against my cheek when I give him a kiss. He only shaves once a week, for church, on Sundays. Most days we go visit him it's Sunday so I'm safe, but any other day I get "the rub" and it really hurts. He doesn't do it to Laurel, only to boys. I have five boy first cousins about my age, two Billys, Georgie, Johnny, and Albert. We all hate getting the rub. Afterward your face stings and is red a few minutes. At the same time, there's something nice about it, because Granddad likes to do it so much and is laughing and giving you a kiss.

"Listen, Laura, I'm telling you, that lion's got to be miles from here by now. And once we get to the beach we can always run out into the ocean. No lion is going to chase us into the water; cats hate water."

"You know I can't swim, Dick. I think I'd rather be eaten by a lion than drowned, anyway."

"You won't drown, I'll carry you. Don't worry about it, honey. We're lucky to have this warm weather so late in the season; let's take advantage of it. Who knows when I'll have another vacation."

Mom smiles at Dad, runs her hands up and down over his bristles, kisses him lightly on his lips. "O.K., it'll be worth it just to have you carry me into the ocean. You haven't carried me since you carried me across the threshold when we got married. Remember going in that half of a row house we rented on Dewey Street with your brother Ed and Emma?"

"You want to be carried, huh? O.K., here we go."

And right there in front of our eyes, in that little room, before any of us even know what's happening, he's scooped up Mom in his arms and is walking around the room with her and then sort of dancing, the way they dance in the movies with black suits and white shirts on, only they don't *carry* the lady when they dance in the movies.

Mom's scared at first then starts laughing and holding her arms around Dad's neck.

"Put me down, you goof. What'll the kids think? Put me down before you strain yourself."

Dad keeps dancing round in circles between the beds. He's never acted crazy like this before. He and Mom have always just been ordinary people, doing the things they have to do, like work and wash and clean up and fix things. There's been more kissing and stuff going on down here in Wildwood than there ever was in Stonehurst Hills. I look over at Laurel and she's laughing. It *is* funny and I know right then I like to see them being silly. It makes life look like so much fun. Up till now I've always been a little bit afraid about growing up, being a grownup.

"So you want to be put down? O.K., here we go."

With that, Dad goes next to their bed and drops Mom right in the center of the bed; her skirt comes up her leg and she reaches to pull it down.

"Dick, I think you've gone crazy. What in heaven's name's gotten into you, anyway?"

"Maybe I'm an escaped lion."

Dad leans down over Mom and goes "Grrrr!!" He holds his paws up the way Cannibal does when she's fighting anything. Mom laughs and pushes him away. Dad takes her by the hands and pulls her up from the bed.

"O.K., everybody who isn't afraid of an old lion, let's get dressed and go to the beach. That sun out there is just waiting for us."

So we all get dressed in a jim-dandy hurry, and we're down on the beach in about fifteen minutes. The sky is blue and the sun is hot. Laurel and I get another swimming lesson, and Dad teaches me how to hold my breath and open my eyes under water. At first I think my eyes are going to hurt having water against them, like it does when you wash your face sometimes, but there's no soap in the ocean and I don't feel anything. It's like looking through a magnifying glass. My hands look at least twice as big as they really are; also I can see shells and things at the bottom of the water. At first I can only go a little ways and I get scared, but after a while I can go for almost a minute, swimming along, looking down at the bottom of the ocean. I even see some little crabs walking around down there. I get to thinking what it'd be like if I saw a big fish like a shark or a stingray. So, I decide to come out. Dad's got Laurel so she can float and strike out with a few strokes of her own.

"You all tuckered out, there, Dickie?"

"No, I'm cold so I'm going to rest for a while."

That's not a lie. I *am* cold and a little bit tired.

"Look at Laurie here, she's practically swimming all by herself."

I stand by the edge of the water with my arms wrapped across my chest, shivering, and watch as Laurel swims at least five strokes before she puts her feet down. She holds her head way out of the water and Mom has her hair in straight-up pigtails so it won't get wet.

"Hey, that's good, Laurel. Soon we can go out swimming together."

I run up the beach to Mom. She has Cannibal out of her box and she's on her lap upside down. I guess Mom's gotten over being afraid of fleas. She has one of Laurel's hair ribbons and is dangling it in front of Cannibal's face, and Cannibal's trying to catch it with her paws. But she isn't really trying because she keeps her claws in and I've never seen her stretched out on her back like that except the day when the lion licked her. I try to put that lion out of my mind, but I can't help looking up and down the beach. I take the towel from beside Mom to dry myself.

"You're all goose bumps, Dickie. Be sure to dry yourself really dry, then stretch out beside me and let the sun warm you up."

She keeps playing with Cannibal, calling her "you little devil" when Cannibal manages to catch the ribbon. I spread out the towel beside her and think about Cannibal being a devil or having a devil in her. I wonder if Father Lanshee would exercise a devil out of her if I ask. I don't think so. Besides I like the devil in Cannibal. I think I'm even beginning to like the devil inside me, if there is one.

Cannibal turns herself over onto her feet and drops off Mom's lap, tumbling into the sand right near my face. She comes toward me sideways, the way she does when she's sneaking up on something. With my head down on the sand she looks big. I try staring her in the eyes. She stares right back at mine and slows down, then stops when she's about six inches from my face. I wonder if I should shut my eyes; she really could scratch an eye out if she wanted to. I keep looking at her. She's certainly a beautiful cat. She's getting darker brown all the time, and the marks around her eyes are almost pure black now, so she looks even more as if she's wearing a mask, like a bandit. Her eyes in the bright sun are just the thin slits up and down so it almost looks as if she can't see at all, especially with the sun behind me.

Then she ducks her head, comes close to me, and pushes her face against mine, especially against my nose, then against my ear, and she's definitely purring. She turns herself to one side and then the other, rubbing against me. I bring up my hand and rub her under the chin, and she purrs even louder. Then she goes around in a circle and settles with her face and her whole body right against my neck, still purring, as if she's purred all her life.

"My goodness, Dickie, that cat really loves you. I can see why you wanted her so much. She's the nicest, craziest cat I ever saw."

Just then Dad and Laurel come running up the beach. Dad drops onto his knees beside me, between me and Mom and right near Cannibal. Cannibal jumps a little but then cuddles closer into my neck.

"Hey, everybody, look what I found. Are we ever going to have fun with this!"

Dad holds out an old tennis ball with the fuzz practically worn off.

I'm afraid he's going to want to play catch. Dad keeps trying to teach me how to play baseball but there's something wrong with me. I'm never going to catch a ball right, especially a hard ball, not well enough to get on any baseball team anyway. It's one of those things I can't do. I like listening to baseball games on the radio but I'm probably the worst baseball player my age on Clover Lane. I'm always the last one chosen to play, if I even get chosen at all. Mostly, I'm afraid of the ball.

But I get up and hand Cannibal to Mom. She can play with her or put her in her little cage. Laurel is jumping up and down the way she does when she's excited, with her arms up and flopping at the wrists. She's been doing that as long as I can remember, even from before she could walk. She'd sit on the floor, laugh and smile and flap those wrists. It's sort of like the way a puppy wags its tail.

Dad turns around and heads down to the edge of the water, maybe ten feet from where the water comes up. I try to act as if I *want* to play ball. I keep expecting him to toss it to me. I'm afraid of being hit in the face by a ball even though it's only a little light tennis ball. I don't know what Laurel's so excited about; she still can't catch a ball unless I bounce it to her, and on a beach you can't bounce a beat-up old tennis ball like this.

Dad gets down on his hands and knees and starts digging in the sand. At first I think he's going to make some kind of a base and we'll be throwing the ball and running back and forth. He looks over at me.

"Give me a hand with this, Dickie. First we have to build up a regular mountain of sand, high as we can get it, and pack the sand tight as we go."

Dad's scooping big handfuls and piling them up, packing them down.

"What're we making, Dad, another sand castle?"

"Something even better than that, you'll see. This'll be something you've never even seen before."

After we've piled up a regular pyramid of sand, Dad pushes the ball onto the top of the hill, then slowly circles it around the hill, rolling the ball and at the same time pushing down and packing a path about halfway around the hill.

Laurel's jumping up and down. Dad rolls the ball from the top, along his path to where he stopped.

"Now look, Dickie. We're going to make a tunnel through our mountain from right here."

He gouges out a little hole where he finished with his ball path. He runs around to my side of the mountain. He looks over to where he made his gouge and measures with his eye.

"To over here."

He makes another gouge on that side, but down lower.

"Now you dig very carefully through the mountain from here, making it go uphill a little bit, and we'll try to meet in the middle."

I nod my head.

"Boy, this is going to be neat, Dad."

"Laurel, I want you to dig a small tunnel right near our mountain here on the ocean side. Dig carefully so everything won't cave in."

Beside our mountain and downhill from it, he scoops up sand and builds a smaller hill. He starts two small scoops so she'll know where to dig. Then he starts digging on his side of the big hill and I begin pulling out sand from my side.

"This is going to take some engineering, Dickie. Keep in mind just how high my hole is compared to yours and see if we can make a straight tunnel between us. We've got to be careful we don't dig at a wrong angle and miss each other completely."

I'm pulling sand out. I'm already in past my elbow when I feel something moving in there and it scares me at first until I realize it's Dad's fingers. He's smiling at me over the top, around the mountain, and he grabs hold of one of my fingers inside the hill.

"We got it just right there, Buster. You'll make a great engineer someday. Now let me clear out some sand so the tunnel's big enough."

He looks over at Laurel. "How's it coming down there?"

Laurel's on her stomach pulling sand out of her tunnel; she's in deeper than her elbow but she hasn't started the other side.

"That's enough on that side, honey."

He gets down on his knees and starts the second hole for Laurel.

She comes around and kneels beside him.

"Gee, Daddy, I want to work on the *big* mountain, this is only a little hill and isn't so much fun."

Dad pulls her to him and gives her a soft hug. For one minute there I'm almost afraid he's going to give her a "rub," but he just kisses her on the forehead.

"It's all part of the same thing, Laurel. Your tunnel is just as important as any part of this whole project.

"Watch."

He takes our ball and puts it in the little dent and gives it a push. It starts down his path and goes round then into the tunnel and out my side. I run to catch it before it gets wet.

"Gee, that's neat, Dad. Do it again."

The next time I wait at my end of the tunnel and catch it as it comes out.

"O.K., now for the hard part."

Dad starts making another path, or ramp, building up high sides on the outside. He goes almost halfway around our mountain of sand again. He keeps checking to see the angles, goes along, then, when he's just on the other side of the mountain from Laurel's tunnel, he stops and digs a few handfuls out of the hill. He runs around to the other side.

"Now, Dickie, you hold your hand up just over from where that hole goes in."

I line my hand up with the hole and Dad checks, then drops down, digging his hole near the bottom of the hill. Laurel runs up to him.

"Daddy, I got through. I came through to my other hole. I have a real tunnel, come look."

Dad goes over to Laurel's tunnel. He pulls out a few handfuls of sand and rolls the ball into her tunnel and it gets stuck inside. He pulls the ball out, then scoops out more sand. On the downhill side, near the ocean, he starts cutting a path in the sand with his hands.

"Now, Laurel, cut a path deep enough so when the ball rolls into your tunnel it can come out on this side and roll down the beach."

Laurel begins digging sand out of the trench. We're close enough to the water so that each mark of each finger shows like a claw mark. Dad looks up at Mom and waves his arms. She waves back. I wave, too. Dad looks quickly up and down the whole empty beach and along the boardwalk. I know what he's doing, watching out for that lion.

"O.K., Dickie. This time you dig from the high side there and I'll dig up from the low side. Dig at just about the same angle down as you dug *up* last time, and we'll try to keep in line."

I dig until I'm dug all the way up to the top of my arm. The only way I can get my arm in any farther is to tilt myself and lift one leg up in the air. I look over and Dad's got his long arm all the way in as deep as he can go, too, with *his* leg up in the air. He pulls out and slides sand out of the hole. He smiles at me.

"Maybe we bit off more than we can chew here, Dickie. Let me take another try at this."

He comes over to my side and puts his arm in the hole. He digs out until he's run out of arm again.

"Well, either we've missed each other entirely, up and down or sidewise, maybe both; or this tunnel is longer than twice the length of my arm."

I watch his eyes: they look up and down the beach again once more, scanning the boardwalk. Laurel runs between us.

"Watch, Daddy. It works. Look."

Laurel gives the ball a push into her tunnel, it goes down then comes up with just barely enough speed to start in her track and go along almost down to the water.

"That's great, Laurel. Dickie, I want you to look for a stick at least a foot long. I'll work with Laurel. Don't go too far. Stay right near the edge of the water. That's where you'll have the best chance to find a stick washed up."

I start running along the beach. I know Dad wants me to stay close to the water because of that lion. I only go about twenty steps when I find a stick. It's all smoothed by the water and at least three feet long. If we wanted to play stickball, it'd make a good bat. I run back. Our hill doesn't look so big against all the whole beach and the ocean.

"Look what I've got, Dad."

"That's great. Look at what Laurel and I have rigged."

Dad rolls the ball with hardly any push from the inside

of his hole in the mountain. The ball rolls perfectly, turns a curve, goes down into Laurel's tunnel then up out the other side and down to a hole Dad's dug at the end of her trench. It's like watching a model train.

"Gee, that's great!"

"Now if we can only get our main tunnel through, we'll have it just right."

Dad takes the stick and pushes it in the top hole, wiggling it around, twisting it from my side. Then he goes around to his side and starts doing the same thing.

"Dickie, you put your arm in at the top and feel for the stick."

"I feel it! Dad, we've made it. The tunnel is all the way through."

"O.K., now we get the sand out."

Dad works fast now, pulling sand with his stick and then smoothing the tunnel and making everything even along the ramp to Laurel's tunnel. Dad stands up, brushes the sand off his bathing suit.

"O.K., Dickie, go up and get Mom. We're going to have the first demonstration of our sand ramp."

I run up for Mom. She looks scared as I come up.

"Mom, Dad wants you to come down and see what we've built. It's really terrific. Dad should be an engineer or an architect or something."

When we get down there, Dad lifts Laurel up and shows her how to put our ball in the little dent on top and give it a slight push.

That ball starts out on the first path going around the mountain; then it ducks into our first tunnel and, after what seems a long time, comes out the downhill side and turns slowly around the side of our mountain and rolls into our big tunnel. I'm about to think it's stuck in there when it comes out again, gets in Laurel's runway, down the hill into her tunnel, up the other side, then on down to the end, like a ball going into a hole in one of those miniature golf courses.

Mom applauds and laughs. Laurel and I are jumping up and down. Dad runs to get the ball.

"O.K., Laura, now it's your turn."

Mom puts the ball on top and gives it a light tap. It rolls slowly and swings around going into the first tunnel but keeps going all the way through everything down to the final hole.

Mom goes back up and brings her towel. She also brings Cannibal in her box down to watch. We run the ball through, over and over. We even make little detours for the ball to go on so it can go through different tunnels and come out different ways.

By now it's beginning to get chilly. Mom's put Laurel's sunsuit on her and then her sweater on top of that. She makes me put a shirt on over my bathing suit. Dad doesn't seem to get cold, and Mom must know because she doesn't ask him to put on a sweater. Dad looks at Cannibal in her box.

"Hey, before the ocean comes and wrecks this ball ramp, let's give Cannibal a turn at it."

I look in her box and she isn't asleep. I let her out wondering what Dad's going to do.

"First, we'll get her interested in the ball."

Dad gets down beside Cannibal and rolls the ball back and forth in front of her. Cannibal tries to attack it. Dad keeps pulling it just out of Cannibal's reach. He's almost mean the way he never gives her a chance.

Then, when Cannibal's really getting mad, he puts his hands under her stomach and lifts her up. She bites at his finger but, as usual, he doesn't notice. He puts her right on top of that sand mountain with the ball in front of her face. He lets the ball go and it rolls slowly down the path. Cannibal goes after it, almost knocking it off before it goes into the tunnel. Cannibal dashes into the tunnel after the ball and comes out as it starts through the long tunnel. She hesitates a moment then goes bravely into that long tunnel under the sand.

I'm scared the whole hill might fall in and smother her, but then the ball comes out again with Cannibal just behind it, pushing along the path with her paws, trying to catch up. The ball rolls down into Laurel's tunnel and Cannibal follows. As it rolls slowly along the last part, Cannibal is striking and jumping at it until it gets to the final hole. Then when it's down in there Cannibal keeps reaching in trying to fish it out, but the hole's too deep. Dad reaches under and lifts Cannibal up to his face.

"You're a brave little devil, all right. I tell you, Laura, we'll never have any trouble with rats or mice at our place again. This here's a champion mouser, even now when she isn't much bigger than a mouse herself."

Mom's worried about it getting cold, so we pack up and go home to our room.

Back there, we get out of our swimming suits, and after we've all showered we hang them up to dry. Even Mom showers this time although she wasn't in the water and was hardly in the sand even. She comes up from the shower all wrapped in towels. She has a towel wrapped around her head. She climbs into bed without getting dressed. Dad's already in bed.

"You kids must be tired so we want you to take a nap. Your father says we can go out on the boardwalk this evening if you two take a good nap. You especially, Dickie, after getting up so early these last couple of mornings. We're going to nap, too. But if either of you gets up or doesn't go to sleep then we don't go out and take any rides or buy any salt-water taffy or anything. Do you understand?"

We both say we understand and I put on my pajamas and climb into bed. Laurel's already in her nightgown because she took her shower with Mom and came back with it on.

I lie there and try going to sleep. I want to. I have Cannibal in her box beside my bed and the top is closed so she can't get out, but she must be tired, too, after all the playing with Mom and then chasing that ball through the tunnels. I try to remember the whole thing, building it and Dad catching my finger in the first tunnel and the long tunnel and the ball going all the way through and then down to the hole. I can see in my mind Cannibal running around the side of the mountain with the sand sliding and that ball keeping just ahead of her and her going through the tunnels. It's something I'll never forget. It's almost more important than catching that sting-ray this morning. But I can't get to sleep.

I lie there and try praying. Saying Hail Marys over and over again can usually help me go to sleep but it doesn't work this time. Also, I can hear that Mom and Dad aren't sleeping either. They're whispering to each other and Mom makes noises like she's being tickled again. I keep my eyes closed but it sounds as if they're wrestling in bed and then both of them start making noises as if they've just finished running a race. I'm a little bit worried and I'm about ready to open my eyes and look up when it all gets quiet.

I try breathing as if I'm really asleep. I try not thinking about the lion. I hope he's all right and that nobody shoots him. I know he killed the motorcycle driver but that's the one who stuck him with the sharp stick, so maybe he was mad at him.

He seemed like such a nice lion when he pushed against my hand. I try to keep out of my mind the part about the lock. When I think about that part, my heart just beats so hard I think I'm going to cry. Then I hear Dad talking. He's whispering, but the room is so quiet I can hear what he's saying. I can hear Laurel breathing and can tell she's really asleep.

"Laura, honey, you'll never guess what Dickie was talking to me about when we were out fishing on the pier."

Mom doesn't answer, and Dad goes on; it's almost as if

he's talking to himself. I wonder if I should stick my
fingers in my ears. I always hate it when somebody talks
about something I said or something I did. I even hate it
when Mom tells Mrs. Reynolds when I got good grades
on a report card or when I was made altar boy so young,
even though Mrs. Reynolds is a Protestant and probably
doesn't even care.

But I lie there still.

"He wants me to quit J.I., the union and everything;
set up my own repair shop for electrical appliances and
things like that. He called it the Kettleson Fix-it Shop.
He's sure a smart little guy. I tried to explain about my
seniority and security and all that and we had some good
conversation. It's nice having him grow up so we can
talk."

They're quiet and I'm hoping they won't say any more.
I feel as if I'm hearing things I'm not supposed to hear.
Then, I can just make out Mom's voice:

"Dick, is that what you'd really like?"

"What?"

"To have your own repair shop the way Dickie said."

"Now don't *you* start being ridiculous. You know we
can't take a chance like that. We're lucky we got through
the Depression as well as we did."

"I'm serious, Dick. You've got the rent paid off for a
year. You know you can always go back to nights waxing
floors if we get stuck. Roy Kerlin will always take you
back. Or maybe you can do it part time."

"Yeah, but they're paying me forty dollars at J.I. now,
that's a dollar an hour. I don't think I could ever beat
that."

"But if you're unhappy and always getting beaten up
and now with that letter about the kids, I'd just as soon
we went out on our own. We should *try* at least."

There's a long quiet. I'm holding my breath. But then I
think I should be breathing if I'm asleep so I start to

breathe deeply as if I'm really asleep, but I don't think they're paying much attention.

"Fabrizio says the company is thinking of making me shop foreman. That means I'll get at least *fifty* dollars a week; think of that. I don't know how I can let a chance like that go by."

"That's wonderful, dear, but how about the union and the terrible men the company pays to beat you up? You don't need J.I. *or* the union. You're the kind of man who should work for himself. You know darned well they're making a lot of money off you."

"Dickie said almost the same thing. You're sure about this, Laura? You're not just scared or anything?"

"Sure, I'm sure. I'm scared, too, but I think you can do it. You could always build porches again with Dickie, too. There's always that. You'll probably have to work even harder than you do now, so it's up to you."

"If it's just up to me, Laura, I quit right now. They can have their lousy seniority and shop stewardship, the shop foreman job, the whole works. I'd rather be my own boss any day. Besides, I like fixing things up. There's a really good feeling about taking something that isn't working because some little part is broken or burnt out or worn and putting it in and having the whole thing work again. It's the kind of work I really like to do. It isn't even work for me, it's like playing."

"I know. It's one of the things I love about you. You really respect things and people; you have a very special feeling."

They're quiet again. I'm afraid I'm going to cry and ruin everything. I don't know why I'm about to cry because it isn't sad; it's just I'm getting that dry feeling in my throat that always comes when I'm trying not to cry.

"I must admit I've been thinking about it ever since Dickie brought it up. I could cut a door between the cellar and the garage; that wall's just two-by-four thick, with chicken wire and plaster over it. If we ever leave the house, I could put it back so nobody'd ever notice. Then I could have my electrical-repair part in the cellar and my carpentry and that kind of thing in the garage. I could cut a small door in the garage door so people could bring their stuff in. I'm sure Mr. Marsden wouldn't mind. He knows I can put it back without any trouble."

"And you could make a little counter and shelves behind on the back wall to store things people bring in to be fixed. We could have one section for the things coming in and another for the stuff you've already fixed. The important part is getting things fixed fast because that's why people would bring it to you instead of going back to Sears or wherever they bought it where they take weeks and weeks to fix anything."

"And you could take care of the records, Laur. We'd need to keep a record of how much time I put in on each repair and when I have to buy parts, what they cost. Then you'd make out a bill and collect from people. I'd rig a little bell so when somebody comes in it'd ring in the house and you could come down. I think it's best if I keep working most of the time instead of gabbing with people. I'm not very good at that part anyway, and I'd probably forget to charge people or do dumb things."

"You wouldn't do anything dumb, but that's a part I *can* do from my experience selling at Penney's before we were married. I like it; it'll make life more interesting, too."

I listen and I can't believe it. It's like a dream coming true.

"I can also go out and do repairs at people's houses, electrical work and a little plumbing, putting in new washers on spigots, things like that. I'll make a sign for the truck. We'll call it 'Kettleson's Snappy Service. No repair too large or too small.' How's that sound?"

"It sounds wonderful, dear, and just think, you'll be home most of the time and we can have so much fun together. That's worth almost everything else."

Then they're quiet again, more or less, at least they don't talk any more and I keep breathing, pretending I'm asleep, until I guess I really do go to sleep because I don't remember anything else.

PART 14

A MAN is standing under a desk lamp in the darkened back of a curio shop. It's the shop next to the Wall of Death. The man is Chinese, middle-aged. He wears Chinese costume; black, with toggle fastenings. He wears a small black silk mandarin cap on his head; his hair is in a long queue.

It could be his age, a desire to maintain the traditions of his country, or perhaps only that the costume lends authenticity, interest, to his shop.

This shop is more than an ordinary souvenir and curio place; it also sells small carved ivory figures, silks, and oriental rugs. At the request of the police, he has stayed closed for the past three days. His shutters are drawn now as twilight descends on the virtually abandoned boardwalk outside.

The room is stuffy from being closed tight during these unseasonably warm days, and he's pushed open the trap door to his attic. It's up there where he keeps his reserves of merchandise, it's also where Tuffy has his lair.

The man stands erect behind an old-fashioned accountant's or clerk's desk. A small lamp is perched on an upper edge and a ledger is spread before him.

He works with a bamboo brush, held vertically, as he carefully checks his records. He's making his final season inventory and preparing order lists for the next year. His intention is to leave on the weekend and go stay with his family in Philadelphia's Chinatown, where he lives most of the year.

Upstairs, Tuffy has been disturbed from his sleep by the opening of the trap door. He gnaws some more at Jimmy's humerus. He's hungry again and confused. He still hasn't completely absorbed the concept of hunting as a way to get food. For the entire life he's known, he's never hunted and Cap has always brought him what he needed.

Tuffy stands and arches his back, yawns, stretches each foot in turn, spreading his toes, baring his claws. He balances carefully as he walks across the attic beams to the source of light from below. The door is propped open with a stick, which Tuffy carefully avoids.

He silently pads down the steep steps, placing one foot tentatively in front of the other; the angle is steep, almost that of a ladder, and difficult for him to manage. He reaches the floor of the curio shop, halfway between the front door and the back wall, back where the man is working. Tuffy is feeling only vaguely hungry, mostly restless, curious. He pads slowly up and down the narrow aisles, between the cloth-shrouded tables holding small articles for sale.

The man thinks he hears something and lifts his head, looks around; Tuffy instinctively freezes, holds still, until the man goes back to work. Tuffy isn't exactly stalking,

but, catlike, he wants to discover before he's discovered.
He moves slowly, quietly, stealthily toward the light,
changing aisles so he comes up behind the man.

He goes to within two yards of him and sits back on his
haunches, runs his tongue lazily across his mouth, lifts
one paw, rubs his face, straightens his whiskers. If it
weren't for the man's age, he would hear Tuffy and surely
smell him. A lion has a strong odor, not of dirt but of
animality, sweat, the general odor of a carnivore.

Tuffy advances cautiously until he's beside the man.
He gently rubs his face against the man's leg, Tuffy's way
of expressing, demanding affection. He's lonesome, and
for all his life man has been his only source of company.
Tuffy, as with all lions, is primarily a social animal.

The Chinese jumps. If it had been a pussy cat or a
child coming up behind him and rubbing against him
without warning, he'd have jumped. He looks down and
sees Tuffy, a lion, a man-eating lion. He stands petrified.
He slowly puts down his brush and feels himself becoming faint. He holds on to the sides of his high desk.

Tuffy pushes harder against the man's thin thigh, rubbing his face, his ears, his mane, his whole head against
him, rubbing so hard he almost knocks this small frail
man to the floor. Now Tuffy sits down. He looks up into
the man's eyes, looking for some return of affection, some
recognition. But Tuffy can smell the fear from the man.
It's a smell he knows; it's the smell from Jimmy, sometimes from Sally.

Slowly the man moves around to the other side of his
desk. Tuffy sits there watching. Perhaps the man will
bring him food, take him to Cap. The man backs down
the aisle toward the front door. Tuffy follows him slowly,
between a stalk and a stroll. Mostly he's only following,
waiting to see what happens next.

The man fumbles with the latch, the locking bar on the
door, the swinging shutter. Tuffy watches. Then the man
pushes the door open and starts running away along the

boardwalk away from the Wall of Death. He's running for help, running for his life.

Tuffy steps out the door. It's a lovely evening. He stands there a moment and then turns toward the Wall of Death. He sees his cage and tries to get inside, but the door is closed. He paces back and forth between the Wall of Death and his cage several times. Where's Cap?

He stands there, first grunts, coughs, then growls. He expands his chest and gives the loud proud roar of a lion searching for his pride, a lion letting other lions in his pride know where he is or defending his territory. This roar can be heard a mile away. The few people on the boardwalk hear it and turn. There is a scampering left and right as people dash to escape.

Tuffy sees something large and colorful turning off to his left. It's the merry-go-round. He starts padding toward it. It's going around in circles the way motorcycles he knows so well go around inside the Wall of Death; perhaps Cap will be there.

Dick and Laura Kettleson are sitting on a bench next to the railing separating the boardwalk from the beach. They're about twenty yards from the merry-go-round on which Dickie and Laurel are enjoying a ride. Cannibal is in her box beside them on the bench. Again, the two children are about the only ones on the merry-go-round. They have outside animals going up and down on brass rails. Every time they come around, they wave and Laura waves back at them. Dick is too involved talking to Laura about plans for his Snappy Service Fix-it Shop. Both of them are involved, so that, with the noise of the merry-go-round, they have not heard Tuffy's roar or noticed the sudden absence of strollers on the boardwalk.

"You know that printer up on Long Lane, Laura, I'll bet I could offer him some work in exchange for having advertisements printed up. Dickie could go around the neighborhood putting them under doors or on people's porches. We'd write out all the things we can do and the phone number so they could call or just come around in the alley to the shop. We'd have to put in a phone for sure; it'd be one of our business expenses.

"You know I never thought about it before, Laura, but there's no one around there who does that kind of work; we wouldn't have any competition at all. When we got a little bit ahead, we could start running a little ad every week in the Upper Darby *News*. That should bring in some customers and it wouldn't cost too much."

Laura waves; she still doesn't notice the quietness on the boardwalk, or the lion, who is now visible at about seventy-five yards, strolling slowly, semi-stalking the merry-go-round. Tuffy might have vague stirrings in his mind as to the appearance of these, his natural prey, giraffes, zebras, horses.

Laura waves again at Laurel. The children don't notice the lion, both because they're turning and because every time they come around to this side they look over at their mother.

"Dick, I'm sure they'll let us put a little notice up on the bulletin board at church, too. A lot of people from our parish keep an eye on these bulletin boards looking for jobs. That way we can get some of the East Lansdowne crowd, too. Those people have more money and things to break down than we do around our way."

Dick looks up to see the children; the merry-go-round has started to slow down. He sees that the boardwalk is empty. Then he looks to his left and sees the lion. Following about a hundred yards behind Tuffy is a group of police and other armed men, closing in on him. Dick is stunned. He looks at Laura and she stiffens. He takes hold of her hands.

"What is it, Dick?"

"That lion is on the boardwalk! You do just what I tell you and I'll go over to look after the kids."

He grabs Laura by both arms and lifts her out of the

bench and over the rail of the boardwalk. He hands Cannibal in her box to her.

"You hold on right there and stay perfectly still. If that lion comes near you, drop down to the sand. You won't hurt yourself. Whatever happens, don't move or make a sound!"

"But, Dick! What're you going to do?"

"I've got to keep that merry-go-round going round. So long as it's moving I think the kids are safe."

Dick turns before Laura can say anything more. He moves cautiously but quickly toward the merry-go-round. Tuffy is already there and watching the animals go past, taking swipes now and then at the leg of a horse or other animal. Dick comes to within five yards of the lion. Tuffy doesn't pay any attention. Dick sees the man who runs the merry-go-round. He's on the other side loosening the straps from a little girl, ready to lower her off her ride. The merry-go-round is slowing, almost coming to a stop.

Dick yells: "Hey, you! Get this thing going again! There's a lion over here and we'll all be safe as long as we're moving."

The man looks up, his cigarette drops from his mouth. He runs and jumps off the other end of the merry-go-round, runs out that end of the boardwalk.

Dick hops up onto the slowing merry-go-round, dashes through the wooden animals to the master control switch. He turns it on, pushes forward the lever engaging the merry-go-round to the motor. It starts going around again. He runs over to the little girl who's sitting on a camel; Dick lifts her onto one of the inside animals.

"Now, you hold on tight till I come get you!"

He dashes out to where Dickie and Laurel are only two animals apart. Tuffy has reared back on his hind legs and is taking swipes again at the animals as they speed past. Dick unbuckles Laurel from her horse, moves her to the inside of the merry-go-round, puts her on a zebra.

"You stay right here! I'll come get you in a few minutes."

He runs back to Dickie. Dickie has seen the lion and what he's doing. He's pulled his leg out of the outside stirrup and is holding on to the inside of his horse, leaning away from Tuffy.

"That's a good boy, Dickie! I think that lion is only playing, but he might hurt you by mistake."

Dick lifts him off and moves him onto another inside animal.

"You stay here! If that lion gets on the merry-go-round and comes toward you, try shimmying up this pole here onto those supporting boards there. O.K.?"

Dickie nods. "What about Laurel, Dad, and where's Mom?"

"Mom's fine, I'll take care of Laurel if anything happens. Most of all keep your eyes open. I think you're safe here. I'm going to keep a watch on that lion."

Dick then goes in and pulls out the long iron bar that slides into the slot to engage or disengage the merry-go-round. He works his way to the edge, where he can see Tuffy, still striking at the animals, retreating, then advancing, making quick charges as the animals go past. Dick stands there with the six-foot-long metal bar in his hand, wondering what he can do.

He yells out to the crowd behind the lion:

"For heaven's sake, don't shoot! There are kids on this merry-go-round! Somebody get around to the other side and I'll pass them off to you."

Just then, Cap breaks through the mob, which has now stopped about twenty-five yards from Tuffy. They've formed a line across the entire boardwalk so Tuffy can't break through. But they're nervous; if Tuffy turns and even looks as if he's charging, they're liable to break out firing. Because of the music from the merry-go-round, Dick can't be sure if they've heard him; also Tuffy is now roaring. Dick sees Cap running toward the lion.

Cap comes up behind Tuffy. He's not sure how Tuffy will react. He calls:

"Tuffy, you bad lion, what are you doing?"

Tuffy turns at the sound of Cap's voice. Cap stares into his eyes. Then, gradually he turns away his eyes, his head. Tuffy stares back almost as if he doesn't comprehend. He puts his tail down and comes, sidewise, toward Cap until he's close. He brushes his face, his nose against him. Cap reaches down and rubs under Tuffy's ear with one hand. With the other he makes motions to the crowd behind him to hold back, disperse.

He grabs Tuffy by the mane and leads him like a very tame dog back toward the Wall of Death. The mob separates, giving him plenty of room. Then it follows on behind, ready to shoot if the lion makes a false move, but Tuffy is happy now. He's found Cap. He's going to be fed.

Cap leads Tuffy to his cage and opens the door, Tuffy leaps gratefully back behind his bars. Cap slips the lock into the hasp and turns to meet the advancing mob. Murph comes forward.

Back at the merry-go-round, Dick has put the lever into its slot again and slowed down the machine, then turned it off. He lifts the little girl down but there doesn't seem to be anyone waiting for her.

"Where's your mommy and daddy, honey?"

"They aren't here. I came myself. Gee, wasn't that a nice long ride?"

"You run along home now and tell your mommy and daddy you shouldn't be out alone."

"I don't have a daddy, I only have a mommy, so there." She sticks out her tongue, turns and runs.

Dick goes across to Laurel and Dickie, helps them off.

"You kids were wonderful. Now let's go get Mother and hope she hasn't fallen onto the sand."

They jump off the merry-go-round and Dick dashes

across to lift Laura over the fence again. She holds on to him.

"Oh God, Dick! I never prayed so hard, not even when I was having the kids. You were wonderful."

"I wasn't so hot. You saw how dangerous that lion was. The guy just took him by the mane and dragged him off as if he was a naughty dog who'd spoiled the rug. I think Cannibal is probably more dangerous than that lion."

"Oh, Dick! Don't be silly. Not now, please!"

Then Laura gives big hard hugs to both the children. Laurel has started crying with Laura, mostly out of sympathy and shared emotion; she doesn't exactly realize what's happened. Dickie is quiet. He's wondering what'll happen to the lion now.

"Dad, I think I was more scared of all those men with guns than I was of the lion. The lion was only sort of playing, the way Cannibal does, but those men all had guns. It would just take *one* of them to start shooting and we'd be dead."

"I think you're right there, Dickie. They had me awful worried, too. Come on, let's go see if they've got that lion in his cage O.K."

"Oh, Dick, do we have to? Hasn't it all been bad enough? Let's just drop down into town from the boardwalk here and get to our room that way."

"Gee, Mom. I want to see the lion. He'll be in his cage and safe. Aw, come on, Mom."

"How about if Dickie and I go look at the lion while you and Laurel go on home? We'll be there soon and maybe we can even go out to a restaurant and celebrate tonight, celebrate our new business and my quitting J.I. Boy, am I ever going to enjoy giving *them* two weeks' notice."

Laurel starts pulling on Laura's arm.

"Gee, Mom. Let's go look at the lion. He can't hurt us now if he's in his cage. Can't I go, too?"

"All right, all right, but if we get eaten up, remember, you're the ones who wanted to go see him, not me."

Dickie takes hold of Dick's hand.

"Oh, I'm not worried. Daddy can take care of any old lion; did you see him with that iron bar? He could've knocked that lion's head right off if he had to. You should've seen him with that stingray; he went clear down near that stinging tail and cut the hook right out of his mouth."

"Ah, come on, Dickie; don't exaggerate. I was scared to death both times. But there's no danger here. If there were any trouble, people wouldn't just be milling around."

The Kettlesons head toward the crowd.

The cage is surrounded. Tuffy is pacing back and forth, waiting for Cap to feed him. There's murmuring from the crowd.

One heavy man in rubber boots, a sheepskin coat, and a peaked leather cap, carrying a double-barreled shotgun, shouts out:

"We oughta put that guy in there with that lion till the lion gets so hungry it eats him the way it did his buddy. That's what I say."

Two young boys are right up close behind the police surrounding the cage:

"Look at them teeth. I'll bet he could bite right through your head and never even feel it."

"Yeah, just a crunch and that's it."

A man with his wife, both local residents:

"I'm sure glad to see that SOB is in his cage. Now all they have to do is get it out of town and keep it out. That damned animal'd wake me up most every night with his roaring; like living in Africa or somethin'."

His wife:

"I think they oughta just shoot it and get it over with. Look at them eyes. He's a maneater all right. He can never be tamed again. None of us are safe long's that animal's alive. He sure has the right name. 'Satan the Dare-Devil Lion.' He's a devil all right."

"You're right there, lady. If one of us killed somebody like that we'd get the chair. Why should a lion be any different? He's a public enemy like Dillinger or Baby Face Nelson. I say shoot it and let's get this over with."

Cap and Murph are close to the cage. Cap has his arm in the cage trying to console, calm Tuffy. Tuffy keeps coming up to his arm, rubbing against it but then pacing. He's hungry, wants Cap to feed him.

"Look, Cap. I've done everything I can. I've even called the zoo in Philadelphia. They say they don't have any place for a ten-year-old male lion that's been kept as a pet like this. They don't want him. They couldn't even tell me what else to do, where else to go. I called the SPCA and they acted as if I was crazy. They're not prepared to dispose of an animal this size."

Cap has his head down listening to Murph. He's trying not to cry in front of the crowd.

Dickie has worked his way up to just behind the police line. He keeps his eye on Tuffy, sure that Tuffy will somehow remember him. He listens to Murph and Cap.

"There's nothing else to do, Cap. We have to shoot Tuffy. Listen to those people. There's no way you could ever use him in an act again. The commissioner'd never have it; it'd be worth my job. You can't pay to ship him back to Africa even if they'd let you."

"He'd die in a week or even days in Africa, Murph. I keep trying to tell you he doesn't know how to hunt. He has no pride, no family; he'd die of starvation. I don't know why he killed Jimmy, but he didn't touch that Chinaman and did you see him with that merry-go-round? Any alley cat could do better than that. He doesn't know how to hunt and I can't feed him any more."

There's a long pause. Dickie looks from one face to the

other, from Tuffy to Murph to Cap Modig. Cap turns and looks at Tuffy.

"Murph, could you let me do it? I know how to handle a forty-five. That's all I ask, let me do it; it's the least I owe him. Clear these people back in case there's a ricochet."

Murph looks at Cap. He motions the other police back. He unhooks the flap on his holster, pulls out his pistol, checks the load, snaps it shut.

"The safety's on, Cap. Do it fast before there's any scene, and make it right between the eyes."

He turns away, motioning with his hands.

"O.K., everybody back. We don't want anybody getting hurt."

Dickie breaks through; he's slipped past the other police. Murph grabs him by the arm with the box and Cannibal in it. "Where you think you're going there, young feller?"

Dickie's crying. Dick is struggling to get through to him but is held back by police. Murph grabs hold of Dickie hard.

"We've got to do it, sonny. There's no other way. All these other people want him killed and there just isn't any place for him any more. Come on, you stay with me."

Cap Modig reaches in and strokes Tuffy's muzzle. Tuffy licks Cap's wrist with his rough tongue. Cap steps back with Tuffy staring him right in the eyes. He's not afraid; this is his friend, Cap.

Cap raises the pistol and flips off the safety. He sights down the dark blue barrel between Tuffy's soft, open, amber eyes, the pupils wide in the waning light. Cap pulls the trigger and holds the gun tight on target so he sees the dark red hole appear directly between the eyes and the slight jolt backward of Tuffy's head as his four hundred pounds absorb the shock from the .45-caliber slug.

There's the noise and then the smell of cordite. Cap lowers the gun.

Tuffy stands a moment, shakes his head, grunts, coughs, staggers, then slowly, gently settles onto his left side.

Cap puts the safety back on and turns. He gives the pistol to Murph. He's crying openly.

"Is it O.K. if I dispose of him myself, Murph? I'll take him inland into the pine barrens and bury him there."

"That's O.K. with me, Cap. I'm really sorry about all this, especially about Tuffy."

"There was no other way. It's not your fault."

Murph's still holding on to Dickie. Dickie has Cannibal clasped to his breast. He wants to edge up close to the cage so Cannibal can visit Tuffy one more time.

Just then, Sally breaks through the crowd, through the police. It's started drizzling. The crowd is beginning to disperse. She runs up to the cage.

"Oh no! Oh no! Poor Tuffy."

She turns on Murph.

"Why'd you have to shoot him? Couldn't he go in a zoo somewhere? He never wanted to hurt anybody."

Murph shakes his head. Cap turns Sally toward him by the shoulders.

"Murph didn't shoot him, Sally; I did. There was nothing else to be done. All this is finished. When you think about it everything was wrong. It was wrong for Tuffy, for you, for me, even for Jimmy and the crowds. We were all somehow fooling with something that's too important."

"Oh, Cap. I'm so sorry; sorry for everything."

"I am, too, Sal."

Cap takes her in his arms and holds her as a light rain starts. He leans and whispers in her ear.

Sally holds Cap tightly and cries harder.

* * *

Dickie breaks away from Murph. He runs past his parents down the boardwalk. He has Cannibal still clasped against his breast. He's running fast and crying so hard he can hardly breathe. As he runs, the lights lining the boardwalk come on. The rain has begun to cover the boards with a slick surface of water so the light shimmers.

PART 15

I DON'T think I ever ran so fast in my life. The rain is coming down hard and I'm getting soaking wet. It's almost as if I'm trying to run out from under the rain. The boards of the boardwalk are slippery.

When all the lights come on, I almost feel as if someone has shot me. I hunch down over Cannibal. I'm holding her box in my arms against my chest and waiting for the sound of a gun.

Then I hear fast, heavy footsteps running behind me. I know it has to be Dad or that fat policeman who was holding on to me. I run harder without looking back.

First I feel his hand on my shoulder, then his other hand on my other shoulder, pushing me down, holding me back. I'm about to twist, try getting away, when I see it's Dad and I stop.

"Hold it there, Dickie. What's the matter? It's not so bad as all that. They *had* to kill that lion. You saw all those people. They were afraid, they wanted him shot. And besides he'd killed a man. Some things just have to be; that's the way it is."

He's out of breath from running and I am, too. He gets down on his knees on the wet boardwalk in front of me. I'm crying so hard I can hardly talk. He takes Cannibal's box out of my arms and puts it down on the boardwalk. I don't think she's getting wet in there, the roof slides in grooves so no rain should get in and no rain will blow in the holes.

Dad takes me and holds me in his arms, hard. I put my arms around him, too. He's so big. It's been a long time since I've had a hug from my dad. I think the last time was when I was in second grade, at Christmastime, when I gave him the copper oil can with the long spout. It cost 69 cents and took almost all my Christmas money.

All these thoughts are running like crazy fish through my head, thoughts about Cannibal, Christmas oil cans, but I keep seeing the lion falling over slowly with practically no blood at all, almost as if he was just giving up, giving up life. I know I have to tell Dad; if I don't tell him, we can never really be friends again.

"Dad, I did it. I let the lion out of his cage."

"What did you say?"

"I let the lion out. I didn't mean to."

Dad holds me tighter. He's quiet.

"That's just your imagination, Dickie; you're all mixed up. How could you have let the lion out anyway?"

So I tell him. I tell him about taking Cannibal to visit that morning, about me climbing under the fence, about Cannibal going in the cage and the lion licking her, about how scared I was and how I took the lock out and how the lion knocked the lock deep into the cage where I couldn't reach it.

"But why didn't you tell somebody, get somebody to help?"

"I was running to tell you when I saw the man who owns the lion, the one who just shot him, going along the boardwalk toward the Wall of Death. I thought he'd get there before the lion got out. That lion had just been rubbing his face against my hand and wanting me to pet him. He was sitting there so quiet in the sun behind his bars. And besides I think something in me, it might be that devil, *wanted* him to get out and walk around without staring at bars all the time."

Dad pushes me away, holds on to my arms so hard they hurt. He looks over my shoulder; I turn and look, too. Mom and Laurel are putting newspapers over their heads and getting ready to come after us. Mom must think we're crazy, standing and kneeling out in the rain, in the dark.

I think Dad's crying, too, but I can't tell, there's so much rain; but his voice is low and he takes deep breaths between sentences. "Listen, Dickie! Listen hard! Don't you say a word to anybody about letting that lion out. It's a secret just between us. You understand?"

He looks over my shoulder again. I nod my head.

"Not even to Mom or Laurel."

I nod my head again. Dad stops a few minutes, looks up at the sky. Then he looks me right in the eyes. He's never really looked at me that way before. It's even more peculiar than winking.

"I want to tell you something, Dickie. You remember this. Nobody can let anybody else, not even a lion, out of a cage.

"The important thing for all of us is never look *at* the bars, look *through* them. Because if you keep looking *at* bars, you'll never get anything done, and you'll never have fun in life, any joy. Do you understand?"

* * *

I don't think I did then; but I do now.

Mom and Laurel come running to us; a wind has blown up and is blowing Mom's dress against her legs. The newspapers are sopping wet, so they're flopping all over their faces.

"What in heaven's name are you two doing out here in the rain? Are you all right, Dickie?"

"I'm fine, Mom. Dad and I were talking. I was sad about that lion being shot, so I ran away and Dad just explained how they had to shoot him."

I'm not crying. Inside I feel warm and the rain seems to be only bouncing on the outside of my skin. Dad stands up and takes the wet newspapers from Mom and Laurel.

"This rain isn't going to hurt anybody. Let's enjoy it; it's probably the last of the warm rains before winter sets in."

He mashes the newspapers into a ball, runs over on the slippery boardwalk and pushes them into a trashcan. I remember the man coming along with the stick with the nail in it. If everybody was like my dad we wouldn't need people doing that kind of work. Dad always said when we'd finish one of our porch jobs and were cleaning up the work site, "One of the ways you can tell a good workman is he covers up his tracks."

I reach down to pick up Cannibal. Dad's come back and takes the box from my hands. He has a hard time sliding back the top because the rain has made the wood swell, but he gets it open. He lifts Cannibal out.

"I think Cannibal's big enough to enjoy a little rain; we can wipe her off when we get home. I don't think there'll be any dogs stomping around in a rain like this."

He pushes the top closed and hands the box back to me. Cannibal is already trying to catch rain drops as they hit the boardwalk. She's dashing back and forth, but they're hitting all around her. We watch and start laugh-

ing, even Mom. Cannibal hardly notices us; she's trying
to beat up every rain drop that even comes near her.

Laurel has her head tipped up with her tongue out and
is tasting the rain. I've done this with snow but never
with rain. I try it, at the same time watching to see I
don't step on Cannibal. Dad has his head tipped back,
drinking rain with us, and he puts his arm around Mom's
wet shoulders.

"Come on, Laura, taste this rain. It might just be the
best-tasting rain you'll ever taste in your whole life."

We walk along drinking rain, and every once in a while
Cannibal will get behind but then she'll dash forward to
catch up. We're her family.